# To Hell and Back

## An Anthology of Horror

### Edited By Joe Mynhardt

HellBound Books Publishing LLC

**Houston, TX**

www.hellboundbooks.com

# CONTENTS

HellBound Books

# Foreword

Lee Murray

"The arguments against anthologies are familiar and obvious," wrote scholar Philip H. Churchman in the opening to his 1922 paper on the use of anthologies in the study of literature. "Instead of an intense intimate friendship with the choicest flowers in the garden of literature, it is felt that they give us a bird's-eye view from the far-off airship that takes in everything and penetrates nothing. Or perhaps the reader may be compared to a traveller in an express train, rushing through province but never knowing a personality. Books of selections, it is argued, are scrappy and superfluous."

Personally, I love a good anthology with their dark chocolate-box story selections on a theme. They're the perfect sampler, the ideal gift for that someone who has everything because you can be sure that in a deluxe box of chocolates there will be something to satisfy even the fussiest palate. And with an anthology, there is the added advantage of accessibility with each bite-sized treat packaged for consumption in a single sitting: on a commute to and from the office, during a tea break, or in the half hour before bedtime. They're the weekend getaway you take when you don't have enough leave saved for a fortnight's rest.

"Books have to be read (worse luck it takes so long a time). It is the only way of discovering what they contain," said novelist E.M. Forster. Not so with an anthology. For readers, anthologies offer a vehicle to discover new authors without the investment required from a novel, and, if the mood doesn't strike for a particular story, you can simply move on to the next.

As for the argument that shorter works are rushed or without depth, any proponent of this statement need only read Edgar Allen Poe's "The Tell-Tale Heart," Charlotte Gilman's "The Yellow Wallpaper," or Shirley Jackson's "The Lottery" to be convinced otherwise. When crafted with skill, short fiction can have all the punch of longer works only without the extended commitment.

For writers, there are advantages to submitting to anthologies, too. Contributing to anthologies can help to build and sustain a career. There is the chance to have work developed and polished by an experienced curator-editor, to practise writing to a specific deadline and theme, to appear alongside some literary heroes, build a network of like-minded authors, gain exposure to a broader readership, and, in the case of charity compilations, to support a cause you are passionate about.

Contrary to his opening statement above, Churchman's thesis is that anthologies do indeed make an important contribution to literature. They are more than the sum of their parts, and Joe Mynhardt is an editor who knows this. As founder and CEO of Crystal Lake Entertainment, a multi-awarding-winning IP company and author hub which has published close to two hundred quality titles and worked with hundreds of writers—including established, emerging, and diverse writers—Mynhardt has built his brand on recognising, nurturing, and supporting artists, and anthologies have been core to this mission. So when he reached out to me to tell me that he was curator-editor of a new horror anthology *To Hell and Back* in conjunction with HellBound Books and asked if I would be interested in writing a foreword to the work, I jumped at the opportunity. A sneak peek at a dark fiction anthology from best-loved and new-to-me voices, and from a discerning editor who knows how to tease the best work from his writers? And as a community-building project for another indie press bent on supporting horror authors? Bring it on.

"It's un-themed," Mynhardt warned. "So it might be hard to preface."

I wonder about that. Can any anthology of original horror stories ever be truly without theme given it provides a snapshot of people's fears at a particular moment in time? What internal or external threats are preoccupying people right now? What issues are affecting our community and beyond? What does this particular chocolate box bring to the genre? There is only one way to find out: I dive in.

First up is "Fix Her" by horror's funnyman Jeff Strand, a supernatural noir on the themes of privilege and the shifting balance of power, delivered with Strand's usual tongue-in-cheek flair. It's the perfect starter: Strand's readers will devour this dark gem.

Our appetite whetted, the next story in the line-up is "The Air We Breathe" by Gage Greenwood, which deals with the trauma of survivors' guilt, and while the pandemic isn't referenced and nor is it the cause of the trauma here, I have no doubt that many readers will relate to this chilling and poignant little tale.

Gregg Stewart conjures every parent's worst fears in "Bunny." With themes of entrapment and abuse, this is a story that will be difficult to digest for certain readers but it's important, nonetheless. Stewart is a new-to-me author, but after reading "Bunny" I'll be looking out for more from him.

In "Come, Save Us, Uberman," UK author and long-time horror commentator Jasper Bark regales with a modern retelling of the Superman fable, a deep-state secret-service romp that is not for the prudish. On the face of it, this explosive adult satire appears to have been written with frivolous and irreverent intent, and yet it explores an important fear: the whittling away of confidence in our institutions and in those appointed to protect us.

"Steel Horses" by anthologist and author Kenneth W. Cain gives us an uncanny take on road rage, which makes me wonder what might have gone down one late night on Cain's way home. Cain makes his story unique with a wonderful Western vibe.

Road rage also features in James Aquilone's story "Get John Flagg" when his character is tailgated by a red Tesla in what is surely the worst day of his life.

With a long career in publishing and media, Taylor Grant is an author who knows how to tell a compelling story, his psychological thriller taking us to a place "where human souls glimmer like a lure" with its lyrical prose. "Glimmergrim" is a story that advocates for confronting one's childhood trauma face to face—although, it's fair to say, results may vary.

The interminable grind of life, of living one chess move at a time and one commute after another, is the subject of Colin J. Northwood's "El Pasant." What's the point really? Why are we here if every day looks the same? Sometimes, all we want is that elusive win to lift us from the ordinary. I expect Northwood to win readers over with this creepy offering of everyday horror.

Chad Lutzke's contribution, "Enough and Then Some," examines the very human fear of being left alone in the world. Who will die first and leave the other to live out their life alone? It's a conversation my husband and I have had many times. Lutzke not only answers the question, he turns the notion on its head in a shocking final twist.

"Going Down" by Felix Blackwell looks at guilt and retribution through a startling architectural metaphor.

Cleverly crafted to carry the reader through all its twists, and reminiscent of Dante's nine circles of hell, "Going Down" is a satisfyingly good read.

J.P. Behrens addresses the horror of war and the helplessness of victims in "Ghost of Chelm," a timely reminder to all of us given the conflicts currently taking place throughout the world. Not your usual golem story, Behrens brushes off the dust and adds a new patina to the mythology in this disquieting cautionary tale.

Then we come to "Hot for Cold" by Bridgett Nelson. In his much-quoted work *Danse Macabre* Stephen King states: "I recognize terror as the finest emotion, and so I will try to terrorize the reader. But if I find I cannot terrify him/her, I will try to horrify; and if I find I cannot horrify, I'll go for the gross-out. I'm not proud." Nor is Nelson proud, because her gruesome tale of bestiality and necrophilia fits squarely in the gross-out category. For lovers of the extreme splatter genre, Nelson's story will likely be their first port of call, while other more squeamish readers might need to work their way to it.

Every good horror anthology needs a haunted house tale, and "One Way or the Other" by Jay Bechtol is a beauty, told in the detail of a paranormal investigations report. Readers are provided with all the evidence, everything they need to make up their own minds. Which way will you fall?

"The Copper Thieves" by Nick Roberts is a graverobbing story. Who doesn't love a tale of death and deception set in a cemetery? Full of foreboding, this haunting tale makes a strong statement on the dangers of addiction and the lengths people will go to for that elusive fix. Told with verve and authenticity, it's a pacy read and great fun.

For me, "The Speakers of Imminent Darkness" by Kyle Toucher is a highlight in what is already a fine anthology. At first, I thought I was reading a climate change horror, beginning as it does with a night escape from a fast-moving California forest fire. But as I read on it morphed into a haunted house tale, with protagonist Ray seizing the moment to torch the offending property, evacuating with barely more than the shirt on his back and his beloved cat. Later, I realised that Toucher's story provides a powerful metaphor for mental illness, the personal demons we try to hide away and isolate others from, but which we inevitably carry with us as we race to escape each new threat. Embedded in the tale is an underlying comment about writers and creativity, with character Ray claiming his art is out of his control, arising instead from this dark muse: "Made me lie, lie, lie. As every word left my lips, every tap on the keyboard when I fell into a writing frenzy, or even more fiendishly when it drove me to paint, I knew it was the house pulling my strings." I've heard other writers say that at times their work is guided by some force other than their own. I wish the same applied to me. Instead, everything I write is prised out of me with a fishhook. Nevertheless, this story gave me so much to think about. As a sufferer of anxiety and depression, I feel sure "The Speakers of Imminent Darkness" is a tale I'll be returning to.

"Fire Escape" by Diana Olney explores an eponymous band's Faustian pact with the Devil and addresses the dual sins of pride and greed. It's a gritty and somewhat sordid tale, and the tale's bar setting and patrons' frantic panic to escape could have been plucked straight from our newsfeeds, but there is more going on in Olney's narrative, which makes it worth the read.

"The Man from the Woods" by Devin Cabrera is a loose retelling of the Little Red Riding Hood fable and represents every woman's nightmare. If the best stories offer a kernel of truth, this one delivers an entire bushel. Hauntingly sad.

Naching T. Kassa offers an unnerving tale of unconditional love and family, wrapped neatly in a secretive layer of the occult, and served up in a cemetery in "A Promise for Rosa Lee."

In "Mount Chocorua" John Durgin cleverly blends New Hampshire folklore and myth in a ghostly tale that examines the universal horrors of grief and longing. This story resonated for me, and I was prompted to do an online search to read more about the underlying legend. Imbued with a sharp sense of place, Durgin's story makes me want to climb the mountain and see for myself, if I weren't so sure I would encounter some ghosts there.

Like Diana Olney, author Francesa Maria offers another contract with the Devil in her story, this time by jaded wrestler El Rompe Huesos, who is desperate to finish up his career with a win, but the similarity ends there with Maria's "Luka and the Luchador," a grim reminder to all of us to always read the fine print.

Loaded with moral nuance, "Our New Church" by James H. Longmore is another favourite, a cautionary word on the dangers of cults and fanaticism. Cult fiction not your thing? I'd recommend you read this story solely for the voice of the evangelist character, Antonio D. Love. Inspired.

Finally, rounding out the anthology with bone-grinding effectiveness is Rowan Hill's "Fur Baby," a rabid tale of revenge and retribution. With echoes of Stephen King's iconic *Misery,* it's a story that stays with you long after you put the book down.

*To Hell and Back* is a veritable cornucopia of terror, a chocolate box of twenty-two dark treats mining personal and universal fears. With tales set in cities and small towns, in office blocks, frat houses, and family homes, on lonely roads, wooded trails, and mountaintops, its writers expose external threats like predators, abusers, and cults, and internal drivers like ambition, mental illness, and moral frailties. These pages are haunted by ghosts and monsters and creepy talking dolls. There are stories of political and cultural tension. Tales of creeping unease and those that make your innards shrink. *To Hell and Back*'s authors expose their fears even as they remind us of our own. But horror literature does more than just scare us, it shows us a way through, a means to confront and reflect on our fears at a safe distance. A way to gird us with hope. After all, it's in the book's title, isn't it? To Hell *and Back*.

I invite you to turn the page and start your journey.

Lee Murray, December 2023

# To Hell and Back

# Fix Her

### Jeff Strand

"Look, he's here already! It's going to be fine. You can calm down. Everything's going to be all right now."

The crying frat boy wiped his nose on his sleeve and nodded. He was seated on the floor, leaning against the wall while his buddy crouched next to him. Sebastian walked over to them.

"Lots of eyes on you," Sebastian said. "Is there a reason so many people are just standing around watching?"

"They live here," said the crouching kid.

"And you can trust them all to keep their mouths shut? Because if a single one of them talks, any services I provide are worthless."

"Yeah, yeah, it's cool."

Sebastian stared at the kid, long enough to make him squirm. "How about you go around and make sure they understand the importance of discretion? I'll handle your friend."

"Yeah, yeah, okay." The kid stood and went to talk to the closest frat boy.

This place smelled like cheap beer, weed, and body odor. Sebastian was thirty years out of college, and he'd never been in a fraternity, so this was new, unpleasant territory.

"What's your name?" Sebastian asked the crying frat boy.

"Randy."

"And what seems to be the problem, Randy?"

Randy sniffled. "Didn't my dad tell you on the phone?"

"I'd like to hear it from you." Sebastian clapped his hands and addressed the other boys.

"Everybody back to your rooms. Nothing to see here."

The boys reluctantly left.

"I understand there's a dead hooker in your room," said Sebastian. "Before I get to work cleaning up your mess, I'd like to know how it happened."

Randy shrugged. "We hired a stripper. She said she'd do a little more if we paid her a little more. I had some birthday money, so she came back to my room, and..."

"And?"

"You know."

"You killed her?"

"Not on purpose! I asked if I could...you know..."

"I don't know," said Sebastian. "I live my life so that I don't have to hire people like me.

Now I'm going to ask you to tell me very clearly what happened so that I can get to work making your problem go away."

"My girlfriend won't let me choke her. I've always wanted to try it. The stripper said it was okay, so I did it, and I guess I squeezed too hard." He let out a sob. "I didn't mean to do it."

Sebastian placed his hand on Randy's shoulder. "I'm going to tell you one thing you already know and one thing you don't. As you already know, it is extremely difficult to choke somebody to death. You did not accidentally squeeze a little too hard. I'm not saying there was malicious intent on your part, but you're giving me a very sanitized version of events. Do you agree with that?"

"I guess."

"And what you don't already know is that I hate when people insult my intelligence.

Fucking hate it. So give me the real story or I'll walk right out of here and leave you to your own fate."

"I just...I got really into it. I kept squeezing and squeezing and I couldn't make myself stop. It was like I wasn't in my own body. I barely even remember it—I swear I'm not lying! I don't even know how long it took. All I remember is that I pulled my hands away and she was dead."

"All right," said Sebastian. "Let's take a look."

Randy stood and led Sebastian into his room. The walls were covered with posters of naked women—not tasteful nudes—and a bong was on the dresser. Dirty clothes were all over the floor. And, yes, a woman in a red bra and panties lay on his bed. She looked underage, although Sebastian would grant the frat boys the benefit of the doubt and assume that she wasn't, and she'd definitely had a rough life even before he put those bruises on her throat.

"You called your father, who called me. Is it correct that nobody else has been contacted?" asked Sebastian.

"Yes."

"And nobody has left the house?"

Randy shook his head. "I don't think so."

"Not a good enough answer. I'll talk to your buddy. What you need from me is to get rid of the body, and to make sure that nobody comes here looking for her. Do I have that right?"

"Yes."

"Good. The first part is no problem. I'll need more information before we can tackle the second part. I'll give your friends a scary speech about how this will blow back on all of them, but after I leave, it's on you to keep the secret. Got it?"

"Yeah."

"Then let me…" Sebastian frowned. "Well, this is interesting."

"What?"

"She's not dead."

"What?"

"She's breathing. See?" Sebastian pointed to the woman. They were weak breaths but she was very much alive.

"Oh." Randy seemed to be in shock.

"Okay, Randy, this situation has just taken a very sharp turn. It's either a reason for you to celebrate, or an unwelcome complication. We can take her right now to the emergency room. Is that what you want?"

Randy said nothing.

"Because if things got a little carried away, maybe some mixed signals, you might be okay. Do you think you'll be okay if she tells the police what happened, Randy?"

"Is there…is there another option?"

"You know perfectly well there is."

Randy nervously licked his lips. "Okay. Do that."

"Kill her?"

"Yes."

"It's a perfectly good choice," said Sebastian. "But I'm not going to kill her. You are."

"What?"

"I'm very sure you heard me."

"I can't do that."

"Yes, Randy, you can. We haven't known each other very long, but considering the circumstances, I have the utmost faith that you can do this."

"Why can't you do it?"

"Because I was hired to clean up after a murder, not commit murder."

"It wasn't murder. It was an accident."

"So, Randy, when you sit here trying to argue semantics, you're wasting our time. And our time is extremely valuable right now. If I'm discussing whether it was a murder or an accident with you, I'm not making sure your dumb-fuck drunk idiot entitled frat boy asshole buddies are going to keep their mouths shut. Do you understand me?"

Randy nodded.

"If you want her to live, I'll take her to the emergency room. If you'd prefer that she not live, then you'll have to finish what you started."

Randy began to weep again. Sebastian smacked him across the face.

"Crying is also a waste of time."

Randy apparently intended to wipe his nose on his shirtsleeve, but since he was wearing a T-shirt, he wiped it on his arm instead. "How do I do it?"

"It's up to you. Obviously you aren't going to shoot her. I'm sure there's a knife around here that you could use to slash her throat. Or you could indulge your sick choking fetish a little more. There's a world of opportunities before you, Randy."

"What…what do you recommend?"

"Well, I assume you're intelligent, since you got into college, so you know that a knife is not the way to go. No reason to add blood to our problems. I suggest that you pick up that pillow, press it tightly over her face, and hold it there for a few minutes."

"Okay." Randy looked over at the pillow. "Are you sure you can't do it? My dad will pay you extra."

"Your dad's bill is already high enough. Make him proud. This will be nice and easy–I doubt she'll even struggle."

Randy picked up the pillow and placed it on the girl's face.

"Press it hard," said Sebastian. "Both hands. I'll be back to check on you after I talk to your friends."

"I don't think I can do this."

Sebastian shrugged. "How old are you? Twenty?"

"Yeah."

"I think you're allowed three years' leeway, so as long as she's seventeen, you're okay. If she's sixteen, well, you become the kind of criminal who doesn't fare very well in prison. Did you check her ID before you choked her?"

"The guys wouldn't have hired a sixteen-year-old."

"Right. I'm sure they did their due diligence. What I'm saying, Randy, is that you're not the kind of person who will thrive in prison. You're a cowardly little bitch with smooth hands and perfectly groomed nails. Your fellow inmates won't respect you, and you're going to have a very rough twenty years."

"My dad's going to find out how you're talking to me."

"Are you saying that your counterpoint to me is that you're going to tattle to your daddy? So when a couple of beefy guys with Swastika tattoos are beating the shit out of you, do you think they'll stop when you warn them that you're going to tell your dad on them?"

"Fine, I'll do it," said Randy, with the whiny tone of a kid who'd been told he had to take out the garbage before he could play Nintendo.

"Press hard," said Sebastian, walking out of the room.

A couple of the frat boys had come out of their rooms. Sebastian clapped his hands and shouted. "House meeting! Everybody downstairs immediately! I don't mean sixty seconds from now!"

Several doors opened as Sebastian made his way down the stairs. To their credit, the kids followed quickly, and he stood in the common area with a crowd of douchebags in front of him.

"Are we missing anybody?" he asked.

The frat boys murmured that they weren't.

"As you know, your brother Randy has been a very bad boy. None of you are going to prison, unless it turns out that she was sixteen, but this could cause major headaches in your life.

This shit doesn't look good on a job application. My first question is, have any of you said anything to anybody outside of this house? Text or whatever. If you have, we can still try to contain it, but you need to tell me now. If there was ever a time for honesty, this is it. Raise your hand if you said anything."

Nobody raised their hand.

"All right. What I'd like to do now is impress upon you how important it is to–"

There was a scream from upstairs.

Definitely Randy, not the girl. And it wasn't the scream of a whiny little bitch who couldn't handle what needed to be done, but a scream of fear. It was immediately followed by a scream of pain.

Sebastian hurried up the stairs. The screams continued, accompanied by "No, God, no!"

Something flew out of the doorway to Randy's room, looking kind of like a blood-soaked wig.

Sebastian stared into the room. Feathers from the torn-apart pillow billowed in the air.

The blanket was almost completely red.

Randy lay on his stomach on the bed, missing the vast majority of his scalp. Both of his arms were broken, with the bones protruding. The girl was crouched on his back, smeared with blood, looking completely feral. She was twisting one of his arms, as if trying to tear it off.

She looked up at Sebastian and hissed.

Sebastian pulled the door closed.

Okay, then.

Tearing off somebody's scalp like that wasn't something you could just do. Same with the broken arms. Those would take tools and effort. And this was a half-dead, skinny little girl.

Sebastian didn't know if she was a zombie, or demonically possessed, or whatever the fuck could wreck Randy like that, and he didn't particularly care. His only concern now was to remove himself from this situation.

Something slammed against the door. It didn't sound like somebody bashing into it, so he assumed it was a large piece of Randy, perhaps his head.

Sebastian hurried back down the stairs.

"Things have changed," he told the frat boys. "You're going to want to leave right now."

Upstairs, there was a loud thump accompanied by the sound of shattering wood. The door hadn't even been locked.

A moment later, the girl bound down the stairs on all fours, like a wild cat. She reached the bottom and leaped at the nearest frat boy. To his credit, he let out a low-pitched grunt instead of a high-pitched scream. Well, at least until she tore out his throat with her teeth.

Without taking a moment to bask in her act of violence, she leaped onto another kid, taking a very large bite out of the back of his neck. She followed that with a second bite, and then yanked his head back until it snapped.

Pandemonium.

One surprisingly brave frat boy rushed at her, a heroic action he quickly regretted when she disemboweled him with two swipes of her hand. She didn't even have very long fingernails.

Nobody rushed at her after that.

The frat boys fled for the exit. Unfortunately for them, the exit was a single normal-sized door, which wasn't suitable for a dozen people trying to squeeze through at once. Three or four of them did make it outside, but the girl (or whatever she was) tore through the remainders like a human lawnmower. She made breaking bones look ridiculously easy.

Sebastian was not a compassionate man. Still, this carnage looked like it hurt.

He sort of hoped that the girl would chase after the frat boys who'd escaped, which would make her their problem instead of his. Instead, after she'd killed or at least seriously maimed everybody who hadn't made it out of the house, she stopped and looked at him.

Sebastian wished he'd brought a gun. He had one in the car, but he hadn't thought he'd need it to clean up an accidental hooker death. For all he knew, she was impervious to bullets anyway.

She regarded him, as if trying to decide if he was friend or foe.

He tried to convey an expression that said "I mean you no harm, and I'm totally cool with what you just did, so let's go our separate ways to try to find happiness in this cold cruel world."

She leaped at him.

Sebastian was better trained in self-defense than the frat boys, which is why he was able to get in a few good punches before the girl broke his right arm and left leg. She took a bite out of his right leg, but it was comparatively small. She raked her fingers across his chest but didn't expose any internal organs.

After he punched her in the nose, generating a squirt of blood that mixed with the frat boy blood that was already all over her face, she snarled, hissed, and then scampered out the door.

There was a bit of groaning from the pile of dead frat boys, but not a lot. Clearly only a couple were alive, and possibly not for much longer.

He used his unbroken arm to dig his cell phone out of his pocket. Pulled up his contact list, and called Vincent White, his biggest competition.

"Hey, Vincent, it's Sebastian. Been a while, I know. Listen, have I got a job for you…"

# The Air We Breathe

Gage Greenwood

Roger came home to find his family dead. He'd had nightmares about this kind of thing, but in those anxiety driven dreams, he walked in to find a mutilated and murdered series of bodies, as if his departure from the house somehow opened the door to serial killers and monsters of the night. But that's not what Roger found. His wife and children were lying peacefully in their beds. No markings or blood anywhere.

He found his wife first, ran to her. "Jessica. Jessica, wake up!" he shouted, knowing something was wrong when she was in bed at 6:00 in the evening. His finger went to her neck, searching for a pulse. Had he ever checked a pulse before? He had no idea if he was doing it right. But it didn't matter. He knew she was dead, could tell by the waxy, pale skin. Truth be told, he knew the second he saw her in bed, maybe even as soon as he opened the house door to silence.

He ran to Dustin's room next. His shades were drawn, and the fall evening drenched the room in darkness. Roger clicked the light, saw the boy lying in bed, and knew. It didn't make sense, but he knew. He didn't check a pulse this time. Doing so meant looking at his dead son, and he couldn't fathom such a thing. Just knowing the lump under the sheets was his boy sent him spiraling.

He fell to his knees and screamed, howled, moaned.

But there was still another room to check. Jesus. Could he do another one? He had to, because what if Rachel lived, what if somehow, whatever happened to his family gave one kindness before exiting?

Rachel's room was blue, but Roger remembered it being lighter, a cooler more inviting shade. Now it looked like a dark ocean ready to drown him within its endless deep. The bedsheets draped over her, covering all but her sweet face. It was almost as if Rachel knew her father would avoid trying to see their faces, and made herself come out of the sheet, turned in the direction of the door, to ensure he couldn't neglect seeing it, her beautiful face, cold and drained of color. Her eyes were open, crystal blues disagreeing with the angry wall shade.

He suddenly felt alone, scared, like some kind of monster might be crawling on the ceiling, hidden in the corners of the dimly lit rooms. He felt it, too, something watching him. Licking its lips. Cackling at his pain.

The bedsheets had little cartoon frogs patterned on it, and they were all looking at Roger, all staring at him with knowing eyes.

As he turned away from it, he tripped on Rachel's Meredith the Mermaid doll, setting off its speech box. "Swim with me."

He'd heard the doll say that a million times, but it never sounded so disquieting. He kicked it, not out of anger or fear, but just to get it out of his fucking way. As it slapped into the dresser, it set off again. "Ride the wave and seize the day."

His legs threatened to quit on him, so he leaned heavy on the wall, using it to help him walk down the long, narrow upstairs hall. He wrapped himself around the banister as he descended to the downstairs living room. Each step felt thinner than he had remembered, steeper.

In the living room, he called 911, fingers trembling over the numbers on his cell. "Help, please."

He screamed into the phone, shouting what had happened, lost, confused. The operator kept her cool and told him to get out of the house. He asked why, not wanting to leave his family. He couldn't look directly at them but abandoning them for the outside felt cruel.

She explained, based off the way he described finding them, carbon monoxide might have been the cause, and he should get out immediately. Once she said it, he realized how dizzy and weak he felt.

The cool, autumn air hit him as he exited the house, but it did not remove the thick dread buzzing around him, pecking at his flesh like mosquitos. This was it. The end of his life. Everything he loved, cared about, woke up for, worked for, dead. It was bigger than picturing his daughter coloring at the kitchen table, hearing her silly way of talking. "I made a picshaw, Daddy. It's a picshaw of dumb ducks." It was more than the haunting film reel in his mind of Dustin begging Roger to play with him, and those regretful daggers that would eventually stab through his ribs and puncture his heart of all the times he said he couldn't. *Too tired. Too busy. Can't play right now, bud.* It was bigger than those cool nights where the air froze still, before the kids, back when he and Jessica sat on the back deck and disrupted the gentle calm with loud fucking, and it was bigger than the opposite spectrum, all those tumultuous nights with his wife, fighting over Roger's lack of energy, his shirking off his responsibilities at home because of his work otherwise. It was so much more than memories, regrets, time given and time lost. It was a balloon and as more seconds passed, the bigger it grew, threatening with its ever-stretching skin to explode within Roger. It was a gripped fist ripping his identity from him.

*You are nothing now, Roger. Nothing.*

He fell to his knees on the loose stones in the driveway. The tiny white rocks dug into his legs. He felt them, those minor annoyances. Red and Blue flashed in the distance. Sirens, so far away. Getting louder by the second. Too far. It was too far.

***

The world moved around him for a while, cop cars, fire trucks, ambulances took over the driveway and street, caging in his house. People asked him questions, but Roger couldn't fit their words together, couldn't make sense of them. Men and women in all different types of uniforms surrounded the house. Some tried to enter, and others told them they couldn't.

"It's gotta drop below 9," one of them said. "We'll check them."

Firemen used some kind of box with a hose at the end around the house before entering with masks on.

The firewoman said things, but he only heard a combination of words that didn't go together. Sniffer. For gas? 4gas? Rusty heat exchanger. Carbon Monoxide. Your detectors are old! Cracks in the furnace.

Roger listened to the words, dead-faced. What the fuck was she saying? An officer approached and asked if he had somewhere to stay. Roger shook his head. Of course he did! He had a house. It was right here.

It wasn't until the street cleared of cars—only one police car and firetruck remained—when Roger realized they wanted him to stay somewhere else. Was that for his mental health, or his physical health? Was the house dangerous? Did they fix the carbon monoxide problem or was that something they couldn't fix? Was the house just a deadly place now? Did death cling to the air?

Finally, a fireman approached him, told him he couldn't return until morning after another fireperson came by and checked the monoxide levels. The windows were all open, and they hadn't removed his family. *They are exposed,* Roger thought. *Anyone can sneak in and do whatever they want.*

He drove to Tanner's Switch Inn after the police officer took his cell number and offered Roger his card, said he'd be in touch. The room was neither nice nor disgusting. Somewhere in between. He fell onto the bed, exhausted, but unable to close his eyes. Did the hotel have a rusty furnace? How could he ever sleep again?

He sat on the bed and stared at the ceiling, the empty whiteness, blank and begging for damage. He stayed that way for a long time. When he closed his eyes, he saw his daughter's face peeking out at him from under the covers. He saw the lump in his son's bed. He saw his wife's pale head and felt her cold skin on his fingertips. "Swim with Me," Meredith the Mermaid said. It echoed in his mind, those three words. But in his head, they were more mangled, more manic, and screechy, the way it might sound with weak batteries or a malfunction. With cracks in its foundation.

He rolled out of bed at one point, probably two or three in the morning. The bench by the front entrance was wet from a brief rain shower hours ago. Roger sat on it and lit a cigarette. A different kind of poison, but one he accepted into his lungs.

Flashes of his daughter's eyes penetrated his mind. She was dead, confirmed by the firemen who refused to allow the EMTs in until the air cleared. When would they remove the bodies? Would they be there in the morning when he arrived back home, still sleeping soundly in their beds?

Could he wake them and pretend none of this had happened?

But his daughter's eyes, they were gone, sure. He had no illusions otherwise, but they seemed so alive, didn't they? They told him something. Just like when the firewoman spoke to him, he couldn't make it all out, but he knew words were uttered and they were meant to make sense. Maybe through the doll. Was that ludicrous? "Swim with me? Ride the wave and seize the day?"

He stubbed his cigarette on the cement and tossed the butt but didn't get up yet. He debated on having another, just to avoid going to the empty hotel room, but his lungs couldn't manage. Instead, he stared at the moon, just a slit in the sky, a closing, winking eye. Not like his daughter's.

Not like hers.

\*\*\*

Back in his room, he stared at the ceiling again, thinking about the doll and his daughter's eyes. He knew he searched for alternatives because he couldn't handle the truth. If carbon monoxide had truly been to blame, it was concurrently "one of those things," and also entirely his fault. When had he last changed the batteries in the detectors? Had he ever had the furnace serviced?

He stayed up all night searching for meaning in the rug patterns. He heard the dying gasps of Meredith the Mermaid in the whoosh that spat from the air conditioning unit every fifteen minutes. Like clockwork. Whoosh. *Swim with me.*

He lay on his side and glared at the space under the door waiting for monsters to appear, demons, killers. He stared intently until his vision blurred and serpentine tendrils crept through the crevice. It hissed like a snake. Or like a gas leak.

His body stiffened, heart rushed, but he freed his mind, waiting for the creature to take him. The wisps grew, stretching fingers inching toward him. Just as it closed in, ready to strangle him, the air conditioning kicked on. Whoosh. *Swim with me.* The monster *was* gone.

\*\*\*

Roger eventually fell asleep and woke at noon. His phone buzzed on the nightstand. An officer talked to him for a while, but again the words came in, never quite marrying into something Roger could grasp. The firemen had cleared the house. Medical examiner. Monoxide poisoning confirmed. Bodies removed.

There was more, but his brain refused to absorb it.

He wasn't sure he wanted to go home, but he wasn't sure he wanted to be anywhere else. It aggravated him that they removed the bodies without discussing it with him first. What if he wanted to say goodbye? See them where they belonged one last time?

\*\*\*

The firemen had left the windows open, making the entire house cold. Roger couldn't turn the heat on, obviously, so he tossed a sweater he'd left by the front door over his shirt and shut all the windows.

Well, all the windows on the bottom floor. He couldn't bring himself to climb the steps yet, enter the yawning void where he'd found his family, where their belongings would taunt him, remind him of every aching memory.

He'd rather just sit in the living room and wait for the monster to creep toward him, enter his lungs and shut his system down. Put a crack in his foundation.

That's what he did for hours, sat on the couch waiting for something to happen. For something to attack, to hurt.

Around 4:00 pm, it happened.

*Swim with me,* the doll screeched, loud and angry, muffled like she shouted through a tube.

Roger ran up the stairs. He found the doll where he'd kicked it the night before. It said nothing. Did nothing.

There were answers here, monsters, and he refused to ignore it. He picked the doll up and tossed it on the bed, right on top of those glaring frogs. With his foot, he slid the closet door open, and tossed Rachel's clothes out, forming a mound on her bed. He wanted to wrap it all under the bedsheet, pressing his hands into it until it all formed together, molding into the shape of his daughter. He slid his hands around the walls behind the now-empty hangers, feeling for cracks that could reveal a hidden door, a place for monsters to hide.

Eventually, he emptied the room, pouring everything the girl had owned onto the bed into a giant, floundering hill. He swore it moved, as if something were stuck under it all, trying to break free.

He went to Dustin's room next, opening his closet. Old toys, arts and crafts, junk, papers, nonsense were piled on shelves around his clothes. When his children failed to clean their rooms, Roger came in and tossed everything off the floor into slipshod piles wherever they were out of the way. This mess was his creation, and the sudden guilt of seeing it made him step away, shut the door tightly. Close it all out.

He had thought himself a good father, but those minor failings, the times he shouted a little too loud, or sunk into his own head, ignoring his children's requests for attention, all the times he tossed their shit into a closet, not thinking of how that might affect them. He was a terrible father. How foolish to consider himself the glue of it all, when now, without his family, he fell apart. Without them he would just rust away, crack.

He went into his bedroom. Jessica's book sat on the end table, a bookmark poking out toward the end of the novel, those last few pages untouched and unread. Two days before he left for his business trip, Jessica had told him they needed a new frame for the bed and he told her to send him some links to ones she liked. She did, and while he sat in a hotel six hours away, he scrolled through Facebook and Reddit, forgetting to go back and check them out, order one. The unfinished business dug into him more than anything else.

So many dangling threads in their story.

He gave up on hunting for monsters, accepting the blame. For all of it. For their deaths. For their lives. For their bad days. For their sadness. He had found the monster.

His fists dug into the comforter, twisting around until he had a ball of fabric in his grip, and he dropped onto the mattress. He squeezed the comforter, squeezed until his fingers hurt. Why was it so empty? So malleable? Why didn't it grip back, and push him and challenge him and yell at him and hug him and wrap itself around his limbs?

*Swim with me.*

The fucking doll misfired again, taunting him. He thought of Rachel playing with Meredith, cutting her hair with safety scissors, and proudly showing the new hairdo to her parents. She painted makeup on the doll's face, grotesquely overdone. Thick red around the lips. Blue that extended beyond the eyelids up the doll's forehead and nearing her hairline. Pinkish blush all over the whole cheek and caking over the clownish lipstick. Roger and Jessica had clapped and told her how wonderful it was, while giving each other eyes that said, "Jesus, it's a monster! It's terrifying."

Roger broke first, laughing hysterically. Jessica followed suit. Rachel, unaware that they were mocking her makeup artistry, joined in, laughing the way children do where it almost sounded like a scream.

*Swim me with.*
*With me swim.*
*Me with swim.*
*Swim.*
*Swim.*
*Swim.*

Roger sat up. The doll's voice had grown more disturbing, as exaggerated as her makeup. It was loud, hissy, and aggressive. He crept out of the bedroom, needing to silence it, but terrified at the same time. It was just a broken doll, he knew, just as he knew his brain manifested the wisps coming through his hotel door last night, a representation of the carbon monoxide that killed his family, and a poor one at that, because carbon monoxide was invisible, scentless, had no taste. It was a silent killer. Hence the need for functioning detectors.

He half expected to see Meredith outside the bedroom, either in the hall or on the stairs, something to indicate her sentience, the monster inside it taunting Roger, but the doll remained exactly as he'd left it, the only item in Rachel's room not upturned and piled on the bed.

He picked it up, stared at the cartoonish face with painted makeup. Waited. *What did it want to tell Roger? What was it trying to say?*

He stared until his eyes watered. *Say something. Anything.*

It said nothing. With a frustrated growl, he stormed down the stairs, clenching the doll in his fist. He flung the front door open and tossed the doll onto the front lawn. There. Now it couldn't tease him anymore, couldn't pretend to give him answers that didn't exist.

When he turned back, the stairs looked too long, too tough to climb a second time, so he went to the couch and sat, staring at the blank screen on the television. He felt

Dustin's head resting on his shoulder, the way he often did when he was playing with the Nintendo Switch, just pressing buttons with his head propped on his dad's shoulder.

Roger's eyes blurred again, and the wisps appeared in the reflection on the television screen, forming behind Roger, twisting and twirling around each other. They formed a shape, a blob of some type. Roger wanted to turn, to see it head on, but he was scared immobile. His heart slammed into his ribs as the formation slithered around the back of the couch.

As it moved around the side, Roger heard it. A quiet hissing.

It undulated as it crept forward. Up and down, the scrim mist went. Roger didn't need the reflection anymore, the monster was right in front of him. He still couldn't move, but he didn't think the fear caused it as much as the monster itself, forcing him into stillness. A face formed in the fog, uneven eyes, slits for nostrils, and a Cheshire smile. Its hollow mouth opened.

"Swim with me," it said in a shrill, painful tone. A thin strip of mist reached for Roger. He flinched, until he realized it wanted to take his hand. He let it, didn't have much choice otherwise.

The mist led him into the kitchen and said, "I drew a picshaw," in his daughter's voice.

"Oh," he said, the word thinly escaping him. His heart plummeted at the sound of her voice, so authentic and pitch-perfect. Something shattered within, even more than it had the night previous when he found them all gone. Rachel's voice penetrated deep within the marrow of his bones, tying his stomach in knots, squeezing his brain. It ripped him apart. He was already a malfunctioning doll, ragged, broken, cracked and leaking battery acid, but the voice finished the job, pulling his stitching apart, shredding him into unrecognizable pieces.

The door to the basement swung open, slamming into a chair at the kitchen table.

"Swim with me," the mist said. "Swim with me."

Then, it's voice changed. "Dad, I got gold on every Mario Kart track in the 200cc."

Had he cared? When his son had told him that, had Roger cared? Did he act excited? Was he excited? Was he too busy? Too in his own head? Did he pull his son close and offer to race him? Was it one of those times where he broke free and let himself have fun? Where he yelled, "I'm Kamek!" and his son shouted back with a smile on his face, "I'm Dry Bones!" or was it one of those times where he gave a mock smile and half-heartedly said "Great job" while otherwise ignoring the kid for his phone or a television show?

It could have gone either way. Roger didn't remember.

As they descended the stairs, the voice played again, changing to his wife this time. "Kids are going to grandma's tomorrow. Should we?"

He remembered that one. He had replied, "Yes, we should! You should wear that black thong you have." And she laughed and said, "Seems excessive for a day of reading on the deck followed by a massage." They laughed. He laughed and she laughed. Together. It was nice. It wasn't the impromptu trip to New Hampshire where they raided the bookstores and spent the weekend naked in a hotel bed, reading and talking and loving each other, and it wasn't when they held hands while Jessica gave birth to the children. Not special, not horrid. Just nice. Sometimes nice was all you needed. Sometimes it held more weight in the relationship. Anyone can pull off special, but to consistently be nice? That took a quality most relationships lacked.

The wooden steps creaked as he made his way down. The voice returned to Malfunctioning Meredith. "Swim with me."

He understood. It lured him toward the furnace, wanted him to turn it on, to climb into bed, to join the family. He wouldn't fight it. They were gone and his entire identity had long been entwined with them, and there was no way to unspool it, to get out the knots. Without them, Roger had no identity. He just had to let the rope pull him in, take him to them. What else was there?

As his feet stepped off the last wooden step and hit the cold cement, he reached for the dangling string by the lightbulb and clicked it on. He startled at the furnace so out of place, standing in front of him at the bottom of the steps, looming like a monster. It was disconnected, removed from the concrete blocks that kept it safe from flooding.

Roger laughed. The house's monsters taunted him more, luring him toward a poetic demise, only to strip it from him. He had no idea how to reconnect the thing, how to make it function. He could probably figure it out, maybe get a YouTube video to help, but that seemed like so much work, removing the whole act of its lyrical nature. The firemen had probably removed it, thinking they were doing Roger a favor.

He climbed the stairs, the wispy monster following behind. He could find another way. His everyday house, like any other house, contained a million ways to die, but again, the purity of the act had been jostled, its base rusty and cracked. Just a few feet from its original place, the furnace had challenged him to go on.

The wisps weren't done with him yet, though. They trailed him, whispering taunts. "Swim with me."

"Picshaw."

"Mario Kart."

"Should we?"

He ignored it as best he could, dragged himself to the living room. Would he ever make it up the stairs again?

He kicked off his shoes and rested his body on the couch, smooshing his face into a throw pillow.

The misty storm surrounded him, grinning something awful at him, sharp-toothed and growling.

"Swim with me," it said. Angry.

"Swim with me." A little louder.

"Swim with me." It yelled, nearly shattering Roger's air drums.

"Swim with me."

It wrapped its tendrils around his throat, pressing tightly. Roger gasped.

"Swim with me."

# Bunny

### Gregg Stewart

"Cover your eyes, kiddo, you don't wanna see what happens next."

Misty sat on the couch, her bare feet bobbing off the edge of the cushion. Evie, the babysitter, sat by Misty's side, eyes locked on the television, munching popcorn.

*Gremlins* was a holiday classic, not the scariest movie ever made, but for 6-year-old Misty, it was a terror beyond anything she'd ever witnessed. Her parents, out on a Christmas Eve date, had left her in the care of 15-year-old horror aficionado Evie Roberts, whose mother had let her watch *The Exorcist* when she was four. Evie had no filter when it came to the fragile minds of children. At the same time, she needed this gig. The Mackenzies were the wealthiest family in town. *Like, 'here, sign this NDA' wealthy.* Getting fired on her first night for giving their child nightmares would destroy her reputation as the coolest babysitter ever.

Evie glanced at Misty. "Seriously, this next part is gnarly, and I don't want your parents getting pissed at me, so—"

Misty threw her hands over her eyes, parting her fingers a fraction on the right hand. Evie grinned. *What was that instinct? How did looking through your fingers somehow ease the anxiety of a jump scare and make it less scary?* She would never know. Though she'd done this same move a hundred times in her younger years, Evie had made it her mission never to do it again, no matter how terrifying the scene. *You gotta look at the screaming bloody monsters head-on, or you won't have the courage to face them when they show up in the real world.*

Misty let out a croaky *'ehhh'* as she watched, and Evie placed a comforting arm around her. The girl ducked her head, peeking from behind her babysitter's Ramones T-shirt.

"It'll be over in a second," Evie said. She'd seen this part a dozen times. In the movie, the mom has a knife and is creeping up on the strange sounds coming from the kitchen. The whole thing bored Evie now, and she absently picked at the white strands of her ripped jeans as green blood sprayed across the television screen.

She reached into her back pocket and pulled out the mobile phone the Mackenzies had given her. No bars. She cursed under her breath. Why hadn't she checked earlier? Maybe it was because they were in the theater room in the basement? No reception underground.

One of the stipulations in the NDA was that Evie had to turn over her mobile phone for the duration of the job. Tim and Claire didn't want her filming or taking photos of their precious mansion. As if Evie would ever post this obnoxious décor on her punk-goth-inspired feed? In truth, the inside of the famous Mackenzie Manor on the hill overlooking town had been a major letdown. Evie had hoped for a Victorian theme to match the gothic stone exterior, but the inside looked like it belonged in Miami or Vegas—all white marble and pastels.

The one creepy thing: There were portraits of Claire everywhere—over the mantel, in the hallway, up the second flight stairs. There was even a photo in the bathroom of a young, naked Claire leaping past a sunset on the beach, right next to another framed image with four lines of block letters: MANI – FEST – DES – TINY. *Fucking rich people.*

"After this," Misty said with her face still buried in Evie's side, "will you read me a bedtime story?"

Evie had seen enough anyway. She clicked the remote, and the massive television screen went black. "Let's get washed up, kiddo, and then I'll read all your favorites."

Misty leaped from the couch, and Evie followed her up the three flights of stairs to the top-floor bathroom for a face-washing and tooth brushing. The Mackenzies had also insisted Evie floss the girl's teeth. *Were all rich folks such sticklers for hygiene?*

After a ten-minute tussle into her too-tight princess pajamas, Misty jumped into bed, ready for her story. Evie perused Misty's bookshelf and picked up *Goodnight Moon*, which seemed a safe bet. "How 'bout—"

"Who's that?" Misty asked, staring out her bedroom window.

"What?" A chill ran through Evie as she clutched the book to her chest and approached the window.

There, at the end of the long drive, halfway down the hill, stood a figure in shadow. Evie peered closer. Was it a person or some trick of the moonlight?

Misty shifted in her bed. "Do you know—"

"Shh," Evie said, red caution lights flashing in the recesses of her mind. Evie pulled out the phone the Mackenzies had given her—still no bars, even on the top floor. *Stupid, useless, fuck, fuck.* She wondered if her own phone would have bars and if she could find where they'd stashed it. She glanced down the long drive. *Had the shadow moved?*

Evie turned to Misty. "You have a landline, right?"

The girl scrunched her face. "What's a landline?"

Evie cursed again, this time under her breath.

The shadow was staring at the bedroom window. *Fuck, fuck, fuck.* Evie yanked the drapes closed and peeked through them like a child who covers their eyes yet still looks through their fingers.

The shadow took a step up the drive. Then another. And then, it was running up the hill toward the house.

Evie pointed at Misty. "You stay here. Don't get out of this bed, you hear me?"

"Where are you—"

"Don't. Move."

Evie closed Misty's bedroom door, raced through the hall and down the stairs, through the living room, past the dining room and kitchen to the entry foyer. Once there, she double-checked the deadbolt. *Locked. Good. But where's the latch? Why don't rich people have latches?*

A hurried knock came at the door.

"Hello?" A woman's voice called, high-pitched, almost desperate. *Maybe she broke down? This is the only house for a mile.*

"If you need a tow truck or something, there's no landline here, sorry." Evie hoped to dissuade the stranger from the door, then winced when she realized she'd given away important information if the woman meant her or Misty harm.

The knocking continued. "Hello?" the woman called again. "I need to speak with you. It's okay, Tim and Claire sent me."

Misty's parents? Maybe they'd tried the mobile and, when Evie didn't answer, they freaked out and phoned a neighbor. "Did they call you?"

"That's right," the woman replied. "They forgot to tell you about Misty's medicine. She needs to take it every night. She isn't asleep yet, is she?"

"Tell me where it is," Evie replied. "I'll make sure she gets it."

"Listen, I appreciate how protective you're being, and I'll be sure to let Tim and Claire know what a good sitter you are, but this will all go easier if I come in and give Misty her medicine myself. I've sat for her before, she knows me."

"Oh yeah? What's your name?"

"Everyone calls me Bunny."

Evie stood with her ear to the door, considering her options. *Bunny?* She dashed to the kitchen and pulled a knife from the block, tucking it into her belt behind her back. She'd seen enough horror movies to know that if someone with a weird name comes to your door claiming they need to administer medicine to the child inside, they can fuck right off out of there.

The knocking resumed, louder and more insistent.

"Hang on a sec!" Evie sprinted upstairs, taking them three at a time. When she cracked open the door to Misty's room, she found the girl sitting up in bed, her face a bone-white sky about to storm.

Evie kept her voice calm and upbeat. "Hey, kiddo, everything's fine, but listen: Do you know a woman named Bunny?"

"Uh-uh," Misty stammered, eyes glassy. "Is it the ghost lady?"

"What? No, she's not a ghost, she's, like, your neighbor or something. You don't know anyone named Bunny?"

Misty shook her head. "Did they leave? The knocking stopped."

Evie's ears perked. *Shit, the knocking has stopped.* "Stay here. Everything's fine." She closed the door to Misty's bedroom and bolted down the hall, almost leaping down the staircase into the living room, past the dining room, before pulling up short, heart catching in her throat.

A woman stood in the kitchen, her hair pulled into a severe blonde ponytail. She couldn't have been much older than twenty, but her face was gaunt with heavy circles under her eyes. She wore a beige trench coat that went to her mid-calf, and who knows what was underneath beyond her muddy hiking boots.

"How'd you get in here?" Evie demanded.

"What's your name?" Bunny asked. "You've got a lot of fight in you. I don't want to fight. I just want my baby girl."

"I don't know what you're going on about, but you need to go, or shit's gonna get real."

Bunny raised her hands. "I'm not here to hurt anyone. You don't know who hired you. This house may look nice, but these are bad people, dangerous people. I want my Misty and then I'll go."

Evie stepped around the dining room table, trying to put a large object between her and this lunatic. "I think you're confused."

"Girl, I haven't thought this clearly in years."

"Fine, wait here and when Mr. and Mrs. Mackenzie get home, we'll sort this out like adults."

"Adults? Is that what you think'll happen?" Bunny stepped around the kitchen island and stood at the edge of the dining room table across from Evie. "Five years ago, when my baby girl was still nursing, the Mackenzies bashed my head in with a golf club and rolled me off a cliff."

Evie crossed her arms, unsure what to believe. "Sounds rough."

"Oh, it was. Thankfully, the park rangers found me. I was in a coma for forty-five months and eleven days, and when I woke up, I couldn't even remember my name. Until three days ago, I was Jane Doe. I'd been working as a housekeeper and living in a group home."

Bunny took another step around the table, and Evie took a step away, hand reaching for the knife tucked behind her. The woman smirked. "But you know what happened?"

"What?" Evie blurted out the word before she could stop herself. *Is this woman telling the truth? Attempted murder? Kidnapping? Amnesia? It sounds super-fishy.*

"I was organizing cleaning supplies under one of my clients' sinks, and I saw a black widow. I hate spiders, so I jumped up and WHAM!" Bunny clapped her hands together, and Evie flinched. "I smacked my head so hard I saw stars. But then… I *remembered.* I fucking remembered everything. What he did to me. What she did to me. So I drove out here, and lo and behold, those two are carrying on as if I never existed. Claire's raising my baby like she's the one who gave birth to her, and nobody in this whole fucking town bats an eye."

Evie held up a hand. "Listen, I'm gonna stop you right here, not because I don't believe you, but because I think you need to call the cops about all this. If what you're saying is true, the Mackenzies are in a lot of—"

"The cops ain't gonna do shit," Bunny scoffed. "The Mackenzies own this town. They've got the police in their pocket and the mayor on speed dial. No one is gonna help some amnesiac teen mother. I don't even care about what they did to me. I want my baby girl. That's it. Give me my daughter."

Evie shook her head. "I'm sorry, I wanna help, I do, but I can't let you take her. Not on my watch."

"Why not? What do you know anyway? You're a kid. You don't know what I've been through. Misty needs her mother. I'm her mother."

*This shit's gone on long enough—time to get rid of this psycho.*

45

Evie pulled the knife. "I'm in charge tonight, and you need to go. What if you're wrong? What if your memories are lying to you? What if you think and hope you have a daughter who lives in some nice mansion on the hill? It's a helluva story, but where's your proof?"

Bunny's eyes narrowed, her irises becoming fierce black dots. "You're making a mistake."

"I don't think so." Evie held the knife outstretched and stepped around the dining room table. "Now put whatever key you used on the counter and get the hell out."

Bunny backed away into the kitchen and set a key down near the sink. "I see why Claire picked you."

*What's that supposed to mean?* Evie took another tentative step closer, hoping to force this crazy woman out the front door.

Bunny lunged for the butcher's block and spun toward Evie, brandishing two large knives, one in each hand. "I told you not to fuck with me. I'm taking my girl!"

"Like hell you are!" Evie screamed. She turned and ran through the living room, sprinting up the stairs and down the hall, headed for Misty's room with Bunny at her heels.

\*\*\*

Bunny stood at the closed door to Misty's room, listening. She turned the knob, easing the door open, and it bumped against something—Misty's desk? The babysitter had moved it to block the entry. *Smart girl.*

Bunny kicked the door, and it rebounded off the desk with a bang. *Gotta keep them moving.* Bunny needed the babysitter to take Misty through the jack-and-jill bathroom and into the guest bedroom. From there, they'd end up in the hallway, where she'd be waiting.

Bunny moved to the top of the stairs. Still holding both knives, she blew on her hands to warm them while she waited. *Fuck, it's cold tonight.* She'd been waiting in the forest at the edge of the property for four hours. She needed to wrap this up and get to the bus station.

The babysitter raced from the guest bedroom, holding Misty in her arms, but the teenager didn't run toward Bunny. Instead, she ran away from the stairs, dashing into Tim & Claire's bedroom at the end of the hall and slamming the door behind her. *Oh, that's perfect.*

Bunny walked to the end of the hall and put an ear to the bedroom door.

She heard Misty whimpering. "We can't be in here. I'm not allowed."

"Shh, shh," the babysitter soothed. "It's an emergency. Your mommy and daddy won't mind."

"Yes, they will," Misty said, choking back sobs.

Bunny nodded to herself. Right now, she's checking for exits—the terrace, the bathroom and sauna room, the walk-in closet. *Sorry, kid, you're trapped.*

\*\*\*

A snowstorm was coming, and the air was frigid on the bedroom balcony. Worse, the ground below was too far down to risk jumping, and there was no way Evie could hold Misty while trying to descend the mansion's outer stone wall.

Misty tensed in Evie's arms as the bedroom doorknob rattled. *Shit, Bunny's found us already.* Evie went inside, carrying Misty into the bathroom—another enormous, white-marbled affair with no exits. *Dammit, we need to find a way out or a better hiding place.*

Evie couldn't take Misty over the balcony railing, but maybe she could climb down the side of the house herself and run for help. She set the girl down on the bathroom tiles. "Misty, I need you to stay in here with the door locked. Don't open it for anyone but me."

"Don't leave," Misty pleaded.

"I have to, sweetheart. I'm going for help, but it's too dangerous to take you with me. Stay in here and don't make a sound."

Misty whimpered, and Evie held up the child's chin to look into her eyes. "You're so brave. It's going to be okay. I'll get us help. You stay here and keep quiet."

Evie stepped out of the bathroom and shut the door, locking Misty inside.

\*\*\*

"Did you stash her in there?"

Evie spun around. Bunny stood in the open bedroom doorway, a knife in each hand.

Evie pulled her knife, and Bunny eased the bedroom door shut. They began moving in a slow arc around the room.

"You're not taking her." Evie was adamant. *This bitch is not leaving with Misty.*

Bunny almost smiled, almost shrugged. "I don't actually want her."

*Don't want her? What's up with this psycho?* "Then go," Evie said, still making a slow circle, ready to stab into this nut-job's guts if she had to.

"Not yet," Bunny said. "My task isn't done to my master's satisfaction." The woman paused in front of the tall mahogany bookshelf against the far wall. She reached behind her, tilted a volume, and the bookshelf slid away, revealing a narrow entryway.

Evie peered past Bunny to look inside. A dull red light bathed the black walls of the secret chamber. Arcane sigils adorned the floor, scrawled in red ink. *Was that blood?* Leather cuffs and collars hung from pegs on the walls, and there was a contraption like a pillory in the middle of the room. Implements of torture lay discarded, and in one corner sat a coffee table with a metal cage as its base. A musty pink satin blanket lay inside of it. The stench of stale urine, blood, sex, and sweat hit Evie's nostrils, and bile rose in her throat.

"You're curious, I can tell," Bunny said. "It's the playroom. I think you'll get to like it."

"What?" Nothing was making sense to Evie. "How'd you know this was there?"

"The Mackenzies have their quirks like anybody. You know, they may be filthy rich, but they're also just like you and me."

"Yeah, whatever," Evie replied. "I honestly don't care. I need you to leave."

Bunny shook her head. "Can't do it. This is the deal."

"What *deal?*"

"Tell me how you got this job tonight. Did Claire call you, out of the blue, and say her sitter cancelled last-minute and she'd pay you triple your rate if you'd help her out?"

A cold chill hit Evie's guts like a sucker punch. It was the exact story.

"And does anybody know where you are right now? Don't answer, I already know. Claire picked you up in the mall parking lot. She asked you not to tell anyone you were working for them, NDA, privacy, privacy, blah-blah."

Evie's stomach turned. She'd wanted to surprise her mother with the extra cash on Christmas Day, so she hadn't told anyone where she'd be tonight.

"Oh, Claire is good," Bunny said with a knowing grin. "She dropped me off in the woods while she went to get you. She wanted a new pet, a special gift for her Timmy for Christmas, and you're it, sweetie."

"What are you talking about?"

"Let's put Misty to bed, okay? She's in there, right?" Bunny jabbed the knifepoint toward the bathroom door. "I think you and me need to talk this out, you know, *like adults.*"

Evie took a step back. "Talk it out? Why? You've been lying to me the whole time. You weren't in a coma."

Bunny smirked. "I had a feeling you wouldn't fall for my sob story, but Claire insisted I sell it hard. She needed to make sure you weren't some bleeding heart."

"So, what's the real story? And I want the truth this time."

Bunny arched a brow. "Sure you can handle it?"

"Try me."

"For the past eight years, I've been living in this room," Bunny motioned a knife over her shoulder at the playroom. "But the Mackenzies are bored with me." She made a pouty face. "They want someone younger, someone with more fight. It's more of a power-trip when they make a strong girl submit. Turns 'em on."

Evie gripped her knife tighter, her angry gaze fixed on Bunny.

"They sure know how to pick 'em, don't they? Had you handed Misty over to me at the onset, they might've changed their minds about you, but no. You fought me, like Claire said you would. Oh, you'll make a great new pet."

"The fuck I will."

Bunny feigned offense. "Such language. What if the child hears?"

"She isn't even yours, is she?"

"Oh, she is. I guess you could call me the Mackenzies' live-in surrogate. It wasn't part of the plan, but it's a nice way to look at it. I popped her out after Tim had a small mishap with his playroom pet. I breastfed her, changed diapers, held her at night when she cried. For years, I dreamed of escaping with her, but they don't let me see her much anymore, and there's no getting away from the Mackenzies once they have you."

"Unless you find them a new pet."

"That's it! Like I said, they're bored with me. I guess I'm a bit long in the tooth for their tastes. Over twenty, *yick.*

So, here's my chance. Get them a new girl with some fight—a lot of it—and once you're safe and secure in there," Bunny pointed at the filthy coffee table cage in the corner of the playroom, "I'm free to go. Start over. Claire even showed me the bus ticket for Atlanta. My Christmas bonus for a job well done. I'm sure my mama's been worried. She hasn't heard from me since I was fourteen."

"You gonna tell her where you were?"

Bunny shook her head.

"Why didn't you just run away when you were in the woods?"

"Like I said, Claire's got my bus ticket home. I get you in there, and the ticket is mine. Everybody wins."

*This callous bitch.* "So you'll walk away from here, forget everything, with no remorse about leaving your child to grow up in this house? No regrets about leaving *me* to the same fate you suffered?"

Bunny shrugged, and Evie saw the grief and resignation behind the woman's eyes for the first time. "I just wanna go. And this is the deal. It's what Claire wants. And I give her whatever she wants. The Mackenzies trained me well. You'll see."

"You're a goddamned idiot. What if they don't let you go? What if they want two pets? You said it yourself. Once they have you, they don't let go."

Bunny grinned, devilish and half-insane. "Oh, they'll keep their end of the bargain after I get you inside the playroom. Look how easy you've made it for me so far?"

Evie lunged at Bunny, knife held high, catching the woman off-guard.

Bunny raised her weapon to block the knife but wasn't fast enough as Evie plunged the blade deep into her shoulder. Bunny gasped and howled, swiping her twin knives at Evie, cutting a gash on the inside of the teenager's bicep with the first and taking a lock of black hair with the second.

Evie shrieked and stumbled back a few steps, leaving the blade embedded in Bunny's shoulder. Evie's breath came in shuddering rasps, and her adrenaline flowed like whitewater rapids. She couldn't yet feel the wound to her arm, but she knew the pain would come soon.

Bunny's evil grin never left her lips as she reached up and pulled the blade from the meat of her shoulder with a sickening squelch. "Nice hit. Made me kinda wet. You know, *down there.* But you're gonna need to hit me way harder than that if you wanna hurt me. I've grown an exceptionally high tolerance for pain."

Bunny strolled to the nightstand and placed all three knives there. "Let's try to avoid tarnishing the merchandise, okay?"

Blood trickled from the cut on Evie's arm, making her woozy. She needed to get away, but she couldn't leave Misty behind. Evie had known the girl for one night but already knew she'd make a better mother than Bunny or Claire. "I don't care what you do to me, but Misty deserves better than this."

Bunny rolled her eyes. "Yeah, no shit, bitch. But it's not my problem, and it isn't yours either."

Evie's vision blurred. She was losing blood fast. *How was Bunny still standing?* She was sure she'd cut the woman deeper. Evie saw the blood running down to her wrist and dripping on the bedroom's pristine hardwood floor. *Had Bunny hit an artery? Shit.*

Evie backed up a step into the playroom to put more distance between her and this nightmare woman. *Was it better to give up? Live to fight another day.* She could reason with the Mackenzies and convince them her mother knew where she was, so they'd let her go. The edges of her vision closed in, grey and gloomy. *No. You need to fight. Face the screaming bloody monster head-on.*

Evie focused her vision as Bunny charged. They met in a grapple, Bunny shoving Evie deeper into the playroom.

Evie shoved back with all her might, but her bloody arm slipped and gave out, sending her toppling backward. Her head banged against the end of the coffee table, and she almost vomited from the concussion.

On instinct, Evie kicked out, smashing a leather boot into Bunny's abdomen. The breath went out of the woman, and she staggered back. Evie, now enraged, leaped to her feet, and charged. The two grappled and fell, rolling end-over-end, biting, pulling hair, and punching. Bunny grabbed Evie's windpipe and squeezed. *Can't breathe!*

Everything went black.

\*\*\*

From inside the bathroom, Misty heard the garbled sounds of her new friend, Evie, arguing with the ghost lady. She squeezed her eyes shut and covered her ears. Mommy and Daddy would be home soon, and they'd make those two stop fighting.

She wasn't supposed to be in here. Evie would get her in big trouble for putting her in here. That was the rule: Never go into Mommy and Daddy's room, especially not after dark.

Something heavy banged outside the door, and Misty jolted in fear. She thought about the mom from the movie earlier tonight, with all those gremlins making scary sounds, but the mom was brave and went into the kitchen anyway. She wasn't scared of those gremlins. That's all the ghost lady was—a gremlin who made strange noises late at night. She would hurt Mommy and Daddy, too. She'd heard them moaning with the ghost lady when they were in here.

Now, she was hurting Evie.

Misty unlocked the door and cracked it open. Evie and the ghost lady weren't in the bedroom. She stepped out, looking around, shaking with fear but trying to be brave.

The bookcase had moved, and there were three knives on the nightstand. Misty thought one of them looked like the knife the mom used against those gremlins.

\*\*\*

The metal grate slammed closed. Evie jolted awake and smacked her head on the underside of the coffee table. Her vision swam, and her arm still bled. The pink satin blanket beneath her reeked of urine, sweat, and now—sticky, fresh blood.

Bunny peered through the bars, out of breath, bleeding, sweating, but grinning wide. "Atlanta, here I come," she said through an insane cackle.

"Fuck you," Evie muttered, drool drizzling onto her chin.

Bunny laughed harder until her cackling choked off in a sudden, high-pitched scream. Her eyes bulged as she fell to one knee, gripping her calf. Blood oozed between her fingers from a slice through the flesh and tendon. A glint of metal flashed, cutting across Bunny's throat—not enough to sever the jugular, but the blood still flowed down her neck and chest.

Bunny twisted in agony, screaming, "No, baby, no!" as the knife blade punched into her side once, twice, three times. Her body went rigid, then slack as she collapsed onto the playroom's sex-stained floor.

Misty stood over the ghost lady's body. As she took in the scene's brutality, the bloody knife slipped from the girl's fingers. Her cheeks reddened, and she vomited half-digested popcorn onto the floor.

Misty wiped her mouth with the back of her hand. She began crying, eyes wide and chest heaving. "I'm not supposed to be in here."

"It's okay. You're okay, sweetheart," Evie whispered, trying to make her weak voice reassuring. She needed to get out of this cage, get them someplace safe. She would deal with Tim and Claire later. "You were so brave. I'm so proud of you."

Misty's cries turned to sobs as she backed out of the playroom. "I'm not supposed to be in here. Mommy will be so mad when she gets home."

The girl bolted.

"Misty? Honey? Come back!"

Evie squeezed an arm through the bars, fumbling for the knife next to Bunny. Resting her fingertips on the hilt, she eased it toward her, cradling it to her chest.

Her mind raced with all the ways she'd show the Mackenzies that fighting spirit they were so eager to tame.

There were monsters in this world—that much was certain—and Evie was ready for them. But first, she had to stay conscious.

*Keep your eyes open. Keep them open.*

# Come, Save Us, Uberman!

Jasper Bark

The World Finance Center reared up over downtown Macropolis, proud, erect and inviting. Lisa Long was glad she hadn't worn panties. She was wet from the minute she entered.

It wasn't her first visit, but it was definitely the most thrilling. Not even a reception for delegates of the Bloomberg Group could dampen her excitement.

Normally, a member of the press, like Lisa, wouldn't get anywhere near a Bloomberg event, especially someone from W0lf News. The international forum for politicians, financiers, experts, academics and their lobbyists, was strictly off the record thanks to the 'Chatham House Rule,' which ensured information and comments were free, but nobody could attribute them. This was the first time they'd held the meeting in Macropolis.

Lisa's editor, Pierre Blanc had given her the invite, telling her to look pretty, stay sober and get all the deep-state gossip she could. He'd gotten the invite from Agent Harris, who'd pulled strings for them in the past.

"Agent Harris says there's a plus-one, in case you've fallen for any lucky guy," Pierre told her with a wink. "He also says you're to have a blast."

Lisa knew who her plus-one was going to be, though he'd miss the reception entirely. She wondered how much Pierre knew. Was he trying to tell her something with that crack? Was Agent Harris? Something about Agent Harris's words made her uneasy. Then again, everything about *Agent Harris* made her uneasy.

Lisa put her time in at the event, doing her best to flirt with foreign dignitaries who'd had too many glasses of Bollinger. But no one's lips were loosened by the thousand-dollar-a-bottle booze. As soon as she could, she slipped away to the Sky Pod Elevator.

The elevator was usually closed at this time, as was the observation deck, but Lisa had the operating codes from Agent Harris. She didn't plan on staring out over lower Macropolis or the Hounslow River. She had another date to keep.

Chris had done a recce of the upper floors, using his sub-atomic vision. That's how Lisa knew where the service staircase to the roof was. One of the perks of having a super-powered boyfriend.

Lisa's heels clattered on the metal stairs and echoed round the confined stairwell. The entrance hatch was stiff and heavy and Lisa broke a nail pushing it open. She stepped out onto the roof and put a hand on the support rings of the 125-foot antenna that dominated it.

When she'd caught her breath, she walked out to the far corner of the roof and gazed down at the streets 1,700 feet below.

Then she prepared herself to jump.

Agent Harris stepped onto the yacht's deck. One of many mobile operating bases used by the Military Interplanetary Bureau. He adjusted his black tie and picked a piece of lint from his matt-black jacket. He'd instructed the captain to sail it up to the mouth of the Hounslow River, so he had the best view of the World Finance Centre.

In less than hour he'd have the monster under control. Hidden away from the public where it should always have been. He'd inherited a shitshow from his predecessor, but this was where he cleaned it up with a few fireworks. A pyrotechnic display for which he had a front-row seat.

He took off his dark glasses and trained his military-grade binoculars on the roof of the skyscraper, the tallest in the country. Was that a figure he saw, just by the antenna? He wasn't sure.

Ice-cold apprehension gripped his gut. All the moving parts were in play, everything was proceeding according to the plan. So, why did he feel so uneasy?

Was it the dream? He'd had it again last night. Sometimes he was in the desert, or an empty lot, other times he was on a boat like this one. Always he looked up to the skies and there it was, hurtling toward him. A giant comet, with a glistening tail, crashing to earth, right where he stood.

The ancient Greeks and Romans had feared comets. Called them bearded stars and thought them omens of impending death. Caesar saw one on the ides of March, before he was murdered in the Senate.

In the dream Agent Harris knew he was going to die. He could neither run nor hide. The comet was as inescapable as fate. It was the comet he had always known would end his life.

On his twelfth birthday an artificial comet *had* fallen to earth in the New Mexico desert. He hadn't known it at the time, but Agent Harris was fated to deal with its aftermath. Today, some three decades later, he was making his play. And if he didn't tame the monster, this comet might not only end his life. It could mean the end of all life on the planet.

He put down the binoculars and thought about his first encounter with Lisa Long. Her name had jumped out from the candidates he vetted for W0lf News. Journalistically, she was one of the least qualified, but her psych evaluation was perfect.

When he'd summoned her to the dimly lit interrogation room, Ms Long actually thought she was there to interview him. The NDAs he produced, in accord with the Espionage Act, soon changed her mind.

Then he placed the first of the photos on the table in front of her.

She frowned. "What's this?"

"This, Ms Long, is a crater in the Chihuahua desert."

He placed a photo of an extra-terrestrial craft before her. "And this is what caused it."

"Is that what I think it is?"

Agent Harris nodded. "Nearly thirty years ago, an interplanetary craft crash landed in the United States. It was intercepted by my bureau, who specializes in these matters. There was a single occupant in the craft, an alien infant, born lightyears from our solar system. It was a shape-shifter, but this was the least of its abilities. Our scientists were unable to dissect the creature because it proved to be invulnerable. Its impermeable hide resisted every blade, bullet or particle weapon we tried. Not even a thermonuclear device could damage it."

Ms Long pouted. "Why are you telling me all this? What's with all the paperwork? Do you want me to report on it or not?"

"The paperwork is to ensure you *don't* report on it. We're telling you all this for your own safety."

"Am I in danger?"

"Yes, Ms Long, you're in grave danger. The extra-terrestrial infant was the responsibility of my predecessor, Agent Brown. He figured that if we couldn't nullify the creature, we would have to contain it. His answer was Operation Smallburg.'"

"What's that?"

"The creature had taken on human form. So, Agent Brown constructed Smallburg, an artificial community with one purpose—to contain the threat of this monster. It was inhabited solely by agents of the Military Interplanetary Bureau, including two who posed as the creature's foster parents. Their job was to indoctrinate the alien in the values of our nation and our culture. It was conditioned never to use its powers against a human being and never to interfere in the power structures of our country."

"Is it still alive?"

"Oh yes, Ms Long, it's very much alive, as you'll find out. You see, as the creature came of age and its powers grew, it developed new abilities that needed to be carefully controlled, for the sake of our nation and the whole planet. Agent Brown decided to encourage the alien to assist in humanitarian crises, without ever revealing its presence here on the planet. It changed shape in order to avoid recognition, but the identity it took was intemperate to say the least, and nothing anyone said could dissuade it."

Agent Harris put another photo on the table.

Ms Long's eyes widened. "Is that…? Oh my days! I'd heard the rumors, but I thought they were an urban myth."

"No, Ms Long, I assure you, this is all very real."

"I still don't understand why you're telling me this."

Agent Harris pulled his dark glasses from the bridge of his nose so he could fix Ms Long with a penetrating stare. "Unfortunately, exposure to the wider world meant it became impossible to contain the creature within Smallburg. It wanted to see more of our country and help more of our people, it wanted a career. It hit upon the media as a way of monitoring the world so it could help more people. When it gets an idea in its head there is no way of stopping it. Reluctantly we found it a place at W0lf News, whose robust ideological position would support the psychological conditioning we'd worked so hard to establish."

Agent Harris put one last photograph on the table.

Recognition flashed instantly in Lisa's eyes. "Wait, is that Chris Klein? Are you telling me that he's…?"

"Yes, Ms Long. I'm afraid we've put you in harm's way, and the situation has proved unavoidable. The man you sit across from in the bullpen is not a man at all. It's a biological weapon of near limitless power. An alien monstrosity that could level a city with its bare hands. You asked me why I'm telling you this. It's a warning, Ms Long. Be as cautious as possible around the creature you know as Mr Klein. I cannot stress too highly how dangerous this being is."

Lisa swayed gently in the crosswinds that tore across the roof of the World Finance Center. She tried to surrender to her sensations. Thought of herself as a leaf carried by air currents.

She couldn't quite do it. Her mind wouldn't let go of her last conversation with Pierre. It was the comments from Agent Harris. She kept picking at them like an unhealed scab. The implications of the first comment were pretty obvious. He was telling her that he knew all about the tristes. Why else would he have arranged for her to attend a reception at the tallest building in the country?

But what did his second comment mean? If it came from anyone else, Lisa would have shrugged it off, but everything Agent Harris said and did had an ulterior motive.

When he'd told her Chris was dangerous he might have well loaded her with bullets and pointed her straight at him. Lisa had always had lousy taste in men. Brutes, bullies and ruthless bastards, that's what got her hot. Nice guys left her cold.

When she first met Chris he'd made her skin crawl. He dressed like someone from the 1970s, in wide-lapelled jackets, bell-bottom jeans and turtle neck sweaters. Squinting permanently through a pair of dweeby bottle-bottom glasses.

But worse than that was the down-home, cornpone way he acted. Like a character from *Leave it to Beaver*, with his *Aw, gee, shucks* and *thank you kindly, ma'am* manner. She wanted to slap him, or retch into a waste basket.

Then Agent Harris revealed the truth. And suddenly she was obsessed. He couldn't stress too highly how dangerous Chris was. And Lisa wanted to be pawed, more than anything, by bare hands that could level a city.

Lisa knew she couldn't come on too strong. Chris had led a sheltered life in an artificially constructed town. To say he was sexually inexperienced was like saying John Wayne Gacy was a poor choice for a birthday clown.

Their early dates were uneventful. They held hands over frozen yogurt or took a lunchtime walk in the park. He treated Lisa like a cross between Nancy Reagan and Mother Theresa, his two favorite women.

Finally, after their third dinner and a movie, she had Chris drive them out of Macropolis in his battered Impala. He parked on a bluff on the outskirts of town and she lured him into the backseat to make out.

As she pressed her lips against his and stroked his tongue with her own, she felt a strange metamorphosis in the alien form to which she clung. His body grew taller, his shoulders broadened and his chest and arms filled with thick knots of hardened sinew.

His biceps weren't the only muscle to have grown. Unable to help herself, Lisa undid his fly and reached inside his trousers. What she found there was the most beautiful cock she had ever seen.

She couldn't keep her hands or her eyes off it. It inspired an aching need deep inside, which is where she longed to feel it. She ran her hands up and down the length of his shaft, massaging the little ridge of sensitive tissue, just below the rim of his helmet.

Lisa increased the tempo as Chris's groans grew louder. His face was a mixture of unbelieving gratitude and raw, animal lust. She was just about to lean forward and take him in her mouth when his moan reached an intolerable pitch.

Then everything happened at once.

The windshields shattered with the force of his cry and the seats were filled with broken glass.

The dashboard collapsed in on itself.

The hood flew up and the front of the Impala disappeared with a shriek and a wrench of torn metal.

Chris's cock lay spent and flaccid in her hand.

The force of his nut was so great it had blown the engine out of the front of the car.

Lisa learned later it had traveled several miles, still dripping with alien jism, before embedding itself in an ancient oak on the property of a puzzled farmer.

If he had come even a second later, Lisa would not have had a head on her shoulders. No single thought had ever turned her on so much in her life.

After he'd come, Chris began to cry. He begged her not to hate him and then he confessed everything. How he came from another planet as a tiny infant, crash landing in a spaceship in a cornfield just outside of Smallburg.

How Mr and Mrs Klein had found him and raised him as the child they never had. How their wisdom and virtue had guided him. Shown him he should use his special gifts for the betterment of all mankind, but especially the United States. Yet he could not reveal his true identity to anyone for fear they would not understand.

That's why he had moved to Macropolis, to work for the most fair and balanced news channel in the world. In this way he could stay abreast of current affairs and learn how to best employ his unique talents under the guise of Uberman.

It took every bit of guile Lisa had not to laugh out loud at that name. Instead she faked surprise. "You mean Uberman is real? I thought he was just a legend."

"Oh no, Lisa, he's as real as I'm sitting here. In fact, I guess he *is* sitting here, cos I'm Uberman!"

*Aw jeez, did he have to ruin everything by being such a cornball?* Worse, he'd just made her use the word *jeez* in an internal monologue.

There was one more thing Chris confessed to her—his undying love. The dumb lummox was smitten. He could raze an entire continent in less than an hour. Single-handedly expunge all life from the planet. And he was mooning around after Lisa like a love-sick kitten.

This put her in a difficult position. Lisa was fine as long as she kept her alien lover sweet. If he ever got pissed, it could mean the end of not only her life, but all life on the planet.

Lisa had to touch herself every time she thought about this.

However much she wanted him inside her, penetrative sex was out of the question. Lisa couldn't risk him shooting too soon and tearing her apart. Being such a boy scout, Chris was concerned about the damage he might do to other people's property every time he came.

To get around this, Chris would fly them as far into the stratosphere as he could go without Lisa passing out, or catching hypothermia. Then she would jerk him off with no fear of leveling a building with his sperm.

On their second trip above the clouds, Lisa was just building to a tempo she knew Chris liked when he asked her, "You remember you told me your dad was in air navigation?"

Lisa thought this strange. "Yes."

"He ever teach you to fly?"

"I practiced all the time on a flight simulator. Even thought about being a pilot for a while. Why?"

"Why don't you steer my control stick to a height of 20,000 feet on a 65-degree turn."

Without losing rhythm, Lisa moved Chris's cock into the position he suggested. As soon as she did he cried out and shot an arc of sperm into the atmosphere.

A second later there was a bright flash and what looked like a shooting star on the horizon.

"What was that?"

Chris grinned. "We just took out a Chinese spy satellite."

They both laughed at this.

On their third trip, Chris came so hard and so fast he forgot himself and let go of Lisa. For a brief second she clung to his magnificent dick, but she'd been using lube and her fingers slipped off.

Lisa had fallen ten thousand feet before Chris came back to himself. He caught her less than twenty feet from the ground.

For a second Lisa lost consciousness.

An insistent pressure in her loins brought her back round as Chris lifted her gently into the air. The pressure felt like a pleasure tsunami hitting underfunded flood defenses. It spilled down her thighs and raced up her spine, overriding every sense in her body. From the follicles in her scalp to the soles of her feet, her nerve endings were screaming with orgasmic overload.

And it kept coming. Wave after wave of it washed over her. Left her gasping for breath and unable to control any part of her body.

Ten minutes later Lisa was still shaking, still wet, still coming.

Chris was terrified, apologizing over and over. Finally, Lisa was able to speak and calm his fears, explaining she'd just had the single best sexual experience of her life.

The big dope had been worried for a long time that he couldn't please her like she pleased him. He'd tried playing with her clit, but when she asked him to go a little faster he'd nearly broken the sound barrier and she'd ended up with blisters where no woman should.

Now he had a way of getting her off.

But the magic soon wore off. After the fourth time of dropping her from a great height she just wasn't able to come like she had before. The problem was she knew Chris was going to save her. There was no danger, no threat of death, so the thrill diminished to the point where she was more likely to yawn than orgasm.

After several more frustrating falls, Lisa hit upon an answer. She needed to reintroduce the element of risk. So, without telling Chris, she climbed to the top of the Colonial State Building and threw herself off, screaming for Chris at the very last moment.

With his hyper-enhanced hearing Chris caught her screams and flew to her rescue. He caught her within feet of the sidewalk. Lisa came harder and longer than she ever had before.

This became their new thing. Lisa would travel to the tallest buildings in Macropolis, and then other cities, and finally other countries, and throw herself off. Screaming for Chris as she fell. He would streak across countries and oceans to catch her just in time. But there was always the possibility he wouldn't reach her in time and this is what kept the magic alive.

Lisa asked, one time, how he could pinpoint her so accurately among all the buildings. Chris told her it was his sub-atomic vision. He had the ability to see the material world at a sub-atomic level, where it was nothing more than particles and waves of energy, but he was still able to discern shape and form. That meant that he could effectively see through any physical object.

Lisa shuffled closer to the edge of the roof. She'd been thinking about nothing else all day, but now that she was here, she was reluctant to toss herself off.

It had something to do with the cryptic comment Agent Harris made to her editor about having a blast. He was planning something, she could tell. She just didn't know what.

Agent Harris used the untraceable cell to call Jamie Osman, a junior anchor at W0lf News. Osman was barely out of his teens and currently relegated to 'youth interest' and 'puff pieces,' but the kid had ambition. He would crawl over his dead mother's corpse if it meant a chance to advance. That's what made him so useful.

His phone rang four times before he picked up. "Osman speaking."

"Mr Osman, I don't have much time, listen very carefully."

"Agent Harris, wow, okay, thanks for calling, do you mind if I record this?"

"Yes, I do, this line is scrambled to prohibit that."

"Um, okay, how can I help?"

"Do you remember we discussed the Uberman phenomena?"

"The urban myths about a flying man who rescues people from earthquakes and hurricanes?"

"That's correct."

"Do you have footage?"

"I can go one better. How would you like to be the first person to shoot some?'

"Oh my God, really? How?"

"We've been tracking him for some time now and I can state conclusively that he's about to make an appearance here in Macropolis."

"Where?"

"Be on the corner of Poulton and West St in the next twenty minutes."

"That's right outside the World Finance Center isn't it?"

"Yes."

"That's more than twenty minutes away."

"Be there, Mr Osman, or miss out on the biggest opportunity of your career."

And with that, he hung up. Jamie Osman would be there, Agent Harris was certain of it. He was too hungry to pass up a chance like this.

The final chess piece was now in play. Everything was going according to plan.

So why did he see flaming comets with glistening tails every time he closed his eyes?

Lisa took a step back from the edge and caught her breath. She'd been looking forward to this all week. She hadn't had a good, full-body orgasm in ages.

So why was she apprehensive? Was it something to do with Agent Harris?

Did his comments suggest the guest pass was nothing to do with crashing the Bloomberg function. Did he actually want her to climb to the top of the World Finance Center and scream for Chris?

Lisa shook her head. Of course he didn't, she was being an idiot.

She took a deep breath, raced to the edge of the roof, took a running jump and screamed for Chris.

As always happened, her stomach lurched as she leaped out over the edge. Cold sweat broke over her body and her breathing accelerated in panic.

Colors and sounds achieved a crystal clarity and her mind began to race, thinking at a rate that was normally far beyond her.

That's when Lisa realized what Agent Harris must have planned. And how much danger she and Chris were in.

"Right here, are you sure?" Colleen pulled her bike over to the curb.

Jamie shouted over the noise of the engine. "Yes, this is where I was told to be."

Colleen climbed off her bike, removed her helmet and shook out her red hair. Then she unpacked her camera equipment. "If this is a hoax, you owe me more than fifty bucks."

Colleen was the only camera person at W0lf News who could have gotten Jamie to the World Finance Center on time. He'd still had to bribe her so she'd drive recklessly. He straightened his tie and smoothed down his jacket. "It's not a hoax. My source is impeccable."

Colleen turned her camera on. "Want me to train it on the building?"

"Yeah, get a good establishing shot to emphasize its height."

Colleen tilted the camera upward.

Jamie caught something falling far above. "Hey, do you see that? What is it?"

Colleen zoomed in. "It looks like a person."

Agent Harris was on the bow deck, watching the security camera feed from the World Finance Center on a laptop. He was pleased to see that Jamie Osman was in place.

The yacht was idling in the middle of the river, under the shadow of the skyscraper. Agent Harris wanted to hear and see the explosion when it happened. He primed the detonator and held his breath.

In just a moment, the monster would swoop down and snatch up Ms Long and their little love game would culminate as it always did. But this time there would be an unexpected coda.

An explosive device planted on the same floor as the Bloomberg function. The minute Ms Long came, Agent Harris would set off a climax of his own.

The device would explode with the intensity of a small star. Everyone at the function would be killed while the alien creature dallied with its lover instead of saving them.

This monumental selfishness would be caught by Jamie Osman and the monster would be exposed to the world as the self-serving pervert it was. Before its fame could spread and people started thinking of it as some kind of hero, the alien's image would be destroyed.

People would see it as the creature that prioritized its deviant sexuality over the lives of some of the most important people on Earth. Then Agent Harris would release details of both its alien origin and the unspeakable acts it had committed with Ms Long.

The creature would be forced into hiding. It would have to give up its heroic acts, it's career and its attempts to fit in with human society. It would be forced into the arms of Agent Harris and the Military Interplanetary Bureau.

Agent Harris would send it deep into space, patrolling the galaxy for hostile alien species. Keeping the monster and the threat it posed far away from the planet. All it would cost were the lives of a few stuffed shirts and corrupt politicians.

It was a sacrifice he was willing to make.

Lisa was close to passing out when Chris caught her. She could feel the intense pressure building in her loins. She had to hold it at bay. Had to keep a level head just long enough to save everyone in the building.

The orgasm pressed insistently at Lisa's body. It wanted to escape, to engulf her in ecstatic oblivion. But she didn't dare give in. They were in too much danger and this danger only increased the orgasm's intensity.

Lisa slipped her hand down the front of Chris's trunks and took hold of his alien member. He stiffened instantly. "This is new."

She was on the point of unconsciousness, concentrating everything on her right hand. Using every bit of skill and dexterity she possessed as she worked it up and down his cock.

She had to fight to keep her words from slurring. "I need you to…use that sub-atomic… vision… I think there's…a device…on the same floor as the Bloomberg function…"

"I see it."

She had to bring him to climax as soon as she could. "Tell me…where to steer your…control stick…"

"Take me down to a thousand feet at a thirty-five-degree angle."

Lisa moved Chris's cock into position.

Colleen wrinkled her nose. "Wait, are they…eew!"

Jamie glanced up and saw what she was shooting. "That's my colleague, Lisa Long. You can't film this."

Jamie grabbed the camera and moved it away. Colleen was not pleased. "Hey! What are you…?"

Something caught Colleen's eye on the viewfinder and she focused in on it. An object was dislodged from the World Finance Center and hurtled toward the river.

Over the next minute, Colleen filmed the footage that would make both their careers. Footage that was syndicated to every news outlet in the world.

The next morning, the authorities would issue a statement concerning a failed terrorist attack in which the explosive device blew itself out of the building and landed instead on the bumbling perpetrators who'd planted it.

While Jamie and Colleen were busy earning their first Emmy, Lisa and Chris were coming simultaneously.

Lisa gave herself over to an intense, full-body orgasm that lasted over an hour. Chris roared and came with an equal intensity.

Thanks to Lisa's careful aim, his enhanced, alien sperm shot downward at a steep angle. It went through an open window on an upper floor and between the closing doors of an elevator, before punching a hole in the elevator's floor and entering the shaft where the explosive device had been planted.

Chris's jism hit the device with such a velocity it blew the explosive through the outer wall of the building and sent it hurtling into the River Hounslow.

Agent Harris had just pressed the detonator when he looked up and saw the device tearing toward him. He was directly in its path.

Before it hit, he just had time to register what it looked like. A bearded star, streaking toward him with a glistening tail of alien sperm. An omen of impending doom.

It was the comet he had always known would end his life. Exploding with the intensity of a small star. Putting paid to his plans forever.

Now there would be nothing to protect the world from Uberman.

# Steel Horses

## Kenneth W. Cain

The car appeared out of nowhere in Mateo Domingo's rearview mirror, two headlights gliding forty yards behind him—the only other car on this lonely stretch of road in Hell, Delaware. Being so late, he couldn't make out the model yet, but the vehicle gained on him, coming within a few car lengths of his taillights. Only then could he make out any details despite the thick fog.

He couldn't believe his eyes, as at first glance, it appeared no one was driving the car. That wasn't possible, was it? "What the fuck?"

"Matty, honey. Are you okay?" Mom said.

"Yeah. Just some car." Why was she even calling him this late?

"You sound distracted" Her concern poured through the phone. "You're not..."

"No, Ma." He sighed. "Really. I promise."

"You sure?"

"Yeah." He shook his head. "Look, I should go." He wanted to get a better look at this car and its driver.

"No, Matty. I mean, are you sure you're doing the right thing; moving out west?"

"Ma, we talked about this. I need a change. A big one. Now let me go so I can focus on my driving and getting there safe."

"Okay..." Again, he heard the concern in her tone.

"I promise, Ma. I'll be okay." But he really wasn't sure. "Bye, okay?"

There was only silence for a beat. "Yes, Matty. I love you. *We* love you."

"I know. I love you, too. Tell Dad I said hi."

"I will." Another moment of silence passed. "Bye."

Mateo didn't respond. He just hung up on her, sat his cell phone in the cup holder, and returned his gaze to the car behind him.

At a glance, he thought the car was a Dodge Charger, maybe one of the older models judging by how its headlights were situated, almost like a pair of eyes framed by thick-rimmed glasses. But he couldn't see much else of the exterior with it being so dark and foggy and the car so black. Even the windows looked tinted, big time, almost as dark as the night itself.

The car slithered back and forth behind him like a giant predatory snake slithering up to its prey. In contrast, the rumble of its engine roared like a ferocious beast.

Mateo did what any other young-blooded man would do: he depressed the gas pedal, quickly putting distance between them. "That'll teach you for riding my ass, dickhead."

To his surprise, the Charger accelerated, matching his speed and now gaining on him. Once more the car swerved left then right, the driver clearly trying to get on Mateo's nerves. And it was working. Anxiousness rose in Mateo's chest, a vice grip pressure on his heart that felt like a python squeezing the life out of him. His eyes flickered from the road to the rearview mirror, back and forth, and he pushed his Shelby GT350R harder. And as if enjoying this engagement, apparently, in doing so, he only further engaged his pursuer, whose vehicle came so close to Mateo's rear that he could no longer see its headlights. The effect cast an almost ghostly glow over what he could see of the car, the surrounding fog almost seeming as though it was being carried by the car, it was so thick.

Mateo just wanted to get away from this crap, to ease that tightness in his chest, alleviate all the worry and anxiety. The city bred road rage, and Mateo had seen his fair share, and that was the main reason he'd left that world behind for a more rural setting. He hoped the panic attacks would stop as a result, that he'd learn to relax, take life one day at a time.

His doctor had said, "You're twenty-nine years old, way too young to feel this bad. You're going to give yourself a heart attack." And Doctor Soval was always right. Had been for as long as Mateo could recall.

Each time Mateo lost his temper, he had this sensation similar to what he imagined it would feel like if a hawk seized his heart in its formidable talons and squeezed. He experienced that now, too, and could almost hear Doctor Soval scolding him, talking him down off the ledge he'd created in his mind. As his psychiatrist had often reminded him, people like that weren't worth the hassle. What if they were going to see their mother for the last time? Wouldn't that make him feel awful?

Mateo wasn't so sure this time, this far out from the city. But letting it get to him like this was like transforming into a monster, and that made him feel ugly and gross, and a bit sad that he still hadn't mastered the art of controlling his temper. That sensation worsened the more he let it bother him, and the way this asshat rode his tail was indeed bothering him. Very much so.

Realizing this, Mateo let off the gas and pulled over. *There, asshole, go ahead and pass if you're in such a hurry.*

But the Charger also slowed, shifting down so fast the resulting rumble made Mateo's seat shudder. This guy—or gal—was just egging Mateo on, it seemed. The unseen person depressed the Charger's gas pedal several times in a row, making the car roar, but it didn't budge an inch—a tiger waiting to pounce on a weaker, more insignificant creature. With every rev of that engine, Mateo's own gears tightened, his chest pounding like a bass drum. He wanted to leave this asshole in his dust, to laugh as he sped away watching the dark car's headlights shrink to nothing in the rearview mirror.

But he suppressed that emotion. And eventually, the Charger swerved around him and passed.

Once the Charger's thin rectangular taillights could no longer be seen in the fog, Mateo pulled onto the road, steadying his speed to make sure he didn't catch up. All he saw was its taillights off ahead of him. And a minute later, there they were, and damned if they weren't getting bigger by the moment.

"You've got to be kidding me."

The Charger slowed until it was a few car lengths ahead of Mateo and then matched his pace. Mateo couldn't even make out the shape of the driver, it was so hard to see through such dark-tinted windows. But the lights of the Charger's dashboard offered a fuzzy silhouette of a person, thin and lanky he would guess, seemingly much older judging by the scruff outline of hair. Other than that, he couldn't make out anything else.

Its brake lights illuminating, the Charger shuddered to a stop before him. His vision flooded with red, Mateo yanked the wheel hard to the right and swerved onto the shoulder, the gravel crunching beneath his tires. A thick trail of dust kicked up behind him in a rooster tail before the GT skidded to a stop.

Sweat beaded on his forehead. "What the literal fuck is wrong with this guy?"

He had to concentrate to pry his clenched fists from the wheel. The anger ate away at his insides, roiling there like torrid waters. He took a deep breath, trying to steady himself, and when that didn't work, he pressed the button to roll down his window. "Why don't you just leave me alone, *asshole*?"

The driver didn't reciprocate, only sat there idling. Whoever this was, they weren't in any hurry. And, even worse, their aim appeared to revolve solely around annoying Mateo. As if to confirm this notion, the driver honked.

"Fuck you, too, pal," Mateo yelled out the window and gave the guy the finger. He floored it, keeping the brake down, and spinning to the side as he carefully turned the wheel. A cloud of dust shot out from behind him, and like a sprinkler, tiny rocks and gravel sprayed out behind him as he spun. He heard a popcorn-like *ping ping rattle ping rattle tink ping* that made Mateo burst out in laughter.

He let off the brake and sped out ahead on the road, and the Charger followed.

A hundred yards down the road, the Charger caught up to him. The driver pulled into the oncoming lane and swerved at him; Mateo almost didn't get out of the way in time. As if to solidify his stance on what Mateo had done to his Charger, the driver rammed the front quarter panel of his GT. Once more Mateo rode the gravel, rocks pinging off his undercarriage, the back-left wheel spinning wildly as he turned the wheel left then right then left.

Once he got the Mustang back on the road, Mateo depressed the gas and pulled ahead of the Charger. The driver pursued. Mateo looked for someplace to pull off— should the need arise—but there were few opportunities on this stretch of the highway. He saw plenty of side streets, but few were accessible from this part of the highway. And he hadn't seen an exit since he first encountered the Charger. He would have to put up with this aggravation until he found an exit. Either that or a cop, whichever came first.

That's a solid idea, he thought.

Mateo grabbed his cell phone and turned it on. "Damn! What happened?"

He waved the phone around the car trying to get a signal, keeping one eye on the road and the other glancing back and forth between the phone screen and the Charger in the rearview mirror. The GT wandered left, right, then onto the shoulder before he righted its path. But no matter what he tried he couldn't even get a single bar now that he'd come to a long stretch of sun-scorched skeletal pine trees.

Mateo half-threw the cell phone into the cup holder and refocused on the road. The Charger's lights grew in his rearview like two curious eyes prying into his thoughts. His anger consuming him, instinct took over.

"Fuck this guy."

Mateo sped up, taking a second to look at the speedometer. The numbers counted up so quickly it never really settled on anyone for long as it approached 100 mph. But the Charger easily matched his speed, coming up behind him but maintaining a position several car lengths back. Mateo accelerated, closing in on 110. Both cars were like rockets in the night, the trees that saddled the road a mere blur. When he pinned 120 mph, Mateo wondered how long it would be before they attracted the attention of a cop. If nothing else, at this pace, he would reach the next exit in no time.

Then he saw the sign.

NEXT EXIT
FAIRPLAY - 4 MILES

"Crap."

Four more miles of this? He was already traveling at an unsafe speed, just trying to stay ahead of this idiot. And no way could he slow down, because this driver had it in for him. The Charger's driver didn't even seem to care if they wrecked, so it stood to reason if he stopped, that would likely lead to a fistfight, maybe even something worse. And while a brawl didn't sound so bad after everything he'd endured thus far, what if the guy had a gun? That made him anxious. Mateo was not a strapping man, but he could hold his own in a dust-up, but against a gun...? Forget about it.

He thought about it a moment. There was that old wooden baseball bat he kept in his trunk, but as much as he couldn't stand this asshole, did he really have it in him to hurt someone like that? To possibly, even accidentally, murder the guy? No, he wasn't sure he had the nerve. Besides, he didn't know what he was up against. For all he knew, lanky or not, this guy could be seven foot tall and tough as a Mack truck, and Mateo definitely wouldn't stand a chance against a guy like that.

Luckily, Mateo didn't have to ruminate on the matter long.

The siren startled him, red and blue lights flashing across his rearview. To Mateo's amazement, when the cop neared the Charger, the driver swerved at the police cruiser. The cop swerved onto the gravel, losing some momentum, but quickly accelerated until it was beside the Charger again. When the Charger swerved at the cruiser this time, the cop sped up, and pulled in front of the Charger. Out ahead of both cars, the cruiser slowed fast, forcing Mateo to jam on the GT's brakes. But the Charger just closed the gap, and Mateo found himself pinned between the two cars, incapable of speeding up or slowing down. As the cop further decelerated, the Charger rammed the back of Mateo's GT and forced the Mustang into the back of the cruiser, as they sped down the road like a train.

Mateo grabbed the steering wheel as tight as he could. "Shit shit shit shit!"

He glanced back over his shoulder and watched the Charger ram him again, pushing him into the cruiser. Surely the cop was calling this in by now, or already had.

*Blam!*

Mateo's eyes went wide as he realized the cop had shot at him. What he'd hit, Mateo had no idea, but he didn't want any part of this...a gunfight.

*Blam bam blam!*

The cruiser's back windshield spiderwebbed and a split second later, the passenger's side of the front window puckered around a bullet hole. That was far too close for comfort.

Mateo needed to get out of this mess, and fast.

The Charger's grill scraped against the Mustang's bumper, ramming him into the police cruiser again and again, and causing the GT to shimmy. Mateo maintained control, but the Charger was persistent if nothing else. When it rammed Mateo again, the GT lunged forward and struck the back-left side of the cruiser. And the Charger continued to push Mateo until the cruiser was at an angle. Then the Charger pulled into the oncoming lane and sped forward, nosing the cruiser.

Both Mateo and the Charger's driver slowed as the cruiser spun down the highway in front of them. The cop tried to regain control but, before he could, the Charger sped forward and rammed the cruiser, sending it over the shoulder and down a steep incline. Halfway down, the cruiser rolled onto its roof and slid the rest of the way down. For a split second, the red and blue lights illuminated a swampy area, then the Charger was back at its side.

"Damn it!" Mateo sped up, pulling ahead of the Charger, but it soared after him.

He glanced in the rearview mirror, saw the water-logged cop reach the road, bend over on his knees to catch his breath, and then he had his gun up.

*Blam blam!*

If the cop had hit anything, it had been the Charger. And that coal black car looked like a panther on the prowl now, wanting only to feed, and Mateo was the meat. It was a notion Mateo felt in his bones, at his core, knowing if he stopped for whatever reason, the Charger's driver would somehow end him. Already, he was going 93 mph, and the Charger was still right behind him, urging him to go faster.

Mateo obliged, paying close enough attention to the roadside mile markers to see he only had one mile until he reached the exit. There, perhaps he could escape this madman, maybe lose him on the back roads. Mateo pushed the GT, reaching 131 mph, afraid to go any faster. Though the Charger matched his pace, it was far enough behind him Mateo thought he could exit safely.

As he neared the exit, the Charger made its move. Mateo prepared to exit, hugging the right side of the road. Then he saw the Charger there too, speeding up alongside him on the shoulder, gravel and dust kicked up in the turmoil. It was almost surreal, the Charger rumbling over potholes, branches, softball-sized rocks, none of it slowing the car down one bit. It traversed all hazards until the strange car blocked any hope of Mateo getting off at this exit.

Mateo shook a fist at the dim shadow inside the Charger. "Son of a bitch."

When they came to the off-ramp, Mateo decided it was now or never. He rammed the Charger, but the vehicle held its ground. The two cars edged past the exit, Mateo looking back in his rearview longingly. A second later, he saw the guardrail and a new opportunity presented itself.

"If that's how you want it..."

Mateo sped to 138 mph, and the Charger matched him, both cars rubbing bumpers. The Charger ate so much gravel, dust and rocks were shooting everywhere now, making it hard to see much of anything. But Mateo saw it just fine, even if the Charger's driver didn't. All his troubles would be over in a fraction of a second if he could just...

The cars reached the guardrail, and Mateo held his breath, gripping his wheel tightly in anticipation of the oncoming collision. It stunned him when nothing came of it at all. He glanced left then right, scanning the rearview and even twisting around in his seat, wondering where the Charger had gone. He'd had them dead to rights, and then...nothing.

It couldn't have just vanished, could it?

"What the fuck?"

Without knowing he was doing so, Mateo let off the gas. The GT steadied to 113 mph, slowing as it approached a large green sign.

NEXT EXIT

EMMITSBURG - 3 MILES

Then, as if out of nowhere, the Charger swerved into the road behind him.

Mateo's face felt like it was on fire. "Dios mio."

He refocused himself on a goal. All he had to do was stay ahead of this creep long enough to get off at the next exit. If he could manage that, he could find help in town.

A mile later, he was still several lengths ahead of the Charger, and he grew more confident by the minute. When he spotted flares up ahead, he knew right away there would be trouble if he didn't put distance between him and the Charger now. But he also saw an opportunity. Having someone by his side would give him a sense of security. Maybe together they could intimidate the driver enough to move on.

Mateo slammed on his brakes, and the Charger tried to reciprocate. Then Mateo swerved right and jammed the brakes again. The resulting contact caused the Mustang to jolt, but Mateo adjusted quickly, this time braking hard and forcing the front right end of the Charger to hit his GT. In his rearview, the Charger spun wildly as Mateo sped away. The driver would probably recover fast, hanging just off the road, but it gave him an opportunity. He watched as its lights quickly diminished in the fog.

Part of him considered bypassing the disabled car just to try to make it to the exit. If he did that, maybe he could find help before the Charger returned. Then again, if he did that, the Charger's driver might go after this easy prey instead. No way Mateo could get past that guilt.

When he got there, Mateo pulled up behind the broken-down car. He threw open the GT's door and leaped out, leaving the car running. Then, remembering the bat, he decided that might not be so bad of a weapon to have right now. He doubled back to his trunk and retrieved the bat, hoping it would intimidate the Charger's driver. Then he jogged over to the Taurus wagon where he spotted an old man peering under the hood.

"Judas Priest!" the old man said. "Son, you just about scared the bejesus out of me."

Mateo was too busy staring off in the Charger's direction. He saw no lights on the horizon. Then, seeing how old the man was, he realized how little help a man of that age would be and sighed.

Mateo considered this. *I'm on my own here.*

The man nodded to the bat in Mateo's hands. "What're you meanin' to do with that, son?"

"Listen, there's this guy chasing me in his car." Mateo pointed off in the distance. "He's about two hundred yards back, and he's dangerous. That's why I have the bat."

"Why didn't you just call the police?"

"I tried. No signal." Mateo glanced back again. "We did see one cop and that guy just ran him off the road. Listen, I'm worried—"

"Bull-malarkey. T'was just talking to AAA." The old man's face melted into a frown. "I'm not sure what planet you think you're on, but we got civilization out in these parts, you know?"

Mateo was lost. "Huh?"

The old man moved to the side of his car. Mindful of his wide berth, Mateo followed the man around to the passenger's side of the Taurus. This man reached in through the driver's side door window and grabbed a cell phone. "Yep. See? Told you. I got full—"

Like the big cat Mateo imagined earlier, the Charger came out of nowhere and pounced on the man. Mateo heard the roar of the engine and less than a second later, the man, the door, his phone all vanished. Blood splattered the hood of the Taurus, so much red and viscera, he couldn't imagine anyone living through that. A dark red trail led up the road like black ice to where the Charger skidded to a halt. There, the driver revved his engine.

"Get in the GT and run," he mumbled to himself, but his legs wouldn't move. He was still traumatized by what he'd just seen.

Finally shaking out of his daze, Mateo spun to do just that when another thought came to him, infecting his brain like a disease. *No. You have a bat. Stay and end this dickhead.* Once the seed was planted, he had to see it through.

The Charger turned back and crept forward like a cat toying with a mouse. When the Charger came within twenty yards of Mateo, its engine roared. The driver pulled his car over in front of the Taurus, off the side of the road where Mateo could barely see the door opening. Mateo tried to get a better look, but the Taurus' headlights near blinded him. He held the bat in his right hand and used his left to shield from the light.

All he saw were two black boots, just below the Taurus, as they lowered from the Charger. A large figure hefted itself out of the Charger and stood, Mateo able to see only a silhouette of the man. The guy had long scraggly white hair covered with a ratty cowboy hat and wore a long black duster. If Mateo didn't know better, he'd swear the guy was a gunslinger right out of the Old West. And he was big, too. *Really* big. And that got Mateo reconsidering the stay-and-fight approach.

The driver's boots clacked along the macadam as he approached, and as he came into view, Mateo almost pissed himself. This wasn't a man—not anymore, anyway. Mateo wasn't sure what he was, only that he was hideous and unearthly and certainly no longer human. His emaciated face wasn't much more than a skull with bloodied bits of flesh sticking to bone, the driver's expression of muscle and sinew and grinning teeth like something out of the movies. The driver lifted a hand and tipped back his hat, the sleeve of the duster sliding down his skeletal forearm.

Blood rushed through Mateo's head so fast, it felt swollen. The heartbeat in his ears sounded like the deafening hooves of a wild stampede beating against the earth. His legs weakened, and he almost fainted. It was like standing on a pair of thin stilts, so weak they could snap at any moment. He couldn't run. No matter how much he pleaded with his brain to move, he just stood there, mouth gaping, eyes wide on this...*thing*.

The creature closed the gap between them, and finally, Mateo's legs sprang to life. He ran without even knowing he was doing so and jumped in his GT, resting the bat across his legs and yanking the door shut. Thank God he'd left the car running. He threw it into reverse and sped backward the way he'd come.

Several yards down the road, Mateo jerked the wheel and hit the brakes hard enough to spin the GT around. Then he shifted into drive, slammed his foot on the gas, and sped down the highway. His eyes remained glued to the rearview mirror where after seconds of bleak hope, he confirmed his worst fears. The Charger's headlights appeared in his rearview mirror.

He pleaded with his car. "Faster. Go faster."

Already the GT was pushing 140 mph. Mateo didn't think the car could go much faster, and he wasn't sure he could control it around turns if it could. He double-checked his seatbelt just in case.

The Charger caught up within seconds and started nudging Mateo's rear, encouraging him to slow down. Mateo did the only thing he could think of; he stabbed the brakes, skidding down the road in tandem. The Charger crashed into the GT, and the two cars slid as one, locked into a single fate. Luckily, the GT gave first, spinning sideways. The Charger slammed into the GT, shattering the passenger-side window as well as its own.

Mateo saw the creature well now, its grinning boney smile seeming to laugh.

The GT skidded away from the Charger, relieving Mateo of the sight, and then it rolled onto its side, leaving Mateo hanging from the seatbelt. Sparks illuminated the inside of his car, his vision nearly blinded by them. The GT flipped back to its wheels momentarily, and the airbag slammed into Mateo's chest so hard it drove all the air out of him. The driver's side window shattered, glass sprinkling Mateo's clothes, burrowing into his skin. He could smell burning hair, and believed it was the sparks igniting the hair on his forearms.

Just when he thought it was over, the Charger rammed Mateo's husk of a car again, and then again, until it flipped over to its roof. Mateo's head banged off the steering wheel, and when it settled, he hung helpless, bloodied and woozy, praying he would survive. Blindly, he felt for the seatbelt clip and, when he found it, depressed the button. His body struck the roof like a ragdoll, the air wheezing out of him as he instantly started searching for anything he might use as a weapon. He spotted the bat in the backseat and clawed for it. Before he could secure it, he felt himself being dragged out through the window.

He kicked with his free leg. "Let go of me, fucker!"

And to his surprise, the creature's grip slipped, and Mateo scrambled back into the car, reaching out as far as he could. His fingers grazed wood, and he almost got it. Then he felt himself being drawn away again, and made one last ditch effort to secure the bat. He pulled and squirmed and pulled harder, inching his way into the backseat just enough to grab the handle.

With the weapon in hand, he allowed himself to be pulled free of the wreckage. Once he lay on the ground beneath this monster, he crab-walked back, putting distance between them before springing to his feet. He wasted no time, running around the car and leaping onto its undercarriage. Atop a heaping pile of twisted metal, Mateo gazed into the creature's pitch-black eyes, his anger overwhelming him.

Mateo lunged forward and swung the bat as hard as he could. He hadn't been a great baseball player as a kid, but he could swing a bat. He made contact with the creature's skull, and the bat pinged off. But Mateo didn't stop there. He leaped down and ran at the creature, striking it in the head again and again. Each time, he swung the bat with every bit of strength he could muster, connecting with the creature's face, its nose, its teeth, over and over until it showed some sign of weakness and dropped to its knees.

But Mateo had had enough. He stood over the creature and struck it again and again, relentless in his attacks. Each time the creature moved, he hit it as hard as he could, until the creature stopped moving. And even then he kept hitting it, harder and harder, striking it until the bat gave and snapped in half.

The jagged handle hanging from his shaking hand, the bat no more than a wooden sliver about ten inches long now, Mateo spit on the creature. "And that's how we do it where I come from, asshole!"

He stood observing the creature a moment longer, convinced he'd killed it, before he turned away. All he could think of was finding his cell phone, see if he could get some reception now, call the cops and maybe an ambulance for himself.

And that's when it happened.

The creature moved so fast. It lunged forward on its hands and knees, coming up behind Mateo like a snake in tall grass. He barely had time to get turned around and get that shard of bat up. He felt bone and sinew against his fist, the length of wood buried deep in the creature's chest. Now that the creature's duster splayed open, Mateo saw the driver's boney frame, the white translucent flesh. At its core, an organ inside the creature glowed violet, beating as strong as any human heart.

He let the bat go and staggered back, watching the creature's face form into a large O. Gurgles and gagging sounds escaped its gaping maw. But something was wrong. Something horrible.

Staggering back, the wretched creature roared wildly, its hands clasped around the wooden stake in its chest. With each failed attempt at removing it, the creature became more desperate, more hopeless. Black bile spilled from the wound, saturating the ground, the road, anything there.

Mateo had barely felt it, but now that he had the time to glance at his hand, he saw it all too well. The fucking thing had bit him.

Holding his hand with the uninjured one, Mateo raced forward and kicked the creature in its gut. "You fucking bit me? You piece of shit!" He kicked it again, and again, but the creature just laid there, seemingly smiling its bony grin.

Mateo went in for another kick, but this time when his foot made contact, it went right through the creature. Its body, as if made of ash, just crumbled around his foot, and a large black cloud burst into the air. The smell reminded Mateo of a cheap cigar smoldering in an ashtray. As if eating the creature, the fog rolled in thicker than ever, and when it cleared, all that remained was the duster and a pair of rugged black boots.

Mateo withdrew his foot and shook off the ash. "What the—"

After several minutes, Mateo readied to leave, but his stomach churned. He bent over, the bile in his stomach wanting to be free of his body but unable to come. He gagged, choking on something invisible, something he could not get to come up, and his mouth opened wider and wider. Mateo dropped to his knees, and clawed at the ground, wishing that doing so could somehow quell his pain.

He crept forward on all fours, still looking for his cell phone, thinking he could dial someone and get help before it was too late. But he grew weaker and weaker by the moment, his clothes on fire, large holes forming in the fabric. The skin beneath sloughed off to the ground in large strips, leaving only bone and muscle and sinew. The coppery aroma overwhelmed him, making him gag harder, and he almost passed out until his face literally slid off his skull. Everything withered. Everything died. Yet everything remained alive…somehow.

Struggling for purchase on anything, Mateo's fingers curled around the boots. He pawed at them, finding some relief in just touching them, and eventually just slid off his sneakers and slid the boots onto his feet.

Experiencing some relief from the pain, he forced himself to his feet and stood on uneasy legs, staring at the duster. He reached down, grabbed it, and threw it over his shoulders and slid his arms through the sleeves. And though the pain abated slightly more, it was there...always there. Like a curse, the pain ate away at him every second, every minute, for so long as this curse remained.

He needed to find a way to be free of this pain!

Mateo staggered over to the Charger and slid into the seat and spotted the hat in the passenger seat. Mateo palmed the hat, placed it upon his head, and looked at himself in the rearview mirror. His hair had whitened, his face no longer so human, but grinning.

The Charger crumpled and pinged, healing itself. A new purpose fell over Mateo here, in the middle of nowhere, on Highway WW. After shifting the car into drive, Mateo steered his steel horse down the road in search of a willing—or even unwilling—soul.

# Get John Flagg

James Aquilone

It began when John Flagg got fired.

Retcher called John into his office on Friday afternoon, after John's shift. Made sure he finished his work for the week. The piece of shit.

As John walked down the hall, he knew with absolute certainty he was about to get canned. It was something he'd been anticipating for years. He could already see Retcher's smug grin.

Bees buzzed in John's ears as he sat in front of Retcher. And there it was—the smug, shit-eating grin. Then Retcher lowered the boom.

The piece of shit told John he appreciated his sixteen years of loyal service and hard work, but that he was no longer needed. He wished him well on his future endeavors and told him to fuck off.

John left the office in a daze, dumped his personal belongings—which amounted to a mug, a pen, and a spare tie—in a small cardboard box, and was escorted out of the building.

Like a chain of dominoes, the rest of his life toppled over.

As he drove home, John thought about how he'd tell his wife Jo he lost his job and had no prospects for a new one. It was a talk he'd anticipated for as long as he had held his job, and in his fantasies, it always went horribly.

A red Tesla tailgated him, because of course that was just what he needed. *Go around, asshole!* The Tesla stayed on John's bumper, but he refused to speed up.

John knew something was about to go down. He could see the hatred in their faces from his rearview mirror. That's what it was. Hatred. He had seen it before. It was in Retcher's smug grin, too. A mix of disgust and aggression.

John maintained his speed, exactly the thirty-mile-per-hour speed limit. When the Tesla got a chance, it swung to the right and pulled up alongside him. The occupants, a mean-looking driver with a cleft palate and two doltish, drooling passengers, were shouting and jeering at him with their windows rolled down.

What did he do to these troglodytes to elicit such anger?

John refused to give in to their intimidation. He cruised down Richmond Avenue at a steady thirty miles an hour.

The Tesla sped off.

John refused to let the encounter rattle him. They were probably drugged out of their minds. He had other things to worry about, like his wife.

*Guess what, honey? I lost my job. Yeah, there's a good chance we'll have to sell the house and live in a one-bedroom apartment with the twins.*

John moved into the right lane alongside Freshkills Park and checked the rearview mirror. He saw the Tesla racing toward him at an angle from the far left lane. They must have circled the block.

"They're going to ram me!" John said aloud.

They were just seconds from plowing into him when John slammed on the brakes.

They went flying by just inches from his front bumper.

They kept going, jumping the curb, running over a bus stop sign, and flying into the wetlands.

No one else seemed to have noticed.

John kept driving. He couldn't believe what he had just seen. It was like something out of a bad action movie.

Meth heads. Had to be. They were all fucked up on dope—and innocent people like him had to put up with this crazy shit. Hopefully, they drowned in the wetlands.

John's head was pounding. The blood in his brain boiled.

He didn't want Jo and the girls to see him like this. He didn't want to upset them. He could never tell Jo about this. Ever. No matter how innocent you are, when something this wild and horrible happens to you, people always think it's your fault. *You must have done something! This type of thing doesn't happen for no reason.*

He stopped in front of the M&N Deli. His headache was reaching nuclear meltdown levels. He needed aspirin and a strong drink. Bad.

He texted Jo to let her know he was coming home early.

"Can't wait for u 2 get here," she wrote back almost immediately. That made him feel good. Hopefully, she was in a good mood. He couldn't handle a contentious day at home.

When he got out of the car, his legs felt like jelly.

As soon as he walked into the deli, the cashier gave him the eye. Did he look completely unhinged? Probably.

"Where do you keep the aspirin?" he asked.

The cashier grunted and sort of nodded at the center aisle. That was good enough for him. John had no interest in engaging anyone in conversation.

He headed to the freezers in the back and grabbed a six-pack of Budweiser for himself and ice cream for the twins (strawberry for Amy, chocolate for Alice). Hopefully, that would shut them up for the rest of the day.

As he searched for the aspirin, he noticed the cashier watching him like he was some shifty teen about to boost a bag of Doritos. *I'm forty-two years old, for chrissakes. I'm wearing a suit. A three-hundred-dollar suit, but still.* Did he look like someone who's going to rob a convenience store? If he didn't need the aspirin and booze so bad, he would have walked out.

Out of the corner of his eye, he saw the guy craning his neck and leaning forward to get a better look. His face burned.

Finally, he found the aspirin—Tylenol Extra Strength—and headed to the counter. The cashier was eyeing him the entire time like he was a dog trailing dirt all over his new carpet. Then the prick's hand flashed under the counter. When he raised it, he shot him with a Taser.

One of the barbs hit him in the side of the leg. The other got him in the balls—or, more precisely, ball. The left one.

Getting Tasered is a bitch. Getting Tasered in the scrotum is like lightning hitting, well, your testicles. There isn't a worse place for lightning to hit you.

He jerked and twitched on the ground like a heroin addict going through withdrawal.

Then it stopped.

Then it started again.

His body felt like one giant muscle and he had the charley horse to end all charley horses.

The third time he juiced him, he rolled over on his side and the lightning stopped. The cashier tried to give him more, but nothing happened. He cursed and then he went limp.

The cashier hopped over the counter and squatted over John. Probably to make sure he was dead.

John thought he grabbed the six-pack, but he got the ice cream container. He shot up and slammed the container against the cashier's head. Never mind that it was ice cream. It was frozen solid. It was a goddamn ice cream brick. He usually hated that. He'd go to scoop out some ice cream, but it's so hard the spoon bends. You either have to wait an hour for it to thaw or throw it in the microwave. This time he was thankful for the over-refrigeration.

The cashier fell on his side and John bashed him again. "I was going to pay for all this crap, you know!" he screamed. The cashier didn't get up. He didn't move at all. John dropped a twenty on the counter as he ran out of the store with the ice cream and Tylenol. He guessed he could have called an ambulance for the jerk, but his generosity has its limits.

Before he got into the car, he plucked out the remaining barb. The one in his testicle. How would he describe the pain? It was like hitting your funny bone with a mallet, except the funny bone is your testicle. Then times that by holy fuck and that's how excruciating the pain was.

He couldn't go to the police. He had just killed a guy. Maybe. Fuck him, though. Self-defense. They would never believe him. He was never good at convincing anyone of anything. He always looked guilty—and he never did a damned thing!

Two blocks away, he tore open the Tylenol and downed four caplets. Then he chugged a Bud. He closed his eyes, leaned back, tried to calm down, but his mind was racing. Was he going insane? Did he really just get Tasered in a convenience store? It didn't seem real.

Home never seemed so attractive. Once he got past his front door he was never going to leave again. Jo could get a job. He'd be a stay-at-home dad. Screw it.

When he got to the house, the girls' bicycles were blocking the driveway. He swore they did this shit on purpose. If he told them once he told them a million times to put their bikes away. But did they ever listen? And today of all days.

He tooted the horn, hoping, praying someone would come out and move them out of the way, save him the trouble of getting out of the car. He only worked his ass off, battled meth heads in Teslas, got Tasered by psychotic convenience store clerks, all so they could have a nice house, ballet lessons, a swimming pool, those stupid dolls with the big eyes. Half a dozen blows of the horn later and no one came out. Of course not, why would he get a break now? Jo, no doubt, was in the yard flirting with their neighbor Mel. He swore one day he was going to find those two in bed together. He didn't know whose throat he'd cut first.

He put the car in park, dumped the bikes on the lawn, got back in the car, and pulled into the driveway.

He walked up the porch steps, a defeated man. He had half a mind to dump the ice cream. They'd only tell him he got the wrong kind. Because now he was thinking Amy liked butter pecan and Alice liked raspberry swirl. Sometimes he thought Jo purposely let the kids run wild just to aggravate him. She never reprimanded them. She just stared at the TV as the girls wrecked the house. His house. He paid all the damn bills.

He took a deep breath and opened the front door.

Alice stood in the middle of the living room. She slapped a fire poker into her palm. Amy was behind her, brandishing a large kitchen knife.

He took a furtive step inside. "What the hell is going on here? Where's your mother?"

The girls came at him.

Alice swung the fire poker at his head. She was a lousy ballplayer, though, and he easily avoided the blow by twisting away. But Amy was waiting and sliced his shin with the knife. He dropped the ice cream, yowled, and stumbled back.

"Are you kids crazy? Put down those damn weapons!"

They stared at him with hatred in their eyes. Like he was the devil himself. What had gotten into them?

He backed up some more.

Jo came down the stairs in a hurry.

"Can you tell me what's going on?" he yelled. "Your daughters are trying to kill me. If this is some prank, it isn't funny."

When she got to the bottom of the staircase, she raised the revolver he kept in his office safe (for intruders) and without a word fired at him.

The bullet whizzed by his head and slammed into the doorframe, splinters of wood exploding all around him.

John ran out of the house.

The children pursued him, whooping and yelling like little savages in a remake of *Lord of the Flies*. If the little brats hadn't fallen over their bikes, he never would have made it into the car. He hoped they skinned their knees.

As he was backing out of the driveway, his wife appeared at the front door. She fired at the car but hit their peeing boy fountain—the one Jo just had to have—in the middle of the lawn. Thank God, she was a terrible shot. He was amazed she knew enough to take the safety off before firing. The last glimpse he got of her...she looked at him with such venom he felt as if he had been bitten by a cobra.

He didn't know how long he was driving. Or how he didn't crash into a tree or a jogger. He wasn't thinking straight. His lunatic family had just tried to murder him. The looks on their faces. The hate. He didn't know what was worse: his wife with the gun or Amy with the knife or Alice with the fire poker.

He racked his brain. Did he do something to them? He hadn't cheated on Jo. He had never even spanked the girls. He did punish Alice last week (no internet for a day after she called one of the neighbors a "motherfucker"; she got off easy, in his opinion). Did that warrant his execution?

The only thing he could think of was that Jo really was having an affair with Mel. She must have turned the kids against him. They'd kill him, say an intruder did it, collect the insurance money, and start calling Mel daddy.

He wasn't thinking straight. This was all insane. The universe was insane.

He drove and drove, down the back streets, away from people. He pulled into the parking lot of a nature reserve where he and Jo used to take walks. He must have been distracted—of course, he was!—because when he parked he hit the edge of the curb and punctured the tire. He got out of the car and saw instantly that the tire was flat.

John got back behind the wheel, on the verge of tears, and cursed his life.

Should he call the police and tell them his family just tried to kill him? Would they believe him? *He* didn't believe it.

He needed to go somewhere to relax, to think.

He grabbed his cell phone and called his only friend, Cedric.

"Are you home?" John asked.

"Yeah," Cedric said. "What's the matter?"

"Just having a really rough day. Like an epically bad day?"

"What's going on?"

"Can I come over?"

"Sure, man."

"Can you pick me up? I have a flat tire and I don't have a spare."

"No problem."

"Just one more thing. Do you have the urge to kill me?"

Cedric laughed. "Are you kidding? Not since you beat me at bowling. Just let me know where you are."

John waited in the car. Cedric didn't live far so hopefully it wouldn't be long.

He thought about texting his wife but he couldn't bring himself to do it. He remembered the pure hatred in her face. She had been mad at him before, but never like that.

*Smash!*

Something hit the side of the car.

A mob approached. It was an odd assortment of people, a completely random mix. A few middle-aged men and women, a few teenagers, and a couple of children. All races. And, John assumed, all religions. They carried flashlights, tire irons, bats.

A young boy threw a rock at the car and hit the back windshield.

John started the engine.

Now the mob was running.

He threw the car in reverse, forgot about the flat tire, swerved to avoid them, and slammed into a tree at the edge of the nature preserve. Someone jumped on the back of the car. Another bashed in the back passenger's side window. Fortunately, he was up against the woods and they couldn't get to him so easily. But with the back window gone, it was just a matter of time before they got in.

John ran into the woods. He heard the mob shouting and jeering him as they pursued. He turned back just for a moment, tripped over a branch or vine or whatever, and fell down an embankment. He rolled to the bottom, banging his shoulder against a large rock.

Despite the pain, he hopped up and ran. His adrenaline was pumping, but he was pretty sure he'd feel it the next day—if he survived.

The woods opened to the street just ahead. He couldn't go back so he had to take his chances on the street. John crept out of the woods.

The street ahead was empty.

As he jogged down the sidewalk, John imagined the occupants of the street bursting out of their homes and pursuing him. He jogged faster. Halfway down the block, his fantasy became reality when people began to rush out of the nearby houses.

They were soon joined by the others from the woods. John dashed to the corner, his heart pumping like mad. When he turned, a car screeched to a stop in front of him.

John was ready to fight. He got into a boxing stance, raised his fists.

It was Cedric.

"Get in," he said.

John ran to the passenger's side and jumped in the car.

"I don't know what's going on," John said, breathing heavily. "The world has gone crazy. It seems everyone's trying to kill me."

"Let's go back to my house, and we can figure this out."

Cedric pulled the car into his garage and they entered his house.

"Sit down and try to relax," Cedric said, leading John into the living room.

"Relax? Everyone is out to get me."

"Can I get you a drink?"

"The hardest stuff you got."

"Okay."

Cedric left to get the drink.

John turned on the TV to break the silence. He didn't want to think about what was going on.

A news bulletin came on. "This is a special report," the female anchor said. "There is a call to get John Flagg. If you see this man, you are asked to kill him." John's photo from his license flashed on the screen.

John turned up the volume. She repeated, "Get John Flagg."

How was this legal? It didn't make sense.

"Cedric! Are you hearing this? On the news, they're telling people to kill me."

When Cedric returned, he wasn't carrying a drink. He held up a revolver. He had the most hateful expression on his face.

"What the fuck is going on here?" John said. "This is a practical joke? This whole day is a joke, right?"

"I'm afraid not. I bet you've always had a sinking feeling something like this would happen. That it was inevitable."

"Things like this don't happen. You can't tell the world to kill someone. What did I do?"

"Sorry, John."

John grabbed the closest thing, a heavy glass ashtray, and threw it with all his might at his friend. It slammed into his nose. Cedric fell back and he fired into the ceiling. John leaped off the couch and tackled him. The gun flew out of his hand. Cedric crashed against the wall. John lunged, grabbed Cedric's head and slammed it into the wall. Cedric didn't give much resistance. He wasn't a very athletic guy. Overwhelmed with fear and adrenaline, John bashed his head against the wall until he put a hole in it. Cedric slumped to the ground, moaning. John grabbed a poker from the fireplace and drove it into Cedric's skull until it was a bloody mess.

John dropped the poker and looked at his friend lying in a pool of blood. His head nothing more than soup.

John thought of the mob and wondered when they'd show up. He searched for the revolver and finally found it under a recliner.

He'd be ready for them when they came.

Blood dripped off his face and hands. He needed to clean himself.

He found the bathroom, placed the gun on the sink, and looked at himself in the mirror. Holy shit. He was a wreck. Blood matted his hair.

Then he saw it.

What all the others must have seen.

And he felt pure hatred. A white-hot feeling of disgust and revulsion.

He understood now. He was relieved.

John Flagg grabbed the revolver and jammed it into his mouth. His final thought, before his brains flew out the back of his skull: *It's not paranoia if they're really out to get you.*

# Glimmergrim

### Taylor Grant

Conner sensed he was not alone.

Amidst the lavender-scented steam of the bathroom, he sensed something shifting, the hint of a presence felt but not seen. Though the tub's porcelain cradled him in a sea of warmth, an uneasy tension grazed his skin. A glass of Merlot was within arm's reach, a velvety promise of momentary peace.

The bath was his sanctuary from Wall Street's unyielding clock and tangled spreadsheets. An escape from the pressures of hitting targets and deadlines, even if for just a few sacred minutes.

He stared at the bath's silver fixtures—silent witnesses to his ritual of water and wine. As his gaze lingered, an unsettling metamorphosis began to take shape. The faucet, a mere shard of polished metal a moment before, began to stretch and distort into a twisted semblance of a nose. The knobs retracted into themselves, morphing into eyes that seemed to calculate his vulnerability with cold precision.

A bemused chuckle slipped from his lips into the steam. "Guess I better lighten up on the wine," he murmured to himself.

But his amusement soon evaporated, to be replaced by a rising tide of apprehension. The apparition that emerged was a hideous distortion of a face, its menacing eyes sunk into the metal, its nose quivering as if it could somehow smell his fear.

He rubbed his eyes with water-softened knuckles, desperate to purge the vision. When he dared to look again, the faucet and knobs had resumed their ordinary forms, as if chiding him for his flight of fancy.

Relief washed over him.

But as his hand reached for the wine glass and another taste of sweet distraction, he froze. A face materialized beneath the water under his spread legs, its eyes two dark chasms. With a strangled cry, Conner recoiled, his sudden movement sending both water and his glass crashing to the floor.

Some of the spilled Merlot tinted the water in the bath as if blood had merged with his sanctuary, forcing him to confront the uncertain boundary between the actual and the illusory. The face wavered and slowly diffused, but its presence lingered in the room like a dark mist.

\*\*\*

In the sterile cold of the Wall Street bullpen—a place where decimals danced, and fortunes fluttered—Conner sat at his desk, haunted. The office's chatter played like an unending Gregorian chant in the background—talk of stock rises, of market trends, of corporate mergers—but it felt like the murmuring of ghosts. A haunting liturgy to which Conner felt he no longer belonged.

For weeks now, unsettling faces were his uninvited guests, materializing at unpredictable moments, hunting him like prey. He had scoured the internet, sifting through medical journals and psychology forums, trying to find a cause or explanation.

He'd researched terms like 'hypnagogic hallucinations,' and even toyed with the idea that his symptoms aligned with some form of optical illusion or stress-induced visual phenomenon. Deep down, he wanted to believe that there was a scientific explanation for all this, that these faces were mere by-products of stress or overwork. But another part of him whispered that this was something darker, more sinister.

His makeshift defense was simple but draining: never let his gaze linger too long on any inanimate object. It seemed that the faces thrived in the stillness of his focus, particularly in reflective surfaces.

Yet maintaining constant vigilance was exhausting. His eyes felt gritty, the strain creating a constant dull ache behind his temples. He could feel his concentration fragmenting over the past few days as he attempted to juggle his work responsibilities, aware that any momentary lapse could provoke another apparition.

Around the office, co-workers were already talking about his odd behavior.

At first, the visages had limited themselves to the confines of his computer screen. But now they crept beyond digital borders. The numbers on the wall clock stretched and congealed into a sneering face.

At the water cooler, an oasis in the arid landscape of numbers and data, Conner's eyes met his reflection. Except now, even his own image stared back with a grotesque grimace. The betrayal of his own reflection hit him like a gut punch, a visceral reminder that nowhere was safe.

Back at his desk, his focus slipped for just a moment. What was normally a grid of comforting numbers and data morphed into menacing eyes that glared at him from the monitor, a malevolent entity born from the electronic void.

Nervously, he glanced around the open-plan space, wondering if anyone else could see the nightmarish vision unfolding on his screen. He glanced over at an old colleague named Bill, who was absorbed in his work, blissfully ignorant.

No, this personal haunting remained his alone.

Beth, the diligent analyst two cubicles over, whose legs could rival any Wall Street curve, caught his eye. Her look was one of unspoken concern, yet she seemed to withdraw into her work, as if retreating from a contagion.

Then, in an instant, all pretense of Conner's composure shattered. A face of grotesque, near-biblical horror spawned from the pixels and darkness. As if transcending the bounds of the screen, its mouth contorted, attempting to bite him. Uttering a sharp cry, Conner's arm lashed out as he leaped up from his seat, sending the keyboard and mouse crashing to the floor.

Time froze.

Conversations halted mid-sentence. A sea of eyes turned toward him, each pair bearing its own microcosm of emotion: pity, discomfort, detached curiosity. His manager, Jerry, who was the closest, stepped up with a thinly veiled mask of managerial concern. "Conner...we need to talk."

\*\*\*

Days had passed since the harrowing episode at his desk, and Conner found himself on an enforced sabbatical. "Think of it as a brief hiatus—for you and the team," Jerry, his manager had declared. He'd even had the gall to suggest a therapist, a recommendation Conner knew was less about personal well-being than it was about workplace liability.

But the isolation had its silver lining. It gave him time to delve deeper into online forums, medical journals, and psychology studies in his obsessive quest for answers. One name kept surfacing in his local area: Dr. Evelyn Stroud, a psychologist specializing in visual phenomena and repressed emotions. Intrigued, he discovered she had authored a paper titled 'The Hidden Psychology of Visual Manifestations.'

Hope swelled within him.

Devouring the content, Conner found it both unsettling and enlightening. The more he read, the more he felt as if the paper described him personally, dissecting his dread with academic precision. There was something comforting, yet unsettling, about seeing his experiences discussed in cold, analytical terms.

Emboldened by the paper's relevance, Conner reached out to Dr. Stroud via email, followed by a phone call. To his relief, she seemed just as intrigued by his experiences as he was by her research. After an in-depth phone consultation, she agreed to meet him. The feeling of being on the cusp of some kind of revelation left Conner in a state of restless anticipation.

As evening pulled its dark veil over the world, he sat, shrouded in the dim light of his apartment, reading more of Dr. Stroud's paper. Suddenly, he felt a tension in the air, as if it were charged with static electricity. The lights flickered, their transient glow casting eerie shadows on the walls. Dismissing it as a power issue, he continued reading until a particularly prolonged flicker caught his attention.

For a split second, he saw a phantom face somehow emerging from the wall across from him—skeletal, ghastly, its mouth stretched in an agonizing expression. A wave of icy fear engulfed Conner, binding him to his chair. His rational mind tried to dismiss the apparition as a trick of the eye, but a low, haunting moan reverberated through the room. It was as if the wall was groaning in agony.

Rational thought clashed with raw terror.

Was the wall, or the thing, trying to communicate with him?

Or perhaps, warn him?

Frozen in place, Conner contemplated fleeing the room. But as he mustered the courage, the room reverted to mundane stillness, leaving him gasping for air, his pulse racing.

He thought about his upcoming meeting with Dr. Stroud, wishing it were sooner. He couldn't shake the feeling that each passing moment was a step closer to a new reality that couldn't be undone.

\*\*\*

The interior of Dr. Evelyn Stroud's office felt like a separate realm, in stark contrast to Conner's sterile apartment and the Wall Street workspace. He found himself enveloped by an artful blend of rich, warm colors, classic literature on psychology, and curated artwork that beckoned one to pause and reflect.

From the moment she spoke, Dr. Stroud's demeanor was unexpectedly warm, even soothing. Her attractiveness was subtle but undeniable, quite contrary to the cold, clinical figure he had conjured in his mind. After an evaluation of his acute situation, her questions shifted from general inquiries to a more pointed, specialized probing. Her approach was as methodical as it was empathic as she guided their conversation through intricate psychological landscapes.

"I appreciate your candor and trust," Dr. Stroud said, her pen dancing across a notepad with calculated grace. "It's essential for our journey toward understanding."

She set down her pen, thoughtful. "I am reminded of symptoms of Pareidolia, when the mind perceives a familiar pattern that doesn't exist. I've had patients who've seen all kinds of things—faces in the clouds, divine figures in toast. You're familiar with the 'Man in the Moon,' I presume?"

Conner nodded.

"But there's also the Troxler Effect," she continued. "Stare into a mirror long enough, and you might not recognize yourself. The brain omits the irrelevant, making the familiar strange—sometimes terrifyingly so."

Conner was struck by the clarity of Dr. Stroud's explanations, impressed by how she dissected intricate psychological concepts with ease.

"You, however, present a unique situation," she said. "Your hallucinations don't fit textbook definitions, based on what you've described, and my own research into visual and auditory manifestations."

"So, is there a pill for this?" he said, half-jokingly.

Dr. Stroud's eyes met his, filled with a compassionate yet resolute expression. "Just to clarify, I'm a psychologist, not a psychiatrist, so I can't prescribe medication. And yes, there are antipsychotic drugs designed to help with hallucinations. But based on my diagnostic impressions, I don't believe you're schizophrenic. And medications are no guarantee. Best case scenario they might alleviate the symptoms temporarily, but they won't address the root issue." She paused to let the weight of her words sink in. "However, given the severity of your hallucinations, a focused and intensive treatment plan may not only be justified, but necessary."

Conner nodded, "Well, frankly, that's why I'm here, Doc. I don't have the luxury of years of traditional therapy. I feel like I'm losing my mind."

Dr. Stroud offered a comforting smile. "Let me assure you that many people find themselves overwhelmed by their thoughts and emotions at various points in their lives. I can't guarantee a 'cure,' per se, but I can promise you a committed, professional partnership to work through whatever challenges you're facing. Mental health is complex and unique to each individual, but modern treatment options have come a long way, and there's good reason to be hopeful."

After a reflective pause, her expression took on a note of reserved anticipation. "I believe we need a targeted approach to understand the intricacies of your condition. In fact, I'm spearheading an experimental project called the 'Perceptual Mapping Sphere.' It's a projective test; think of it as a much more sophisticated version of the Rorschach inkblot. It delves deeper into the subconscious mind and can give us unprecedented insights into your unique situation. If you're up for it, we can do a simple test now."

Curiosity piqued, Conner agreed.

Dr. Stroud led him to a dimly lit room with an academic feel; bookshelves lined with psychological journals and diagnostic manuals. In contrast, a spherical digital projector in the center of the room stood as a modern juxtaposition, sophisticated yet unobtrusive. The setup suggested a blend of established knowledge and cutting-edge technology.

She offered him a seat and started the projector. Clouds of swirling light materialized on the wall facing him, morphing, and dissipating rapidly. "Simply relax and observe the patterns, Conner," she instructed. "Then speak your thoughts freely." Her fingers poised over a keyboard to take notes.

Conner hesitated. "I see them...the faces...they're everywhere. They look angry, menacing."

"Remember now," she said gently. "You're only looking at a projection. They can't harm you." She adjusted a dial on the projector. The lights transformed into fractal patterns, intricate and chaotic. "What does your mind interpret now?"

"A labyrinth," Conner replied, his voice shaky. "But there are faces embedded in its walls.

Male...female...adults...children. A mix of emotions. Too many to describe."

"Interesting. Please, go on," she said, her interest evident yet professionally controlled. She clicked a remote, and the images changed into a pulsating, singular light. "What about now?"

He spun away, as if what he'd seen was too horrifying to witness. "I can't..."

Dr. Stroud's hand reached for the projector, switching it off, plunging the room into total darkness except for the ambient light from her desk lamp. "What did you see?"

He wiped a tear from his eye as he said, "It was the same hideous face I saw in my office. It was lurking in that pulsating light. Waiting."

"Do you have any idea of who it was?" she asked.

"No," he said, trying to shake the image from his mind. "But whatever it was...it wasn't human."

\*\*\*

Leaving the office, Conner felt the twilight's chill air turn heavy. Streetlights came on, spotlighting the darkness that his mind was struggling to parse.

He saw his car parked some distance away, the walk seeming longer now as the sky turned from twilight blue to pitch black. Then, an unnatural sound—less than a roar but more than a growl—rang out behind him. Turning, he saw it. Standing eerily still beneath a flickering streetlight was a figure, its features indiscernible yet menacingly familiar. He realized what it was: the terrifying specter from his hallucinations.

*Confront the root cause*, Dr. Stroud's voice echoed in his mind.

He paused and stood his ground, his breath shallow. Yet this situation felt more threatening than before, more visceral. With that same guttural sound, the figure began to crawl—slowly, ominously—toward him. Its movements unnatural, each motion deliberate yet distorted.

Panic gripped Conner as he spun around and sprinted toward his car, each pounding step punctuated by his thundering heartbeat. A raspy, malevolent hiss emanated from behind him, and he dared not look back.

He yanked his keys from his pocket and nearly dropped them. A wild, guttural shriek pierced the air. He noticed a shadow gaining on him and ran even faster. Slamming into the car door, he unlocked it, jumped in, and jammed the key into the ignition. Something monstrous began to press against the driver's side window, but he didn't look. He revved the engine to life, tires screeching against the asphalt as he peeled away. In his rearview mirror, he saw the dark figure come to a halt, as if letting him go.

Or perhaps postponing the inevitable.

\*\*\*

Weeks had passed since Conner's nightmarish encounter. Given the severity of his experience, Dr. Stroud had recommended more frequent sessions, several days a week, to delve into what she believed was underlying trauma. Her office had become his haven of calm. Soft lighting, lavender scent, the predictable tick-tock of the wall clock—he needed such a sanctuary.

Today was their first foray into Regression Therapy.

"Hypnosis enables us to explore deeper layers of the subconscious," Dr. Stroud said ten minutes into their session, her eyes locking onto his. "Just remember that you'll remain in control and be safe throughout. Are you comfortable proceeding?"

"Comfortable? No. But I'm willing to try," he replied. The lingering fear in the pit of his stomach was overshadowed by a stronger urge to unearth and confront whatever lay buried in his psyche.

"Excellent," Dr. Stroud said. "Let's start by getting comfortable. Close your eyes, take a deep breath in, and as you exhale, allow yourself to begin relaxing."

Conner followed her instructions. The soft fabric of the couch seemed to embrace him as he inhaled deeply.

Her voice flowed like a soft current, "Imagine yourself at the top of a staircase with ten steps. With each step you descend, you'll go deeper into a state of relaxation and openness. I'll count down from ten, and when I reach one, you'll be in a deep, receptive state."

Conner visualized the staircase in his mind. It was an elegant structure, bathed in a soft, diffused light. He placed his foot on the first step as Dr. Stroud began to count.

"Ten."

His foot sank into the soft carpet that covered the step, and he felt a noticeable release in tension.

"Nine."

He descended another step, the muscles in his neck and shoulders loosening, as if invisible hands were kneading away his anxiety.

"Eight."

Another step and he felt an unfamiliar lightness in his chest, a weight being gradually lifted. With each descending number, Conner moved further down the staircase, and deeper into a trance. By the time Dr. Stroud reached 'one,' he was submerged in an intense state of relaxation, as though floating in a tranquil body of water, far removed from the turbulence of his daily life.

"In this deeply relaxed state," Dr. Stroud continued, her voice now hardly above a whisper, "you're able to access memories with greater ease. Let your mind drift back to your childhood, like flipping through an old photo album. Stop when you feel like you've reached a moment that seems significant."

Feeling anchored by Dr. Stroud's words, Conner let himself sink deeper into the labyrinthine recesses of his mind. The room dissolved around him; the scents of lavender and leather receded, replaced by a different smell—musty, damp, like a place long forgotten.

A maelstrom of images flickered onto the theater screen of his mind, but one scene bubbled up with striking clarity. He found himself standing in front of an abandoned building, its windows shattered, the facade crumbled and peeling away. Beside him stood Liam, his childhood friend—wide-eyed and full of youthful mischief. Conner's heart raced, not from fear but from the sheer exhilaration of youthful adventure.

"What do you see?" Dr. Stroud prompted.

"It's the old Tunison building," Conner said, his voice tinged with a kind of awe. "Liam and I... we'd heard rumors about this place. People said the Glimmergrim haunted it. We wanted to see for ourselves. We were just kids," he said, the regret palpable in his voice.

"You're safe," Dr. Stroud said with encouragement. "Take all the time you need to experience this memory."

"We've entered the building," Conner continued, his eyes still closed, his body visibly tense on the plush couch. "It's dark, really dark, and our flashlights barely cut through the blackness. I can smell the rotting wood and crumbling bricks. We...start exploring, laughing nervously at every creak and groan of the old structure.

Liam moves ahead, crossing a floor that looks unstable. And then... Oh God, then we hear it—the howl of the Glimmergrim. My stomach twists in knots, and for a brief second, I feel light-headed, like the room is spinning around me."

Conner's hand clenched involuntarily. "Liam... He gets scared. He starts to back away, but then these hands...these horrible, inhuman hands reach up through the floorboards and yank him down into the darkness. I hear him scream and then...a thud. A sickening thud." Conner's voice broke, choked by emotion he had long buried. "I...couldn't save him, And then I saw it, in the darkness below, staring up at me. The Glimmergrim! It was real! I ran, I had to. I left Liam and I ran."

Then, as if the weight of the memory was too heavy to bear, Conner's eyes snapped open. He looked disoriented, as if he had physically stepped back from the precipice of a dark abyss.

Dr. Stroud leaned forward, locking her gaze onto Conner. His eyes were brimming with tears, a fragile veneer barely holding back years of repressed emotion. "Conner," she began, her voice imbued with empathetic warmth. "It was brave to go to that place and bring these memories into the light. They've clearly weighed heavy on your heart for a long time. This emotional journey you've embarked upon is crucial for healing."

She reached over to her side table and pulled out a box of tissues, offering it to Conner. As he wiped his eyes, she resumed the conversation. "This…'Glimmergrim.' Is it local folklore, or does it possess a different kind of significance for you?"

Conner swallowed hard. "When we were kids, we all thought it was a silly myth—like the bogeyman. But after that night...."

"It seems of great significance to you," she said. "I find it intriguing and would very much like to explore its role in your experiences further. However, let's save that for a future session. Today, the focus is you."

She paused for a moment, contemplating her next words carefully. "Have you ever tried visualization exercises, Conner?"

He shook his head, bewildered.

"In moments when you're overwhelmed, you simply close your eyes and confront these phantoms that haunt you. Picture yourself standing strong against them, reclaiming your own narrative."

A flicker of doubt passed across his eyes, but Dr. Stroud pressed on.

"It's a mental exercise to help you gain control over what terrifies you. The power of the mind is not to be underestimated."

Conner swallowed hard. "I'm willing to try anything at this point."

"Then perhaps this exercise is the first step in confronting whatever it is you believe you encountered," she suggested, her gaze never leaving his.

A shiver coursed through Conner's body. He had come to Dr. Stroud as a last resort, putting all his hopes on her expertise. But what if it failed? What if, in trying to reclaim his narrative, he only empowered the very apparitions that haunted him?

The thought left him paralyzed, weighed down by a newfound dread that maybe, just maybe, he was unlocking a door that was better left unopened.

\*\*\*

Conner sat in the back corner of the Coffee Shot, staring at his laptop screen, his eyes bloodshot, his fingers tapping nervously on the tabletop. A myriad of tabs were open on the screen, each offering pieces of lore about the urban legend known as the Glimmergrim.

Two weeks had passed since that strange regression session with Dr. Stroud, and he'd been driven by an incessant urge to unravel the threads of the monster that had resurfaced in his memory. He'd taken the doctor's advice and attempted the visualization exercises she mentioned a few times; surprisingly, it had seemed to diminish the intensity of his visions somewhat.

Yet despite the fleeting respite, he still felt tethered to the haunting entity from his past; his focus was solely on unraveling its mythology. *Glimmergrim*, the word was almost a hiss, an urban legend whispered among children but now haunting his adult life.

He had been delving into online forums, old books, and even interviews with people who claimed to have had encounters. The Glimmergrim were said to have once been human but cursed with a life of darkness and despair. Creatures that roamed urban labyrinths, drawn to the emotional intensity of teeming cities, to places where human souls 'glimmered' like a lure.

As Conner sifted through his research, he noticed patterns that extended beyond his current obsession. The Glimmergrim were part of a global tapestry of myths designed to enforce good behavior in children and serve as cautionary tales. Striking parallels existed with dark figures from other cultures, like Latin America's shape-shifting El Cucuy, or the weeping La Llorona, or even the Eastern European Baba Yaga.

According to several sources, the urban legend of the Glimmergrim was wielded as a warning by parents: be home before the streetlights flicker on, and stay away from decrepit, abandoned buildings. "Don't stray after dark," they'd say. "Avoid the vacant, derelict buildings that litter the city."

These places, parents warned, were treacherous not just because of decaying structures and hidden hazards. They were also the lairs of the Glimmergrim, where they would collect the souls of the reckless and disobedient.

But Conner couldn't shake the feeling that the Glimmergrim was more than just a story. Could the faces that haunted him be the souls reaped by the Glimmergrim? And rather than haunting him, might they be warning him?

As the folklore went, if you found yourself outside after dark, the only way to save yourself was to find a reflective surface—like a puddle or a window, and chant the words 'Glimmergrim, Glimmergrim, I heed your warning, please let me return home before morning.' By repeating the chant three times while looking at the reflection, it was said that you could evade the clutches of the Glimmergrim and make it safely back home.

Conner took a sip of his now cold coffee, the ritualistic words resonating in his mind.

*The night Liam died; I didn't make it home safely.* He thought. *Because I never did the ritual. Maybe it never stopped searching for me. And now, all these years later, it's come to collect* my *soul. too.*

Just then, the café door jingled, and Olivia walked in, her eyes—blue like Conner's but colder somehow—scanned the room before finally settling on him. Her features, although sharing familial resemblance with Conner, were sharper, as if years of life's vicissitudes had sculpted them to a finer point. She wore a simple but elegant blouse paired with a charcoal skirt, an ensemble that spoke of practicality but with an eye for detail. Her face, framed by faint lines, lit up with a controlled smile as their eyes met.

Conner glanced at his watch—she was punctual for once, a rare occurrence that bordered on miraculous.

"Hey, stranger," she said, her voice tinged with a warmth that barely concealed the underlying tension.

"Hey, big sis," Conner replied, rising from his chair to hug her. He felt the rigidity in her frame as they embraced, a subtle reminder of the emotional distance that had grown between them. They both sat down, and the atmosphere thickened, weighted down by a litany of words left unspoken.

After a brief interlude of awkward pleasantries and drink orders, their conversation turned to more serious matters. "I heard about your leave of absence from Mom," she said. "You OK?"

Conner fidgeted with his coffee cup, gently pushing it back and forth across the tabletop. "Not really. But I'm working on it. And to be honest, that's not what I asked you here to talk about."

"I see," she said, never one to mince words. "So, what then?"

After avoiding her eyes for an uncomfortably long moment, he found the courage to ask, "Do you remember…the Glimmergrim? From when we were kids?"

The randomness of the question was clear from her expression. "The Glimmer…" Olivia set down her drink with a puzzled look. "Is that a serious question? This is why you wanted to meet after three years of radio silence?"

Olivia's reply hung in the air like a thick cloud. They hadn't spoken since their father's death when they had argued over the funeral arrangements. It was an argument so meaningless he couldn't remember the details. But those details had never mattered; it had been a result of their own stubbornness and a lifelong power struggle coming to a head. The funeral had simply been the final nail in the coffin.

"Olivia…look. I'm in a bad place. You know me, I never ask for anything. But right now, I need my big sister. I need you to humor me and answer the question."

She sized him up and, after a moment, her clenched jaw loosened and her cold eyes softened. "OK, sure," she said, her eyes locking onto Conner's. "Yes, I remember. How could I forget?"

Conner sighed, and the tension in his body seemed to lessen just a notch at his sister's admission. It was as if her acknowledgment of the Glimmergrim had somehow validated the fear that haunted him. If his logical, buttoned-up sister, Olivia, remembered the bogeyman from their childhood, then perhaps he wasn't losing his mind after all.

He leaned forward and, in a bold move, reached over and held her wrist, almost pleading. "Please, Olivia. Tell me what you remember. I have these huge blank spots in my memory around that time."

She didn't remove his hand, which was a good sign. For now, it seemed, she was willing to entertain such a strange question. "Well...I remember you were terrified of it as a child. You and your buddy Liam would sneak out at night, and when you'd come back, you were afraid to even look in a mirror. I used to tease you endlessly about it."

Conner looked up, intrigued and surprised. "Mirrors...strange. I don't remember that at all."

Olivia sighed. "Well, it was a long time ago. I remember that you and Liam were always up to no good. I think they call it 'urban exploring' these days, but there wasn't really a name for it back then. You guys loved going into abandoned places you weren't supposed to. But you were both too young to understand the dangers of old buildings, so maybe it was a good thing that you were afraid of the Glimmergrim."

But after what happened to Liam...you became obsessed. Nightmares every night for a year, waking up in a sweat screaming about the Glimmergrim. You said you thought you were living on borrowed time because you hadn't done the ritual chant the night Liam died."

"I said that?" Conner's voice carried an undertone of disbelief, mixed with a sense of haunting revelation.

"Yes, you did. And then one day, it all just stopped. No more nightmares. And you never mentioned Liam again. It was like you locked it all away somewhere inside you."

Conner felt an involuntary shiver. His sister's words were like missing pieces in a puzzle he had long given up trying to solve. "Olivia, I know this will probably sound insane. Hell, it probably is insane. But...do you think it could be real? The Glimmergrim?"

Olivia hesitated, her eyes searching his face to see if he was serious. Just then, her phone buzzed on the table. She glanced at the screen and her expression tightened. "It's work. I have to take this."

She stood and moved to another table as Conner took a sip of his cold coffee, grimaced, and put the cup back down. Olivia was whispering, but he heard her say something about "my brother" and "he's lost it."

She put her phone on mute as she returned to the table but didn't sit down again. "I'm sorry, Con. I have to get back to the office. Then her gaze softened, clouded with concern. "I don't believe in the Glimmergrim. But I think it's real enough for you. Please consider getting some professional help, OK?"

She went back to her phone call, mouthing a silent 'I'm sorry' to Conner as she walked away.

He was left to his thoughts under the dim café light. Through the window, he watched as his sister got into her car and drove off, leaving him alone with a chill in the air and his unease. His eyes fell upon a group of kids playing in the distance. Their laughter, so carefree, so uninhibited, made him think of simpler times, times when Liam was still around.

A sense of urgency washed over him then; perhaps it was time to confront the ghosts of his past rather than skirting around them. The Glimmergrim tale, as absurd as it sounded, gave voice to his fears—fears that were no longer confined to the realms of childhood or mere superstition. What if the answers he sought lay within those very fears? Dr. Stroud's words echoed in his mind: *confront these phantoms that haunt you.*

*Maybe it's time to visit some old ghosts,* he thought. *Starting with you, Liam.*

\*\*\*

Conner stood at the wrought-iron gates of St. Mary's Cemetery; his eyes drawn to the familiar rows of graves stretching toward the horizon. The twilight sun cast long shadows over the weathered tombstones, each a sentinel of eternal rest.

Taking a deep breath, he pushed open the creaking gates and made his way toward Liam's final resting place.

As he walked, he felt a weight lift off his shoulders, as if he was shedding layers of the past, but also bracing for a confrontation with whatever awaited him. Liam's grave was a modest stone marked simply with his name and the years that bookended his brief life. Conner knelt, brushing away some moist autumn leaves stuck to the gravestone.

"Hey, Liam," he whispered, "It's been too long."

As the words left his lips, he felt as though he'd unlocked a door within himself, one that had been bolted shut for years, holding back a reservoir of unshed tears and unspoken words. His voice quivered as he spoke to the cold slab of marble. "I never got to say goodbye...never apologized for running away that night. I wish you could see me now—how much I've changed, and how much I haven't. I'm still running, Liam, running from the goddamned Glimmergrim."

His throat tightened, as if the air itself struggled to convey the gravity of his words. "I'm scared, buddy. Scared that the visions I've been having aren't just in my head. That they might be real."

Just then, a soft glow caught his eye. He looked up to see fireflies starting to emerge, dancing among the tombstones, their luminescence contrasting the ever-encroaching darkness. It was as if the universe itself was offering him a moment of respite, a poetic juxtaposition that made him think—life persists in the presence of death.

Suddenly, a gust of wind swept through the cemetery, carrying with it a distinct scent, stirring a memory. It was the earthen smell of the countless explorations he'd had with Liam in their neighborhood. He was reminded of their innocence. Children playing together, full of imagination and eager for adventure, unaware of the tragedies that would befall them. It was a potent reminder that his past wasn't just made up of fears and monsters; there was beauty there, too.

As he basked in this short-lived moment of nostalgia, a low growl reverberated through the air, shattering the tranquility. The fireflies dispersed, and the wind carried a new scent—one of rot and decay. Shadows began to elongate and distort, tendrils of darkness stretched out like dark fingers—reaching for him.

The air grew denser, almost suffocating, and he heard something circling but saw no one. A voice came from behind, as cold as a tomb's embrace, *"You...can't...run...forever."*

It was the Glimmergrim. Conner didn't look over his shoulder. He simply ran for his life.

It chased him. He could feel it only steps behind as he sprinted out of the cemetery gates toward his car. As he reached the vehicle and scrambled to unlock the door, he saw his own terrified reflection in the driver's side window. Behind him stood the towering figure of the Glimmergrim, its nightmarish visage only inches away. It had him where it wanted him. There was no way he could get into the car without facing it.

Something triggered in him, a memory from childhood. *The ritual.* The one he never performed that fateful night. Staring at his own reflection with the monstrous thing behind him, he whispered, "Glimmergrim, Glimmergrim, I heed your warning, please let me return home before morning."

He repeated it three times and watched the demonic entity behind him fade into nothingness. He stood there for several moments. Frozen. Had that really worked?

Finally, he breathed again and spun to face whatever might be waiting for him. But he was alone. No Glimmergrim, just the parking lot of a silent cemetery bathed in the light of the rising moon and a twilight chill.

With a newfound resolve, Conner climbed into his car and revved the engine. *You can't run forever*, it had said. "You're right," he muttered to himself, acknowledging the lingering memory. *Maybe it's time to face what I've been running from.*

***

The respite Conner earned through the cemetery ritual was ephemeral. His life remained a theater of inescapable visions—both the ghastly Glimmergrim and the nameless faces that troubled his dreams and waking hours.

Dragged down by relentless dread, he was continually exhausted. Recognizing his fragile state, Dr. Stroud suggested a shift in their therapeutic approach. Firm in her belief that her experimental device, the Perceptual Mapping Sphere, could facilitate the unlocking of his underlying trauma, she felt this change could accelerate his journey toward recovery.

Re-entering the familiar setting of Dr. Stroud's office, Conner felt a resurgence of determination. Encircled by an intricate assembly of mirrors and cutting-edge sensors, he steeled himself to confront the specters of his past.

Maneuvering herself behind the control panel, Dr. Stroud activated the machine. The sphere hummed to life, unleashing a panoply of lights swirling across its surface, casting shadows that danced and melded on the wall. They began to morph, insinuating the outline of faces—faces that gnawed at the murky depths of Conner's subconscious.

"Describe what you see, Conner," Dr. Stroud's voice cut incisively through his reverie.

Clenching the armrests as if anchoring himself to reality, Conner replied, "Men, women, and children, their eyes wide open, their mouths wide open, as if screaming."

She jotted down some notes. "Are they the same faces?"

"Yes," he confirmed. "They're always the same faces."

"I believe they are not illusions but rather obscured memories. Memories you've suppressed."

He swiveled toward her, "What do you mean—?"

"Don't resist this, Conner. I believe we've reached the cusp of a pivotal revelation. Please turn back toward the wall—focus on the projections."

Resigned, Conner returned his gaze to the undulating lights. He felt a nascent awareness bubbling within him, a sensation that hinted at an imminent breakthrough. Yet a shiver of apprehension coursed through him; he was uncertain whether he was ready for those revelations.

With calculated intent, Dr. Stroud manipulated the machine's settings. The lights intensified, coalescing into forms that were hauntingly familiar, almost tangible. "What do you see now, Conner?" she inquired, her voice infused with anticipation.

A searing flashback cleaved through Conner's consciousness. He was back in the derelict Tunison building, his childhood friend, Liam, standing in front of him. He saw his own hands shove the boy through a gaping hole in the floor and fall to his death. A gut punch of shock and disbelief coursed through him.

"No…that's not what happened!" he shouted.

"What didn't happen?" Dr. Stroud inquired, tilting her head subtly, as if relishing the unfolding drama.

"It wasn't me…the Glimmergrim killed my friend."

"Was it, now," she uttered, her words forming more of a statement than a question.

The haunting image persisted, looping endlessly in the crevices of his mind—an infinite loop of him pushing his best friend to a gruesome death.

Then, his perspective shifted. He approached the chasm in the floor, its wood rotted and brittle. Below, enveloped in the black void, he saw eyes. Staring back was the Glimmergrim, its face twisted in a hideous smile.

"It was there," Conner whispered. "It was down in that hole. It made me do it. It *compelled* me."

As Conner's attention remained fixed on the oscillating lights, Dr. Stroud stepped closer, scrutinizing his face. "I believe you, Conner."

Tears began to stream down his face. "You—you do?"

She nodded. "I've also specialized in Anomalous Psychological Studies, differentiating the genuinely possessed from the merely delusional. And you're not delusional, Conner. You're just confused.

"I researched peer-reviewed journals on paranormal psychology. And I delved into the lore surrounding this so-called Glimmergrim. Obscure manuscripts trace its history back to a human origin, allegedly a malevolent person cursed to harvest souls to extend its unnatural life. According to myth, it can only reclaim its humanity by finding a suitable successor—a vessel already tainted by moral corruption. That, Conner, is you."

He shook his head in denial and started to rise. Shockingly, Dr. Stroud shoved him back in his seat. A sudden unease gripped him, as though the room itself had turned hostile. Her voice intensified. "You must confront your true nature. Now is the time."

The import of her words sunk in, deflating his initial defiance. His voice took on a desperate tone as he asked, "My true nature?"

With a chilling calculation replacing her usual warmth, Dr. Stroud asserted, "You wanted to do it, yes? You resented Liam; he was your better in every way—looks, courage, intellect."

His eyes vacant, Conner found himself immersed in a mental cinema, reliving those charged moments. "I...yes," he conceded. "I suppose...deep down, maybe I did resent him."

He looked up at her, distraught. "What am I?"

"*Stop* resisting," she said. "Your conscience wants to protect your fragile ego, to preserve the cognitive dissonance you achieved regarding the things you've done. Not just your childhood friend, but against all those you've murdered or harmed throughout your life. Liam was simply your first kill."

Dr. Stroud's words shattered Conner's constructed reality, laying waste to his illusions. Understanding dawned; he just needed to unlock the door to his repressed self.

And so, he did.

The floodgates opened, releasing a torrent of horrific images long contained, bursting forth into his mind like a dam giving way. The faces that had tormented him for weeks now screamed their accusations, their condemnations. Their anguished cries reverberated within his psyche.

Gripped by this shocking epiphany, he held his head as if trying to contain a mind that was fracturing.

Dr. Stroud spoke, her voice eerily composed, "Your mind fabricated false memories to create a more acceptable narrative...to shelter you from the truth. But you're at the mental breakpoint, Conner; what's left of your conscience has lost the war against your authentic self."

She thrust a hand mirror toward him. "Hold this. See yourself for what you truly are."

Conner was reminded of his childhood fear of mirrors. He hesitated, terrified of what awaited him.

"I said *take it*," she demanded.

His hand trembled uncontrollably as he took the mirror and faced his own reflection. What he saw there revealed the truth.

Dr. Stroud edged closer; her voice soft yet chilling. "You see now... don't you? Every soul carries a shadow, a secret darkness. Most deny it, lock it away, but not you. Together we've given it life. I've been searching for someone like you my entire career. Someone who could shatter the barrier between the psychological and the paranormal."

The thing that was once Conner continued to gaze at its reflection. In embracing the horrifying truth, it felt a perverse sense of liberation, lips twisted into a grotesque smile.

"Come," Dr. Stroud said, extending her hand, "The world is full of...opportunities."

Hand in hand they strolled through the exit, leaving behind an unsettling quiet, as if the very walls held their breath in dread of what was to come.

# En Passant

Colin J. Northwood

*K* *night to c6.*
Gary cocked his head slightly to the side. His eyes shifted about slowly, searching the walls of the well-stocked office for confirmation that his move would bring him victory. They found none.

Blades of orange light pierced the air of the ranger station, launching their assault from the sunrise outside. The broad wooden slats of the blinds offered meager defense, and were overrun. Gary looked through the window and surveyed his domain, paying little heed to the conquering light. It was the early shift, and he was alone. He adjusted his badge, then checked his watch.

Another day, another move.

The humble chessboard sat on a stool near the back of the room. It must have looked grand, once—a stark, clean lattice adorned with elegant pieces. A primordial ichor, which must have bled from the night sky itself, alternated with a heavenly white in a triumph of order over chaos. The immortal struggle of light against darkness, rendered in microcosm, was once trapped in this single perfect square. But time's yellow venom had crept into its veins. For a moment, Gary reminisced about the elegant, black-and-white films of vintage Hollywood; they too had since been invaded by color. Barbaric!

What had the old thing seen? Was it an heirloom, even older than its owner? Gary wouldn't know. He was young, and Arthur, who owned the board, wasn't telling.

Despite the insistently peaceful summer morning, Gary managed to convince himself that there was no time for such questions. It was the Fifteenth of August, 1976, and Eighty Rivers National Park needed its keeper.

The small station was manned by only one ranger at a time. Gary worked the morning shift, and Arthur the evening. An hour for lunch between the two shifts ensured that the two men rarely came face-to-face. Save for the occasional vacationer in the park, Gary rarely saw another human face. He liked it that way.

Therefore: chess! One move per shift. One move, carefully planned during the station's ample quiet time. One move, the fruit of a day's scheming. One move, to vindicate. One move, to prove a general's mind lay hidden in a lowly park ranger's head. For this, there was time.

Gary rubbed his gold engagement ring. It was crafted in the shape of the Ouroboros: a snake swallowing its own tail. To the ancients, it represented Eternity. Gary twisted it around his finger in a valiant attempt at perpetual motion. But Anne was still gone.

He frowned slightly and looked out the window again, at the here-and-now. It was summer and there were visitors to serve, at least until lunch.

Like most men of his time, Gary lived in a box. Each morning, the box gave birth to him, and to an iron steed. Caffeine permitting, the rider and his mount charged headlong into an indolent world, taking it by storm. Each evening, like Cronus before it, the box devoured its offspring, forestalling its obsolescence. Like most men of his time, Gary understood that he would one day find himself in a different wooden box, swallowed instead by Mother Earth. Until then, the cycle continued, sacred and inviolate.

And so, the next morning, Gary returned to the road, atop whirring wheels and groaning metal, and beneath the endless firmament. The same stars watched over him always, despite the best efforts of the Earth and Sky to conceal them. Some days, their bodies slung low in their celestial thrones. Some days, they went into hiding. But they always returned, with a dutiful resolve (an inevitability!), to their posts in Heaven's lighthouse, guiding the way for an ascendant soul prepared to match their grandeur.

Gary had begun to believe he was prepared for anything. He would win, this time.

The early-morning city lights fled into the distance in his rear-view mirror. Through the thickening trees, he threaded his path with the deftness of a skilled tailor. The road was his herald, its serpentine, asphalt body painted with streaks of gold to trumpet his coming. A concrete bridge spanned a small canyon, just beyond the park's gate. Into this gate he entered each morning, and from this gate he returned each day.

A short distance further, Gary arrived at work. He parked his car and stepped out onto the gravel, stopping at the station's front window for a moment to admire himself in his well-fitted uniform. One hand stroked his hair while the other searched for the correct key. The jingle of the door chime welcomed him back inside. He switched the lights on.

Everything was in order. Maps and brochures, in neat upright rows, were perched in a display case at the front of the office, each one waiting its turn to instruct some tourist on the local wildlife and scenery. A water dispenser, flanked by a few chairs and a stack of paper cups, was on the right side of the room. A washroom and a supply closet were on the left. Near the back wall was a handsome oak desk with a rotary phone and some stationery. Beside this desk, in the most distant corner of the room, was the chessboard, upon a stool. Gary eagerly attended to it.

Today, Arthur's move had been a predictable one. Gary had the old man in his clutches, he thought to himself with a smug hand on his hip. This was going to be a good day.

Between his rounds of the park, Gary sat at his desk, planning out the downfall of Arthur's forces. A wily advance, seizing control of the center with his bishop, would surely set the dominoes in motion. It was a *fait accompli*. All that remained for Gary was to spring the trap. The game itself was a mere formality; his victory was sacrosanct.

Another day, another move. And the following day, another move still. Gary preferred to think that with each move, the chessboard commanded another day to pass, and the clockwork universe obeyed; with his imminent victory, Gary would assert his own sole command of the chessboard itself.

Surely, Arthur would realize in short order that he must resign. But alas, there was no hurry. The old man's fate had been sealed. He had only to realize it. Gary didn't mind a few more days of cat-and-mouse; they'd allow him to savor his predatory glee.

Nevertheless, on one of those days, the telephone had something else in mind. Like a bastard infant child announcing its loathsome birth, it cried out for Gary's attention with a metallic shriek. Resentful of its interjection, Gary scowled as he lifted its earpiece with one hand and strangled its umbilical cord with the other.

"Eighty Rivers National Park, Station Number Five. How can I help you?"

A gruff, familiar voice responded, "Gary, this is Frank. I need to ask for a favor. Could you do me a kindness and stay late next Monday?"

"Sure thing, boss." The word left a bitter taste in Gary's mouth. He glanced at his coffee, wishing it had been the culprit. "What needs doing?"

Frank spoke in a softer tone than usual, but in a higher register. "We've found a new guy for the late shift. We're going to schedule him to start soon. I'd like you to meet with him. Show him around the grounds a bit. Can you do that for me?"

"Yessir."

"And there's some catching up to do." Frank coughed. "You know, for the late shift. Paperwork."

"Hm." Gary rubbed his fingertip against the desk. It wasn't like Arthur to neglect his duties. "You want me to tell Arthur?"

"Oh." Frank paused for a moment. "You haven't heard."

Gary's eyes shot to the chessboard.

From the telephone came a deep breath, and then the news. "Gary, I'm sorry," Frank said, his voice creaking ever-so-slightly with the timbre of a waning bonfire. "Arthur's been dead since last Wednesday."

Gary's hand slackened, and the telephone handle broke free. Frank's voice continued, pitiably faint. The world receded, and only the chessboard remained, still and at peace.

When time resumed its dutiful march forward, Gary's heart began to beat again, and he stood. He made his way to the corner, his eyes transfixed by the board, and began to pace around it, slowly, with a lion tamer's caution. Arthur was dead, but the game was not. And no one else had access to the station. Gary interrogated the board with his eyes, but it confessed to nothing. He intensified his terrible glare, but still it did not give up its accomplice.

These were ordinary days, the chessboard would have him believe, and nothing was amiss.

Gary returned to his desk, sat down, and took stock of the situation. The prospect of victory over Arthur was gone. Gary felt a flash of cinder-red blood burning in his cheeks, furious that death had dared to pilfer his glory. And yet, the game had continued. The armies of light and darkness had not given up their fight. The bishop waited, still, to spring his trap. Gary smiled slightly upon realizing that some kind of win could still be salvaged.

"But who are you?" Gary sneered, demanding someone over whom to prevail.

As if in response, a draft made itself known. It was a wintry thing, gone far astray on this summer morning. Gary closed his eyes. The cold air caressed his neck and shoulder, gently at first, then with a gradually building vigor, and finally with a *tap* that jolted his eyes open.

Gary stared, motionless, at an empty spot on the opposite wall, looking for some reason—any reason—why it should continue to hold his attention. For the barest moment, he almost began to believe it was this rapture which held him paralyzed, and not the catatonic dread taking hold of his every nerve. The telephone, still unhooked and lying pathetically on the desk, sputtered out a dial tone. Gary's watch ticked, trying to lull him with its hypnotic rhythm.

Then came another *tap* on his shoulder.

With a jolt of adrenaline, Gary stood upright, slamming his chair into the wall behind him. He scrambled around the desk and bolted toward the door, hurling it open violently. The tiny brass chime cried out in protest.

He charged across the gravel parking lot, fumbling for his keys before stabbing them haphazardly into the car door. On the second try, the door yielded. In one swift motion, Gary leaped inside and slammed the door behind him, shoving the key into the ignition. The engine roared to life and the tires screeched. Rider and steed fled the scene.

The vehicle careened down the road. Trees flew by in a blur. Gary stared straight ahead, holding the steering wheel tightly despite the sweat on his palms. His breathing slowed a bit when he saw the familiar bridge by the park's entrance. His eyes darted to the mirror, but there was nothing behind him. Nothing but trees, road, and more trees.

Gary's foot released the gas pedal, and the car decelerated as it crossed the concrete bridge. He pulled over on the opposite side, and looked around. No one else was here. He closed his eyes and felt his heart thumping against his chest. He tensed and released his grip on the steering wheel a few times. Then, for a moment, he closed his eyes, and just sat.

The affable songs of birds filled the warm summer air. Gary recognized a robin. He opened his eyes, allowing himself a sigh. The sun was at its apex. Shadows meandered across the ground as the arms of the roadside trees swayed in the gentle wind.

Wind. It was just wind. Gary laughed briefly, expelling his confusion. He stepped outside, feeling the solid ground beneath his feet, and wiped a bead of sweat from his brow. Reassured by the soft breeze, he leaned against his car, closed his eyes, and spoke to himself.

"Only wind."

He forced a smile.

But still, maybe it was best not to go back to the station. Not just yet. Frank would understand. A little bit of alone time at home might be a good idea. Arthur was dead, after all, so Frank would have to understand.

Gary returned to the car seat and started the engine. He spoke to himself again as he pulled away from the shoulder and back onto the road.

"What's gotten into you? You nutcase—you really had yourself going for a minute there."

He continued forward, waiting for the gate to emerge between the trees past the next bend. He turned on the radio, and rock music flowed from the speakers. Gary thought he knew the song, but he wasn't sure. The reception was less than ideal. He didn't mind, though. It's the price one pays for staying far from the city.

Gary continued around the bend, but the gate did not appear. Instead, there was another twist of the road. He must have gotten confused. It was understandable. After that stressful episode from earlier, it's no wonder. The gate must be around the next turn. It had to be.

It wasn't. No gate here. Just more road and more trees. Gary wondered briefly if he had taken a wrong turn, before remembering that there were no intersections on this stretch of road. He knew the gate was here. Five days a week he came this way. It *had* to be here. He *knew* this road.

Instead, around the next turn, the ranger station lay ahead.

Gary hit the brakes, and pulled over again to the side of the road. He stared blankly at the building. The door was ajar and the parking lot empty. The birds sang, the shadows danced, and the sun lazed in the sky.

He turned around. Back to the road, across the bridge, and around the bend he went. Several minutes later, he arrived again at the station.

This time, he drove past it. Eighty Rivers National Park was large, but there were other exits.

Gary's foot pushed harder on the gas pedal. "I don't know what the hell is going on, but I'm getting out of here," he told himself. "I'm going to live through this. I'm going to live through this. I'm going to *live*." The gold engagement ring dug into the underside of his finger as he gripped the wheel tightly. He sped down the narrow road, as fast as its curves would allow.

Bursts of static bled from the speakers, interrupted by the occasional guitar riff. Was that the same song again? Gary turned off the radio.

This way, too, circled back to the station. Time for another try. He sped off again, this time intending to take an unpaved service road he knew was just ahead. But again, he arrived back at the station.

After returning a few more times, Gary could no longer muster another attempt. The way out was not away, but through. He parked his car at his usual spot and stepped out onto the gravel.

Gary looked up and saw a blazing golden ring. *Eternity*, he thought, as an ill twilight bedimmed the sky. No eclipse was scheduled for today, but no matter. The heavens must have had other plans. What is a serpent, if not full of surprises? Gary lowered his eyes to the structure in front of him, and stared it down. The wind began to whip fiercely at the trees, each lash provoking a howl more wretched than the last.

The station door rattled on its hinges as Gary stepped forward. He seized it roughly by the handle, punishing it for its impudence. He stepped into the office once more, and the door slammed behind him.

And then there was peace. The wild cries of the wind had vanished. The tiny chime on the door delivered a cheery welcome. Through the windows, a bright, sunny morning was visible. The trees outside were motionless in the still air. A tiny, brown bird flitted by.

The office itself was untouched—just as Gary had left it. The telephone's earpiece had been kept alive by its umbilical cord; it emitted its soft cry from across the room, pleading to be returned home. Gary checked the washroom and the supply closet, but nothing else was out-of-place.

The chessboard, too—the wicked seductress—sat innocuously on its stool, eagerly awaiting Gary's next move. And in exchange, it offered victory. Glory. Order over chaos. Mind over matter. Another move. Another day.

But Gary knew better. He would not give in to temptation. Not for all the kingdoms of the world. The devil must be expunged!

Gary leaped forward and kicked the stool, knocking the board to the ground. The pieces were routed, their tidy formations scattered across the carpet. Their battle stations, their feudal hierarchies, their rules about who-may-go-where—all were upended in one fell swoop. Gary felt like a force of nature.

"Your move," he chortled, exhilaration creeping across his face. And for a moment he loomed menacingly over the vanquished armies. *But enough of this*, he thought, as his laughter died down. He picked up the board and lifted it high overhead, imagining himself as Moses holding the Decalogue. "Enough!" he shouted, and slammed it loudly onto the edge of the desk.

The board suffered only a small dent. It was of a sturdy build, but it was not invincible. Gary lifted it high, and with a bestial cry he slammed it down upon the desk again, harder than before. Both board and desk were wounded this time. Gary was delighted to see splinters forming in the wood. Defense may be imperative in chess, but no barrier is impenetrable.

"Not so tough now, are ya?" he cackled.

Again and again, Gary battered his enemy, relishing the soreness of his own hands. He squealed in delight as he picked up the pace, smashing the board until, finally— *Crack!* Now Gary knew the wooden board could not withstand much more. He held it against the desk with both hands and delivered a violent kick. The board buckled, and splinters emerged from its back side. The next kick nearly broke it in two. Gary roared and threw it against the wall, where it collapsed into a heap.

Elation washed over Gary, and he began pumping his bleeding fists into the air in a victory dance. "Yes!" he bellowed. "Damn right!"

The massacre was over.

Gary sat on the damaged desk, then stood up a few seconds later to get a drink of water from the dispenser. Then it was back to the desk to cool down. He hung up the phone, and the room was silent once more. He took a sip of water, noticing the blood smeared on the paper cup, and grinned at a job well done. For the ruin of one's enemies, a few drops of one's own blood were a price well worth paying.

The conquering hero lingered on his throne. For this, there was time—maybe a minute, maybe a lifetime. Such distinctions were insignificant trifles in the wake of such resplendent majesty. Gary thought for a moment about Arthur. Pity he couldn't be here. Then he thought about Anne. He took off his ring and set it down on the desk, ready for whatever tomorrow may bring.

# Enough and then Some

Chad Lutzke

The day Elizabeth talked about dying, we were at a faraway park that seemed everyone else on the planet had long forgotten. It was our place. We could make love in the middle of it, right there in the spotlighting sun, with never the worry of being seen.

Strangely, even the ducks steered clear of our pond, perhaps favoring the other one some ten miles down the road. This was our haven. It's where we had our first kiss, our first heavy petting, sledding together on the northern hill in the middle of winter. Picnics, naps, stargazing.

She brought up the topic moments after we'd witnessed a catfight. The fight was loud and violent. A tom and a calico were going at it. And by the end, the calico lay down and never stood again. The tom walked off and sat next to the tree line, licking blood from its paws.

"You can't die before me," Elizabeth said. She took my hand in a hurry, like I was a kite that might fly away. "Promise you won't die first." She was gazing at me, her eyes darting to each of mine. They wore a worry I'd never seen before. Two graying clouds waiting for the downpour.

"I'm not in control of that, my love." I squeezed her hand tight for reassurance that all was well, that we were okay and going nowhere. Life was good. We were healthy and careful.

"I want you to quit smoking." Her eyes continued to dance with mine.

I entertained the thought of quitting and realized in the grand scheme of things—and my role in her life—it wasn't a big ask. When you share your life with another, you give. And you do it unconditionally. You sacrifice. If they're worth your time—and she certainly was, my sweet Elizabeth—then your generosity can trigger a comparable response. Only self-centered asses smack the face of one who's offering their all. And we were not asses. Nor were we self-centered. It's why things still worked even decades into us.

"Okay," I said. "Consider this my last one." Before even taking a final drag on the half-smoked cigarette, I drew my finger behind the butt and flicked it into the grass, where it stayed lit for the next few minutes, snaking smoke like a teasing wave goodbye.

Elizabeth leaned in and put her head on my shoulder. She sighed deeply before saying, "Thank you."

Weeks later, when winter had gone and spring was pregnant with blooms-to-come, we happened upon a squirrel that lay dead over a tree branch as though it'd missed its jump and broken its back on the way down. Rain and rot had pulled the black hair from its body, leaving behind a glistening blue-white patch of skin where the body curved over the limb.

Elizabeth blew a kiss to the squirrel and said to me, "Promise me you'll not die before me, my love." It wasn't the second time she'd said it. There were other times. Several of them, ad nauseam. At first it was endearing and romantic, almost Shakespearean. But her anxiety regarding my premature death was contagious, and rather than find any flattery in the obsession, I found myself concerned.

"I'll never leave you," I said. "May the Lord allow my ghostly return should I exit before you, even if just to cast a chilly breeze on a warm day."

She failed to see the humor in my words. "I don't want a haunting. I want you, Sedrick. Right here, by my side. Always. I can't live without you. And if you love me, truly love me, you'll see to it I'll always have your hand to hold, your lips to touch, and your manhood to carry me to the edge and back again."

Her innuendo triggered a laugh between us. Then we carried each other to the edge and back, there in the park, under the clumsy squirrel. Not a stitch of clothing on us.

The next time we met Death, a cardinal lay sprawled on our bench, ants having burrowed deep beneath its crimson wings. Eyes closed in a peaceful, everlasting wink, and its talons curled in on themselves like a spider's lifeless legs.

This time, I didn't wait for the obsessive request and told her I would always be here. "We have so much to do, my love. We've yet to travel to so many of the places we've longed to go. There's still our golden years to reach, when our wings will spread further yet."

She hugged my arm. "Were we ever meant to love this much, Sedrick? Does anyone else share a love like this? Or are we made special? Like two genuine soul mates God planned before even giving light to the world?" She looked at me, deep into me. "Are we His prideful example of how it's supposed to be?"

"Yes, I think we are." I'd never really considered how much different our love may be from others. I only knew where we stood. Neck deep in a bliss that no one could ever pull us from.

After reveling further, we made love in the grass like we'd done a hundred times before. But after, when she drove her arms through mine and held me tight, caressing me, her hand found its way under my arm, and her fingers lingered, touching something new there. Something that caused her brow to furrow, her eyes to go wide and fill with tears.

"There's a lump," she said, and I knew right away the abnormality would send her into a downward spiral. "A lump! Do you hear me?"

I felt the area. The hardened bulb was buried deep but most definitely existent. I tried to settle her. "I'm sure it's harmless, Liz. It means nothing."

"You can't do this to me, Sedrick. You can't die. I've told you. I can't live without you."

"And I told you, love. I'm not going anywhere. We have decades to go yet."

"The cardinal." She pointed to the bird covered in ants, its chest inviting the infestation of tiny eggs. "Don't you understand? It's a bad omen. This is a sign."

She broke down like I'd never heard before. Inconsolable. Trembling to the point of near seizure, her teeth chattering chattering chattering. I carried her home, and we spent the night in each other's arms, until the sun spoke through a crack in the curtains.

That day, I called to schedule an appointment. The earliest I could get in was six weeks away. When I relayed this to Elizabeth, she became catatonic, quietly mumbling that she can't wait that long, like some kind of dreadful mantra. Nothing I did calmed her. The obsession had excelled to a dangerous point I feared she would not return from, and that even in obvious health she would cling to this idea that she would be forced to one day live her life alone.

I spent the day by her side. Not by choice but necessity. The few times I did wander from the bedside, whether to fix a meal or use the restroom, she called out to me in a panic, begging me not to leave. Several times a day, her hand would wander to the lump under my arm, judging whether or not the thing had grown. For her sake, I offered more than a few prayers, requesting the tumor to shrink or disappear completely just so I could get my dear Elizabeth back, because from the moment she discovered the nodule, our carefree love seemed to have ended.

Days went by. She stopped eating. I was able to make her smile exactly twice, but the smiles were charitable things that lacked any semblance of joy. I think she started to realize the burden her obsession had caused. Finally, on the fourth day of bedridden grief, she said, "Take me to the park, Sedrick. I want to see the pond and make love in the grass."

I filled the picnic basket with her favorites, hoping the scenery would be enough to get her to eat. As we walked through the grass on our way to the pond, she held onto my arm, purposefully keeping her fingers away from the spot that had conjured this new-found trauma. Her gait was weak and clumsy on frail legs, and she leaned on me as we made our way.

I spread our blanket out, the same one that'd met this grass a thousand times before, and we sat eating sandwiches, as well as Elizabeth's favorite: cheese with crackers. She'd even brought wine that we drank from the bottle like a couple of free-spirited winos.

"We're getting older," Elizabeth said as she ran a pinky along the corner of her lips, wiping away the tiniest drop of wine.

"Nonsense," I said. "We have years before we're even considered seniors."

She frowned. "You have three more years. I have nine. It's not a lifetime, Sedrick. It's a season."

"Then I suggest we get back to enjoying it." I tried to smile but was distracted by the wilted cat floating in the pond, bloated white with a halo of flies. Elizabeth had already spotted the poor creature, and I knew to her it was another sign of the dread to come—a tell that death was waiting to devour me, starting at the pit of my arm.

Her hand ran up my leg, caressing it. Her eyes grew heavy with seduction. "Make love to me."

Under the influence of her touch and a belly full of wine, I laid her back, kissing every inch of porcelain flesh, from head to toe and back again. We moaned and grunted while covered in spit as the cat bobbed against the ripple of the wind. She rode me with a ferocity I hadn't seen since we were young, when the word death didn't linger in our vocabulary.

She sat on me with trembling legs, exhausted from climax, and set her eyes on mine. "Kill me," she said. Her face was made of stone, clearly serious. "Death is all around us, my love. And if it comes for you first…" Her eyes bubbled with tears, breasts hung, reaching out for me.

I sat up on my elbows, still inside her, shriveling. "We don't know that I'll die first, Liz."

"The lump is bigger." The statement was so matter of fact, filled with so much surety that I reached under my arm and felt the bulb which had indeed doubled in size, even more tender to the touch. Something I had kept from her was how painful it'd been since the discovery. It would have only exacerbated her fear.

"Kill me, Sedrick. Drown me in the pond." She swung her head toward the water-logged cat, which had made its way to the far shore. "If you don't do it…" She held the rest of her words for what felt like years. "…I'll do it myself."

"And what of me?" I asked. "Who's to say I could ever find joy again without you?"

"You're stronger than me. And you'll be with me again soon." She touched the lump, caressing it as though the feel of it now gave her solace. "Very soon. What a beautiful thing to die knowing you loved me enough to fulfill my request."

The nodule throbbed, as though communicating with me, clarifying that it indeed was sent to end us and who am I to deny my wife peace of mind.

I grabbed the bottle of wine and downed the rest. Each swallow was a step toward the pond, a hand to the back of her head, a plunge under water. I'd decided. And she knew this, because a smile curled her lips. She knew the wine was for courage—or poor judgment. It's exactly why she'd brought it.

She stood, dripping the last of me, and reached her hand out to mine. I felt the warmth of it. The calm. And together we walked through the lush grass and to the pond.

A fish with milky eyes lay on the shore, its gaze stuck on the graying sky above. Death had become such a frequent visitor. A voyeur. The signs were there. Was I a fool to miss them? Or a fool to follow? To create a superstition that meant nothing more than coincidence.

My dearest Elizabeth knelt and crawled down the embankment, her bare skin like ivory against the wet dirt, much like the rotting fish next to her.

We looked at one another in the reflection of the water. She seemed so distant, and the sparkle of her once lively eyes was gone, eaten by the murk.

"I know you love me enough," she said, attempting one last smile, then held her face to the water as though going in for a drink. "I'll see you soon, my lo–"

I dove at her, forcing her head below, shouting at the death that'd surrounded us these past few weeks, cursing the park and all its decay. The place we once called our safe haven.

While the end came, Elizabeth never struggled. Not once. She gave freely to a lungful of everything but air, as I trembled violently, my grip unforgiving and determined to fulfill the morbid request, even if it meant the spiderwebbing crack of my own sanity.

I could actually feel the moment she left, the pulse of her carotid silencing its spastic rhythm. Without context, her hair weaved through my fingers was a violent sight. I caught my breath and released my grip, lay back on the embankment as her hair swam like celestial arms in a black void. She'd found peace. And I loved her enough to give it.

But what of me?

She claimed I was stronger, yet my voice was impossibly hoarse from screams of anguish—the first session of many to come, no doubt.

But I loved her enough.

I left her there in the park and went back to our empty house, where I spent the next few weeks gazing at pictures of her while waiting for my upcoming appointment. The only thing that kept me afloat was knowing I loved her enough. Otherwise, I was a miserable wreck, wishing the lump under my arm would metastasize at a profound rate, shortening the road traveled in which I'd see her again.

For the next six weeks, I tolerated the lump's ache, willing it to grow. And I stayed clear of the park. It was nothing but an ugly reminder now, no longer the sanctuary it used to be. Even the countless memories seemed to rot away with everything else in it.

When the day of my appointment finally arrived, the doctor inspected me, taking a biopsy that would leave me waiting yet again on another plane of hell filled with bitter excitement for bad news.

Two days turned into three. Three to four. The clock's hands and the sun seemed to conspire together, stretching the days into tortuous years. Finally, the phone rang on the day expected, and I wasted no time in answering.

"Hello?" Having not spoken a word all week, my voice cracked desert dry.

"Mr. Sedrick Bava?"

"Yes."

"We have your test results. Is there a convenient time in the next few days you could come in?"

"Yes, of course."

"Actually, how's today look for you?"

It was a good question.

# Going Down

## Felix Blackwell

Preston Lyle closed the manila folder and pushed himself away from his desk. The chair rolled backward a foot or so and stopped. He spun around to face the big window. A sickly orange Philadelphia sky loomed beyond it. Minutes before, the sun had dipped behind the ring of distant skyscrapers. It was 7:20 PM.

Preston peeled off his glasses and wiped a forearm across his oily face. He grabbed his briefcase and loosened his tie, then hobbled down the hall toward the elevators. Empty cubicles lined his peripheries. If someone had been sitting in one of them, he'd not have noticed; his eyes were glued to the cell phone in his hand.

*Finished both portfolios today,* he typed with a chubby thumb. *Sending them to you and Bryan first thing in the AM.*

*Excellent,* his partner replied. *You carried this one, Pres. Owe you a steak.*

Preston smacked the Down button on one of the elevators. As he waited, he glanced down the hall he'd walked through. The sky was changing to a deep purple. When he first began working at Wessman & Schultz, Preston spent an inordinate amount of time gazing out his office window, admiring the city. As the years passed, he barely noticed it anymore. For some reason, today the view beckoned to him. The compulsion to look was almost foreign. It sort of felt like he'd never see it again.

A soft *ding* pulled him from his reverie. The elevator doors slid open with a gentle hum and Preston stepped inside.

The phone buzzed in his hand. While checking it, he poked the Level 1 button by mistake, then corrected himself and hit P1.

It was a text from his wife, Beth.

*Are you still at work?*

*On my way home*, he typed. *Ever been to Milan?*

The phone rang.

"Hi sweetie," he answered.

"You didn't," Beth said. Preston could almost *hear* her grinning.

"I did. Booked 'em today. Figured it was about time. Closed a major project today."

Beth squealed in excitement.

"Get home quick," she said. "Let's go out to celebrate."

Preston obliged and hung up the phone. He glanced up at the digital readout above the button panel.

*21…20…19…*

He compulsively scrolled through the emails on his phone. There was a message from Alison Briggs in management. He stuck the phone back in his pocket.

"Not tonight, y'old hag," he muttered.

*13…12…11…*

He tried to clear work from his mind, but ended up going through mental lists of things he had to finish the next day. The job was never far from his thoughts. It was medication to him; the busyness of it all helped him avoid the things in life he couldn't control, the memories he tried to bury.

Preston found himself instinctively reaching back into his pocket for the phone. The elevator lurched.

*3...2...1...*

The doors slid open. The ground floor of Wessman & Schultz was empty, spare a lone security guard reading his paper. A set of huge glass windows near the entrance framed a scene of twilight streets. People in suits walked by, laughing and chatting. Cars passed now and then. Preston stared out for a while, longing to be outside, then tapped the Close Door button repeatedly. He wanted to get home as fast as possible.

The doors slid shut and the elevator lurched again. As it descended, its mechanical hum made Preston feel anxious.

*Too much coffee today,* he thought.

The readout glowed its soft blue light.

*1...P1...P2...*

Preston's brow furled. He pressed P1 repeatedly, but the elevator did not stop.

"What the hell," he complained. "Parking, you stupid shit. *Parking.*"

The elevator didn't respond to his command. He tried pressing several other buttons, but none of them lit up.

*B1...B2...*

"Great. This is great." He smacked P1 over and over with his fist to no avail. He loathed the idea of walking up several flights of stairs to get back to the underground car park.

*C1...C2...C3...*

Preston stared in disbelief at the display above the button panel. He had no idea there were this many floors beneath the parking structure. He didn't even know what C stood for.

A shrieking sound of metal on metal deafened Preston. He clutched his ears, then nervously paced around the little room. The elevator seemed to speed up as it descended; it almost felt like it was in freefall. The metallic sounds alternated between high-pitched whines and deep, shuddering groans. Floors flew by.

*C18...C19...C20...*

A waterfall of sweat poured off of Preston's head, smearing down his face and glasses. He stumbled to the emergency panel and opened it, revealing a button marked "STOP" and a red phone. He slapped the button but it didn't give; upon further inspection it was stuck. When he picked up the phone, it rang and rang endlessly, but no one ever answered.

*C36...C37...C38...*

The air went out of the room. Preston's old claustrophobia crept back into his conscious thoughts. He smoldered under his heavy suit. He couldn't breathe. He fumbled for his cell phone, but forgot which pocket it was in. When he finally found it, he dialed Beth. The call refused to connect. Preston was alone.

*C43...C44...C45...*

"Somebody help me!" he screamed at the top of his lungs. "Stop this thing!"

As if in response to his cries, the elevator came crashing to a halt. The jolt almost knocked Preston to his knees, but he caught himself against the button panel. The readout flashed in bright red letters inches from his face:

*C46. C46. C46. C46. C46.*

The doors struggled to open, but finally did so with a loud rumble. A single drop of water collected on the carriage's metal ceiling and dripped onto his neck. He didn't notice.

Preston practically threw himself out of that god-forsaken elevator. A wall of musty air assailed his nostrils. He strained to catch his breath. Before him lay a long, dark hallway, dimly lit with yellow tube lights every few yards. The hall was strangely, incomprehensibly, terrifyingly long. It vanished into a distant, dark point. He could hear water dripping somewhere far ahead.

Preston found his phone in his hand again. He couldn't remember reaching for it. No service. He whirled around as the elevator doors slammed shut behind him. He heard the carriage heading back to the upper floors.

"Wait!" he shouted, bashing his palm against the metal. There was no button panel on this floor. He could not recall the elevator.

Shaking and sniffling, Preston shuffled down the hallway, wondering where on earth he was. His footsteps echoed all around him, the sound of Italian leather scraping on concrete. The ground and walls were unmarked gray surfaces.

He walked for what seemed like a mile. After a long time, he reached the distant point. It was a single door in the otherwise barren hallway. Preston pushed the door open. Beyond it lay a wooden staircase that descended down, down, farther into the dark. There were no lights here. The dripping noises grew more intense, but he still couldn't see any water.

"Hello?" he called out. His voice bounced off the unseen bottom and returned to him warped and faded. "Anybody here? I have no idea where I am."

Again, the cell phone appeared in his hand. Preston used it to illuminate the stairs as he made his way down. He clutched the railing with his other hand; its metal surface was warm to the touch. The stairs, like the hallway before them, seemed to go on forever. He made his way down, counting the steps as he went.

*72, 73, 74, 75...*

With each step, Preston felt the growing urge to turn around and run back to the elevator. It felt like he was heading in the wrong direction, like he was going to a bad place. The sense of doom grew with each footfall.

After one hundred one stairs, the wooden thuds beneath Preston's feet turned back to concrete scrapes. There at the bottom, the light from his phone revealed a metal door. Rust had nearly conquered it; the handle looked unturned for centuries. With a bit of strain, he forced it open.

It was another dimly lit hallway, similar to the one before the staircase - only, this one made a left turn. A frantic fear now gripped Preston. He walked faster. There were little metal pieces strewn everywhere, as if some appliance had been disassembled and tossed onto the ground. As Preston rounded the corner, a strange sight came into view.

An ancient, rusted bicycle leaned against the wall in front of him. It was badly damaged; one of the tires was missing and the entire frame was bent. For a moment, Preston imagined some sort of animal crawling around down here, powerful enough to crush a bike and eat its rider whole. The chubby man squeezed past the bike, careful not to touch it. His designer suit dragged against the concrete wall behind him as he snuck by. His foot came down on a puddle of water.

Still glancing at the bike over his shoulder, Preston tripped over another piece of it and nearly fell. He looked down at the ground and saw that it was no longer concrete. Heavy asphalt lay beneath him. It looked like a road. Pools of water collected everywhere. Baffled, he spun around and checked in both directions. Black pavement covered every inch he'd walked on, and spread out before him toward another door.

This door was made of old, rotten wood. Dust collected across its surface, spare one area at the center, where some sort of sign or plaque had once rested. Its outline was in the shape of a shield. Preston looked back at the bike once more; the lights flickered as he did. The scene felt distantly familiar. He carefully opened the door and stepped through.

Preston wasn't sure if he was in a hall anymore. He wasn't even sure he was inside a building. The asphalt path he walked on stretched out before him into the yawning black. Only the light from his cell phone guided him now. It was so dark he couldn't see the walls; he wasn't sure there were any at all. The air smelled like rain, and the sound of rushing water met his ears from far off. He took a step forward, and something clanked under his foot.

It was some kind of metal sign. Preston bent over and scooped it up. It was soaking wet. Its familiar shape fit the outline on the door he'd just come through. He studied its blank surface, then turned it over.

"California Highway 46."

Preston gasped and instinctively dropped the sign. It clattered to the floor, but the noise did not echo. A breeze kicked up.

Heart thundering, Preston turned around and went back for the door. Its lock clicked audibly as he did. The sound sent him into a panic.

"Let me out!" he screamed. "I didn't want this!" His voice was drowned out by the rising sound of water. He bashed his fists against the door, but it didn't give at all. It felt like a brick wall now. The handle broke off when he grabbed it; it had been glued on.

"No, please," he panted, trying to avert an anxiety attack. He didn't have his medication. It was back at his desk, far, far up above somewhere. In another world. "Please, God. Please no."

Preston stood there in the dark, cell phone clasped in one shaking hand, the other brushing cold sweat from his face. Repressed memories rushed to the surface of his mind – things he'd trained himself for years to forget. The watery cacophony died away, leaving him in silence. He plodded onward, sucking in huge breaths in an attempt to maintain composure. The highway marker clattered under his foot once more. He didn't look down.

Preston's round face went flush. His glasses fogged with perspiration. His heart boomed inside his chest. He imagined himself walking a plank. The scraping sound of his good shoes on asphalt gave way to stickier, wetter noises. The sickly smell of metal overwhelmed him as he pressed on.

The dying phone's light reflected off the wet ground. It looked like black liquid, but when Preston lifted his foot and ran a finger across the bottom of the shoe, he saw dark red. A path of it stretched on another few steps and stopped at a large circle in the asphalt. When his eyes found that circle, Preston's muscles loosened. Warmth rushed through his gunky veins. A relief washed over him – not one of redemption, but one of certain doom. For Preston, it was less terrifying *knowing* what was about to happen. Before this moment, he only worried about what *might*.

The man walked past the circle. He shuffled through the dark with purpose, knowing exactly where to go. Up ahead there was an SUV; its cabin light glowed and the driver's side door hung open. He slid his hand beneath the seat and retrieved the crowbar. He didn't need to look. Then he returned to the circle and pried it open. He tossed the manhole cover aside and listened as the blood dripped down into the hole. The reek of long-forgotten death made him swoon.

He'd seen it all before. Each morning he blinked those dreams back into the depths of his mind. This place was a bit different, but Preston knew exactly where he was. He knew what he had to do to wake up again. He pulled in a half breath and surrendered himself to the darkness of the hole. His wet shoes smacked against the ladder bars, and his hands picked up the blood they left behind.

Soon he reached the bottom. Preston laughed morbidly, and begged God one last time. But he knew that even God could not hear him where he was: a long elevator ride from the surface, and a short walk to hell. Water splashed and sloshed all around him. The air was musty and freezing cold; it made the sweat on his body sting.

The cell phone appeared in Preston's hand again. He dialed 911, but did not dare to hope the call would connect. Of course, there was no service. Not down here.

But then, the phone lit up brightly, and a name flashed across the screen.

*Beth.*

A flicker of hope sparked inside him. With a shaking hand, he answered.

"...Hello?" he said.

"Hey, you!" a familiar voice chirped.

"Sweetheart?" Preston asked in disbelief.

"How are the boys?" she asked. "Sorry to bother you. I just wanted to let you know that I'm still out with my mom."

There was something strange about Beth's voice. Beneath the static and poor reception, her speech was different. It was brighter, younger.

"Uh...the boys?" Preston asked.

Beth laughed.

"Uh, yeah, you said it was Robb's birthday. Didn't you get drinks?"

The will to lie bubbled up inside of Preston. It was such a primal feeling that he barely noticed it as his lips moved.

"Robb's fine. I'm on my way home now."

"Okay great," Beth replied merrily. "You'll probably beat me home. Are you alright? You sound upset."

"I'm fine," Preston sighed.

"You okay to drive?"

"I...I hit a deer," he blurted out. "Didn't even see the fucking thing 'til it was too late."

In that moment, Preston had no control over his words. His subconscious simply vomited them up.

"Oh my God," Beth said. Preston heard her say something to her mother. She gasped. "Honey? Are you hurt? Do you need me to call an ambulance?"

"No! No," he replied. "No, I'm fine, don't worry. Don't call anybody. I'll be home soon. Everything's fine. I'm fine."

The call abruptly cut out. Preston pulled the phone away from his ear and examined it; *no service* flashed across the screen. He fought back a sudden urge to cry. For all these years he'd carried on in silence, wearing a thin smile over his terrible desperation.

A hair-raising sound erupted from behind him. It was the sound of someone taking a deep breath. Someone who hadn't breathed in ages. Every inch of Preston's skin crawled when he heard that noise.

He turned around and shined the phone's light out in front of him. Filthy water rushed past his ankles and flowed through a giant metal grate. Its smell was overpowered by the stink of rotting meat. Above him, something metal scraped and dragged, then clunked into place. The manhole cover had been replaced. The way out was shut.

A dozen feet away, illuminated in faint blue light, a torso rose from the water. It looked like a young woman – or what used to be one. She groaned and sputtered and threw up black water. Her face was dark and mangled; the cheekbones were crushed and jutting beneath her bloated skin. The head sat wrong on the shoulders, indicating a broken neck. The form rose to its feet and lurched toward Preston.

"Jesus...Jesus Christ, help me!" he screamed. He backed into a wet cement wall and pressed himself against it, as if trying to disappear into one of the little cracks. He shrieked uncontrollably as the woman came within arm's length.

"Please don't hurt me!" he begged. He held the phone out in front of him defensively. Its light revealed a face like rotten porridge, with two cloudy eyes set deep beneath the surface. They peered into Preston's. They gazed past them, right down into his soul. The woman reached a flayed arm out and traced the lapel of the man's suit. She ran a brittle finger across his lips.

"What is your name?" she gurgled. Stinking water dribbled down her lips as she spoke.

"P- P- Pr-" he tried to speak. His teeth chattered and chopped up the words.

"What is your name?" the woman asked again, drawing even closer. Her face stopped inches from his.

"Preston," he managed to get out. "M- my name is Preston."

"Aaah," she breathed. "I never knew."

The man stood rigid and kept his eyes closed.

"What is my name?" she asked.

Preston whimpered and opened his eyes.

"...Katie," he said, after a long pause. "Katie Alvarez."

The woman inhaled sharply.

"Now I remember," she said. Her daisy-slaying breath did to Preston's nose what her appearance did to his eyes. She smiled, revealing a set of broken teeth, and laughed a nightmarish laugh. Water droplets splashed and sprayed all over Preston's face.

"Please," he whispered.

Katie's hands ran all over his face as if to help her remember him. Her fingers felt like slimy eels as they glided across his skin.

"How long?" she whispered back. Her eyes widened. She wrapped those fingers around his throat.

"Th- thirteen," Preston choked. "Thirteen years."

"Mmmm," she replied, digging her nails into his neck. She jumped backward, dragging Preston with her, and threw him down with unholy strength. The chubby man collided with the water and the mossy cement beneath it.

"Why did you come back?" she demanded, striding toward him. Her wet hair slapped her bare skin as she moved. Some of it fell into the water.

"I'm so sorry, Katie," Preston said, shielding himself with his arms.

"Thirteen years!" she screamed. Her voice boomed across the dark sewer and portended a horrific vengeance. "Thirteen years!"

"Please don't!" Preston sobbed. He fell silent as Katie lifted him out of the water and slammed him against a wall. She pressed her face against his; it sapped what little warmth was left in his cheeks.

"I want to hear it," she commanded. Preston desperately wanted to lie to her, and to himself, but the force in her voice pulled the words right out of his mouth.

"Okay," he breathed, shaking violently. "Okay. Okay. I was coming home. It was late. It was the last year of my Master's program. One of my friends had a birthday. I was visiting him way out in Paso Robles. We drank. I'm so sorry, Katie. I'm so sorry." Preston began to cry.

"Tell me," she pressed.

"I...I didn't see your bike until it was too late. I swear I didn't do it on purpose. It was raining so hard that night. So hard I couldn't see. I'd been drinking...I was going fast. Too fast."

Katie growled. Her lidless eyes bore into Preston. They yearned for his blood.

"I didn't know what to do. It happened right off the exit. I thought about calling the police, but it was too late. The second it happened, you were gone."

"And then what?" she asked, baring her shattered teeth.

"I got your bike off the road. Kicked all the little pieces into the tall grass. The rain took care of the blood." Preston dreaded the words spilling out of his mouth, but he couldn't hold them back. "Th- there was a sewer line. So I got my crowbar. I put you down there, Katie. I put you down there in the dark. I didn't know what else to do. I'm so sorry."

Katie did not respond. She stood there, holding her victim, frozen in thought.

"Every time I saw you on the news I wanted to die," he added. "The feeling never left me. They stopped searching after a while, but I thought about you every day. Every time I shut my eyes. Every time I dream. I wish I could take it all back."

Katie set Preston down gently and took a step back. She examined her hands, her arms, the bones that protruded from them.

"You broke me," she said, rage and anguish intersecting on her voice.

Preston sobbed. Her words sliced into him like claws.

"And you put me here," she continued. The woman dry-heaved suddenly, then spewed black water all over herself. She wiped an arm across her lips. The skin sloughed off like wet dough.

Katie's pathetic state, her misery, broke Preston's heart. His disgust with himself overtook his terror of her. He cried harder.

"And while you were off living your life," she said, "getting promotions and nice suits, I was down here in the cold. Where my mother would never find me. For a long time it was all black. I felt nothing. Like a deep sleep. But then, I began to dream. You lay in your bed and dreamed of me, Preston, while I lay here in the water. I dreamed of you. I never saw your face, but somehow I knew you all along. And though the water washed away my body over time, and scattered my bones over all those dark miles, I keep coming back to this place. Over and over."

Preston's cries fell to silence. He wished for the relief of death. He sank into the water and sat against the sticky sewer wall.

"I can't leave," Katie said. "I have nowhere to go, and so I keep waking up right here. Maybe it happens each time you dream of me, and what you did. For so long I dreamed you'd come back and carry me out of here, up into the sunlight. But you never came back."

"Katie," Preston breathed.

"No," she interrupted. She waded toward him through the water.

Preston still held the wet cell phone in his hand. Its light flickered.

"I can take you out of here now," he said, desperation welling in his voice. "I'll show you the sun. I'll tell everyone what I did."

"It's too late," she replied. "It's my turn to show you something. I want to show you what thirteen years in the dark feels like."

Preston burst into tears and begged for his life.

"Don't cry," she whispered. "I won't do what you did to me. I won't abandon you." Katie sat down on Preston's lap and put her arms around him. She leaned her wet and rigid body against his, and nuzzled her rotting face into his neck. The cell phone flickered once more, then went off. A veil of inconceivable darkness fell, and Preston's cries of anguish were muffled by the sound of running water.

# Ghost of Chelm

JP Behrens

The eyes of the statue began to glow a fiery red. A grinding, as if the very earth were waking up and moving for the first time since creation, rumbled through the room. Great clouds of dust billowed from the statue. Only the blazing red eyes pierced through the unexpected storm. The crowd gasped and coughed, frozen with fright, wonder, and curiosity. A deep voice, like the roar of an avalanche, intoned, "Hechatev'bee." Children cried as the waves of sound coursed through the unsettled audience.

Staring into the face of the past, surrounded by terror and uncertainty, Dr. Ibrahim Zolozhin whispered, "No..."

"Ladies and Gentlemen!" bellowed the carnival barker standing beside the statue in his velvet jacket. "Boys and Girls! Welcome to Carnacki's Carnival. Tonight, you have seen wonders and oddities from across the globe. Proof of alien life. Evidence of the magic Fae Folk, fairies and pixies. Mutant creatures from the depths of the New York

City Sewers. Now, I bring you our newest discovery. Behold the Living Statue of Khem!"

The statue repeated the word over and over. Vibrations of its awakening stirred the crowd into a minor frenzy. Just as the general panic threatened to burst forth into the open carnival grounds, the barker stepped forward. "Fear not, my friends! With a swipe of my hand, I return it to sleep." He flourished a handkerchief and smeared one of the charcoal-written symbols on the statue's head.

Everything became still. The crowd fell into a fit of relieved laughter and applause. Many of the audience began theorizing and debating how the illusion was performed, claiming inside knowledge. Only Ibrahim remained paralyzed, staring at the clay statue with a combination of disbelief and horror.

The audience swarmed around Ibrahim, sweeping him out of the tent. He stumbled along, in a daze, past fake, stitched together Fiji Mermaids and formaldehyde filled jars containing the unborn fetuses of children suffering from a variety of birth defects. Horrific memories and nightmares left behind long ago flooded back. He tried to shake them off as the crowd drove him closer to the carnival exit. The press of bodies, the smell of sweat, the flickering lights, all brought back the days he'd spent trapped in a wooden box with so many others, rattling along a train track towards something so much worse. When the crowd broke apart outside the main gate, the families spread out into the fields toward their cars. Ibrahim shuffled onward as if in a trance. He blinked and found himself standing next to his car. He leaned against the cool metal of the driver's side door and drew a haggard breath of cold air, relishing in the open space and reality of the present.

"You ok, Mister?"

Ibrahim found a young man peering at him with concern. Behind him stood a worried woman and two children, poised to get into their car and leave. The children dropped into their seats, eyes glazed over and drooping under the weight of sleep. Ibrahim smiled, his own exhaustion crashing down on him, as well.

"Yes. The noise and lights overwhelmed me for a moment. I am fine." Ibrahim tried to rub the soreness from his over-tired eyes. "I will be better when I discover a place to sleep for the night. At some point, I lost my way along these long stretches of fields. I stopped here for directions; however, none of the carnival employees were very helpful."

"Yeah, it can be tricky to get around these parts at night. A lot of the roads around here aren't much more than dirt paths." The young man thought for a moment while checking on his kids. They had already fallen asleep in the back seat. "If you'd like, follow us. I know of a motel nearby that's decent."

"Please, I do not wish to burden you. If you could just direct me."

"It's on our way home. Just follow us. Like I said, the roads around here can get tricky at night."

Ibrahim nodded and got into his car. The family pulled out and Ibrahim followed. The young man hadn't been exaggerating. The roads they led Ibrahim down were a network of dirt paths feeding into gravel ones. When they turned onto the asphalt roadway once again, a great neon sign flashing "MOTEL" seemed to sprout out of the darkness. Considering the twisting series of back roads, Ibrahim was thankful for the young man's persistence in guiding him. Ibrahim honked twice as a thank you and pulled into the parking lot. The family drove on.

After paying for a room, Ibrahim sighed with relief at the sight of a bed. He eased himself down onto the mattress, slipped off his shoes, and lay back on the cool linens. Sleep claimed him in an instant.

The world came back into focus a moment later. The sounds of muffled screams and gunshots seeped into the basement of the home he'd shared with his father in Poland. A boy once again, Ibrahim watched his father sift through his research and tools, scrambling to put the finishing touches on the colossal statue of clay he'd been working on for the last week. The shouts of soldiers ordering families into the streets grew closer. For weeks, they had been coming to the village. At first, they took people at night, claiming them as traitors or terrorists. Daylight raids began soon after. Whole families dragged into the streets while their neighbors and friends stood by, silent, afraid to speak up for fear they would be next.

Father, a local historian, recognized the atrocities as a new wave of pogroms. When the village elders could do nothing to prevent the approaching evil, father turned to the myths and legends of the past for a solution. He found a way to defend their community and people, but at a great cost.

"Son, we don't have much time. Do you understand what you must do?"

"Papa, I can't…"

"You must! Once I give life to the statue, you will need to take control and command it."

"But why must you—"

"My son, only God can create life from nothing. Though the secrets of creation are in the ancient texts, I am only a man. My ability is limited; therefore, I must give of myself to protect our people."

"Papa…"

Both father and son fell into each other, hugging for the last time. When his father broke away, his face was wet with tears. He withdrew a weathered folding knife and pushed the handle into his son's hand. "Carve the word I taught you into the forehead so no one will be able to deactivate it. Once it is awake, breathe your name into its lips, and command it to protect our village." He gripped Ibrahim's quaking, scrawny shoulders. "Have care with your instructions. The golem will do as you say in the most literal sense. Good luck, my son."

The sound of crashing doors and families screaming thundered closer. Ibrahim's father stepped up to his creation and turned his back to it. He locked eyes with young Ibrahim and leaned back into the clay giant. Ibrahim couldn't understand the words his father chanted, but he watched in dismay as the clay rippled to life, latching onto his father's body. The clay statue consumed his father's form, and Ibrahim saw the flicker of a sad smile before the clay enveloped him.

Their front door exploded with an earth-shattering crack. Angry voices barked unfamiliar words and boots thudded above Ibrahim's head. Ibrahim dragged a stool to the front of the golem before they could discover the hidden door to the basement and unfolded the knife, intent on carving the letters that would bring the golem to life. With the tip of the blade hovering over the clay face, a premonition of death and destruction flashed in his mind. The golem would burst from the basement, crushing all the soldiers. His neighbor's screams would be replaced with the screams of soldiers. Tears coursed down his cheeks. Ibrahim wanted to protect his friends, but he didn't want to be responsible for the death of so many.

The crashing of furniture grew louder. He stepped down from the stool and assumed that if they found only him, a child, in the basement they would just leave him be. He folded the knife and found a crack in a dark corner of the basement to hide it in. No one would harm an unarmed child. He piled bundles of cloth over the crack and returned to the center of the room. Maybe they wouldn't even find the door.

Just as the thought finished, the door to the basement slammed open and three foreign soldiers stomped down the stairs. They found Ibrahim standing alone with his hands in the air. They shouted both commands and questions, but Ibrahim couldn't understand any of it. As they dragged him up the stairs, they laughed. Ibrahim found more soldiers in his home, smashing furniture and heirlooms for no other reason than to destroy.

Out on the street, Ibrahim found fire, pain, and death. The soldiers separated the men from everyone else and shot them along the sides of the streets. Women and older children were gathered in the center of the village, weeping at the sight of their sons, husbands, brothers, and fathers lying dead in the gutters. As the soldiers began marching the women and children away, Ibrahim heard another sound drifting along the winds. Somewhere, babies wailed, but he noticed there were no babies with the mothers in his group. The sharp retort of a gun. The wet thud of a club. The crying stopped. Innocence erased to the sound of heartless laughter.

A loud *pop* broke Ibrahim from his nightmare.

The retreating lights of a car suggested the noise was a backfiring engine. Trying to shake off the ghost of crying children, Ibrahim paced the room. He tried to distract himself with work, a book, or the radio, but he abandoned each activity for another in an endless cycle. He was desperate for anything to exorcise the dark memories from his conscience. He reached into his pocket and withdrew the knife his father had given him all those years ago.

He'd returned to his home after surviving the camps. The basement lay empty, the golem and all his father's papers gone. The knife remained hidden in the crack, and he'd pried it free. Staring at it now, scuffed by history but well-maintained since its retrieval, he knew walking away from the golem was not an option.

Ibrahim made his way back to the carnival. The pink glow of dawn and deep tire ruts made navigating the back roads easier. The carnival came into view, its tents sagging under the gray fog forming all around. Ibrahim shivered. He thought back to his village, abandoned and razed. He parked his car in the empty field and made his way toward the front gate. A few lights glittered in some of the trailers, but no one patrolled the grounds or came to investigate his arrival. In the diffused light, everything in the carnival appeared drained of color, leaving behind limp fabrics, threadbare and tattered. The smell of oil and sugar permeated the air.

Inside the Hall of Wonders, the lights were off. Ibrahim made his way through the tent and followed the pitch-black tunnel into the room of the golem. The barker hadn't covered the golem with a sheet or curtain since the show, so Ibrahim found himself standing before the monster, feeling like the child who had watched his father die. Fear and shame flooded through him as he thought of all the people he'd allowed to suffer by not finishing the work his father died for.

The hard, dry clay felt rough under his old fingers. The layers of charcoal smudged over the statue's forehead marred the creature's colorless visage. He removed the folding knife from his pocket and carved the word *emet* into the clay, slicing through the charcoal. As he finished the last letter, the golem's eyes flared to life, and the room began to shake, resonating with the power of the construct.

"Hechatev'bee," the golem intoned.

Ibrahim searched the room for a stool or chair to bring him up to the golem's mouth and take control of the construct. A low, satisfied sigh revealed another's presence in the room.

"I have to thank you for correcting my sigil, old man." The carnival barker from the show stepped out of the shadows, still dressed in his ostentatious garments, holding a simple wooden stool in his hand. The kind Ibrahim always pictured a lion tamer waving about to keep the well-trained lions at bay. Tipping the large, shabby top hat at

Ibrahim, a slick smile cut across his face. "I saw you during the show. I wasn't sure you'd returned, but one must always give himself over to hope."

Two men entered the tent from the side and back entrances and seized Ibrahim before he could react. "No, you don't understand," he begged as the barker shoved him aside and mounted the stool.

"I understand more than you know. I managed to decipher quite a bit from the texts found with the statue, but much of the lore was lost to rot and time. I could activate the statue with my incomplete sigil, but never take full control of it." He leaned forward as if to plant a gentle kiss upon the golem's clay lips.

"No…" Ibrahim struggled against the two strongmen holding him, but it was no use. He'd failed once again. "It must be destroyed. The golem is dangerous."

"I am very aware of what this monstrosity is capable of. It will be a great use to me as we travel the country. Imagine, a side show attraction that everyone thinks is nothing more than an illusion, but is capable of tearing through any door, any wall, unlocking treasures hidden in the most secure vaults. All that is necessary is the Breath of Life. Or so says the book I acquired when I purchased this wonderful creation."

Ibrahim stood aghast at the base greed of the man before him. "Others will know how to stop you."

"Easily managed." The barker breathed his name into the golem's mouth. The eyes flashed orange as its limbs began to loosen and stretch, able to finally come alive for the first time since its creation. Ibrahim sobbed at the thought of his father's spirit being misused for one man's avarice. His father's legacy reduced to petty larceny.

The barker motioned for the strongmen to pull Ibrahim out of the way so he could stand before his new toy.

"Golem," began the barker, "I command you to eliminate any who have the knowledge or attempt to destroy you."

Ibrahim gasped as his stomach twisted with dread and bleak understanding.

The barker sneered as the golem's eyes blazed red as the command set in. The golem reached out and took him by the head and began to squeeze. The screams of the barker spurred the strongmen to his aid. Their strikes at the golem proved ineffective. With its free arm, the golem swung out and basked the two men aside, crushing them with a single swing. One lay broken on the floor, twisted as no human was meant to be. The other twitched, still alive, cushioned from the blow by his companion, but only barely. Ibrahim fell to his knees, surrendering to the inevitability of what came next.

The crunching of bone as the golem crushed the barker's skull echoed in the tent. The body toppled across the wooden planks with a mixture of the clatter of loose planks and the deep thuds of lifeless limbs.

The golem stomped up to Ibrahim and stared down at the man who woke it up. Ibrahim stared back, lost in the knowledge of his many failures. The golem reached a blood-smeared hand to Ibrahim's side.

"Papa?" For a moment, he imagined a faint whisper of the ghost of his father within the expressionless statue.

The golem seized Ibrahim, pressing the air out of his lungs. The floor fell away as the golem lifted him. The eyes blazed a dark, angry red.

"Visn," it growled while the grip tightened.

In the sound of his cracking ribs, his father's warning echoed. "Have care with your instructions."

He'd woken the golem in the hope of protecting his father's legacy. Visn. Knowledge. The golem listens and does as it is commanded. Exactly as it is commanded.

The golem dropped his broken body to the dirty floor and stomped out of the tent to continue its mission. As shock washed over Ibrahim's mind, erasing the pain rattling his thoughts, an instant of clarity flashed through him. Ibrahim choked on his blood as the last vision of the retreating monster burned itself in his mind. The golem, a creature powered by sacrifice and vengeance, would march across the earth, destroying and killing until no one remembered it. An impossible, unending mission.

Ibrahim drifted away, asking forgiveness as the screams rang out under the steady thunder of immortal feet.

# Hot For Cold

Bridgett Nelson

I held her cold, lifeless hand, and my body physically responded.

The icy, mannequin-like condition of her skin provided exquisite contrast to the feverish warmth of my own. I gazed at this girl I'd been friends with since kindergarten, lying on the baby-pink satin lining her white metal coffin, and realized it was my first time actually seeing her. My first time *wanting* her.

The first time I'd felt my penis twitch with want. The first time I'd felt any sexual attraction toward anyone—ever.

Her eyes were closed, most likely held in place with body glue. Yet I could imagine how those dead, staring eyes would look opened—the corneal clouding making her normally onyx-colored irises a pale bluish-gray.

The dim lighting glinted off her waxy pallor, emphasizing the stiffness of her formaldehyde- and ethanol-filled body.

I *craved* her.

Not the memories of her laughing, telling jokes, playing third base on the school's softball team, or watching movies. Nothing about the living version of my friend appealed to my sexual nature.

No. I desired the dead, slowly-rotting corpse lying in front of me.

Its frigidness.

Its lack of blood.

Its dilated pupils.

Its shrunken skin.

Its unbeating heart.

Its *lack of judgment.*

The implications were not lost on me, but I shoved them all aside. Right now, I just wanted to focus on the feeling.

I held her inanimate hand for as long as I could, but the line of mourners waiting to view her body began to back up, so I reluctantly relinquished it and took my seat for the funeral service.

Hours later, though, I could still feel the chill of her skin on my hand, and I wondered what it would be like to revel in that glacial love forever.

\*\*\*

The feelings evoked that day didn't fade with the passing of time. They grew, and eventually overwhelmed me. I found myself spending more and more time in the shower, trying to relieve the pressure building inside me.

I never mentioned my longings to my friends. I knew without being told that their reactions would be anything but positive.

But then…the dream.

*Dark. So very dark. I couldn't see anything. But I could feel. Feel the thrust of my cock into something cold. Wet. Icy. The smell of decay spurred my lust. Groaning,*

*breathing hard, thrusting...fucking. Nothing had ever felt
so good.*

*But, wait.*

*Was that...* fur?

*As if my subconscious had been waiting for the big
reveal, an absurdly large sun rose over the horizon,
illuminating my partner.*

*A doe.*

*A deer.*

*An oozing female deer.*

*Why, yes. I did enjoy* The Sound of Music.

*And yes, I was making sweet love to venison.*

I woke up screaming, disgust and self-loathing writhing
through my veins like a parasitic infestation, followed
quickly by lust so hot and heavy, I ejaculated without ever
touching myself. My confusion was real.

The desire and longing stayed with me for days, weeks,
months. The more I thought about it, the more titillated I
became. Since I didn't have access to a multitude of dead
bodies—not even one, in fact—I decided to lose my
virginity to a girl.

A *breathing* girl.

***

Poppy had developed a long-term crush on me in fifth
grade. We'd been lab partners, and she'd found me
irresistible. I'm not sure why. I wasn't a particularly
handsome, athletic, or witty guy, but that didn't seem to
matter. I had never encouraged her feelings, because I
didn't feel the same.

But now, things had changed.

Was I a necrophile? A zoophile? Both?

Did I even *like* girls whose pussies could get wet
without using synthetic lubrication? Would a living body's
warmth turn me off?

I needed to know.

I approached her in the cafeteria at lunch. She was alone, reading a giant tome of a book.

"Hey, Poppy," I said, sliding onto the bench across from her.

She looked at me, surprise and curiosity etched across her face, and closed the book's cover. "Hey, yourself. What's up?"

I paused, trying to figure out what to say. I'd never done this before. "I was…well…I was wondering if you'd like to go out Friday night. Maybe see a movie, get some ice cream?"

She smiled. I saw something flicker in her eyes. Something like hope. "Okay, sure."

"Awesome." I smiled back. "Think about what movie you'd like to see, and I'll be in touch."

I left the cafeteria as fast as I could without downright sprinting, blowing out the breath I'd been holding.

\*\*\*

"Put it in slow," she whispered.

We were in the backseat of my beater car

I could feel her heart frantically pounding as her body anticipated the probable painful arrival of mine.

It turned me off.

We'd had a good time at the movies, stopped for ice cream afterward, and now here we were. Ready to…*make love.*

I choked back laughter. Maybe she *was* in love with me. Hell, she probably was—she was giving up her virginity, after all. But I felt no love. Or arousal.

She'd told me I didn't have to wear a condom…that she was protected, and wasn't worried about sexually transmitted infections since we were both virgins.

"All right. Sounds good," I'd replied.

But my dick was a limp noodle.

We kissed.

She fondled me.

She briefly put it in her mouth and sucked.

*Nothing.*

Trying to save myself from further embarrassment, I said, "Lay back and spread your legs. Don't move."

I masturbated, looking at her still body. My dick showed some signs of life, but it wasn't enough. "Will you do me a favor, Poppy?" I asked in my most innocent voice.

"Yes. Name it." She was determined. I could tell my lack of response to her body was cranking up her insecurities.

"Will you stare at the roof of the car and try not to blink?"

The look that crossed her face was comical, though it quickly disappeared. "Uh, sure. I can do that, I guess." She seemed to understand what I wanted, as her eyes rolled slightly back in their sockets and stared blankly at nothing.

I gazed at the pale body staring sightlessly into oblivion.

My cock sprang to life.

"Don't move. Don't blink. Don't speak. Don't even make a noise," I said, as I slid inside her.

She gasped and squeezed her eyes shut as I pushed through her hymen, but then, not wanting to upset me, resumed the original pose.

I hated the warmth. I hated the oily slickness. I hated the clean, girly scents emanating from her body. But I would make this work. I settled deep inside my head and imagined I was lying in that pink-lined coffin with my friend's cold corpse.

I thrust…hard.

To her credit, Poppy kept her pose. I felt her relax slightly as my body responded to the rotting carcass I saw inside my head.

"Yeah," I whispered. "That's it."

But something wasn't right. *Why is she getting warmer? Wetter?*

I looked between our bodies and saw streaks of crimson blood crisscrossing my shaft.

My anger and loathing was immediate. *It isn't right, goddammit!*

"What the fuck, Raven? Blood? You're fucking *dead*."

"Don't threaten me!" the corpse responded, its voice gravelly, the jaws not quite moving with the words. "And who the hell is Raven?"

"Corpses don't *bleed*!" I screamed and slapped the sloughing skin on her face.

She let out a startled gasp as her cloudy eyes widened, and her hand covered the fiery red cheek. "Get off me, asshole!"

"Dead whores don't tell me what to do." I kept fucking her.

"GET OFF OF ME!" She pushed hard against my chest, her fingernails digging into my flesh.

Just like that, I was back inside the car with a furious Poppy.

*Not Raven.*

*No caskets in sight.*

"I'm not a whore, and I'm sure as hell not dead," she said as she pulled on her panties and straightened her dress. "That…whatever that was, it was sick! Take me home!"

I listened to her cry on the short drive and dropped her off at her front door without saying another word.

\*\*\*

Less than a week later, I drove to a remote section of highway, scanning the sides of the road. I finally found what I was looking for and pulled over.

The deer had been dead for a while, and the smell made me hard. Not wanting to fuck it where anyone driving by could see, I attempted to drag it into the woods.

Its legs came off.

*This won't do. Its holes will be mush.*

Leaving the deer where it was, I trekked farther up the road, until I found a groundhog sprawled across the yellow lines in the center of the blacktop.

I'd pictured something more...*human*...sized, but beggars couldn't be choosers. It was slightly bloated with decomposition—an aphrodisiac to me. I snatched it up and ran into the forest.

Laying the dead groundhog on the cool grass beneath a giant maple tree, I unzipped my jeans. Fondling my dick in one hand, I ran the other over the coarse fur covering its body. It reminded me of the German Shepherd I had growing up...the wiry outer layer, with a thick, soft undercoat.

I pushed my pants down and sat, leaning against the tree. Picking up the groundhog, I rubbed the rear of the furry corpse over the tip of my erection, until I felt something give...then I pushed. I didn't care if it was male or female. I just needed a hole.

It was so goddamned tight, I felt myself ready to come within seconds, but I held off, savoring the chilly feel surrounding my sensitive flesh. I held it around its middle and slid it up and down.

Up and down.

Up and down.

Its head hung limply to the side, the dead eyes staring into infinity. I pictured Raven riding me, her putrefying joints creaking as she moved. Her gravelly, croaking voice saying, "Oh God, yes! Fuck me harder!" Pustulant fluid running down her thighs and into my pubic hair, causing the curly strands to clump together in smelly green coils.

I edged for as long as I could, knowing this was going to be the most mind-blowing orgasm of my life...so far. When I finally came, I let out a guttural roar and unloaded inside the decaying rodent. Pulling out, I noticed the hole (ass or vagina, I was none the wiser) was now a ragged, gaping maw with my cream dripping from the rim.

I threw the carcass aside, flipped a few maggots off my cock, zipped up, and walked back to my car, realizing it wasn't the animal that made the experience so satisfying…it was the cold, lifeless corpse. I'd happily fuck more dead animals, but they weren't my fetish.

I needed a deceased human.

\*\*\*

I drove her to an isolated pond near a rarely traveled stretch of road. She was so absorbed by the burger and fries I'd given her, I'm not sure she noticed how long we'd driven.

She was gaunt, with greasy bleach-blonde hair and acne-riddled skin. Her eyes were wild as she gulped down the food. I wondered when she'd last eaten.

As she put the last fry in her mouth, this one covered in too-bright ketchup, she finally realized we were no longer in town. "Where're we at?" Her voice was surprisingly high-pitched, like that of a much younger girl. I could see the last remnants of the fry as it vanished down her gullet.

"We're heading to a romantic little spot I know. Waterfront," I said. "And I brought this." I pulled out the bottle of premium whiskey I'd pilfered from my dad's liquor cabinet.

I watched her eyes brighten and the tip of her pink tongue lick her dry, chapped lips. I couldn't guess her age. She could have been anywhere from twenty to sixty. Life hadn't been kind to this woman.

I could feel her sneaking peeks at my face.

"Could I ask ya a question?" she finally asked.

"Sure. Can't promise I'll answer, but you can ask whatever you'd like."

"All right." She cleared her phlegmy throat. "Why's a good-looking, young feller like you have a need fer the likes of me?"

"Good looks don't necessarily equate to charisma with the ladies," I answered, pulling my car into a secluded spot between some trees. I shut it off, pocketed the keys, and looked at her. She let out a muffled burp. "I've always been pretty awkward. Not terribly suave. This just seemed easier."

"That's fair." She put her hand on my thigh and rubbed. "Should we get started then?"

I placed her hand back on her lap. "How about a drink first to get us loosened up?"

"I could get behind that plan." She grinned in anticipation.

I filled two cups I'd also stolen from my house and handed one to her. "Cheers!"

She tapped her cup to mine. I didn't drink—just mimed as I watched her polish off the amber liquid in one giant swallow. A dribble ran from the corner of her mouth.

"I'm impressed." I handed her the other. "Want the rest of mine?"

She snatched it greedily from my hands and chugged it down. "Thanks," she said, wiping her lips. "Was thirsty."

"Clearly."

"Let's get this party started!" She reached down as if to unzip my pants.

I grabbed her wrists and gently pushed them away. "What's your name?" I asked.

"Kitty." Then, in falsetto, "Meow, meow." She let out a peal of laughter, and I could see beneath the wrinkles and neglect that this woman had once been beautiful.

"Come on, Kitty. Let's walk down to the lake. We can stretch out and take our time."

"Purrr-fect!" She laughed harder, but I noticed she was having a hard time opening the passenger-side door.

I went around the car and opened it for her. Her wheezing breaths echoed throughout the late-summer air as she stumbled out.

"I...I...Imma not feelin' so good."

I picked her up and carried her skeletal frame to the water's edge. Tears trickled from the corners of eyes now sporting hugely dilated pupils.

As soon as I set her down, she fell to her knees and vomited across the coarse, grainy sand. When she looked up at me, her expression was confused and the wheezing was more pronounced. "Who...what did..." Her skin had taken on a slightly blue hue.

It was the last thing she said. Then she toppled over and began twitching.

I gave myself a prideful pat on the back for getting the cyanide dosage right, then sat and watched Kitty's body shut down and die.

\*\*\*

As I waited for her body to cool, I built a fire, set up a small tent, and roasted some hot dogs over the spitting flames.

It was Friday night. My parents weren't expecting me home until Sunday evening. I had time to play with my Kitty. Hell, I might even leave her out here and come by after school for more visits. If she got too ripe, though, I wouldn't be able to risk my mom smelling it on my clothes. Then again, I could strip down, wash off in the pond with a cheap bar of soap, and enjoy Miss Kitty for weeks to come.

Shortly after the seizure, a gurgling sound had released from her throat, and her eyes had opened. I left them that way, giving her an unobstructed view of the star-filled sky and surrounding fir trees.

I should have probably felt guilty for taking a life, but the truth was, I'd put the poor woman out of her misery.

I'd once read an article about a tribe who lived on the Ganges River, worshiped the God Shiva, and, in order to reach enlightenment, ate the flesh of, and fornicated with, their dead loved ones. They made dishes and jewelry from their bones and used various body parts to build altars.

*Does their enlightenment give them information I'm not privy to? Do their loved ones like post-mortem attention? Should I eat Kitty parts?*

I liked to think dead Kitty would get some enjoyment from my…services.

I looked at my phone. Three hours had passed since Kitty stopped breathing. After the sun had gone down, the temperature had dropped to the low seventies. That meant her body was probably five or six degrees cooler now. It was enough.

I went to her, my erect penis uncomfortable within the confines of my jeans. I'd already stripped her down and burned her clothes in the fire. Her legs were splayed. She was ready for me.

I crouched over her and licked the line of her jaw. She tasted bitter, acidic, with just the faintest trace of rot.

*Delicious.*

Kitty had released her bowels when she died—I didn't care. And the chlorine-like odor coming from her pussy told me I wasn't the first guy she'd been with that day…but I'd certainly be the last.

I took off my clothes. I wanted nothing between my too-hot body and the soothing coolness of hers. I wanted to get lost in her frigid love. Finally, after all this time, I was getting what my heart—and body—desired.

A dead plaything.

I knelt between Kitty's legs, took a deep breath, and slid my throbbing, rock-hard member into her slit.

She was tight. Wet…likely the spooge from her last customer. And so much colder than I expected after such a short time.

She wasn't in full rigor mortis yet, and although her skin already felt hard—concrete-like—I could still move her extremities. I spread her legs even more to give me better access and placed her hand on her own tit.

As I pounded my cock inside her, I noticed how pale her skin had become. How her mouth hung open, displaying gaping holes and grimy teeth. How her hair already looked dull and straw-like.

It all turned me on. Within seconds, I ejaculated into her smelly pussy.

I rolled off and laid my head gently on her softly-rounded belly. I could already hear noises in there, as the bacteria in her gut prepared to begin the putrefaction process that would cause her body to bloat.

I couldn't wait.

\*\*\*

"Uh! Uh! Uhhhhh!" I gave one final thrust, praising the gasses that caused the tissue in her pussy to swell and tighten.

Blowflies were everywhere, landing on her clouded eyes and inside her mouth. Soon, her body would be riddled with maggots.

Again, I couldn't wait.

\*\*\*

"That's right, Kitty, I'm fucking you so good, baby. Tell me how you like it."

Her body made a wet, farty sound in response. It sent me over the edge.

When I finished, I studied the green-hued skin of her face. Microscopic life moved in the corners of her eyes and inside her nostrils. The skin around her mouth had shrunk and pulled back, causing a gummy, macabre smile to spread across her zombie-like face. Blackened gums and a few yellowed teeth were on full display, as was the dried, desiccated chunk of her tongue. I licked it, giving my lover a French kiss.

Tomorrow, the maggots would overtake her.

Unsurprisingly, I couldn't wait.

\*\*\*

I made love to my lady—slowly, softly. Beneath my bare skin, thousands of maggots squirmed and feasted. It was the most erotic thing I'd ever experienced. I pulled out and spurted my jizz all over their white bodies. It made them wiggle even more.

\*\*\*

I covered her body with my bright red sleeping bag, weighing down each corner with a large rock. I knew it wouldn't completely protect her from animals and the elements, but hopefully there would be enough left for me to enjoy when I drove out for another visit.

Throwing the rest of my gear into the trunk, I gave Kitty one final adoring gaze and said a silent goodbye. Then I climbed in my car and headed back to the highway.

Daylight was fading quickly—I'd stayed longer today than I'd planned to; I'm sure my mom was ready to send out the National Guard—so I flipped on my headlights as I turned right onto the main road. My tired brain fell into a video montage, flashing scene after glorious scene of my weekend with Kitty. My body was satiated to the point of torpor.

What I needed now was a long hot shower, a home-cooked meal, and my bed. And maybe a sock. Once I got into bed, I had no doubt I'd start thinking about Kitty's sexy carcass.

Images of her purple backside sprang to my mind. I'd rolled her over to have some backdoor fun and her back and buttocks had been a mottled magenta. I had freaked the fuck out until I'd looked it up on my phone. Apparently, it's called livor mortis, and it's caused by the blood pooling in the dependent parts of the body after death…like a post-mortem bruise. That aroused me. I grinned thinking about how I'd spanked the hell out of her ass as I fucked its hole.

My daydreams were interrupted by a blaring horn. Flashing red and blue lights penetrated my retinas. A police car blocked the road. I slowed to a crawl and heard a cop yelling at me to vacate my car and get on the ground.

Somehow, they'd found out. Somehow, they knew.

Thoughts blasted through my mind, and I made a decision. No way was I going to prison, where I'd be raped and killed simply because I loved the dead. I'd go out on my own terms. I slammed my foot on the gas and drove full-speed at the officer.

An explosion.

Bright light.

Sounds of glass breaking, followed by metal grinding and screeching and grating.

The light was no more.

\*\*\*

*Where am I?*

My eyes popped open. The lights above hurt them, but my lids refused to cooperate. No matter what I did, they wouldn't close. Whatever I was lying on was hard and freezing cold.

I'd never been this cold before. I tried to stand, but none of my body's muscles were working. I heard a noise to my left and tried to turn my head, but couldn't. *Am I paralyzed?*

I heard someone humming. A girl. Her voice was nice. Soothing.

*Is that "Bohemian Rhapsody?"*

I tried to grin, but my mouth wasn't functional.

Footsteps sounded. Something blocked the light above me. It was the humming girl, all blue eyes and auburn curls.

"Well, *hello* there, good-looking!"

Had I been able to blush, I would have.

She continued, "I'm sorry about the death and all, but I'm gonna take *such* good care of you tonight, baby."

*Death? What death? Does she know about Kitty?*

"You've got some pretty nasty injuries, but we'll work around them."

*What the fu...?*

"I've had a very stressful day, and I need some relief. You're gonna be my best friend, tiger."

I heard the sound of clothes falling to the floor and shoes being kicked off.

"You're a sight for sore eyes!"

She stopped talking and took my dick inside her mouth.

*Fuck! This girl can suck cock!*

I was riding high on the sensations when she abruptly stopped.

"I can't wait anymore, tiger. I'm so wet." I felt her knees press against my hips, followed by the sensation of her fluid warmth throughout my pelvis.

*This is nirvana.*

"Oh my God, you're so big," she moaned, then paused. "What's that? You like having your nips pinched? I'm happy to oblige." She bounced up and down on my cock, pinching my nipples...hard.

Her searing heat was so much better than Kitty's arctic pussy.

*Is this karma? Had I made Kitty feel good in death, so now this random woman is giving me my due?*

Hell, I just wished I could push myself deeper inside her. I never could have imagined the ecstasy getting fucked *as* a corpse could bring. God help me, it was *better* than fucking a corpse. I'd die all over again to keep experiencing this euphoria.

"I'm so close," she said, her breathing ragged. Seconds later, her panting and moaning became louder and more intense. I could feel her pussy twitching around my dick, as she gradually stopped moving. "That was incredible. Thanks, tiger."

She crawled off me, giving my nipple one last twist, then put her clothes back on.

Already, I missed her heat. Her lifeforce.

"You might be the best I've had. Damn shame they want you cremated."

*Wait...what?*

Whatever I was lying on began moving dizzyingly fast.

*No! Don't do it! Stop! I'm still here! Don't burn me!* I tried to scream. I tried so hard.

"Okay, sweet cheeks. Any final words before you become ashes?" She giggled. "Didn't think so."

One final shove and I was inside the cremation chamber.

I wanted to cry, thrash, and escape this enclosure that would eventually end all human sensation. But I could do nothing. Just lay there.

Seeing.

Hearing.

*Feeling.*

"Have a good afterlife, tiger. I'll never forget you!"

The door slammed shut.

# One Way Or The Other

Jay Bechtol

There is nothing inherently terrifying about butterflies. Unless you are a four-year-old kid at a birthday party and one of your grandparents thought it would be a good idea to put a bunch of the little buggers in a box so that when you opened it, they all burst out. The flurry of motion and color would be shocking. Then, say, one of the butterflies lands on your four-year-old nose. You've seen a butterfly in those kiddie books with the thick cardboard pages, but they don't do justice to the alien thing on your face. Long antenna, huge unfeeling eyes, a tongue or whatever it is uncurling, trying to determine if you are edible or not. That's fucking nightmare fuel.

I know nightmares, but what I really know is people.

I fiw rotea sen tencel iket his, would you be able to read it? Maybe. All the letters are there, even in the right order. But the gaps are in the wrong places. For a second, even a tiny fraction of a second did you assume you misread something? Had a stroke? Lost your ability to process things? The human brain goes to work in those gaps. Gaps of knowledge, gaps of experience, gaps of understanding. The human brain hates those gaps if they aren't in the right place and gets busy filling them in. Your brain needs to have it all make sense because if it doesn't, it will leave you screaming like a four-year-old kid with a butterfly on his face.

The human brain is one fucked-up piece of hardware.

I think if more people understood that, I'd probably be out of a job. But, as it works out, people don't. They'd rather believe whatever shit their brain fills the gaps with than what is real. So people call me when they have a haunted house or some other paranormal event they can't explain. They need someone to convince them that the things their brain is telling them are wrong, or, on rare occasions, right, and they hire me to make it all go away, one way or the other.

Either way, it's lucrative.

I'm not one of those idiots hawking my wares on Discovery or some other ass backward cable channel. Paranormal Caught on Tape or whatever. I'm the guy people call for realsies. Am I worried that some of my clients might see this and figure out it's a stupid scam? Not really. My clientele isn't so much into the reading part of life, if you know what I mean.

Anyway, this is how it usually goes. I carry my notepad to write a few things down as I'm going through the place. I also carry my phone and record things. When it's all done, I'll type up my notes and give the client the report. Then their brain has the information to fill the gaps so it can stop making ridiculous assumptions about ghosts and evil presences. They feel better, I feel richer. Life is good and on to the next place.

Tonight I'm in a small town called Bomont, standing on the front porch of The Melnick House. It's the only house at the end of a deserted cul-de-sac. A little history? The previous three owners all moved out/ran away based on "feeling watched," "a malevolent presence," and "unexplained noises." As a side note, any homeowner who uses the word malevolent to describe their house is probably a douche. Rumor has it there were grisly murders committed here back in the forties by the guy that built the house. Talking to people in town about the rumors, a lot of them laugh, but it's that nervous laugh. They say kids sing songs about it. Everyone knows someone who knows a real story about the place, but none of them have ever experienced it personally. Another side note, it's always a small town and it's always a grisly murder.

Before I got here tonight, I stopped at City Hall and went through a pile of records. I've made copies for my final report, of course. The guy that built it, Mark Melnick, did so in the late fifties. No reports or stories or arrests related to any grisly murders. Two parts of the mythology already debunked. Like I said, my clients aren't much into the reading part.

It's a two-story house with a partially finished basement, detached garage which, according to the City, was built later. Sits on an acre. Was supposed to be a model house of some kind that he was going to use to build up this area, but then Melnick died before he could get the rest of the houses in his little cul-de-sac going.

The outside paint is green, covering aged wood siding. Lots of windows with old curtains, mostly hardwood floors, a couple of rooms with carpeting, the appliances look to have been updated back in the 90s or so. Couldn't find anything specific to that, just how it looks to me.

I haul my stuff inside. I don't use a lot of equipment, just a few necessary things. I have one of those noise detectors, not fancy. Found it on a used medical supply website. It's the kind of thing you'd find in a hospital to remind the nurses and orderlies to keep it down around all the recuperating patients. I have it cranked to the highest setting so it can pick up something like a footstep in a silent room. It's good for verifying that the house is actually making noises rather than the owner hearing things. Nine times out of ten, that's all I need. Houses make weird noises. And if your brain doesn't like it, the gaps get filled in. I'll often record the noises and then find the source. That's another piece of equipment I have. A good recorder. It can pick up the sound of a mouse running through the attic and reliably tell me if it's one mouse or a whole family. I also have three flashlights, regular, infrared, and UV. The UV one comes in handy especially when it's people fucking around, people leave fluids and DNA shit everywhere that the UV light picks up. Ghosts don't leave anything. My cell phone doubles as my camera. But my most important piece of equipment is my Fitbit. My brain is as susceptible to gaps as the next guy. And as the heart rate goes up, the more your brain is willing to fuck with you. So I keep it on and it alerts me if my heart rate gets going too fast. Reminds me to take a step back and not believe the nonsense my brain is feeding me.

Usually works.

For the first few hours, I wander around the place. Half empty. Test outlets, find the various pipes hidden in the walls, check out the house's innards. No electricity—new owners never switched it over, and were only halfway through moving in furniture when they freaked and bolted. Water works fine, although no hot water because the gas is turned off. Means it's much less likely any strange noises are coming from some of the bigger appliances or pipes.

There's half an attic. Half because the master bedroom is open above to the rafters like an old farmhouse which has been converted. It's a rustic effect. I poke my head into the attic which is nothing more than storage space, no room to stand up. Empty, as well.

The new owners did get their bed into the master bedroom, but I won't be sleeping tonight—too much to do.

My routine is simple, I set up shop in each room then sit and listen for an hour. Waiting for sounds or feelings to hit me that are akin to what the owners describe.

Tonight I start in the dining room from 8pm to 9pm. Nothing.

The front room/living room 9pm to 10pm. Again nothing. Some noises outside, but distant.

The kitchen from 10pm to 11pm. A floorboard creaks in the hallway which runs from the back, through the middle of the house, to the front foyer. I glance at the noise detector, but I missed it. My Fitbit chimes an alarm, set to do so for every ten bpms above seventy. Eighty-one. I slide the noise detector into a better position so I can see it and the hallway at the same time. It takes another five minutes for the floor to creak again. The detector flashes green meaning it heard something, too. I stand up and walk to the doorway and peer into the hall. Nothing there.

I shine the flashlight toward the floor, hard wood. Worn in the middle, still almost brand new at the wall. Wood floors are one of the biggest culprits. All that wood which once fit together so nicely is now stressed, compressed, and worn, at least in some places. Other places, like I said, good as new. Old and new don't always mesh together so well. And as wood cools down or warms up, those old pieces that used to fit together so nicely now fight against each other. I don't let my brain get distracted with gaps.

I check my Fitbit, back at seventy-five.

I stay in the doorway for another fifteen minutes. No more creaks. I go back into the kitchen and sit on the floor.

The floor of the kitchen is cold so I visualize the house. The washer dryer hookup in the basement would be right below me, pipes and dryer vents running out through the walls, lots of places for air to sneak in down there and cool things off. Drafty down there. A slightly cold sensation in this location is explainable.

The hallway creaks again. Like the sound of a heel rolling toward the toe. At least that's what my brain wants me to believe as it searches my memory for something that replicates the sound. I'm not falling for it. Just a creak. If another one happens, I'll go check it out. Fitbit at seventy-nine.

The remainder of the time in the kitchen is uneventful.

The hallway from 11pm to midnight; I hadn't planned on spending an hour in the hallway, but since that's where the only noise I've gotten a reading came from, I figure it can't hurt. I walk the length of the hallway five times. Stepping in different locations, finding spots that might be more likely to creak. There are several, the most prominent is the transition from the kitchen to the hallway. Makes sense. Kitchen is generally the heart of the house, going to see the most traffic. I am not able to successfully replicate the creak I heard earlier, further validating that it was the house settling rather than a supernatural footstep.

At five minutes to twelve I hear a sound in the kitchen. The detector hears it, too. Flashes orange, meaning louder than the earlier noise. My brain tells me it's a chair sliding on the floor. Chairs don't slide on floors by themselves I remind my brain. I step quickly down the hall and as I peer around the corner, I see a person sitting on one of the chairs at the kitchen table.

It's gone before I can focus on it. My Fitbit beeps. The window over the sink is open, not much, but a little. The curtains flutter as air pushes into the kitchen from outside. Moonglow fills the yard. All enough information for me to determine that the figure at the table was nothing more than a shadow caused by moving curtains and my eyes adjusting from the darkness of the hallway to the moonlit kitchen. I hadn't noticed the window being open earlier when I felt that chill.

At midnight I go upstairs. Three bedrooms and a bathroom.

The smaller bedroom toward the front of the house from 12am to 1am. Zip. So far, this is a relative nothing burger.

I move to the rear bedroom from 1am to 2am. It's slightly bigger than the front bedroom with a big window peering out into the backyard and the emptiness beyond. There are no curtains on the windows in this room.

Before I can sit down, I hear a creak in the upstairs hallway. Followed by another. My brain tries to convince me it's footsteps. The roll of weight, the time between the creaks, all clearly reminiscent of footsteps.

There's a group of people that have set up a page on Reddit to discredit me. Sometimes, when I'm not too careful, they figure out where I'm going next and show up at the place and give me grief. To be fair, the harder they try to prove I'm fake only further ensconces me as the real deal. Funny how that works. But I wouldn't put it past them to show up here at the house and walk around. Try and surprise me, spook me, throw me off.

All of that goes through my head between the second and third sound that might be a footstep. Definitely a footstep, my brain tells me. My Fitbit beeps in disagreement. Eighty-nine. A fourth footstep, this time clear and unmistakable. Beep, ninety-five.

"That you, Gregson85?" I call to the hallway. "Coming to make a point?"

A fifth footstep. The sixth sounds to be in the doorway as if whoever is walking down the hallway has stopped and is staring at me. In the dim light coming through the bedroom windows, I can see there's nothing there. Because there *is* nothing there, I remind myself. I shine my flashlight into the hallway and startle a shadow. At least that's what it looks like as the beam reflects off the doorknob and onto the hallway wall giving the illusion of movement. Creaking footsteps retreat down the hallway toward the staircase and then it's quiet again.

I turn back toward the window to see if Gregson85 or one of his Reddit buddies runs out the back door.

Nothing.

For the next fifty-two minutes I don't hear anything else. It takes almost the full hour before my heart rate Fitbit is back in the acceptable range.

When it gets to be two, I debate sitting in the bathroom or the master bedroom. Two to three bath, three to four bedroom, four to five basement I figure. That seems to be a good plan.

In the bathroom from 2am to 3am I get nothing.

Into the master bedroom from 3am to 4am. The open ceiling is a little disquieting. So different than the rest of the house. At 3:14am the chair in the kitchen slides again. At least that's what my brain would like me to believe. What else might make that sound? I wrack my brain, search for a hidden reference that I've forgotten about. I've heard plenty of sliding chairs in plenty of houses. All explainable. Sloped floor, heater coming on and vibrating underneath. In one case a guy had it rigged to mess with his wife. But this one? Sounds different. My brain tries to fill the gaps, but I don't let it. At least my Fitbit isn't beeping.

Then muffled footsteps from the downstairs hallway. Settling floorboards, I tell myself. The detector picks them up from the second floor. Coincidentally in a pattern that sounds like someone moving from the kitchen, down the hallway, and toward the stairs.

I feel it. The sensation the new homeowners told me about. That feeling that someone is watching me. That same feeling I used to get in third grade on the playground when Mike Gunderson came to school with a new bruise. I knew to stay sharp and not make eye contact with Mike, because he was looking for retribution. I watched out for all the third graders, too, kind of like the way I watch out for grown-ups now. It wasn't fair that Mike got bruises, no, but that's the way it was. In the master bedroom it felt like Mike Gunderson was watching me and I knew what was coming. Up the stairs.

The creaks do not stop or falter.

I sit down on the edge of the bed and check my Fitbit. It hasn't beeped in a while, but my breathing suggests it should have. The small face of the little device is black and empty, like the house, like the neighborhood.

"Shit," I mutter.

I always charge the battery before a new job. Maybe I didn't plug it in all the way at that knock off Motel 6 back by the interstate where I stayed last night. Maybe I forgot to charge it at all? Maybe that kitchen window hadn't been open. My brain starts filling gaps I didn't even know were there.

I hold my fingers to my wrist. It takes a second because everything's jittering more than it should. When I find my pulse, it is jumping though my skin. The creaks are now coming down the hall.

"Footsteps," I remind myself out loud.

My phone tremors in my hand as I thumb the camera button and swipe to video. I try to hold it steady toward the doorway. Try.

And then the shape comes around the corner.

I turn my face and squeeze my eyes shut like I'm sitting too close to a campfire. I try not to see the fog that enters the room. My brain wants to convince me that the fog has human legs extending to the floor and arms reaching toward me. But that is my elevated heartrate and some significant gaps doing the thinking. I suck shallow breaths and shove them out as quickly as I can without hyperventilating, willing my heart to slow down and running through possible scenarios. A fog from temperature differentials, an open window I missed, no sleep. Just seeing things.

"Ruuuuuu," the shape intones.

Not a word. Simply a sound from an old house at night. If the thing spoke, I might have a different problem. Except it can't because amorphous clouds of imaginary gas do not speak. My breathing shortens further still. Pathetic little gasps. I squeeze my eyes tighter and keep my phone directed toward where I remember the bedroom door to be. Butterflies aren't fucking scary, and neither is a meaningless trick of the eye. Nothing but a gap in my understanding.

I close my lips and fill my lungs through my nose. Something steadies within me. A very little something, but better than nothing. I open one eye, the one farthest from the doorway, and peek at my wrist, hoping the Fitbit would be telling me everything was back to normal. Its blank face reflects the darkness of the room. Nothing else.

"Loooo," the shape says. Followed by two creaks that might be footsteps if the shape had legs or feet.

My teeth grate together and my brain tries to convince me that the shape *is* speaking. Trying to communicate. *Is* walking. Getting closer.

The phone had to be picking it all up. I could review the footage once my heartrate dipped. Nothing in the room, nothing in the house, just gaps in my brain. It takes everything I have to push the air in my lungs up and out through my nose, in a slow, controlled exhale. I open my other eye and turn my head in the same direction I pointed my phone.

A face bursts from the shape. Only it isn't a shape anymore. Not a billowing cloud of anomalous something or the other. It has legs and arms and eyes. It is a man. Naked. Breath seeps from his mouth, fetid and lonely, and fills the room.

"Ommmm," it says. A length of rope slides through his hands.

My brain does not permit me to move, or I would reach out and touch the naked man., to verify he is there and real.

That would explain everything; this man escaped from somewhere and just my luck, wandered into this house tonight. Or maybe he was casing the place. That is a logical assumption.

The man wraps the rope around my throat. Once, twice. The rough fibers scratch my neck. My breathing returns to short, uncontrolled bursts. Almost like sobs. The rope goes around a third time. I hear my phone clatter to the floor.

He tightens the noose. It slides through his hands silently. From the corner of my eye, the sound detector on the floor verifies this.

"Who are you?' I gurgle.

He tosses one end of the rope up over the exposed rafters and catches it as it falls back to him. No sound. Until he starts pulling on it. The rope buzzes across the wood of the rafter in short bursts. The detector flashes green with each tug.

I am in the air. Dangling from the rope while a naked man stares at me from the floor of the master bedroom in the Melnick house. I claw at the rope, try and loosen its grip, watch my legs flail uselessly and swing back and forth three times before I start to black out. Images flash through my mind. Butterflies, Mike Gunderson, my parents, that house in Reno and a dozen others like it. The hotel rooms, the diners, those fuckers on Redditt.

Then I am Mark Melnick. Standing in the master bedroom of the house I've built for a woman who didn't see me. Dead parents, no friends. Alone in the world. A life spent searching for meaning without ever finding it.

I gasp, and the rope tightens further. "Please…" I try to say.

My feet kick one last time and I see Mark. He built a house. Which fixed nothing other than giving him a place to hang himself. The wave of emptiness and loneliness and desperation is a tsunami. Melnick didn't have a choice, couldn't get out of the way. He built a coffin for himself and hoped someone would hear him. No one did.

Until tonight.

I wake up on the floor a little after six a.m. My Fitbit working again. Not a huge surprise. It shows I've gotten two hours of deep sleep. Not bad.

There are a couple messages on my phone. I lean back against the bed and scroll through. One from the new owners. I told them they could come by the house at seven and I would give them an oral report in precedence of my final written report. They want to know if we are still on. Yep, we are still on. The second is from a family in South Carolina, some weird stuff happening in their house, they'd like a consultation. It's after eight on the east coast so I text them back. I'll be there tomorrow.

I think I mentioned earlier, I'm the guy that makes it go away, one way or the other. Most times it is one way, listening to noises and filling in the owners' gaps, telling them there's nothing wrong with their house. Probably forty-nine times out of fifty that's how it goes. But every now and then, like this one, I gotta do it the other way. It's a lot to carry, all that trauma and loss and anger and desperation. But it's what I do. I absorb that shit and then tell the owners everything is fine. It's more than just the brain that is a fucked-up piece of hardware, it's humans in general.

The Melnick House is clean now. My report will not include anything that happened in the master bedroom. It will include a loving biography of the man who built the house, who wanted someone to care about him. Someone to notice him.

I still have a lot of gaps in my understanding, in my knowledge, but I'm getting better all the time. One of these days though, I'll get those gaps filled in.

And in the meantime, it's still pretty lucrative.

# The Copper Thieves

Nick Roberts

12:35 AM, Columbus, Ohio, 2012

Two men rocked in the front seats of the white Chevy truck as it rumbled down the wooded path. Fulmer, the thirty-six-year-old driver, had stringy red hair that he hadn't cut in years. He covered it with an Ohio State Buckeyes hat that was beginning to tear across the brim. His beard was just as unkempt. At well over six feet tall, with his gaunt, skeletal frame and disheveled appearance, he was the kind of guy you'd cross the street at night to avoid.

Oxycontin will do that to a man, though.

Fulmer tolerated his partner in the passenger seat, Menke, though he'd never call him a friend; junkies don't have *friends*. The two men had worked together as HVAC repairmen for an old veteran whose business had a reputation for good work and reasonable prices. Menke was a hell of a ductwork fabricator, and he did most of the copper soldering. Fulmer ran the show though, whether it was diagnostic or a full installation. Menke was always second in command.

But when they started selling parts or overcharging customers to fund their burgeoning opioid addiction, the old man finally put two and two together. He shitcanned them, giving them a lecture about all the soldiers he'd served with who'd had similar problems and got help, but they didn't want to hear it and were out the very next day, uninstalling units they had just put in. Stealing copper rapidly became their new full-time gig. After the local law started cracking down on HVAC unit theft, they had to find a new way to get scrap metal.

The bright idea came from Katie, Fulmer's girl, even though she was fair game for Menke, too. She lay sideways in the folded-down back seat of the truck, her legs bent at the knee and her shoulders crammed inward to fit in the tight space. It didn't help that Fulmer hadn't had any pills that day and was taking his withdrawals out on her. His bones ached, he wanted to crawl out of his skin, and every time she pushed her knee into his seat, he glared in the rearview mirror.

Fulmer had met her at the recycling yard, and she caught onto their scheme during Fulmer and Menke's first visit. She was just as trapped by addiction as they were and had resorted to getting what she wanted with what she had, and her biggest bartering chip had nothing to do with money. With a steady supply of Oxy in her system, they could do anything they wanted with her.

The rocks on the one-lane access road made it feel like the earth kept punching the truck from underneath. Trees lined both sides, but it would soon open into the rear maintenance entrance of Green Lawn Cemetery. Over twenty-seven miles of roads and pathways cut through the 360 acres of private land that made up the second-largest cemetery in Ohio. The truck's headlights—one slightly brighter than its dimming counterpart—fought to illuminate their way through the crippling darkness. They had to wait until night, though. This, Katie had said, was the only time they could come.

From 10 PM to 6 AM, the cemetery only had one man making rounds along the grounds, and with such a large area, it would be easy enough to avoid detection. Fulmer, Menke, and Katie had arrived at 9:30 and parked in a clearing hidden by trees in front of the main gates.

***

Katie knew this was where the guard would enter, so he could lock up behind him. A fact she'd found out one day at the scrap yard when a man had come in with two bags full of copper vases, twelve in each one. The insides of most of them were still dripping from the watered flowers that had been freshly removed. She remembered seeing something in the paper about the VFW putting flower vases on the graves of every known serviceman, and the junkie in front of her probably saw the same article and got a lightning strike of an idea when he saw the picture of the vases; they were solid copper. And less than a day after the VFW and other volunteers decorated all of those headstones, this addicted little weasel scored $19 per vase. He managed to go back three more times after that, each time bringing a heftier load and rolling out with a few nights' worth of feel-good.

When she finally got up the nerve to ask him what his scam was he, of course, would only tell her after they did some Oxy in his car. The nasal cavity full of the cool blue euphoria greatly outweighed the mouthful of *him* she had to ingest. He finally got around to telling her about the vases. She said she already knew *where* he was getting them; he just had to tell her how. This was how she acquired the knowledge of the lone security guard, mindlessly patrolling the endless labyrinth of death or remembrance, depending on one's outlook.

Katie never saw him after that. She'd assumed that he'd cleaned them out or moved on to some other score. Had he been caught, it most certainly would've been on the news. They would've had his drug-addled mugshot front and center on the local paper for everyone to cast judgment and heave mental stones at.

*\*\**

"Cut the lights," Menke said and looked at Fulmer.

"I suppose so," Fulmer said, killing the headlights and slowing the truck's pace to a crawl until his eyes adjusted to the darkness.

He was thankful for the full moon, or he wouldn't be seeing shit. They had a bag of flashlights, crowbars, and a sledgehammer, tightly bundled by tarp and twine so they wouldn't roll around and cause a ruckus in the metal truck bed.

Menke kept the best flashlight on his lap, though—the Maglite he'd neglected to return to his previous employer. He pointed it straight up and turned it on. The bright beam lit up the interior of the truck like a lightsaber.

"God damn," Fulmer said, cupping the right side of his eyes and trying not to drive into a row of tombstones. "Point it out your window."

If they found more copper vases, they wouldn't exactly leave them behind, but salvaging those wasn't the reason they were here tonight.

*\*\**

After Katie told Fulmer about the vases, he had researched the other potential treasures that lay at rest. Graverobbing was nothing new, and not something he was interested in, frankly. It wasn't any kind of moral obligation that prevented him from doing it; it just seemed like too much work for not enough of a payoff, if there was even one at all (Geraldo Rivera opening Al Capone's empty vault live on network television replayed in his mind). The research that he did find interesting was the amount of copper used in the construction of caskets.

Copper, being naturally resistant to corrosion and rust, made this precious metal a go-to for many families wanting to send their loved ones off the best way they could. Finding a bronze casket would be even better as it commanded a slightly higher return. Fulmer had no intention of digging up graves though, especially when there were plenty of easier ways to hit the jackpot. In his research of Green Lawn Cemetery, he discovered it housed approximately 150,000 graves, but it was the mausoleums, notably the historic ones, that piqued his interest. He guessed, no, he *knew* that they belonged to families of generational wealth.

All they needed to do was break into a few of them and strip them of their parts. Ideally, he would like them to just get in, grab a coffin, load it up, and be on their way, but he knew that wasn't feasible. They would use their expertise in removing any metal worth scrapping, and if anything of value rested with the dead, well that would just be a bonus.

\*\*\*

"Hey, I think I see one of them copper vases," Menke said, shining the flashlight at a tombstone in the shape of a cross.

The vase did have a copper color and reflection, but what sealed the deal in Fulmer's mind was the miniature American flag embedded in the flowers. He stopped the truck and looked at Menke.

"Run out there and grab it," he said.

Menke shifted in his seat as if he was thinking about it.

205

"The fuck's the matter? Go grab it. Quick, before rent-a-cop spots us," Fulmer ordered.

"Yeah, OK."

Menke opened the door and swept the flashlight left to right, scanning the area and seeing tombstones of various sizes, shapes, and ages that were between him and his target. As carefully as he could, he sidestepped grave marker after grave marker until he came to the vase. He shined the light on it; it was solid copper. Just as he was about to reach for it, he pulled back.

"Good Lord, Menke," Katie shouted from the backseat in that nasally yet raspy voice of hers. "Just grab the fuckin' thing!"

"Fuck it," Menke said and snatched the vase.

The cool metal was heavier than he anticipated, which he supposed was a good thing. He quickly dumped the flowers, water, and flag on the ground and turned around to head back to the truck. He moved much quicker this time, feeling the darkness behind him. With his gaze fixed firmly on the open truck door and the welcoming interior light, his right knee banged against the arm of a cross-shaped tombstone. He hissed and fell forward, arms extended and juggling the vase until he bellyflopped on the ground.

"Fuck," Menke said, wincing at the pain now pulsating from what was surely a fractured rib from hitting the corner of the headstone.

Katie burst into a fit of manic laughter from the back of the truck.

"Damn it, Menke, get up!" Fulmer said, her squealing laughter grating on his frayed nerves; he needed a fix bad, and he knew it.

Menke pushed himself off the ground and hobbled to the truck, leaning on his banged-up knee and holding his injured side. His boot kicked the metal vase he'd forgotten about in the last few seconds. He bent to pick it up, but a stabbing pain pierced his ribs, and he had to right himself back up.

"Shit, Fulmer. I think I broke my rib."

"Just pick it up, you pussy," Katie said.

"Why don't you get your bitch ass-"

"Hey!" Fulmer shouted. "I'm not in the fuckin' mood for either of your all's shit. Just get in the truck."

Fulmer erupted out of his door and stormed around the front of the truck just as Menke limped back into his seat.

"It's right there," Menke said, pointing to the vase near the front right tire.

"I see it," Fulmer said.

He picked it up and tossed it on Menke's lap.

"Ouch! Goddamnit, why'd you do that?"

Fulmer smirked as he walked back around the truck. Katie laughed from the back seat.

"If I wasn't hurtin' so bad, I'd turn around and smack the shit out of you."

"Ohhhh," Katie taunted. "So scary."

Just as Fulmer rounded the corner of the truck, he noticed a soft whiteness off in the distance. He squinted at the rectangular structure and immediately knew what he was looking at. His grin widened, and he got back in his seat.

"Found one," he said.

"One of what?" Katie said.

"There's a mausoleum less than a hundred yards that way," he said and pointed to his left.

He shifted the manual transmission into first gear and coasted a little farther along the dirt road. With the mausoleum being that far away, he began to worry about transporting their tools and whatever loot they'd find in there. It'd be a lot easier if he could just back the damn truck right up to the...

And then he saw it.

A small path on the left ran straight to the front of the structure. Tombstones lined both sides, and it looked like it was built for something no bigger than a golf cart or an ATV to access, but his narrow S10 could fit. He thought about those cool blue Oxy 80s just waiting on him when he finished the job, and he knew he would make this work. He drove past the path and stopped, shifting into reverse, and then looking over his shoulder as he turned the back of his truck into the path.

"Damn, be careful," Katie said as she looked through the back window.

"Keep an eye out," Fulmer said. "We can make it."

Menke watched from his side mirror as they slowly cruised the length of the path. Fulmer hit the brakes just six feet shy of the mausoleum's entrance.

"And here we are."

Fulmer put it in park and shut off the engine. He looked at both of them.

"Y'all ready to do this?"

"Fuck, this is going to hurt," Menke said.

Fulmer patted Menke's knee. "Only one thing will make it better. Let's go get 'em."

Everyone exited the vehicle. Fulmer eyeballed the five cement steps leading to the entrance, smiling when he saw the simple padlock under the handle.

"Well, that'll be easy enough to get into," Menke said as if reading Fulmer's mind.

Fulmer opened the back of the truck and took out his side-mounted cut-off tool, one he'd considered pawning several times, but knew he wouldn't get shit out of it. Plus, it came in handy on too many occasions. He gave it a quick test whiz and then looked at his two partners.

"Just keep watch for *any* lights out there once I get this thing going, OK?"

They both nodded. Fulmer ascended the steps and turned on the tool. The little circular saw spun fast and loud in the quiet night. He pressed the tip of the spinning blade into the metal arch of the lock. Tiny sparks emitted like a miniature fireworks display. The teeth of the tool chewed through the metal with a loud, mechanical scream. Fulmer knew how much noise he was making and pushed harder, just to get it over with.

The heavy base of the padlock fell to the cement and clanked its way down the steps.

"Got it," Fulmer said.

With the hack job finished, Menke and Katie closed in on him as he removed the broken piece of lock from its holder. He examined the freshly unlocked door. Two handles—one above and one below the padlock area—were drilled into the door. Just as Fulmer reached for the handles, Menke spoke from behind him.

"Gloves."

"Huh?" Fulmer said, turning around and pushing the brim of his hat up, revealing an aggravated look.

Sweat glistened across his taut forehead in the moonlight.

"Put your gloves on," Katie said, clearly in synch with Menke. "Fingerprints."

"Oh, yeah," Fulmer said, pulling a pair of workman's gloves he'd used during his HVAC days.

He turned back and faced the door.

"All right." He gripped both handles. "Here goes nothing."

With one swift jerk, the door opened so easily that he nearly stumbled backward.

"Holy shit. Definitely wasn't expecting that."

"Well yeah," Katie said in that tone that made him want to knock her teeth out. "They're meant for families to come visit. The lock's the only thing meant to keep you out."

She shut up when she saw Fulmer's bulging eyes and his wild hair swaying around his face, some of it sticking to his moist cheeks.

"You want to do the honors, little girl?" he asked. Before she could respond, Fulmer said, "Menke, give her your flashlight. It's time for Katie here to pull her weight."

Menke held the flashlight out for her. She gave it one disgusted look.

"Get that fuckin' thing out of my face. I'm not doing shit," she snapped back. "You want to know *my* part? *My* part was setting up this whole fuckin' score, assholes. That's what my part was!"

Menke gripped her by the wrist.

"Keep your goddamn voice down,"

"Get your fuckin' hands off me, you piece of shit!"

"Girl, you got two seconds to shut your trap," Fulmer said from the open doorway.

"Or what?"

Menke jerked her arm so hard her shoulder could've popped out of socket. She winced and then spun around, kneeing him in his broken ribs.

"Fuck!" he screamed and doubled over. "Stupid *cunt*!"

Fulmer's eyes widened when he saw this girl that he didn't *really* know do what she was about to do. Katie lifted the metal flashlight and slammed it into the back of Menke's skull like she was splitting wood with an ax. Menke hit the dirt and didn't move. Fulmer ran down the steps and looked at his former coworker lying on the ground motionless. The small crack in Menke's skull leaked dark blood in a steady stream. Fulmer's shocked eyes found their way to Katie who was stepping back with the flashlight, holding it like a baseball bat.

"Don't you try nothing, motherfucker, or you'll end up just like him," she said, trying to sound tough, but he could hear the fear in her voice.

He squatted beside Menke and looked at his face. The man's expression was frozen like the universe just hit the pause button on him mid-scream. Fulmer removed a glove and placed two fingers on Menke's throat, but he felt no pulse.

"Holy shit, girl. You killed him."

"No," Katie said. "No, there's no fuckin' way. It's just a flashlight. I can't kill nobody."

Fulmer stood back up. He stared at the dead body on the ground and then at Katie, still in her defensive stance. His heart was beating so fast that he thought it was going to give out. The withdrawals weren't helping. He thought about the Oxys and the rush they provided, and his brain temporarily tricked him into feeling better. His mental obsession thickened.

"We're going to finish the job," he said.

Katie looked confused as she lowered the flashlight and relaxed her body posture.

"We came here for the scrap," he said. "We're not leaving without it. Give me that flashlight."

She took cautious steps toward him and handed him the flashlight when she reached the mausoleum stairs.

"What are we going to do about him?" She tipped her head back at Menke's corpse.

Fulmer smiled; he couldn't help himself.

"We're breaking into a casket. Where else would we put him?"

Katie looked back at Menke and then at the darkness behind Fulmer and crossed her arms like she knew she was in over her head. Fulmer clicked on the flashlight and turned around.

"You just stay out here and keep an eye out for headlights," he said as he walked into the damp, earthy structure.

Two caskets rested atop their concrete slabs. Fulmer shined the light all around the small, square-shaped room. Little concrete statues of children's faces ran along where the ceiling met the wall. Someone had spent some money on these intricate designs. The walls were smooth and cool to the touch.

Fulmer walked to the center of the room with his back to the door and the two caskets in front of him. He looked back over his shoulder and saw Katie out there with her back to him, watching for the guard. With a deep sigh, he approached the caskets, feeling more claustrophobic with each new step—a fear he didn't know he had until now.

A gold-plated plaque clung to the foot of each casket. He read the one on the left:

Jonathan Spythe

1867 – 1935

Devoted Husband

Fulmer moved the light to the other plaque. It read:

Garnett Spythe

1874 – 1941

Beloved Wife

"Everything OK in there?" Katie whisper-yelled from outside.

Fulmer jumped, shaking the flashlight, and then spinning around.

"You trying to give me a heart attack? Just be quiet and keep a lookout."

He heard her scoff as he turned back around, carefully approaching the caskets and scanning them with the light. Each one had a copper band running along its base. The inside would also be lined with it. After looking at the gold plates and the caskets, he could practically feel the Oxy coursing through his system.

\*\*\*

Katie watched Fulmer emerge from the mausoleum and skip down the steps. He didn't even look at her. His focus was on the back of the truck.

"Well, we good?" she asked.

Fulmer pulled the tailgate down and hopped into the uncovered truck bed. Katie walked closer and peered in, watching him as he unwrapped his tools. She saw him grab a chisel and a mallet and leap out.

"Fulmer, we're good, aren't we?" Katie said, the excitement in her tone rising.

"We're definitely ahead already," he said as he walked back up the steps. "Come in here and hold the flashlight. We'll see how good we are once we pop the tops."

Her stomach rolled over at how casually he said, "pop the tops" and what that truly entailed, but like Fulmer, her obsession for a few lines of one of those blue pills overruled all judgment. She quickly followed him into the dank room.

"Here," he said and handed her the light. "Shine it on the plate on this one first."

The tip of the chisel wedged tightly under the plate. With the light tap of the mallet, the delicate metal popped off. He picked it up and examined it, surprised at the light weight.

"Holy shit," he said.

"What?" Katie asked like she wanted to know what was inside of a Christmas present.

"It's not just gold plated. It's solid."

Fulmer stood up and repeated the same process on the other plate.

"Here, hold these," he said and handed them to Katie.

She stared at them in awe, having never seen that much gold before.

"This is going to be the tricky part."

Fulmer tried to pry off the copper that ran along the base of the casket, but the chisel wouldn't go in, no matter how hard he hit it with the mallet. He dropped both tools and marched out of the mausoleum. Katie walked to the door and watched him grab a crowbar out of the truck and a sledgehammer.

"Goddamn, Fulmer," she said.

"You're going to have to hold the crowbar," he said, walking past her.

"What?"

"I'm going to need you to hold the crowbar. That would've been shithead's job if you hadn't killed him."

Fulmer jammed the flat part of the crowbar into where the copper met the casket.

"Here, just hold it with both hands right like this," he said, gripping the long piece of the tool in a demonstration. "I won't miss. Don't worry."

Katie did as she was told. She squatted and held onto the bar the same way she did the flashlight when she'd killed Menke. Before she could look up to see when he was going to swing, Fulmer brought the heavy metal sledgehammer down on top of the crowbar at just the right spot. She fell back, dropping the crowbar with a CLANK against the stone floor, as the entire bar of copper broke off the casket.

"That's what the fuck I'm talking about," Fulmer said. "Quick, get up. Let's get the rest of these sides real quick and then we'll open them up."

After a grueling few minutes of wedging, holding, and praying not to get hit, Katie had managed to keep a firm grip as they broke off all the bars on both caskets except for one.

"Last one," Fulmer said. "You ready?"

"Yeah, just do…"

Before she could finish her sentence, Fulmer swung the crowbar and cracked her head open. The metal head was buried in the top of her skull, and the handle jutted out like a unicorn's horn. Katie's eyes rolled up as rivers of blood poured down her face like a juicy watermelon. She spasmed, and then fell forward, face-first, onto the ground.

\*\*\*

"That's what you get, bitch."

Fulmer grabbed the crowbar's handle and put his boot on the side of her face. He wiggled the embedded metal top until it popped from her head like a loose tooth. Her blood spread across the fine stone ground like it was trying to escape.

The crowbar rested on the other side of her. Fulmer stepped over her, picked it up, and shoved the blunt end into the casket. He used the full weight of his gaunt body to get it as far in as he could, not wanting to completely demolish the casket. Once it held good enough for him to whack it without having to hold it, that's what he did.

The top of the casket popped open, but not all the way. He maneuvered his way around it, carefully repeating the process until the lid cracked enough to where he thought he could open it. After placing his tools on the ground, he stared at the jarred top. His palms began to sweat at the thought of what he was about to see. He decided to delay it for a few more seconds by walking to the mausoleum door and scanning the area for the security guard, but he knew he wouldn't see him. The chances of running into him on the massive lot were slim to none.

"All right," he said and approached the casket.

He walked to the middle of the casket, gripped the lid, and lifted. The stench of decades of rot and decay wafted in his face. Dusty debris of the dead caked the back of his throat when he inhaled. He coughed and spat on the floor, hitting Katie's face by mistake but not really caring.

Once he looked inside, he felt like a fool for having been so unnerved before. Garnett Spythe was a skeleton with tattered clothes that had once been the mark of high society. Fulmer's pulse quickened when he saw the pearl necklace hanging from her bones and the gold, diamond ring on the bone that once was a finger. Disassociating his abhorrent actions by thinking only of the Oxys was what gave him the ability to reach in and take her jewelry, which he quickly pocketed.

The velvet lining inside of the casket hid what he came for. He reached in and ripped the corner, exposing copper plating that lined the inside. It was a big sheet, and he'd have to be careful getting it out if he wanted this casket to remain intact. That would mean removing Garnet, prying it off without damaging the structure, and then putting her back in. Every time he thought that the job was too much, he just calculated how many more Oxys this extra effort would yield him.

It took him thirty minutes, but he did the job exactly like he'd planned, and the copper plate actually came out easier than he'd thought. He gently laid Garnett back how she was and smiled when he examined his completed job. Everything looked exactly as it had before he'd messed with it.

"Hey, Garnett," he began and then looked down at Katie's body and back at the skeleton in the casket. "You want some company?"

Katie was heavier than he thought when he picked her up, carrying her like a bride across the threshold of their home. Gently, he lowered her down on top of Garnett. The sickening sounds of the long-dead woman's brittle bones crunching made him queasy, but that sensation went away as soon as he closed the lid.

Fulmer let out a long sigh when he realized he was only halfway finished, but he wasn't going to stop now. He might as well go for the gold, metaphorically speaking. First, he ran outside to where Menke was. He gripped the poor bastard by the ankles and began pulling him across the grass, up the stairs, and eventually into the mausoleum. He stopped beside Jonathan Spythe's casket and let Menke's feet drop with a THUD.

"Round two," he said, and then repeated the exact same process he'd just done with the two dead women from different eras.

The only difference was that the skeleton in this box had a wedding band, no necklace, but a few gold fillings in his teeth, which Fulmer had no problem snapping off and adding to the collection in his pocket.

Once he slammed the lid on the two dead men, he rounded up the copper bars and began loading his truck. He grabbed the gold plates and his tools and hauled that load. The smaller pieces of the precious metals went in the front seat where Menke had sat, while the tools and the larger pieces went back in their regular spot in the back of the truck.

Fulmer looked at his dollar store cell phone that was in the truck and saw that he'd been there close to four hours, and Christ, he felt like it. The last thing he had to do was go back in the mausoleum and make sure everything looked as close to normal as possible. Aside from the pool of blood on the ground and the missing copper on the outside of the caskets, he thought that it could've looked worse.

Judging by the age of that lock he'd cut through on the door and the dates of death of the inhabitants, he reckoned that these two didn't get many visitors. It'd probably been decades since someone other than him had been in here. Satisfied, he shut the mausoleum door and realized there was one more step that he had to do: the lock. He had no desire to try to find someplace open that sold locks and come all the way back out here to replace it. He decided to return in the next few days during visiting hours to replace the lock.

Fulmer trudged back to his truck, starting it up, and creeping out of the cemetery with his headlights off, the same way they'd all came in.

It didn't take long for him to realize that he'd fucked up. He hadn't been paying attention as well as he should've been when they entered the cemetery. The dirt path bumped the truck, sending the metal clanging in the cab with him. He heard the tools slide from one side of the truck bed to the next. Slowing the truck to a crawl, he eyed the fork in the road in front of him.

"Shit."

He looked at both paths for any sign of familiarity, but they were identical. Katie had said it was easy enough to get lost in the cemetery during the day if you didn't know where you were going. Forget about driving around in the dark with no clue. The longer he stared, the more he realized how much time he was wasting. It felt right to go right, so that's where he went.

Fulmer kept the headlights off just in case the security guard would be lurking near the access road from which they'd entered, but there was no sign of an exit anywhere. After ten minutes of this, he realized he'd made a wrong turn and slammed the brakes. The copper and gold shot forward and almost tipped over on him.

"Gotta turn around," he muttered to himself, attempting to look through the army of trees surrounding both sides of the road.

Another slight bend in the rocky road lay ahead of him. Just another part of this hellish odyssey that he didn't remember. Everything looked the same. But he realized that if he cut the truck at just the right angle at the bend, he could possibly turn around. The one thing he absolutely could not do was let his back tires get caught in what looked like a deep ditch by the road.

Fulmer slowly pulled forward just enough to angle the rear of his truck into the bend. He shifted to reverse and, inches at a time, began to back up. Glancing back and forth between the rear and the front, he was just waiting for an acceptable angle that would give him enough clearance to whip his truck around and head back to that fork in the road where he'd made the wrong decision.

"Just six more inches, baby," he said and shifted back to reverse.

He lost his footing on the pedal for only a second, but that was all it took. The truck tipped backward; the runner lights crawled up the trees in front of him as the back two wheels sank into the unassumingly deep ditch behind him.

"Fuck!"

Fulmer shifted to first gear and tried to ease his way out. Once. Twice. But it was no use. He was stuck.

"Fuck! Fuck! Fuck!" he screamed as he punched the steering wheel.

Deciding to give it one more go—more out of frustration than any pragmatic form of escape—he floored the pedal, which did nothing but cook the tires and fling the earth. His stomach got that cold feeling that it often did when he knew he was in a jam. He thought about calling Skully, his dealer who had a much bigger truck than he did and could probably pull him right out of this predicament and hook him up with some Oxys to boot, assuming he'd front Fulmer the pills and follow him to the scrap yard.

Fulmer sat still in the truck, looking at the darkness surrounding him. He had to get out of here. If anyone found his truck, they'd see the copper, and eventually find the mausoleum with the brand-new bodies. He slapped the steering wheel and climbed out. It took him a minute to find the flashlight between the tools, but he did. He hopped out of the bed and bent down to examine the rear tires. The beam of light in the darkness confirmed what he already knew. He'd dug his tires too deep in the ruts to get out on his own.

"Shit."

A door shut. Fulmer shot up and pointed the light at his now closed driver-side door. His heart was in his throat. No one stood near the truck. He shined the light in the general vicinity but saw no one. Gripping the flashlight harder than he realized, he approached his truck with the interior lights still on.

Someone was sitting in the front seat, his seat.

Fulmer jumped at the sight and felt the urge to run, but that flight instinct switched to fight when he realized he had nowhere to go. He took a step forward, never removing the light from the silhouette of the person in his truck.

Just as he approached the side to get a clear view, his flashlight bulb flickered and then turned off.

"Damn it," he whispered and gave it a smack, hoping to jar some juice in the drained batteries.

The door squeaked when it opened, but it was so dark that Fulmer couldn't see six inches in front of his face. He heard the footfalls of someone getting out of the truck. He banged on the flashlight until a quick flash of light shot out of it. The truck door was open, and someone disappeared into the trees just as the light went back out.

Fulmer's abdomen tensed. He had no idea who or what that was, but he was all alone, sightless in the night with it. Twigs snapped on the forested earth behind him. He stepped toward his truck and noticed that all the copper and gold had disappeared. He looked at the bed and saw the long pieces were gone, too.

"What the fuck?" he said as he bent over and scanned the interior.

Not one single piece of the precious metal remained.

*How is this possible?*

The truck rattled as a hefty weight landed in the bed with a THUD.

"Son of a bitch!" Fulmer yelled with a crack in his voice which hadn't happened since puberty.

As he backed away from the truck, he saw a figure standing in the darkness with slivers of moonlight illuminating it.

"Who…who is that?" Fulmer said, still trying to shake the flashlight alive.

When it finally came on, he wished it hadn't.

The grinning corpse of his dead buddy Menke somehow stood there, staring at him. But the longer Fulmer examined the grotesque sight, the more his body hairs began to stand on end. It was Menke's face, but it hung loosely from the skull underneath. His eyes looked lifelessly in two different directions. As Fulmer dragged the flashlight down the length of the monstrosity, he noticed the same pattern; the skin was too big for the bones underneath. This thing wore Menke's remains like a fleshy poncho.

Before Fulmer really had time to accept the unbelievable, the TING TING TING of metal hitting the ground made him spin around.

"Oh, Jesus Christ," he said as he gazed upon the hideous counterpart to the thing in the truck.

A deformed version of Katie stood about fifteen feet in front of him on the road, and all the copper and gold lay at her feet. But it wasn't the same Katie he put in that casket in what seemed like a lifetime ago. The version of the junkie girl he'd hooked up with, used, and abused, stood at least a foot shorter. Her hands were empty gloves because the bones inside didn't reach the length of the arms. It was the same deal with her legs. Her empty feet flesh trailed the cadaver like a child playing dress-up in his or her parents' clothes.

Fulmer wondered how the hell it even got all that metal out of his truck so fast, let alone carry it this far. It must've sensed his confusion. It laughed and began to shuffle toward him, arms extended with draping hand flesh wobbling back and forth as it moved.

Fulmer screamed as he stumbled backward. The thing on the truck landed behind him with a thud. He turned sideways to keep an eye on both of them. Menke's corpse smiled enough to reveal missing teeth, and though Fulmer couldn't process the shock, that's when Fulmer figured out what was going on.

Somehow, the skeletons of Mr. and Mrs. Spythe had done what Fulmer did to the deer he'd shot during hunting season; they had field dressed them, stripped them of their flesh and useless parts, and kept the essentials. Their skeletal remains now had fresh new suits. He thought about the dead, rich bastards and how this must be a treat for them, one they hadn't experienced for quite some time. All dressed up for a night on the town.

As the two of them cornered him against the truck, he did the only thing he knew to do. He gripped the door handle and slid back in the truck in one quick motion, making sure to lock both doors for good measure. He turned the truck on again and tried like hell to get out of the ditch, but it didn't budge.

Something heavy whacked the windshield and it splintered like rock candy. Fulmer hit the high beams and saw Mrs. Spythe holding one of the long pieces of copper, which now dangled at her side.

"What the fuck do you want?" Fulmer pleaded.

The thing that was Menke now stood at his door. The loose flesh hung forward, nearly touching the glass.

"What?" Fulmer begged. "I'm sorry, OK? Just let me go, and you'll never see me again!"

The Menke-thing shook its head. It raised a copper bar and jammed it through the window like it was spearing a fish. Fulmer felt like he'd been whacked in the forehead with a hammer. He fell to his side, rolling around on broken glass that pierced the taut flesh of his ribs. The interior of the truck swirled in his vision. He knew he was dazed but had no idea of the severity of the blow to his head until he touched his forehead and saw no blood.

A cold, claw of a hand clenched his belt and jerked him right-side up. Fulmer was still finding his bearings when he turned to see the grinning face of the ghoul in the Menke suit leaning in his window.

"Please..." Fulmer began.

With a ravenous growl, Menke lunged in face first and bit Fulmer's nose, his primary source of Oxy ingestion. Fulmer let out a howl and tried to back away, but the devil just clamped down its decayed teeth and shook back and forth, tearing through cartilage like beef jerky. It laughed as blood and drool poured down Fulmer's face. Fulmer gripped the seat to pull himself to the passenger side, but a shard of glass pierced the webbing of flesh between his index finger and thumb.

Just as he let out another whelp, Fulmer's nose snapped off. He fell back and hit his head on the passenger door, where he let it rest as blood drained down his face. The thing at the window in front of him chewed his severed appendage like it was a wad of bubble gum. Its taunting smile gave Fulmer the rage he needed to fight back. He raised his right leg and stomped the bottom of his boot into the thing's face with a crunch that sent it to the ground.

Fulmer leaned back against the door just as someone pulled it open from the outside. His head fell back like an open Pez dispenser, and he looked upside down at the hideous cadaver standing in front of him. She tilted her head as far as she could to meet his eyes. The flesh did not cling well to the skull inside and folded over on itself like a burlap sack. He watched as she lifted a piece of copper and rubbed the end against his temple.

"Fuck..."

She tapped it, tauntingly, and then she began to speak.

"*This*...is...what...you...want?" she said, somehow producing the words that sounded like crisp leaves burning in a fire.

Fulmer could only stare in shock. She slid the end of the copper across his cheek and rested it on his lips. It was cool and smelled of pennies.

"*This*…is…what...you…get."

In one violent push, the copper pipe broke through Fulmer's teeth and tore through his throat, ripping free his innards like a hand yanking a strand of pumpkin guts. His eyes involuntarily widened as he felt the cold pressure burrow past his heart and pierce through every part of his abdomen. It wasn't until the tip exploded out of his sphincter, that he began to spasm. His eyes drifted uncontrollably downward, and he saw the Menke ghoul with the busted face standing there. It gripped the viscera-soaked end of the copper, and then Fulmer felt himself begin to rise upward toward the roof of the car.

\*\*\*

Sam the Night Man, as the "normies" on dayshift called him, was making his final rounds of his shift. The sun began to emerge and stain the sky copper. The off-road vehicle, that the kind members of the Green Lawn Cemetery Board of Directors had finally bought him after two years of asking, made all the difference in his job. He used to have to use his own truck. Sure, they'd reimburse him for gas and wear and tear, but his Ford pickup could only make it up and down certain access roads. The other ones had just been too narrow. Being that he had to cover the entire cemetery all night long, this meant he had to patrol certain parts on foot (he'd tried a mountain bike once but laughed at himself when he tried to ride up the first hill).

This vehicle could go anywhere in the massive cemetery, making him much more efficient at his job. That was the selling point that eventually got the Board to approve the expense—efficiency. He would be able to cover more ground multiple times, and they'd never have to worry about him getting injured by falling off a bike or twisting an ankle while walking a rough path. Once he got his way, however, he realized that he could cover the grounds effectively and have plenty of free time to catch up on his shows in the field office or even take a cat nap.

As he rounded the corner on the part of the cemetery he liked the least and the best simultaneously, he slowed his pace as he approached the path that led to the Spythe mausoleum. He liked the road because it was always the last route he made. This was the case ever since he'd heard the stories about the Spythe family. He felt icky driving by their eternal resting place when it was still dark; now he waited until the sun came up. So, yes, the rumors of Mr. and Mrs. Spythe being sadistic murderers, particularly of stolen children because they had been incapable of having their own, was a deciding factor on only coming by this part of the cemetery at dawn. On slow nights, he'd read up about the wealthy couple and how they were always suspected of butchering vagrants, prostitutes, and the city's forgotten, but no one ever said a word to them. Money talks in this city, he thought. *Always has, always will.*

Something was off about the area surrounding the mausoleum that morning, though. Sam put the vehicle in park and stepped out with his flashlight that he still needed because it wasn't completely daylight yet. He shined the beam across the tire tracks in the manicured grass. He turned around and looked at the area on the other side of the road and saw discarded flowers. The light moved amongst the tombstones and highlighted an empty spot where he knew a copper vase had recently been placed.

"Damn junkie thieves," he muttered as he climbed back into his vehicle, put it in drive, and cruised down the path that led to the Spythe mausoleum.

The closer he got, the more he realized someone had definitely been here. He gripped the wheel and felt his hands getting clammy, not just because he hated to be near this place, but because if there was a break-in, the higher-ups would have his ass.

Sam stopped at the steps of the mausoleum and got out. He pointed the flashlight at the spot where a padlock was supposed to hang. That's when he saw the broken pieces lying on the concrete.

"Ahh, hell."

He continued forward, shining his light around the surrounding grounds. Just as he was about to place his foot on the first step, he saw the crimson puddle to his left. He gulped and wiped the sweat from his forehead as he approached it. The closer he got, the more certain he was that it was blood.

"Good Lord," he said and turned back to the mausoleum.

As he walked, he looked for more evidence but found none. Once he reached the Spythe family door, he pulled it open. He'd never seen anyone in all his time here open that door. A metallic smell with hints of dirt and decay invaded his nostrils. He recoiled and lifted the flashlight, nearly dropping it at the sight before him.

"What in God's name…?"

The two coffins were in pristine condition. His fear of copper thievery was assuaged when he saw the coveted metal still lining the caskets. Even the gold plates were in their proper place. *Whoever came in here must've done something with the bodies.* Slowly, he walked across the room until he could see inside the coffins.

"Oh, shit," he said and looked away.

There were two cadavers in there, but they weren't rotting skeletons like they should be. He took a deep breath, preparing himself for another look. He shined the light again at the freshly skinned bodies. One had been female, the other a male. Every inch of their flesh was gone, leaving nothing but exposed muscle tissue and lidless eyeballs that stared at the ceiling, gathering debris.

*If these are new bodies, then where are the old ones?*

Sam spun around and hurried back to the vehicle. This shit was above his pay grade. His plan now was to get back to the main office as quickly as possible and call this in. The fastest way back was the access road in the direction he'd already been heading. He'd drive out through the back exit and drive on the outside of the cemetery around to the front gates where he'd let himself in and phone the authorities.

As he sped down the bumpy road, he couldn't stop wondering where Mr. and Mrs. Spythe's bodies were. His only conclusion was that this was the work of some cult who knew about the Spythe's history and carried out some sort of sick sacrifice.

Just as he came to the fork in the road where he knew to turn left, he noticed headlights straight ahead through the trees. It looked like they were angled up as if the truck was on its side or tipped at an off angle. He let out a deep sigh and drove down the right side of the fork.

After a short ride that felt like an eternity, Sam came upon the vehicle. It was a white Chevy S10, and the back of the truck was stuck in one of the steep ditches that had nearly caught him once when he wasn't paying attention. As he got closer, he heard the low idle of the engine and realized it was still on. He parked his vehicle and hurried out, fearing that someone could be in there hurt or unconscious.

Sam stopped when he saw the broken windshield. His eyes scanned the rest of the truck, and that's when he saw the driver's side window had been busted out, and something protruded from inside. His nerves were doing their best to get the better of him, but he kept breathing and reminding himself that he got paid to do this.

"Hey, is uh, somebody in there?"

No response.

Sam crept up to the window and stretched his neck to look in, afraid of what he might see. He froze as he attempted to accept the reality of what he saw. A copper pipe the length of a coffin—in fact, it was the same pipes they used in the coffins, now that he thought about it—was balanced on both broken windows with about six inches of pipe sticking out on either side. A man, perfectly impaled on the pipe like a hog roast, hung belly-up with limbs dangling. Glass and blood were strewn about the seats.

"Oh God," Sam said and stepped back to vomit.

After three good upchucks, he turned to head back to his vehicle, determined to make double-time and get the hell out of there. He hopped in and drove in a small circle to turn around in the agile, off-road machine. Pressing the accelerator down, he went back the way he'd come until he reached the fork in the road that led to the exit. He floored the pedal on the straight stretch, seeing the closed gate in front of him.

Just as he was about to stop and get out to input the access code, the doors gracefully swung open on their own. *What the hell? When did they get automatic doors?* He'd suggested automatic doors for exiting the cemetery to the Board several times, but it always came down to not having the funds in the budget. *They must've finally listened.*

Sam slowed at the exit. There were a few cars on the main road that ran parallel with the cemetery gate. He pulled out past the gate and waited to turn left and head to the main entrance. As the last car flew by, he realized he hadn't made sure the new automatic doors had shut. He looked in his tiny rearview mirror and froze in terror at the two twisted bodies watching him from beyond the closed gate. One was taller than the other and had its arm around the shorter one. Their faces were slabs of rotten meat dangling from the skulls beneath, but he could still tell they were smiling.

When he turned around to see with his own eyes, they were gone.

In just a few hours, the cemetery would be open for business.

# The Speakers of Imminent Darkness

Kyle Toucher

Fire violated the cathedral of the Santa Monica Mountains.

Ranches were leveled to ash, horses that hadn't been evacuated choked on smoke. Rich people lost Ferraris. Poor people lost it all. The roads winding through blackened canyons were stained red from air-dropped fire retardant. It looked as if dragons had fought there, and their war had been brutal.

I was still up when Ray called. He said he was doing ninety on the 101, with the hills ablaze in his rearview mirror, and that his heart nearly stopped when the Sheriff's Department rolled up in the middle of the night, speakers blaring: *A dangerous wildfire is approaching this area. For your safety, an emergency evacuation order has been issued.* To Ray it was tantamount to *Enemy Missiles inbound, get to your shelter.* He packed a bag, then grabbed his cat Renfield and hit the road.

"The fire's everywhere, David," Ray said. "We just got the evac order. How could it grow so fast?"

"The Santa Ana is pushing it," I said. The Santa Ana, annual dry, hot winds that roared westward from the desert, were often a wildfire's greatest collaborator. "If firefighters can't get a handle on it, it'll burn all the way to Malibu, so just get here."

Ray's voice turned to static. By then, most of the cell antennas near him were likely in flames, but I thought I'd heard him say, "This tumor of a house."

At seven the following morning, Ray rolled up in his bruised and beaten Ram 1500. Renfield peered out from his carrier, wide-eyed and relieved to be anywhere but Ray's truck. In Ray's other hand was a half-finished bottle of Balvenie and a gym bag. He was filthy as a Victorian-era chimney sweep. Behind him, eastward, the sky roiled cancerous, ugly with smoke.

"Jesus, Ray, I tried to call you all bloody night."

"Everything is down," he mumbled.

Ray stomped into the house, hooked a left to the guest bedroom, and opened Renfield's crate. The old fella hopped right up to the bathroom sink. He wanted water.

"Around four AM, I began to worry, nothing but an out-of-service message from Verizon. You said you were flying down the freeway at ninety miles an hour. I watched the news; the chopper footage was crazy. The freeway above the Conejo Grade was shut down, and traffic backed up for miles. You came to a screeching halt, I imagine."

"Wasn't the traffic, David. It was that witch."

"Witch? Oh hell, were you with *Janice* last night?"

"Hah. No. That *house*."

Okay, I thought. *Here we go.*

"Made me lie," Ray said as he opened the faucet, and the cat drank. "I never left the driveway. Near everything I said beneath the roof of that place was false; my new novel's coming along just super, Janice says she'll move back in this fall, the spots on my X-rays are nothing, I don't own too many knives, there's no altar half-buried on the property. All bullshit."

I'd known Ray since high school, when Led Zeppelin was king and you could hitchhike to the beach without ending up wrapped in a shower curtain. He'd been blessed with imagination, making his living as a musician, illustrator, and, later, writer. He created several movie posters you'd recognize, composed commercial jingles you'd know, and penned two fringe science fiction novels that somehow merged H.P. Lovecraft with Phillip K. Dick. When he bought his house in the hills near Seraphim Lake, he thought he'd found what realtors call A Forever Home. Perhaps some of his best work had come out of that place, most notably his 2016 six-hundred-page weirdfest, *The Speakers of Imminent Darkness,* which revolved around a man misdiagnosed with schizophrenia as voices dragged him into madness and isolation, fueled by a house that remembered every single thing that happened not only within its walls but upon the soil on which it was built. I read it, and it gave *me* the willies.

"Again with that house," I said.

Ash sprinkled to the floor and his expression turned to haggard resignation. "Those are old hills, David—with even older rules."

"You need to rest, my friend, and I'm glad you made it."

"Here I am."

"And here you'll stay until the evac is lifted." But I had to ask, "So your house is okay?"

"Oh God, no. *Shit* no. It's torched, homie."

I gasped, the news a fist. "I'm so sorry, really. I had—"

"Rabid dogs must be put down," he interrupted, his voice brittle as clay. "Except the house screamed."

*Alright, watching his house burn snapped his cap.* I could only imagine the shock of it. Ray must have read my face because he set one hand on my shoulder and looked me straight in the eye.

"You don't understand. *The house would not let me leave.* Fire raging, trees exploding, deer fleeing—but it *insisted* I stay. Once the house knew its fate was sealed, it wanted me to die with it."

"Wait. What?"

"I was there. I watched the house burn to the ground. I was never on the freeway headed toward you when I called. I stayed, man. I was its bitch to the bitter end, still taking its orders while it refused to accept death. But in the end, like all of us, it had no choice. When it screamed, when that house finally, goddamn *finally* screamed, I took an enormous pull from this bottle in celebration. It *suffered*. It felt every nail boil between its boards, every tile split, every bone and floorboard warp and incinerate. A weight lifted. A glorious end to a ravenous monster."

He raised the bottle, sloshing the contents around. "Care for an early-morning snort?"

"I'll pass."

"Made me lie, lie, lie. As every word left my lips, every tap on the keyboard when I fell into a writing frenzy, or even more fiendishly when it drove me to paint, I knew it was the house pulling my strings. Some prefer a house dipped in ooga-booga to follow the established rules of the Gothic haunt, yeah? Creaking doors and billowing curtains, a stone angel overlooking the graves of restless ancestors, maybe a spooky housekeeper named Esmeralda. Well, not so much at Uncle Ray's Shitshow Pavilion. That *house* isn't haunted, my friend. That house haunted *me*. It was built on ground damned before any European set eyes on North America, before some Chippewa named Spitting Pebble took a dump in Lake Erie."

He looked at me and smirked.

"Something crawled here to hide from the Pleistocene, and that house sprang from its blood and bones. Hah! Take *that*, David Attenborough."

*Hide from the Pleistocene? All well and fine as a device in one of his novels, but—*

"You're saying that the house was built on top of something alive?"

"X-ring, my friend," Ray said, bottle in hand and head down, staring at the space between his filthy shoes. "A cosmic tragedy thousands of years ago marooned them. Fallen lunatics, you may say. Most remain in stasis, kept alive by the network. The *Machine* network."

His mouth shut like a spring-loaded trap, and he snapped his eyes to me, the face of a kid who'd accidentally spilled the beans. After a long sigh, he rolled his shoulders and turned to the window. In the far away, a dark smoke ribbon rose into the morning sky, backlit by the sun's raging eye.

"But now it's gone, either asleep or back to Hell. It's in that smoke now, the spell—hopefully—broken."

Renfield hopped onto the bed and licked away a layer of ash. Poor little guy probably inhaled a pile of smoke last night, too.

"You don't believe a word of it, and I get that, but I have *photos*. Well, not photos in the traditional sense; it's not like I shot them with an Instamatic. Still, I defy you to look and not see what I saw." He unzipped his gym bag and rummaged around. I saw a few pairs of socks, T-shirts, a money clip stuffed with C-notes, and a scuffed leather bag. He removed the bag and motioned to it like Vanna White.

"Listen, pal, be thankful you and Renfield made it outta there alive."

Ray blew past that. "They're sloppy, a little blurry even, but they're *there*. Transmitted then emblazoned to anything within my reach. Passed through me to the medium, dig? An unintended effect, I think, of the...of its...*influence.* But the picture isn't the issue. It's the *message.*"

I recalled the ESP craze of the seventies and early eighties when spoon benders and mentalists frequented talk shows. One stood out, Ricardo Montalvo, able, he claimed, to will descriptions given to him from his mind to film. The gag worked like this: as Montalvo stood on the stage with a camera in hand, someone in the audience offered a prompt—a cathedral in Barcelona, for example—and that's when the performance began. The first beat was a series of deep breaths and unintelligible muttering, soon escalating to clenched teeth, a sweating brow, and eyes pinched tight as a frog's asshole, culminating in a sudden, violent thrust of his forehead toward the lens. After the audience floated upon a sea of tension, he ripped the film from the Polaroid and, after much fanning to supposedly dry the stop bath—*presto!*—a blurry image of a cathedral spire. Mysterious and hurried, urgent with motion blur, an image from beyond the veil, captured on film. The same stink rose from Ray's claim, but I couldn't be shitty about it. *He* believed it.

"And the subject of these photos?"

"The ones I wrote about. *Them.* The Speakers of Imminent Darkness. For a man forced to lie every time he opened his mouth, the cruel irony is that every word in that book is true."

*The Speakers of Imminent Darkness.* Ray's novel met with moderate success and had been film-optioned twice, once by an independent producer named Barry Grueller, who died soon after when his Range Rover burst into flames outside Ruth's Chris in Beverly Hills, incinerating him, his mistress, and disfiguring the valet. The second came from Sheila Daily at Warner Brothers, who quickly released her hold on the book after two writers she'd hired terminated work on the project within days of one another, claiming their lives had gone into awful spirals since the adaptation began. Jo Freeling lost her twelve-year-old son to sudden, unstoppable pancreatic cancer, and Michael Kason developed a rare form of skin necrosis—a derivative of the flesh-eating bacteria you've likely heard about—which cost him three toes, half his left calf, and, as he told Ray from a hospital bed via Zoom, "That shit also took one of my balls and was headed for my dick, so you can keep your fucking psycho book. I'll not mention whatever I saw in the black glass of the microwave door every time I walked through my kitchen, but here's a pro tip, Ray: find your original manuscript and burn it."

That particularly juicy Hollywood story never saw the light of day, and for Ray it was fine the secret stayed unknown, as he had attempted his own screenplay adaptation but failure repeatedly slapped him down. It doesn't want to be watched, he'd said one night over cigars and bourbon. It wants to be experienced.

"Not that my writing matters now; all the computers are slagged." He shrugged and petted his cat. "Of course, all my canvases went up in flames, too. Now that I think about it, maybe *that* was the source of the scream. It wasn't the boards and the plumbing. Its soul was buried in the *work*, and when that went, oh God, the terror that seized its heart. See what I mean, David? Scattered to the wind."

"I think I get it," I said. "So—"

"Maybe my safe survived. The property deed, title, and all that is in there, but I'll wager that you wouldn't recognize a word if the paper's still intact. It's probably no longer in English, written in Aramaic at best, or some long-dead language from God knows where. Things changed over time there, you know. Did I tell you about the fireplace mantle? Over the years, the grain pattern transformed into eyes peering out from the swirls, galaxies turning in the knots, and lines connecting these features like an alchemist's astrological chart. The leather elbow pad set calls it *Pareidolia*, the sighting of order or images where it does not exist. I call it totally bananas, but true.

"As I wrote the book in that little den of mine; that room *never escaped winter*—and it took me seven months to write the manuscript. Get up any July morning, and it'll be ninety degrees by noon. But in my den it was perpetual January, pouring ass rain, the porch flooded, that nutjob fireplace going like hell. Renfield didn't know to shit or go blind, but he liked the cozy atmosphere, so he stayed with me. Janice was smart and kept a safe distance. And by that, I mean her sister's place in Chatsworth."

I hadn't heard that story. Impossible of course, but again, *he* believed it. Ray believed everything he made up about that house.

"Look, it's crazy, I know. But I tell you: something that shouldn't exist was in—no, *part of*—that property, and last night it got its ass kicked, and for all I know, the Machine network doesn't reach down this far to rescue it. So, good riddance to you, Fuckface Manor."

He took a pull of Balvenie and held it out to me. When I again refused, he swallowed and sang a line from an old Jim Croce song. "*If I could put time in a bottle...*"

I looked at the scratched leather bag, a shaving kit really, and back to him.

"I'm curious to see the photos."

"Then you'll definitely want a drink, buddy."

"I'm fine. You thought to snag these pictures instead of your manuscripts and canvases. That says something."

"Not pictures. *Transmissions from Elsewhere.*"

I nodded.

"Sure you got the stones? Perseus wisely chose not to eyeball Medusa, you know."

Ray's diatribes and accusations had become increasingly bizarre over the years, and by the time Janice left him for good and the story of the screenwriters reached my ears, I had become concerned for his state of mind.

When we spoke last night, my primary goal was getting him here, near the beach, away from those hills, his estrangement, and, of course, the relentless fire fanned by desert winds. Still, I *needed* to see the contents of that bag; I'd be able to tell if it was some type of Photoshop prank, crap grabbed from urban legend message boards, or whatever. Although he knew I did not see the world through his filter, warped and dark as it may be, my job was to listen.

And sometimes listening meant looking.

As much as I ached for him, a tug of suspicion had my sleeve. What if he took advantage of the wildfire and torched the house? Who the hell would investigate it?

No one. Crimes of opportunity walk hand in hand with disaster all the time. Looting is the lowest hanging fruit, but I'd wager murder rides the tide of almost every natural disaster. Law enforcement stretched to the brink. The chaos of lights out and phones down. The lure, for some, is too great.

*This tumor of a house*, he'd said.

So would Ray murder his house?

Like a broken woman returning to her abuser, Ray was a prisoner in a poisoned relationship. But for Ray, it was bent time and manipulation of will, stories of buried altars, and images from an ethereal plane. The harried history of his novel and the twists of life had been rough enough, but now his nemesis had been reduced to ashes, and with no one to fight, his mind spiraled for purchase.

"Let's go where the light's better," Ray said as he grabbed the bag and stood. He looked out the window to a sun red and angry, blasting its dragonfire through a grotesque canopy of incinerated trees and structures. "I can't have the shadow of that house on me."

*He's unraveling.*

"To the kitchen," I said, "and I'll feed you and Renfield."

***

Renfield was not impressed with the feeding spot I chose next to the sliding glass door. He jumped onto the counter, planted his ass next to the blender, and thumped his tail.

"He doesn't like windows," Ray said. "He knows what's out there."

I fed the cat, and Ray set his bag on the counter. He plopped onto a bar stool and swiveled around to me.

"Have at it."

The case was cold to the touch. I snatched my fingers away, surprising myself with a girlish, startled gasp.

"Oh yeah, sorry, didn't mention that. Kind of goes with the territory. Remember, it *fled* the Pleistocene, the goddamn Ice Age, so I imagine it was already witch-tit cold by the time that happened, eh?" He uncorked the bottle and filled his cheeks, swallowing hard and exhaling like a leaf blower.

Grimacing, I pulled the zipper. Frost, immediate and purposeful, eddied from the gap and pushed its way across the countertop.

"God almighty," I said.

"Not too late, David. No shame in looking away. But, I am curious if you see what I saw. Perhaps it's different for everyone, I don't know."

Fearing frostbite, I yanked the case open and removed the first thing my fingers lit upon, then dropped it to the counter with a hard *clack*. If it was a photograph it had either frozen solid or had been printed on the toughest damned paper imaginable.

The object, however, was a shard of wood, barely thick as that fake paneling my old man had used to nail up all over the house, but there, in the grain, an unmistakable image.

*Pareidolia?* True, I'd seen a sailboat in the clouds, a snarling face in the grille of a car, who hadn't...but never believed it anything other than illusion. But I saw a human-like figure in the bends of the wood grain, little more than a rim-lit silhouette, peering out from behind a curve in the pattern, a slight, slender hand wrapped around its edge as if rounding a corner. Its eyes, dark, true, *alive,* stared at me from...wherever. Sex I could not determine despite grim, bleached skin, lips yawning in either sorrow or emptiness. But inside the hollow of its mouth, hypnosis gathered, an abyss swarming with vertigo. Immediately overcome with that inexplicable weight one feels in dreams of pursuit, my bones felt like rusted pipe, my muscles bags of sand, yet downward momentum swelled through my body in a heady, relentless rush.

I fell. It spoke.

*The end is rebirth, smoke and bloody skies.*

"It's speaking."

"Damn Skippy, pal."

*We will all be shadowless in our last raving days.*

Ray snatched it from my hand and laid it face down on the counter. As the vertigo tapered off, my arms and shoulders prickled into chicken skin. I ran my hand through my hair and felt the slightest hint of frost. Flash-frozen sweat.

Ray said, "You'll never forget your first time, am I right?"

"Jesus, Ray, *what was that?*"

"Good thing you picked one of the lesser Speakers. Change your mind on that drink?"

Renfield looked up from his dish, eyed the frost oozing from the maw of the leather bag, and hightailed it to the bedroom. I waved the vapor away, and inside, the case lay crammed with a variety of items: a twist of sheet metal, a jagged tooth of glass, crinkled notebook paper, a split wine cork, aluminum foil, a cracked ceramic tile, even a tiny rodent skull.

I fished the cracked green tile from the bag, recognizing it from Ray's downstairs bathroom—a beautiful example of late 1920s Art Deco—but this tile's pattern of fissures was unique, not the fractal lightning-shaped scars that ordinarily occur; these were sweeping and elegant, dare I say approaching artistic. Organic? *Intentional.*

My attention narrowed into a dream grip, a vise not of pain but force of will. And within the galaxy of those cracks, one of *Them.* An awful thing, a split being conjoined at the base of the neck and jawline, emaciated and warped—retaining enough human countenance to turn my stomach—but with so much more happening beneath its shroud of flesh. A prehistoric knowledge dwelt in its eyes—three eyes, actually—as the center was a shared, wet, gelatinous thing housing a merged iris, a ghastly figure-eight shape, cell mitosis frozen in mid-spawn.

Its voice was not heard, it was *felt*, ringing in my skull like the subsonic concussion of a gunshot.

*The Nightworld cast us out, through the Gate. Speak now, the history of your ancient future sleeps in oblivion beneath the Sentinel mountains of the world.*

The entity burst into laughter as that shared center eye became a maelstrom, the dual iris a windstorm of dust and light, a womb of shadows. As the cyclone turned, the sadistic laughter throbbed rhythmic, mechanical. Something artificial prowled the center of that dark, dirty hole, powerful enough to squash the lunatic ravings of the Speaker.

*Whurrrmp-Fwack—Whurrrmp-Fwack*

"That's The Machine you hear." Ray's voice from a mile away, a man screaming across a chasm. He snatched my shoulder, and the haunted compound eye vanished, leaving me gawking at a green tile with curved cracks. But the reverberations of laughter morphing into that slurping, reciprocating sound remained tamed as a wave of nausea wormed through my body.

Sweat gathered at my chest and armpits and, like my hair a moment earlier, stiffened with brittle frost. I pushed back from the counter and looked at Ray, neck tendons tight as bridge cables as he contemplated another slug from the bottle.

"I feel ill," I said. "Dread."

"A front row seat in a witch's theatre," he breathed. "Ever notice the sinister always telegraph their intent? A law to which they are bound. A cosmic demand. One of the old rules I spoke about."

"No more, Ray. No more." I nodded toward the bag.

"You sound like that screenwriter in the hospital. I wonder how he's feeling these days."

"I'm serious, we should take it outside. Torch it like that house of yours."

"I only wish it was that easy. You've come so far, don't stop now. One more and you'll see their plan, the monstrous future they have in store. Nice to know the fate of the world is in the hands of lunatics never invited to the party, am I right?"

"Normal people rescue family photos from a burning house, and you chose *that*?" I pushed the tile to the floor. It didn't shatter. "What the hell were you thinking?"

"I told you I was their bitch, and in a way, the Speakers *are* my family now. They've shown me so much, and they want *you* to know, too."

"I don't think so."

Ray shrugged and continued as if I hadn't said anything.

"The substrate, or medium, I guess, doesn't matter, as you've figured out by now. Like I said, they aren't *really* photos in the traditional sense." He rummaged through that bag of winter and produced two pieces of Lucite held together by big, heavy screws. Between these blocks, an iridescence, a kaleidoscopic shimmer of a thousand colors.

He placed it so that it was backlit by the blood-hued, smoke-choked sun.

"I have to give them credit. Their approach is unique. I scraped this oily water out of Janice's old koi pond. Fun fact, David: the koi changed over time, like everything else in that place. Their eyes *moved*. I don't mean darting around in their little koi faces, no way, José. Their eyes moved to the *front* of their heads. Deep sockets, a weird scaly version of a brow ridge, the whole shebang. Evolution in play right under the kitchen window. One morning, they were just gone; a little trail of goo and a few arcane drawings on the flagstone were all that remained. Janice was clueless, of course—having lost interest in them the summer before—she assumed raccoons snagged them. Truth is the fish simply *left* and, in their way, spoke through symbols on stone. But the real story is in that water sample."

Some time during Ray's soliloquy, his voice dropped away and my eyes snapped to the Lucite blocks, the colors willed into motion by my attention. I don't know how I knew that, the thought simply came to me: *Acknowledgment is existence.*

Images bloomed in that oily iridescence, a hybrid of video and penny arcade picture show, a flickering tragedy played out in the micron-thin layer between the Lucite blocks.

I saw a mountain, a granite talon scratching a bruised sky. A hole opened at its base, excavated from within, belching millions of tons of debris like noxious factory smoke. The landscape froze in a blinding white blight wherever this ejecta touched it, plunging uncounted square miles instantly into the Ice Age.

"Sweet Jesus! Is that Everest? Denali?"

"Neither," Ray said. "The Eiger. Switzerland. Keep watching."

The sun plummeted, trailing a comet's tail of bloody fire. Upon impact behind the mountain, a discharge of energy eclipsing any nuclear holocaust wrapped the morning sky in a terrible sanguine blanket. Death had fallen to Earth, and from the world's darkest places, a horror resurrected.

Born of that open sore at the foot of The Eiger, limbs, crab-like, too many to mention. A flood of creatures the size of school busses swarmed just inside the lip of the hole, grotesqueries scrambling over one another, pulsating bags for bodies, eyes on stalks, glistening as if turned inside out. They waited, their excavation work done.

"They're called Harvesters," Ray whispered. "They tend to what's inside."

What followed wormed from the throat of the Eiger, pushing the Harvesters aside like an angry child. The creatures tumbled, limbs splayed, their sphincter mouths yawning open—until they crossed the threshold of the tunnel into the open air, where they became shimmering, watery outlines, mewling pods of refracted light skittering like a nest of spiders. Rendered invisible.

The colossus approached, mouth agape—*mouths* agape—pulverized earth tumbling, its flesh a sinewy network of greasy sores, each one fastened to a monstrous cable; bloody, dripping lengths, like those old photos of the first atomic bombs, but alive and hideous, bleached to albinism by centuries of subterranean blackness. It pushed through the opening, sending cracks and fissures crawling through the north face of The Eiger.

The mountain excreted its load, an unholiness dragging miles of apparatus, a snarl of giant pumps breathing life into membranous sacs. But unlike the Harvesters, this thing retained visibility. It bloomed, swelling into existence, a wretched butterfly wet from the cocoon, unfurling, *becoming*. Tethered to the Machine, the behemoth ached its way over the terrain, the hint of a limb here, the silhouette of a mammoth segmented leg there, slamming down to earth like a mighty ingot. The impression of a wing swept through a wall of upturned earth and ice, translucent and vile, an orgy of veins and arteries glistening in the glow of a suicidal sun. It kept coming, more mass, more Machine, an invalid chained to its life support system, yet free to roam the world.

The semblance of a head, a shape-shifting titan the size of an airliner, gazed upward as several mouths opened, some horrible with teeth, others throbbing with hairs. Gills hissed in the frozen atmosphere, the tender meat bristling with sputtering machine parts. Too hideous to behold, too marvelous to turn away, my eyes burned as I hadn't blinked in over a minute.

"The Shadowless Ones," Ray said.

Dear God in Heaven, it spoke:

ȸḩӪRƬ ÎƧ ƮĦʝΞ ĐƠɯƗƆĮŐƝ ŏ°F ИƎИ

I squeezed my eyes shut and slapped the blocks away. When I opened them, Ray stood with his back to me, watching the eastern sky. "And there's one convalescing beneath every great mountain on Earth."

Dumbstruck, I had little to say on the matter.

"I said the house wanted me to die with it. But now, watching the smoke, I think it had another plan entirely. Opportunity. Maybe the only way out was fire."

I shook my head.

"It is the smoke, you see? Now that it's been atomized, it'll spread. I was wrong. The fire liberated it. It didn't scream as it died; it screamed as it was *reborn*. And here I am, still nursemaid to its messengers. The Speakers, exiled in this bag, will follow the house wherever the winds take it, infecting the world with its cancer—starting with you. I'm so sorry, David."

I looked past Ray to a sky rife with hospice, its fate

sealed, the sun identical in hue as in that awful future prediction, bleeding fire as it plummeted behind The Eiger.

Hot desert wind pushed the smoke, and within it, that Goddamned house—the imminent darkness—toward the sea.

Toward us.

# Fire Escape

## Diana Olney

The band was still backstage, and the crowd was getting restless. The kind of restless that necessitated earplugs—not that any of the Off Ramp's inebriated patrons were wearing them. Within the freshly graffitied walls of the club, swells of tempestuous flesh churned beneath an empty stage, rocking to their own beat as they awaited the arrival of Fire Escape, the latest addition to the booming Seattle grunge scene. Yet even without the band's incendiary fanfare, the room was burning up, sweltering in the heat of so many fevered bodies that the ceiling itself was breaking into a sweat.

Mort took a final swig of Jack Daniel's as he approached the dressing room. At the bar, the party was in full swing, but for Fire Escape's thirsty front man, last call was coming early. Everything was riding on this performance, and if he didn't deliver, there'd be Hell to pay. Though between the sounds of rising bedlam and the spiking temperature, he couldn't help but wonder if he was already there.

*Chill, man. You've got this.*

Mort inhaled, drinking in the energy of the club. Even backstage, he could taste the violence in the air. And the cheap beer. The disgruntled rockers out there were more interested in chaos than entertainment, seething with the slurred bloodlust of drunken peasants swarming the gallows of a public execution. The opening band had bowed out early, thanks to a volley of curses and empty bottles—an occupational hazard they should have been better prepared for—and now, the mob was ready for seconds. But unlike their amateur-hour predecessors, Mort's band had a secret weapon, one that was guaranteed to win over the raucous crowd. In fact, they were about to become Fire Escape's biggest fans. They just didn't know it—yet.

Assuming the band actually made it onto the stage.

"Yo!" Mort hollered into the hall, searching for a sign of his miscreant bandmates, who were running more than fashionably late. "Let's get movin' guys!"

His request was met with a barrage of indecipherable expletives.

Mort scowled, balling his free hand into a fist. Not that he intended to use it. If last night hadn't taught these burnouts to get serious, nothing would.

"Ugh, dude..." a familiar voice groaned, filling the corridor with the somber tenor of Glenn, Fire Escape's guitar player, as he emerged from the dimly lit dressing room. "I don't think I can do this, man. I've been scrubbing all night, and I still can't get this shit out." He glanced down, cringing at the splashes of dark red detritus smeared across his flannel.

Mort gave Glenn—and his filthy shirt—a brusque once-over. "Just leave it, dude. No one is gonna notice. This is the *Off Ramp*, for fuck's sake," he spat, holding his temper between bared teeth. Granted, his guitarist did have a point: his attire was more Hitchcock than Jagger, from his blood-splattered flannel all the way down to his mud-encrusted Levi's—but wardrobe was last on Mort's list of Give a Shit's tonight.

Glenn was less than convinced. "Really? I dunno, man...this is pretty gnarly. You don't have anything I could wear?"

"*Dude.*" Mort raked a hand over his aching forehead, the site of a burgeoning migraine. "We don't have time to worry about *clothes*. The opener finished twenty minutes ago." He held up his whiskey, aiming the bottle at the stage door. "These bastards are out for *blood*."

"I guess they're in luck then," Glenn muttered, still eyeing his shirt.

"Don't be a smart-ass. Just get your gear, and let's *go*. And no flashy solos, got it? Stop trying to be Jerry Cantrell. It's not working. Sharing a dealer with the guy hasn't taught you any new tricks."

Glenn reeled back, shrinking in defense. "*Come on*, Mort. You know I'm trying to get clean."

*That's what they all say.*

Without a second thought, Mort grabbed his guitarist by the arm, zeroing in on the track-marks constellating his ghost-white skin. Most of Glenn's scars were faded, but not enough to paint even a sloppy picture of sobriety. Mort scoffed and stepped back, dropping his companion's lacerated limb like a bad habit. "Sorry, bud, but if we want to pull this off, we can't afford distractions. So, it's up to you—the Rock and Roll Hall of Fame, or smack in a gutter. Your pick."

Glenn threw his hands up in acquiescence. "Hall of Fame, man. All the fuckin' way."

\*\*\*

"You'd better get back here, Mort," a shaky voice called out from the dark depths of the dressing room, scraping through the hall like nails on a chalkboard. "Emergency band meeting!"

*Emergency, my ass.*

Mort shook his head. There wasn't time for cold feet. Or warm-ups, even. Not that warming up would make a difference for Static, his bassist/aspiring backup vocalist. Static wasn't his real name, of course, but there was a reason the nickname stuck. Three months of professional training, and he was still pitchy.

That, and he was always whining.

"Forget it, man!" The fuming singer threw his voice at top volume into the shadows, hoping one of them belonged to his target. "It's showtime!"

Glenn took a step toward the dressing room. "I'll deal with him," he murmured sullenly.

Mort sighed. "You'd better."

*We've only got one shot at this...and they're gonna blow it.*

As his guitar player shuffled into the distance, Mort looked down, staring longingly at the bottle in his hand.

*Screw it.*

He guzzled another shot of Jack, then tossed the near-empty bottle onto the floor. Whiskey rarely failed him, but right now, the monkey on his back was about to go rabid. Fortunately, Mort's DIY anger management program was a multi-step process. And step two was right in his back pocket.

He grabbed a cigarette and lit up, slipping into a cathartic cloud of tobacco. All vices carried a little virtue, if you knew where to look. And three drags in, Mort found his: a cool, clear head, haloed in a ring of smoke.

*Thank you, Marlboro.*

The singer sighed in relief, reminding himself that he had no need to panic. Or wage war with his band. Fire Escape had a penchant for doom and gloom—their first single, "Hell-Rager," was a dirge of dread-inducing tritones, the dissonant notes superstitious composers once called the "Devil's interval"—but this show wasn't a gimmick. Tonight was the real deal, the climactic second act in a performance for the dark lord himself. And that was a lot of pressure, even for Mort. Before last night, the closest he'd ever come to Devil worship was a graveyard party with some freaky goth chicks last year. A party that Beelzebub failed to attend.

*But he'll come through...*
*He's already been paid.*

That's what Mort assumed, anyway. To his knowledge, the ritual had gone according to plan, though truth be told, he had cut out a little early, before the ensuing splatter had a chance to stain his shirt—or his conscience. But that was his prerogative. He'd orchestrated every gory detail of the blood rites, so once his band started slashing up their sacrifice, Mort saw no reason to get his hands dirty. He was the frontman, after all, and every once in a while, it was important to remind them who was calling the shots. Or stabs.

His ex-drummer had just learned that the hard way.

*Tough luck, man.*

But Mort had no regrets. The sacrifice was a necessary evil—he knew it, and so did his band. His buddies may have been junkies, but Fire Escape was their life, and they all agreed that it was going to take more than another album shrink-wrapped in recycled heroin-chic to make their mark on the charts. Hence their choice to call in the demonic favors—the band needed a guarantee, and the way they saw it, a few pints of blood was fair trade for musical acclaim.

Mort checked his watch. His bandmates should have been back by now. He stepped forward, stomping his cigarette out on the floor.

"Hey!" he bellowed. "What's the hold up? You guys find new groupies and forget to share?"

No response.

Mort pressed on, marching to the melodic crunch of broken glass as he delved deeper into the dregs of the club. The place was a wreck; when he reached the dressing room, he nearly fell in the door, tripping on a heap of forgotten gear that looked like it had been there since the eighties. Grumbling under his breath, the aggrieved singer caught himself, first on a smashed-in amplifier, then again in the mirror on the adjacent wall. That, at least, was a pleasant surprise. Mort wasn't a classically handsome guy, but his reflection had all the makings of a rockstar—and an apex predator. He was dressed the part, naturally, his attire an ensemble of tailored shadow that would have made Alice Cooper's head turn. But in any performance, on or off stage, style was secondary, merely an accessory to the arsenal of his facial features. If looks could kill, Mort knew his would draw first blood. He was all jaw and hard angles, every expression pre-sharpened and ready to cut. Only his eyes betrayed a hint of softness, shifting from powder blue to a light seafoam green. But Mort wasn't about to go soft now. It was time to give his band a swift kick in the ass, courtesy of his new pair of Doc Martens.

Turning from the mirror, Mort called out again. Still no reply from his entourage. But it didn't matter. As he wormed his way through the mausoleum of abandoned amps and smashed bottles, the room answered for them.

The back door was open.

*Those assholes… Are they trying to bail?*

Mort passed through the doorway. Outside, the Seattle skyline was starting to clear. Above the parking lot, the glow of the moon partitioned the smog-choked horizon, illuminating the wet pavement like a spotlight on a midnight stage. And sure enough, there in the center of the theatrical haze stood his bandmates, encircling the van. Mort's anger management skills were of little use now. His fury was fully loaded—lock, stock, safety off.

"What the fuck is this, guys?"

Static leaped back, nearly dropping his cigarette. "Sorry, Mort," he whispered into the unraveling smokescreen. "But this whole thing is just too much. We've gotta call it."

Mort re-clenched his dominant fist. "Screw that! It's a full house out there. We're not calling shit."

"Dude, relax," Dodge, the new drummer, chimed in, though his feeble tone suggested he was a long way from relaxed himself. "We just came out here to get some air. We'll still play and everything, let's just cut the creepy bullshit."

"*Creepy bullshit?*" Mort growled, feral with indignation. Usually, he enjoyed Dodge's easy, docile company. He was neutral, like Switzerland, or Canada, and his eagerness to earn his keep in the group made up for the fact that his drumming was mediocre. But now, Dodge hadn't just crossed the line, he'd taken a piss on it. "You guys are just as invested in this as I am," the singer continued, lowering his voice to a gas-leak hiss of warning. "So, if you want to feel guilty, go ahead, but it's *way* too late to back out now."

Glenn crept forward, tentatively approaching Mort. "Look, man, there's something you don't know."

"Oh, yeah?"

"Yeah," Static echoed in agreement. But he couldn't face his infuriated leader. He stared down at the pavement, as if the courage he sought was at the bottom of the puddle at his feet. "We wanted to ask you…the, umm, instructions you got…from Vedder? What exactly did they say again? About the…you know…"

"You know *what, WILL*?" Mort snapped, reverting to his bassist's real name in all capitals.

"The…uhh…" Will, aka Static, looked up, shifting his gaze to Glenn.

"The sacrifice," the guitarist finished for him.

Mort rolled his eyes. "I never said I got *anything* from Vedder. So, stop asking—unless you want us to get our asses kicked." He stepped closer to the group, asserting his dominance. "The only instructions that matter are *mine*. Got it?"

Glenn held his ground. "Okay, well, we did what you said. You saw. You were there for…most of it. But we should have…" He gave Mort a pleading look, the moonlit gleam of his pale, bloodless countenance violently polarized by the dark red stains on his clothing. "We should have done it differently. Used a goat, or something."

"That wouldn't have *worked*," the singer retorted. "Remember?"

"Yeah, okay." Glenn heaved into a sigh. "But Dave didn't deserve that. He was a good dude…"

"He was a crap drummer," Mort reminded him.

Glenn shrugged. "Sure. Whatever. But that didn't make it easy."

"Maybe not. But the amount of dope you guys shoot should have."

"*Mort*—Jesus, man," Will interjected. We haven't touched that shit in months." As he finished his cigarette, his breath quivered, bursting from his lips in visible shudders. "But that doesn't matter right now, so just…just *listen* for a second, okay?"

"Alright." Mort caved, pity dulling the barbed edge of his anger. Will was shaking from head to toe, and for once, it wasn't withdrawals; the fear in his eyes reflected much more than the need to score. "What is it, man?"

"Well, we're just not a hundred percent sure that Dave…umm…" The bassist trailed off, glancing nervously at the rest of the band.

Glenn nodded his approval. "Go ahead, dude."

"Well, we're not sure that he…that he died. There's a chance he might still be alive."

\*\*\*

A chorus of primal howls surged through the Off Ramp as Fire Escape took the stage. The band had yet to play a single note, aside from a rushed soundcheck, but the clubgoers didn't care. Beneath the fading house lights, corkscrewed shadows rose and fell in entropic waves, limbs gnashing like teeth. The crowd was hungry.

*And so are we.*

Mort tore into the opening track, filling the room with the electric wail of his Fender. Then the drums kicked in, and the band behind him opened fire, launching an ear-piercing cannonade into the airwaves. That was his cue. As the spotlight flared, slow-cooking his skin, Mort grabbed the mic, breaking into a battle cry of raw, undiluted testosterone.

"Yeeeaaahhh-*ah-ah-ahhh!*"

His grand entrance complete, Mort slid back to his fretboard, pouring his ego into the tight spaces between the notes. But he couldn't seem to find his rhythm. Every amp in the house was cranked, yet somehow, he could still hear the whine of his neuroses, droning like feedback in the back of his head.

*What if it doesn't work...*

*It WILL.*

*But they said he wasn't dead.*

*They're just chickenshits. Of course, he's dead. You saw the blood. No one gets stabbed that many times and lives to tell about it.*

Or so he hoped. The ritual guaranteed a lifetime of success, but according to Mort's source, the sacrifice was non-negotiable. And given the number of platinum records the guy had under his belt, it was safe to say he knew what he was talking about. In the immortal words of the legend himself, "If you're gonna dance with the Devil, you've gotta get all your moves right." A tall order, but he was willing to give lessons—for a price.

The start-up cost was reasonable, as far as Faustian bargains went, invoking the trade of a triple-digit bar tab for a Satanic to-do list. It wasn't easy to read, thanks to the tell-tale stains running down the page, but fortunately, Mort's instructor was fluent in blood splatter. "You can't half-ass this shit," he'd insisted, murmuring between swigs of gut-rot whiskey. "So, just hacking up an animal won't cut it. And forget what you've heard about virgins. That's total bullshit. You need a symbolic offering, and it can't be just anyone... All the real rock legends were born from tragedy. And do you know why? Because greatness requires *sacrifice*. You get what I'm saying?"

Mort got it. The guy was cryptic, but his meaning was clear enough: if Fire Escape wanted a hit single, they would have to pay for it. With their own flesh and blood.

*Drummers are a dime a dozen anyway.*

\*\*\*

The singer's restless mind was back in sync by the start of the next song. "Cobweb King" was Mort's opus, and the crowd was hooked. While the rock fans raged, lapping at his heels, a susurrus of low whispers spilled from his lips, slipping into the mic like secrets into a lover's ear.

"*Walk* behind me. Your footsteps...fall empty."

"*Hard* as stone. Show me to the throne..."

It worked like a charm. As the melody surged, cascading from verse to chorus and back again, Mort let himself sink, following his band into the beating heart of the song. And he took his audience with him. Beneath the stage, the crowd swam, awash in streams of heady, Dionysian chords. They were drunk on the music, and for a few minutes, so was Mort. But by the time he reached the third verse, he sobered up. There was a storm gathering in the strings of his guitar, a fiery tempest that in a matter of seconds, would part the sweat-soaked sea below with an explosive solo written by the Devil himself.

"...where the kingdom *lies*. In a crown of thorns..."

"...secrets *hide*."

*NOW.*

Mort stepped back from the mic, his fingers flying down the neck of his Fender. Deep, thunderous notes soared into the crowd, unleashing an ancient refrain rarely heard by living ears. This was the final step in the ritual, the diabolic pièce de résistance that would bring the power of darkness into the light. Power that was ripe for the taking.

*HELL yes!*

But right in the middle of the last chord, the unthinkable occurred—Mort's hand slipped, torn from the fretboard as a violent shockwave burst from the strings. Then the room went dark.

*What the—*

Scattershot gasps and shouts erupted from beneath the stage, jetting like hot steam up from the floor. The audience was livid, clearly, but when Mort looked down, he couldn't make out a single face in the crowd. The walls of the club were washed in black, masking his fans in greyscale obscurity. But they wouldn't be his for long. Soon, they would forget all about him. The spell of the ritual was broken now, and without it, his dreams of stardom were lost, eclipsed by the dark dawn of every musician's worst nightmare: a mid-show power outage.

*"Fuck."*

Mort spun around, spitting a slew of additional curses between desperate calls to his bandmates. But it was no use. The blackout was ravenous, leaving no man behind. All that remained was the sound of mayhem, choking the room like a swarm of angry wasps. Noise came from every angle, crashes and scuffles and panicked, profane outbursts intertwining into one inseparable tangle of discord. The result was both disorienting and disheartening. Mort was center stage at a sold-out show, yet suddenly, he felt completely alone, adrift on the tide of insatiable shadows swallowing the club.

Until one of them spoke.

"Hey, man. Nice set."

A stunned silence fell over Mort, pricking his nerves with warning. The greeting was friendly, on paper, but the voice behind it wasn't. It was sharp and grating, a slivered hiss honed with such deliberation, it sliced through the surrounding cacophony, sliding like a needle straight into Mort's ear.

"I dig that new song," the voice continued, edging closer. "But I know someone who could play it better."

Then, it laughed.

The startled singer leaped back, recoiling from the baying laughter as if it were a spray of bullets. The voice's bark was even worse than its bite, a sensory attack serrated by the kind of subversive malice that in his experience usually led to a black eye or a loss of teeth. Slowly, he curled a hand around the neck of his Fender, clinging to his only weapon like a lifeline.

Mort never got the chance for a rebuttal—Hell literally broke loose before he could raise a fist. The Off Ramp had never ended a show early, but it was clear the party was over when the stage started to shiver, echoing the arrhythmic vibrato of the singer's frantic pulse. Then, like the metastasis of a cancer, the shiver began to spread, rolling through the club in a scale of mounting distention until the darkness itself was stretched to the gills.

Mort tensed and tightened his grip on his guitar, bracing himself against the sudden spike in air pressure. Around him, the room was holding its breath, suppressing an inclement terror too heavy to be contained. And half a heartbeat later, that terror burst free, dissecting the swollen shadows with whip-cracks of light that rose like an electrical storm from below the stage. But the power hadn't come back. Mort knew that, as well as he knew the hermetic knot of dread that was coiled like a serpent around his heart. This wasn't a storm, or an earthquake, or an electrical surge. This was something else, something infernal, the spark of a conflagration that had been burning for centuries—right underneath his feet.

Mort wasn't sure what had become of his mystery heckler, nor did he care. He had much bigger problems, as did everyone else in the club. The light, which had been sporadic at first, was heating up like a stovetop burner, forming a fluorescent ring in the center of the room. The glare was painfully bright, yet Mort couldn't look away. It was as if he was watching the climax of a movie, glued to the edge of his seat in a chamber of horrors too terrifying to walk out of. Even when the next scene leaped into fast-forward. Mort froze in the front row while smoke bloomed black as death and the floor split into spiderweb fissures smoldering with hot neon, holding the horrified crowd as captive as he was. But it didn't hold for long. Just as the glare between the cracks came to a boil, the concrete shattered like a pane of glass, leaving a gaping hole in its wake.

Then, as if on cue, the hole burst into flames.

There weren't many survivors. Not that Mort tried to recruit any. That would have been suicide. He'd seen some wild pyrotechnics in his day, but this was no parlor trick. This was biblical fire and brimstone, the real Old Testament kind. And he had invited it here, pouring his own hot-blooded hubris like gasoline onto a funeral pyre.

But Mort's offering wasn't enough. The flames were hungry, and they demanded to be fed. As panic tore through the crowd, driving herds of human cattle toward the door, the blaze followed, lashing at the stampede with molten tongues. The collective scent of sweat and fear and burning flesh was a nauseating miasma of an olfactory cocktail, even for Mort, who before starting his first band, once worked on the killing floor of a slaughterhouse in Eastern Washington. For tonight's livestock, the survival rate was almost as bad, too. A lucky few made it to the exit, but for the bulk of the group, doom was inevitable, lighting up bodies like wicks of wind-torn candles before dragging the whole screaming vigil into the lake of fire below.

Except for one unwelcome guest.

The second the hand hit his shoulder, Mort knew it didn't belong to any of his friends. The appendage was ice cold, digits stiff and frost-burnt, like meat left too long in the back of a freezer. The singer shivered, chilled to the bone despite his proximity to the flames. Then he pivoted, turning to face his assailant, and in that splinter of an instant, Mort's neuroses were torn, divided in a snap assessment of which was worse: the gaping Hell-mouth at his feet, or the sinister saw-toothed grin of the man who put it there. The man who was supposed to be dead.

"Sorry to crash the party, bro," Dave whispered, dropping his hand. Between his lips, something twitched, slithering worm-like between the clamp of tar-black teeth.

Mort sputtered and staggered back, stifling the urge to vomit onto the waking nightmare standing before him. His ex-drummer looked like shit—even more so than usual. A true devotee of the grunge movement, Dave habitually forsook most forms of hygiene, including showers, shaves, and antiperspirant. But the unwashed, unclean, un-*dead* thing currently stinking up the stage was a multi-sense offender, a walking ode to filth and decay that made George A. Romero's work look like family entertainment. But that wasn't what scared Mort. What scared him was the smile his ghoulish companion was wearing, the smile that in spite of its owner's septic state, kept on spreading, stretching so impossibly wide, it was as if an invisible knife was carving the gash of a grin into his face.

"What's wrong, Mort? Can't take the heat?" Dave sneered. His eyes flickered, mirroring the flames.

Mort was still too stunned to scream. Or move. Or speak. His bandmates, on the other hand, had no trouble breaking the silence.

*"What the Hell?"* Static's jagged tenor tore across the stage, scraping an octave higher than he'd ever attempted in back-up vocals.

"Is that…" A second voice followed, harmonizing in clarion terror. *"DAVE?!"*

"In the flesh," Dave declared. His grin crept up even higher, nearly splitting his face.

Mort looked over his shoulder, watching Glenn and Static slink out from the recesses of the side-stage sound booth. Seeing their leader in peril, the two rushed to Mort's aid, stopping only when they got close enough to catch a whiff of Dave.

"What the—" Glenn grimaced, his expression twisting into a tortured medley of shock and disgust. "What the *fuck* are you doing here?"

Cocking his head at a near horizontal angle, Dave regarded the trio with mock disapproval, as if they were schoolkids who had just flunked a pop quiz for the second time. He rolled his eyes haughtily, pupils trailing into yellow clouds that were probably cataracts but looked more like piss stains. "Oh, Glenn. Are you really that dense?" he taunted. "You dipshits were the ones who *invited* me. Hell, I've even got a backstage pass."

*Backstage…*

Mort clenched his jaw, sinking his teeth into an idea.

Discreetly, the singer turned to his band—minus one member, who had yet to be accounted for—and nodded subtly toward the side of the stage. The main exit was out of the question, but if they were quick, they could make a run for the back door. Unfortunately, Mort and company weren't quick enough. Dave's sunken eyes saw everything, including their escape route. But he didn't say a word. Apparently, he didn't need to. As he followed Mort's gaze, the ceiling above the hall collapsed like a cartoon-style cave-in, spilling its insulated innards with a bone-rattling avalanche of TNT.

Dave let out a sulfuric sigh, satisfied with his work. "You guys weren't gonna skip the encore, were yah? You know that's not fair to the fans."

The band exchanged horrified looks. There was no backup plan. None of this had been part of the deal, if there even was one.

Mort turned to the inferno that was growing ever closer to the stage, then across the room, surveying the club's single window. Outside, there was no sign of rescue, no lights or sirens or booming megaphones seeking survivors. He wasn't surprised; he had a sneaking suspicion that when help came, it would arrive moments too late. He frowned and lit a cigarette—his second to last one.

Mort took a long drag. Then, in an act of knee-jerk desperation, he extended the near-empty pack to his ex-drummer. A flimsy peace offering, but an offering, nonetheless.

"Smoke?"

Dave reached out, but only to knock the pack from Mort's hand. "Thanks—but no fuckin' thanks. That's not even my brand. Not that you ever gave a shit," he said, glaring as his former leader stooped to retrieve the fallen Marlboros. "In fact, I bet you still don't even know my full name. You sure as shit didn't put it on the album credits."

Mort wrinkled his brow. He could neither confirm nor deny the accuracy of that statement.

"Dude," Glenn, always a team player no matter the risk, chimed in. "We're...*sorry*." He winced, as if the word had stung him on the way out. "For everything. Really."

"*Sure,* you are. I was always a has-been to you," Dave snarled, grin fraying at the edges. "Just another deadbeat drummer you could stab in the back." He leered, sizing up the group through a slivered stare. "Over and over again."

Mort stepped back, averting his gaze. His companions followed suit, shrinking behind him.

"You can't hide from me," Dave scoffed. "I know everything. I heard your whispers. Your plans. Your secret meetings. You would have cut me out...one way or another. Even if that *hack* hadn't put the blade in your hands. But I've got news for you, assholes." He inhaled sharply, and the curl of a lip hooked his signature sneer back into place. "You think drummers are expendable? Well, think again."

The band froze. Dave snapped his fingers, then proceeded to flip them the middle one. And just like that, the offending finger went up in flames.

But Dave didn't scream. Instead, he laughed, convulsing with maniacal howls as he blew out the immolated digit like a candle on a birthday cake.

Across the stage, Dodge, Dave's successor, finally crawled out from behind his drum kit. From his lips, came the only word befitting the mood of the room, "*Fuck...*"

"Yes, you are fucked." Dave smirked. "And on the first date, no less."

*So much for the Hall of Fame.*

Mort looked somberly to his bandmates. "This is all my fault. I should have listened..."

"But you get an A for effort!" Dave interjected. "I've gotta hand it to you guys—that ritual was *hardcore*." He glanced down, eyeing the tableau of angry wounds carved into his chest. "And you almost pulled it off—*almost*."

"Look man," Static pleaded. "We can still fix this. We...we'd be happy to have you back in the band. Dodge wasn't that good, anyway."

"Yeah..." Dodge nodded. "I can bail...no hard feelings."

Dave whirled, staring daggers into his replacement. "It's too late for *feelings*, bro. You shitheads broke the deal. And now, you're going to pay."

*Like Hell we are.*

Mort glowered. At his side, sparks flew, rekindling the rage in his veins.

"But hey, look on the bright side!" the demonic drummer declared. "Fire Escape is about to go on tour. And from what I hear, it's almost sold out!"

Dave turned and raised his arms, limbs held aloft in a parody of martyrdom as he stood with his back to the conflagration. In response, the fire rose behind him, shadowing his silhouette in a curtain of crimson flame. If Mort had been a God-fearing man, he would have dropped to his knees right then, praying to all the merciful deities he could name.

But he wasn't. And he didn't.

He did something worse. Something blasphemous, an offense to the only division of faith he'd ever truly believed in.

Rock 'n roll.

Mort didn't feel good about it. At all. But from where he was standing, he didn't see a better option. With a heavy sigh, he reached for the guitar tethered to his waist and unhooked the strap, releasing his instrument. Then he gripped his two-month-old Fender Mustang by the neck and hiked it into the air, aiming right for Dave's head.

It should have been an easy win. Mort struck without hesitation, letting his predatory instincts run wild. Yet somehow, his weapon never made contact. Not with its target, at least. It did, however, find its way to the floor—courtesy of his vindictive ex-bandmate.

"I can't believe you bought this hipster piece of shit!" Dave exclaimed, slamming Mort's beloved Fender into the concrete. Its neck broke instantly, snapping like a twig on impact. "A Mustang—*really* Mort? Who do you think you are? Kurt-fucking-*Cobain*?"

*No.*

Mort had *never once* thought that. Certain strung-out musicians reveled in the deconstruction of their instruments, but to Fire Escape's devout front man, the Fender wasn't just an instrument. It was a friend. A friend he had dreamt of since he was fifteen years old, fumbling through "Smoke on the Water" on an off-brand thrift shop acoustic. A friend that was supposed to take him to the top, to stick by him on every treacherous step of the Stairway to Hard Rock Heaven. A friend that now, thanks to one sick, twisted, talentless drummer, wouldn't even get a proper burial.

*Unless I bury him first.*

Temper flaring high as the adjacent inferno, Mort donned his grief like armor, flesh bristling with righteous fury as he charged back into battle. Little did he know, fate had just upped the stakes. He started out strong, putting a hefty dent in Dave's deceptively decrepit façade, but Mort's bravado was no match for the power of Hell— power that had given his enemy both the stamina and disposition of a comic book villain. Laughing hysterically, Dave brought the hapless singer to his knees, forcing him to bow before the altar of fire. Mort tried to resist, commanding his battered bones to rise, but to no avail. His skeleton crew had a new master now, and when Dave's iron fist came back down, he folded like a house of cards, muscle and marrow and hot-blooded rock-n-roll gusto poised to stage-dive straight into a sea of flames.

*There'd better be some hot groupies down—*

"Step off, man!" Dodge cried, interrupting Mort's inner monologue. A percussive crash followed, punctuating the outburst with the assault of an airborne snare drum.

But nothing could surprise Dave. When the projectile came his way, he didn't even flinch. Nor did he lose track of his captive. Grinding a steel-toed boot into Mort's spine, Dave caught the drum in mid-air and cast it right back, taking down his rival without missing a beat.

From the back of the stage, an agonized groan hung in the air, wavering like a white flag.

"Nice try," Dave snapped. Then he burst into laughter—*again.*

For Mort, that laugh was the last straw. A barbed, snaking straw that had taken root inside his skull like a parasite and was giving him a bloody, screaming juggernaut of a migraine. Someone had to shut Dave up, and since the rest of his band was afraid to act, he'd have to take the lead. But Mort didn't mind. Deep down, he always knew he'd go solo eventually. That was the way all rock stars went out, and if this was truly his last song, he'd be damned if he was going to let a *drummer* sing back-up.

*Show's over, asshole.*

Tensing against the heel in his back, the fallen front man breathed in, inhaling the unfiltered heat of the Off Ramp. For most singers, the lack of airflow would have been a problem, but Mort wasn't just a vocalist; he was a smoker, a two-pack-a-day Marlboro man with lungs as black as the smoldering ashpit around him. And he always sang best after a smoke break. So, he took another hit from the blaze, then spit it back out, lighting a pitch-perfect fire under his tone-deaf drummer's ass.

*"FUUUUUCK YOUUUUU!"*

His audience was not entertained. Side-stepping off Mort's crumpled frame, Dave gave the singer a swift kick in the ribs, knocking the wind out of his solo. But this time, he didn't fight. Not for long, anyway. His ego resisted, at first, yet after accruing a few more wounds, Mort began to realize that he was only delaying the inevitable. The fire was spreading, rapidly closing in on his bandmates, but suddenly, he knew who it was really after. And it wasn't going to stop until it had him.

\*\*\*

In hindsight, Mort should have put it together sooner. Even while he swung, and missed, and bruised, and bled, over and over again, the truth was staring straight at him, reflected like a mirror in the lambent glow of the blaze. And the truth was that there was no escape—not for him, at least. His band, on the other hand, still stood a chance. A chance not just to escape, but to thrive, to climb even higher than the rising flames. All he had to do was give them a leg up—on his way down.

*Greatness requires sacrifice.*

Granted, his friends didn't know that yet. In an explosive display of eleventh-hour valor, they were fighting tooth and nail, discharging a fusillade of fists and musical artillery that had yet to make an impact on the battle. But Mort knew they'd come around eventually. Maybe one day, they'd even thank him, praising him as Fire Escape's musical messiah in the glossy pages of *Rolling Stone* and *Entertainment Weekly.* Hell, maybe that was how it was always meant to be. After all, Mort was about to make a comeback of his own. Eternity was waiting, and it was a full house tonight, packed wall-to-wall with screaming fans. There was only one problem: he was going to have to share the spotlight.

"You know… that solo wasn't too bad. But you're a little rusty, bud," Dave sneered, grin stretching Glasgow-wide as he raised his offering over the flames. In his grip, the tendons of Mort's neck pulled taut as piano wire, straining against a chokehold forged from rigor mortis. "I think it's time for a warm-up."

Mort bit his tongue, resisting the urge to snap. Not an easy task. His head had taken such a beating, he was literally seeing red. When he blinked, blood rained down from his wounds in rivers, pooling in the periphery of his vision until all he could see was the decrepit face of his enemy, floating like a twisted archipelago of flesh and teeth in a scarlet sea. Mort shook his head vigorously, attempting to clear his vision and splattering his captor in the process. Dave found that hilarious, as he did most things, but even if he'd had more gas in the tank, Mort couldn't do much better. His hands were bound—with the same gore-stained rope he'd used to restrain his drummer last night, which he supposed was only fitting. He'd given Dave the upper hand the moment he bailed on the ritual, and now that very same hand was preparing to drop him.

Mort couldn't let that happen. Not until he found a way to turn his ticket to Hell into a two-for-one.

Tilting his head back to staunch the bleeding, he peered over Dave's shoulder to his bandmates, who had just run out of ammo—even Glenn's Gibson lay in ruins, yet another sacrifice that didn't make the cut—but still had a surplus of shock and awe. He was tempted to try to signal them, but that would have been a fool's errand. Even if he could communicate without tipping off Dave, he knew his comrades wouldn't go for it. They had their shortcomings, but they were loyal. Far too loyal to do what needed to be done. So, Mort finally gave in, turning to the same clichéd, last-ditch petition of all desperate sinners:

Prayer.

He didn't care who was listening—God, the Devil, Zeus, Hades, a vengeful, many-tentacled-Lovecraftian-man-eater. Anyone was welcome to step in. Or reach out. As a matter of fact, if a zombified arm were to burst forth from the underworld right now and grab ahold of his decomposing drummer, that would have solved all his problems.

But that seemed like a lot to ask for, especially for someone who had never been to church, except on the occasional misguided bender. So, Mort stuck to the basics.

*Please...*

*Something…anything…*
*Please…*
And lo and behold, his prayers were answered.

\*\*\*

Mort may have been a sinner, but he knew a miracle when he saw one. And it was beautiful, curving in a brilliant, gilded arc around the stage. The flames had Dave surrounded, both above and below, but they weren't about to give him a halo. They had something better in store. Directly over his head, the blaze had taken the ceiling, and once it burned through the rafters, there would be nothing left to hold up the steel scaffolding of the stage lights. Ironic, given its target's affinity for theatrics. Like a hammer of poetic justice, the metal beams would fall, forcing the vainglorious drummer to take his final bow.

The aforementioned drummer, however, saw none of this. He was too busy gloating, milking his presumed victory for all it was worth. Behind his shit-eating grin, Mort could see him salivating, joy and decay bubbling in brackish clots between his teeth. And no matter how many bad jokes he told, he still hungered for more.

"You hangin' in there, dude?" he jeered, digging his fingers into Mort's neck.

Mort grimaced. He knew he should play along—realistically, he would be singing covers in Perdition already, had Dave not been so desperate for an audience—but if he didn't spit out a few drops of the venom that was flooding his tongue, he'd choke before he even got there.

"Go. To. *Hell.*"

As if a little venom would inhibit Dave.

"Been there, done that," the undead drummer declared, soaking it all up. "You can try to keep the Devil down…" he added, snickering under his breath, "but he always comes back."

"I suppose that's true," Mort admitted, changing his tune. "Because the Devil…he's the oldest legend we've got, right? And legends never die," he mused, holding his captor's attention as he shot a pointed look across the stage and onto the fearful faces waiting in the wings. It was time to say farewell to his friends. And they were *good friends*, despite all his complaining. The trio hesitated, at first, but like any band worth a damn, they knew how to follow a cue. As their eyes met, Glenn gave Mort a slow, solemn nod, then led his companions out of the blast zone, guiding them into the shadow of a tower of amplifiers.

Remarkably, Dave didn't catch on. Still beaming, he leaned forward, dangling his quarry playfully over the edge of the stage. Then, just for kicks, he loosened his grip, watching Mort squirm as the flames seethed at his feet. "Well, he *is* dying…" he chortled impishly, "to meet you! He might even help you with that new song!"

Mort hoped so. His music would live on, if the band did their part, but even with a Hail Mary, he was still fucked. Six-hundred-and-sixty-six ways to every foreseeable Sunday. That was the deal: as a relatively wise man once said, all the real rock legends were born from tragedy. And honestly, Mort could think of nothing more tragic than an eternity spent in the company of his ex-drummer.

On the bright side, he'd have plenty of time to work on the next album.

"I could be down for that. But…" the singer retorted, raising his voice over the tell-tale crackle of burning wood. "There's one thing you're forgetting."

Dave cocked his head, and his smile slanted in tandem, tilting with the shifting gravity of its owner's axis. "What's that?"

Before Mort could reply, a sudden crack rang out from above, lashing like a whip through the room. Dave reeled, half-turning in a frantic corkscrew and nearly losing his victim in the process. Around them, smoke billowed, lowering a dense, black curtain onto the stage. But the grand finale wasn't over yet. As Mort swayed, pendulum-swinging inches from his doom, he lifted his gaze, scanning the smog-choked ceiling. And sure enough, there it was: a sharp, silver gleam of steel, jutting like a blade through the backdraft. The rest of the framework was impossible to see, but there was no question where the closest beam was headed. Any second now, the flames would devour the remaining rafters, and a hundred-plus pounds of heavy metal would come crashing down, returning the damned to Hell.

Now it was Mort's turn to smile. "*You're* not a legend," he hissed, giving Dave his best Fuck-You smirk. "You're just a deadbeat drummer, remember?"

Dave didn't argue. Finally at a loss for words, he gaped in horror, embers of epiphany lighting up his soulless eyes like the Fourth of July. Even as the smoke thickened, churning in dark, ominous clouds above him, the drummer saw what was coming. But for once, he had no comment.

"And guess what?" Mort laughed as the clouds parted, dropping a guillotine onto his adversary. "Drummers are a dime a dozen."

# The Man from the Woods

## Devin Cabrera

The skies seemed to open up as Katie made her way home.

Rain poured against her windshield and her wipers struggled to keep up.

To make things worse, her vehicle seemed to be losing power as she drove.

Her old car had been through its fair share of storms, but she feared this might be the one to put her car to rest.

"Come on girl, just a few more miles," she said, patting the dashboard of her car.

Her car seemed to respond, but not in the way that she had hoped.

Smoke poured from the engine compartment, making her already blurred view of the road just about impossible to see.

"Fuck!" she shouted to no one in particular.

She pulled over into the nearest driveway she could find, which just happened to be a short dirt road that ended at a clearing in the woods.

Her car lumbered to a stop, blowing smoke like a pothead on April 20th.

Katie checked her phone, but the storm must have knocked out a tower—there was no signal to be had. She was going to have to figure this one out on her own.

Cursing to herself, she pulled the lever next to her seat which disengaged the lock from the hood, then she ran out into the rain and pulled it open.

Katie brushed away the smoke with her hand and took a look at the engine.

Yup, that's an engine, she thought. She had no clue what she was looking at and had no idea where to begin looking to fix anything.

She heard a noise in the bushes behind her.

She jumped and spun around, leaning back on the car in the process.

"Ow!" she yelled as her butt touched something hot.

Now I did it, she thought. *Now the bear or moose or whatever is in the woods is gonna come eat me.*

She waited in fear as the bushes parted and a man stepped forth.

Katie was frozen in place, feeling like she would have rather seen a bear. She was alone in the woods with a random man and had no way to call for help. Her mind ran through all the possible ways this could go wrong.

The man stopped on the outskirts of the clearing, staring at Katie. He noticed the car smoking behind her.

"Could I take a look at that for you?" he asked.

Katie hesitated before replying. The guy didn't look crazy, but he was also soaking wet in the middle of the woods. But what choice did she have?

"Um, go right ahead. I don't think you'll be able to fix it though. She's really old and should probably be put out to pasture soon."

The man moved forward, and Katie stepped back, putting some distance between them.

The man seemed to notice, but didn't take offence.

He bent under the hood of the car, inspecting the engine below.

While he was occupied, Katie reached into the pocket on the side of her door, checking to make sure her pepper spray was still there.

Her hands clasped around its smooth, round shape, and she let out a breath of relief. If things should take a turn for the worse, she felt better knowing that she had a weapon readily available to defend herself.

Katie glanced at the man while he worked, taking in his impressive figure. He really wasn't that bad looking. He was tall, with a closely trimmed beard that barely hid a sharp jawline. Katie couldn't help but notice how his wet clothes clung to his muscles.

Katie took a few steps closer, examining what he was doing.

The man took a cloth out of his pocket and wiped down one of the belts, then stood up to admire his work.

He turned to face Katie, who failed to hide the fact that she was checking him out.

"You can go and start it up," he said.

She did as she was told, making her way into the driver's seat before putting the key in the ignition and turning.

The engine flared to life.

"Give it a few revs," he said.

She did so and was relieved when no smoke appeared from under the hood. If anything, it appeared to be running better than usual.

The man closed the hood, and Katie got out of the car to thank him.

"It was just a wet belt," he said. "Sometimes cars may kick up some water and the belt will just slide right off. This is a temporary fix. You may have to get your timing looked at when you get the chance."

"I can't thank you enough Mr….," Katie said, waiting for the man to fill in the blank.

The man hesitated for a moment before offering up his name.

"Riley. Benjamin Riley."

"Is there any way I could repay you, Benjamin?" Katie asked.

Benjamin looked back at the woods.

"Anyway you could give me a ride to the nearest motel?"

"I could do that," Katie said.

Benjamin got into the car beside her, and that's when she noticed the blood.

"Oh, you're bleeding!" Katie said.

She pointed at his arm, where there appeared to be four long scratches dripping with red fluid.

Benjamin looked down at his arm, then brought out the cloth from his pocket to stanch the bleeding.

"It's not too bad," he said. "I must have walked into a branch while I was in the woods."

Just then, a loud clap of thunder brought Katie back to reality, and she knew they needed to move before they got stuck again.

\*\*\*

Katie pulled in to the parking lot of the Havarest Motel just as a bolt of lightning lit up the sky above them.

"I guess this is my stop," Benjamin said.

He reached for the handle to get out, but Katie stopped him.

He looked back at her, and she pointed at a neon sign on the office window.

It said *no vacancy.*

"Everyone must have come here to get out of the storm," Katie said. "I'll tell you what. If you promise me that you're not a serial killer, we can go back to my place and wait out the storm there. By tomorrow you should be able to go wherever you need to go."

"Oh, I couldn't impose," he said.

"It's the least I can do since you fixed my car. Without you, I would probably still be stranded in the woods with a broken down car."

Thunder clapped overhead as another beam of lightning zapped across the sky.

Benjamin looked at the storm above, then relented.

"If you insist."

Katie pulled into her driveway.

"Welcome to my humble abode," she said.

Benjamin got out of the car, staring up at her house. Then he looked back as if he were checking out the surroundings, or looking for something.

"What a wonderful place you have out here," he said.

"It's a one-bedroom, so I hope you're okay with crashing on the couch," Katie said.

The two made their way inside, where Katie gave the man a pair of clothes left behind by an old boyfriend of hers.

They both went into separate rooms and changed into dry clothes. Katie finished first, and she went up to the bathroom he was in, planning on asking him if he wanted a drink.

When she got there, she found that the door was open just a crack.

She put her fist up to the door to knock, but hesitated.

Through the crack, she could see Benjamin putting his shirt on, and she couldn't help but notice the impressive set of abs he had underneath it.

She was still staring when he opened the door, and she took a step back, trying to compose herself.

"Um, I was just going to ask if you preferred red or white wine," Katie said, looking down at the floor to avoid meeting his gaze.

"I'm a fan of red myself," he said.

Katie made a beeline for the kitchen, eager to get out of that situation.

They both took a seat on the couch, wine glass in hand as the storm raged on outside.

The lights flickered above as a rumble of thunder shook the house. It looked like it was going to be a long night.

"Something has been bothering me this whole time," Katie said. "What were you doing in the woods when you found me?"

The man nearly choked on his drink. He looked like he was trying to formulate his words carefully before he said them.

A man who thinks before he talks, what a change, Katie thought.

"I was hiking on a trail nearby," he said.

"Oh, you're a hiker?" Katie asked.

"Not really," Benjamin said. "I'm not much of a hiker, but I needed to think about some things, so I started walking on the trail. Pretty soon it began to rain and I lost sight of the path. I was beginning to think I would die out there of hypothermia when I heard your car. If you hadn't shown up when you did, I would probably be dead by now."

The two talked for a little while, laughing and drinking until they were red in the face.

Finally, Katie looked at the time.

"Oof, it's late. I don't want to keep you up," she said.

She chugged the rest of her wine glass and stood up, going into a closet nearby and producing a set of blankets and an extra pillow.

"I couldn't thank you enough for your hospitality," he said, taking the blankets from her and beginning to set up a place for himself on the couch.

"It was my pleasure," Katie said. "After the day I had, I needed a night like this."

Katie left Benjamin to make his bed and walked into her own room, shutting the door behind her. She turned on the TV as she got ready for bed, changing the channels until she got to the news station.

She wanted to check to see if there were any updates on the storm, on when it would be over and if there were any roads washed away that she needed to know about. She didn't think she would mind being stuck in the house with the man for another day.

A commercial came on where a mother was filling a minivan with what seemed like an entire soccer team, and Katie took this as her cue to brush her teeth. She came out a moment later, toothbrush in hand with a mouthful of toothpaste.

The news was back to its regularly scheduled programming, and a red banner at the bottom of the screen read, "Breaking News."

Katie took a seat on the edge of her bed as she brushed her teeth, eager to find out what was happening.

The camera panned to a man sitting behind a desk, the local anchorman whose name was Bob Fields.

"We are just getting word that a body has been found along River Road this evening."

Katie stopped brushing. Hadn't she been on River Road today?

The picture changed, and suddenly Katie was watching from a bird's eye view as a cameraman in a helicopter circled the spot where they had found the body.

Katie recognized it as the clearing where she had pulled in earlier with her car.

"We are now going to Jim Thurston who is live at the scene. Good evening, Jim," Bob said.

The screen split, with one side showing Bob behind his desk, and the other showing a man in a yellow raincoat holding a microphone.

There was a delay as Jim received the signal from the studio and began to talk.

"Good evening, Bob!" Jim yelled into the microphone, trying to be heard over the rain coming down around him.

"Could you tell us a little more about the scene on the ground?" Bob asked.

Once again, there was a delay before Jim replied.

"It appears that earlier this morning, a man drove his car into this clearing behind me," Jim said.

He backed away, allowing the camera to get a full view of the scene behind him.

The screen showed the little dirt road Katie had driven down only a few hours before, except now it looked almost unrecognizable. The area was swarming with police cars, and officers dotted the scene.

As she watched, an officer began to unravel a length of police tape across the road, effectively blocking off the area from the public while they collected evidence.

"Is there any news about the body that they found?" Bob asked.

"Yes. According to the police chief who I spoke with earlier, the body of a woman was found beaten to death in the trunk of a car hidden behind some trees along the edge of the clearing. The police say that the person who'd parked the vehicle there had then doused the car with gasoline, as if he intended to set it on fire. Police say that something must have happened, which caused the suspect to refrain from setting the car ablaze. It may have been the torrential rainfall at the time or something else. Excuse me," Jim said, making his way over to the police chief who was attempting to walk past the reporter without being seen.

The camera didn't follow Jim. Instead, it seemed fixed on one spot, facing the road going into the clearing. As Jim spoke to the police chief, a group of medics rolled a stretcher underneath the yellow tape.

Atop the stretcher was a human-sized mound underneath a white sheet. The sheet wasn't exactly hiding the body from anyone, as the heavy rainfall was making the sheet stick to the body as well as making it see-through in the process.

Katie could make out the blood stains on the sheet, and the dark marks on the woman's skin, visible even through the fabric.

The medics hit a bump in the dirt road with the stretcher, just as it was crossing the line of sight of the camera, and Katie looked on in horror as a pale white arm fell from beneath the sheet. At first she thought the arm was covered in tattoos, but then she realized it was bruises, and she had to look away.

Had she imagined it, or was there blood under the woman's fingernails?

Katie remembered that Benjamin had four scratch marks on his arm, and he had brushed it off as something that had happened when he walked into a tree branch in the woods.

The screen changed, going back to Bob sitting behind his desk.

"We apologize for the graphic imagery you have seen here tonight folks. We do advise that anyone uncomfortable with violent imagery change the channel at this time," Bob said, warning the public a little too late.

"I'm getting word that Jim is back on the scene. Jim?" Bob asked.

The screen split between the two again, and Jim was once more standing in front of the camera.

"Hi, Bob. I was just debriefed on the situation by the police chief. He said that witnesses had seen another car enter the clearing shortly after the first, and that a man had been seen driving away in the passenger seat of that vehicle. We do not know at this time if the second car is in cahoots with the man or not, but we want to warn the public that the man is to be considered dangerous. The police have extracted a name from the registration of the first car, and it was last registered to a man named Raymond Taggart."

Katie breathed a small sigh of relief. The man she had picked up was named Benjamin Riley, though she then realized that he could have given her a false name.

"I'm getting word that our news team has pulled up a picture of the suspect at large, and the image will soon appear on the screen," Jim said.

Katie held her breath. What happened next could alter her life as she knew it. Had she invited a murderer into her home? Or was there a chance that she had picked up some random hiker in the middle of the woods?

Even though she knew that the chances were very slim, she felt stupid trying to be an optimist in this situation.

Still, nothing could have prepared her for what happened next.

An image popped onto the screen, and Katie's toothbrush fell to the floor.

It hit the ground with a clatter, and Katie bent down to pick it up, then listened to see if the man in the other room had heard the commotion. She didn't hear anything from the other side of the door, and she didn't know if that was a good thing or not. Even so, she turned down the TV so the man wouldn't hear it.

On the screen was a picture of the man who had killed his wife earlier that day. It was also the man she had picked up that evening.

It took everything inside her not to scream. She knew nothing would come of it, and she lived too far away from the nearest neighbor for anyone to hear her. Katie knew she needed to think through her next few moves. She needed to call for help, or find some way out of the house. The problem was that her house was built on an embankment, meaning that the front of it was one story and the back was two stories.

Katie wouldn't be able to escape through her bedroom window without potentially breaking her neck. The only way out was through the front door, which was in the living room where the man was currently.

Maybe he was asleep already and she would be able to sneak past him.

She slunk over to her bedroom door as quietly as she could, then with bated breath, she turned the doorknob as slowly as possible.

Katie eased the door open just a crack.

From her spot at the door, she could see the living room couch.

The man was standing over it, gently placing the blanket down in a position where he could comfortably lay on it.

Katie gently closed the door, careful to not make a sound, then she pressed her back against it as she thought about her next move.

I could call the cops and wait for them to come and take him away, she thought, piping up at the thought of not having to leave the room and see his face again.

Katie walked over to her purse and dug out her phone.

The screen lit up and she was dismayed to see that she still didn't have any service. *The storm must have really done a number on the cell towers.*

Katie looked around, spotting the landline on the bedside table.

It was days like this when she was glad she hadn't removed the thing yet.

Katie walked over to the phone, picked it up, and dialed 911. She pressed the phone to her ear and her face dropped, realizing that all she heard was a dial tone.

The landline was out of service, as well.

Had a tree fallen across one of the nearby telephone cables? Or had the man in the living room cut her phone lines?

Katie shook her head. She didn't need to think about the logistics of options that wouldn't work at this moment, she needed to think of a new plan. The only way out of her situation at this point would be to escape through the front door and go get help.

Katie walked back over to the door, taking a deep breath as she slowly opened it once again. She prayed that the man would be asleep by now, and was hoping that the wine had taken effect.

She opened the door slowly, looking out into the living room.

But the man wasn't there.

The couch was empty.

Katie's heart dropped. She turned around, for some reason expecting him to be standing behind her. Thankfully the space behind her was unoccupied, but it left her wondering where he could be. She opened her bedroom door a little wider and noticed that the light was on underneath the bathroom door.

She saw her chance and decided to take it.

Katie tiptoed across the living room, feeling her heart rate increase to the point where she felt like it would jump right out of her chest. She didn't want to take the time to put her shoes on, so she picked them up from where she had left them near the door. Katie grabbed the keys hanging by the door, closing her fingers around them tightly to prevent any noise from escaping.

Katie glanced back at the bathroom door once again, making sure that the light was still on.

Then she made a break for it.

Katie threw the door open and ran outside, her bare feet splashing on the wet earth below.

She raced down the front steps to her car, fumbling with her keys as she did so. She kept looking back at the front door to see if she was being followed, and because of this, she accidentally dropped the keys.

Katie scrambled around barefoot in the dark, in the pouring rain, trying to find her keys on the ground.

A searing pain arced through her foot as she stepped on the keys. She screamed.

She had found her keys.

Katie picked up the keys and ran over to the car door, unlocking it with a press of her key fob.

*He heard me. He definitely heard me.*

Katie nearly yanked the handle off the door as she pulled it open and jumped inside, slamming it shut and locking the doors. She threw her shoes into the passenger seat before gripping onto the steering wheel.

Katie stared up at her living room window, expecting the man to show up and come after her. She could barely see the window, whether it was because of the rain pouring down her windshield or from the tears blurring her vision, she didn't know. All she could do was cry tears of relief that she was able to get out of that house alive.

Katie looked into the mirror as she fumbled with her keys, trying to get her car key into the ignition. In her haste, she dropped the keys again.

"Fuck!" Katie shouted, then bent down to pick it up. She brushed around with her hand in the dark, not wanting to turn on the light above her head.

Her fingers touched dirt, leaves, and some loose french fries which had fallen below her seat. Finally, her hands closed around her keys, and she breathed a sigh of relief.

Katie sat up, and this time she calmly inserted the keys into the ignition and started the car.

The headlights sprung to life. The light reflected off the house and illuminated a face in the mirror that she was hoping she would never see again.

There was a figure in the seat behind her.

"Going somewhere?"

# A Promise for Rosa Lee

Naching T. Kassa

The room smelled of oxygen and death.

I sat beside the hospital bed and somehow managed a smile. Mama, white-haired and wizened, gazed up at me. She seemed so much smaller, swaddled in the blankets. So fragile, hooked to the machines.

My brother, Ron, sat across from me. Twice in my life, I'd seen him cry. This made for a third. Looking into his face, I finally understood why they called it a broken heart.

I took Mama's hand and squeezed it gently. This had come so quickly, too quickly. Wasn't there a way to turn back time? Or, at least, to freeze it in place?

"I'm so glad you came, honey," Mama said. "I've missed you so much."

Guilt drove a razor-sharp rapier into my chest, and I swallowed, unable to speak. Why had I stayed away? The question rang out within my mind, but I already knew the answer. It was to avoid moments like this. I wanted to remember Mama as the strong and vital woman she'd been. Not the woman confined to a hospital bed, too weak to move.

The words seemed like a lie, but I said them anyway. "I came as soon as I could, Mama."

"I'm glad you did. I have to tell you something...about your mother—your real mother."

My heartbeat quickened. Mama had never spoken of my birth parents, not even when I'd begged her to. They'd remained a mystery for most of my life.

"Ron, would you bring me my purse, honey?"

My big brother rose and retrieved a leather bag from a small closet. He opened it and set it on the bed, just within Mama's reach. She rummaged in it with one hand and withdrew a little box wrapped in brown paper.

"Julie, I want you to take this. No, no, don't unwrap it. It's for your mother if you ever see her again. She'll try to contact you...once I'm gone."

I bit my lip to keep the tears from falling and turned the little box over in my hands. Something rattled inside.

"I was there when you were born, my girl. Born with the cord wrapped round your neck, clinging to life. One moment longer, and you would've been dead. They cut it off, and they handed you to me. From that moment, you were mine. I wasn't about to give you back." She lay back against the pillow. "Your mother...she didn't want you then. But I knew one day, down the line, she'd change her mind. If she comes for you, Julie, give her..."

She turned to me. Her eyes had lost their focus and, like a candle, the life within them flickered. She clutched at my wrist. "Promise me you'll give her what's in that box. Promise me."

"I will, Mama."

She lay back, and Ron took her hand.

"I love you both. The boy who issued from me and the girl who's still my blood. I love you..."

Her strength faded, but still, she held on. We didn't know she'd gone until the last breath left her lips.

***

The world blurred after Mama died. Ron and I became sleepwalkers as we carried out her wishes. We didn't wake until we'd slipped into Ron's car on Parking level A. As the shock slowly slid from our minds, the tears came.

Sometime later, Ron started the car, and we left the hospital. When we reached the highway, and the asphalt rushed on beneath us, I finally found the courage to ask my questions.

"Did Mama know my…my…"

"Your birth mother?" Ron said in his bass-baritone. "Yeah. She knew her. About as well as anyone could. I guess I knew her, too."

"You did?"

"I was nine when you were born. Maybe other people forget what it's like when you're little, but I don't." He glanced at me, and his face grew grim. "Mama tried to tell you in the best way she knew how, but she still couldn't get it out. I suppose it's up to me to finish it. You weren't a stranger's child, Julie. You're blood. Your mother was Mama's sister."

My head spun and shock threatened to veil my eyes once more. "Mama had a sister?"

"Her name was Rosa Lee, Rosa Lee Henry after she married. But Joe Henry wasn't your father, Julie. Mama didn't want me to tell you, but I think you should know. Your father was Jake Tappert, and he was put to death for killing Joe Henry. He died three months after you were born."

The secrets that came spilling out of Ron as we drove stunned me into silence.

"Rosa Lee was always a bad one but, after she had you, she just got worse. I think it drove her a little crazy. She tried to take you once, but Mama wouldn't let her. She chased old Rosa Lee off and she never came back."

We pulled into the driveway of Mama's house. The manufactured home stood silent and lonely, like a lantern without a flame. Ron pulled up beside the door and turned to me.

"Mama may have wanted you to make peace with Rosa Lee, but I don't think you should. Stay away from her, Julie. Far away. That woman is a witch. A *real* witch. She doesn't love you and she never will."

I remained silent for many minutes, listening only to the humming of the engine and the beat of my heart. Ron bit his lip, then reached out and clasped both of my small hands in his.

"I'm sorry, Julie. I shouldn't have told you the way I did. But I've never liked secrets, and I didn't want to keep these any longer than I had to."

"It's alright. I understand."

He glanced up at the house. "There'll be a lot to do in the next week. We'll have to plan the funeral. And we'll have to talk about the will."

"We don't have to do it today, do we?"

"No. Not today."

He shifted in his seat, sorrow creeping into his face once more. "Is it okay if I drop you here? I…I have to go to the grocery store and get some dinner. It'll just be a few minutes."

"Of course. You go ahead."

"You sure now? I won't leave you alone if—"

"Ron, I'm not twelve anymore. I've been to college. I can handle myself."

"Sorry. Every time I look at you, I still see that skinny girl in braids. Sometimes it's hard to see the change in people."

"I know what you mean. But I'll be alright. Really." I stepped out of the car. "See you in a few."

He nodded and pulled out of the drive. I watched him

go and then hurried into the house.

Cold darkness greeted me. The house had become an empty void in Mama's absence. I entered the bedroom, which had once been mine, and fell upon the bed. My cell phone buzzed to life when I turned it on. The text message I'd received a few hours before Mama's death remained unanswered.

I hadn't recognized the number. I didn't know how the caller had gotten mine. Maybe Mama had given it to her.

Guilt stabbed my heart once more. I didn't want to keep this secret from Ron, but after he'd revealed how he felt about her, I felt I had no choice.

I read the message for the third time:

JULIA, MY NAME IS ROSA LEE HENRY. I'M YOUR MOTHER.

I KNOW I HAVEN'T BEEN A GOOD ONE. I KNOW THEY HAVEN'T TOLD YOU ABOUT ME.

I'M ONLY ASKING FOR A CHANCE. WILL YOU MEET WITH ME?

I read the message a fourth time and then a fifth. Finally, I messaged her back.

WHERE?

A minute later, she answered.

DO YOU KNOW THE OLD PIONEER GRAVEYARD? MY SISTER AND I PLAYED THERE AS CHILDREN. MEET ME THERE AT NOON TOMORROW. WE'LL HAVE A PICNIC.

My fingers hovered over the screen as my stomach became one large knot. *A picnic? In a graveyard?* I crossed my legs and stared at the words on the screen. Why there? Why not in a diner or a fast food place? I wasn't asking for much. Certainly not a five-star restaurant.

And then, it came to me. Maybe this cemetery had been a special place, special to her and to Mama.

At last, I answered.

Ok.

She followed my response with a heart.

I started to type in a new message, telling her Mama had died, but decided against it. It didn't seem right telling her in a text. She should hear the words firsthand.

I tossed the phone aside and reached into my pocket to withdraw the box Mama had given me. It rattled in my hands as I unwrapped it. A crystal on a silver chain lay inside. Mama had worn it for years. I held it up to the light, and it swung before me. Within the crystal lay something small and pink. A memory flowed into my mind.

I had been eight, sitting on Mama's lap in the kitchen. She'd been baking bread and the room smelled of it. Sunlight shone through the window and gleamed in the crystal about her neck.

"What is it, Mama?" I asked. "Whatcha got in there?"

"It's a charm. For good luck."

"It's lucky?"

"It is now. It wasn't when you were born."

"Why?"

"Because, back then, it was wrapped about your neck."

"It's bad then."

She shook her head. "No, now it's good. I turned it into something good."

"How?"

"Magic."

"What kind of magic?"

She squeezed me. "Love."

"Love isn't magic."

"Love is the best kind of magic. Love can save you and protect you. Even from beyond the grave."

I took a breath. The question I needed to ask wouldn't

please her. "Mama, is my mother…my *real* mother, is she dead?"

Mama frowned. "No."

"Does she love me?"

She didn't answer.

"If I had your necklace, would she love me?"

Mama squeezed me tighter, so tight I couldn't breathe. "You don't fret about such things, Julie. As long as I'm here, you'll always be loved."

"But what if you're not here? Can I have your necklace? Just in case?"

She smiled. It seemed brighter than a kitchen full of sunshine. "I'll give it to you later. When you're older."

I rubbed my thumb across the crystal, a sudden bitterness cleaving my soul. Mama wanted me to give it to Rosa Lee. Made me promise to do it. Why she wanted to give it to a sister she didn't love instead of me was more than I could fathom. The childish part of me wanted to keep it.

Another memory flowed in then, one I wasn't particularly proud of. I was five at the time, dressed in a little yellow dress and braids, my hands on my hips, screaming at Mama. She stood before me in the kitchen, peeling potatoes, her lower lip a thin and bloodless line.

"You can't tell me what to do!" I screeched. "You're not my real mother!"

She turned, and I thought she might paddle my butt, the way she had before. But she didn't. She just stared at me, her eyes brimming with tears. It was the only time I ever saw her cry.

I returned the crystal to its box.

\*\*\*

It wasn't hard to get away at noon. Ron had made an appointment with the funeral home for that time, and I'd complained of a splitting headache. He'd left without me.

The graveyard wasn't far from Mama's house, maybe a mile or less. I'd considered inviting Rosa Lee over, but I knew Ron wouldn't like it.

The sun had burned off the morning fog and left a brilliant blue sky in its wake. The world seemed so different from yesterday. It didn't seem fair that it should move forward when Mama could no longer enjoy it.

I strolled along, the little box clattering in my jacket pocket, my thoughts drifting to my birth mother. For years, I'd wondered what I could have done to make her hate me. What the reason was for giving me up. Now, I thought I had some inkling. I was the daughter of the man who'd murdered her husband.

Was she an innocent in all of this? Or did she play a part in her husband's death? Ron seemed to think so. Was he right?

Perhaps she had changed. Wanted to make amends. Ron didn't believe people could change, but I did. I would give her a chance and allow her to explain.

A few minutes before noon, I arrived at the graveyard. No one waited outside the gate. No cars stood in the parking lot.

I pulled out my phone and messaged Rosa Lee's number.

WHERE ARE YOU?

The answer came after a thirty-second wait.

BY YOUR GRANDMA'S GRAVE.

I pocketed my phone and set out on the path.

The pines whispered around me, and shadows pooled at the base of their trunks. Theirs was the only sound. No bird lifted its voice in song here.

293

Tombstones leaned in odd directions, as though the occupants of the graves had pushed them up from beneath. I hurried on before my imagination got the best of me.

Sunshine warmed my back as I climbed the hill which led to my grandmother's grave. I halted when I reached the top and glanced about. A large elm cast its shadow over my grandma's stone. No one stood near it.

"Hello?" I called. "Rosa Lee?"

The chime on my phone sounded, announcing an incoming message. I checked the screen.

By the tree.

A cloud passed over the sun, and the shadows in the graveyard lengthened. One seemed to slither over the mound near Grandma's grave. When the sun returned, it vanished.

Rosa Lee was nowhere to be found. Was she hiding? Why couldn't she just come out and see me? Was she afraid?

As a child, I had often fantasized about the day I would meet my mother. I thought she might cry and hold me, hold me so tightly that I could never escape her grasp. She would love me always and we would never be apart again.

As a teen, in full rebellion against Mama, this fantasy became part of my daily life. Whenever Mama did something I considered unfair, I thought about running away to find my *real* mother. I thought of her, and what she might look like. And how she would smile when I told her I was her daughter.

And now Mama was gone. My world had shattered like so much glass and all I wanted was for Rosa Lee to hold me and call me her own.

I approached the tree as the sun continued to play hide and seek with the clouds. A woman leaned against the trunk. She wore a dark sweater, her dark hair trailing down her back. A purse lay on its side nearby. The contents had tumbled out. Her cell phone had fallen near the mound. I picked it up. The last message Rosa Lee had sent me was displayed on the screen.

"Rosa Lee?" I whispered. "Are you Rosa Lee?"

The woman didn't answer. I reached out to touch her shoulder.

The most famous scene in *Psycho* came to me then. And for a moment, I was Vera Miles, reaching for Mrs. Bates. The scene replayed over and over in my mind, until I withdrew my hand. I left the woman as she was.

The sun, which had secreted itself behind a cloud, now reappeared. Something glinted in the grass before me, something buried in the dirt. I peered at it, trying to figure out what it was. It resembled a human eye.

I halted, studying it. Perhaps, someone had lost a button, or part of a favorite toy. I leaned forward just as the eye blinked.

A voice in the back of my mind warned me that I should run, that I shouldn't stop until I reached Mama's house. But my feet wouldn't obey me, no matter how hard I commanded. It was as though they no longer served me.

The earth around the eye rose and crumbled under my gaze. Skeletal fingers pushed through the soil, followed by arms sleeved in torn, white silk. The skull came next, crowned by stringy black hair. As the skeleton rose from the dirt, the woman leaning against the tree fell over and faced the sky. Never have I seen such terror frozen upon the features of the dead.

"Yes," the skeleton said, its voice not unlike sandpaper rubbing stone. "I am Rosa Lee."

My shriek died in my throat and, like the most horrific of dreams, I found I could make no sound. I couldn't express my terror nor alert anyone to it. I simply stood there, staring into that malevolent eye.

My heart thundered in my chest as my birth mother

advanced upon me. Bony fingers reached for my hair and pushed it back from my eyes.

"Do you know how long I've waited for this moment?" Rosa Lee cried. "At last, I'm reunited with my baby." She laughed, the sound grating on my ears.

With a tremendous effort, I wrenched my gaze from that terrible eye and turned to run. Unfortunately, my foot caught on something and I fell, sprawling into the grass. When I tried to scramble up, the same thing which had tripped me, held me tight. I turned, and this time, nothing hampered my scream.

The corpse had caught me by the ankle and no matter how I kicked, it wouldn't let me go. The phone I thought was Rosa Lee's went flying. It slid across the grass, far out of reach. The corpse used my body to drag itself forward. It reached my shoulders. It stared into my face.

"Look at you," the corpse whispered. "There's nothing special about you. Yet, my sister chose you over me."

I shook my head, unable to speak. The thing pinned me to the ground by my wrists.

"I was going to spill your lifeblood upon the altar the moment you were born and offer you as sacrifice to my Lord. But she stole you away and hid you from me. Worse still, when I finally found you, she murdered me and buried me in the ground by the grave of our mother. She sought to protect you, but I knew I need only bide my time. I knew she would die someday and when she did, I would be there to take my baby back."

I whimpered. She seemed to savor the sound.

"My Lord will accept your sacrifice gladly. He has promised me life eternal in exchange for you."

Rosa Lee leaned over me and opened her maw. It smelled of dirt and decay. A tongue, long and black, slid out toward my left eye.

"Tell me you love your mama," Rosa Lee crooned. "Tell me before I leech the life from your body."

I forced the words out. They felt like ice upon my tongue. "M-Mama...M-Mama made me promise."

"Promise what?"

"T-To give you this. In my pocket."

Rosa Lee rifled through my jacket pockets. The cold she radiated was like nothing I'd ever felt. It sapped me of my strength, my will. She pulled the box out and opened it. The crystal fell into her boney hand.

The moment it touched her, the crystal burst. Something long, pink and sinuous grew from within the shards. It pulsated and swayed like the tentacles of some eldritch beast, then wrapped itself around Rosa Lee. The cord which had nearly killed me at birth, splintered and crunched the bones within its grip.

"Julia, stop this!" Rosa Lee cried. "Stop it at once!"

I dragged myself away from her, the warmth returning to my limbs.

"Julia!" she screeched. "Listen to me! Do as I say!"

"No."

"Julia!"

"You're not my real mother," I whispered.

She screamed again. And kept screaming, as the cord ground her to dust.

# Mount Chocorua

John Durgin

"You sure about this, Andy?"

Andy Kraus stood at the base of Mount Chocorua, surrounded by the majestic White Mountains, with tears in his eyes. After three months in rehab and a lot of time to reflect on what led him there, he was ready to heal. He turned to face his best friend, Sean Layne.

"Yeah. One of the things we talk about in recovery is a way to mend, to overcome."

Andy and his ex-wife, Lidia, had lost their eight-year-old son, Brett, to brain cancer a year ago. Instead of being there for her, he reverted to self-pity mode, drinking away his sorrows. He'd always had issues with drinking, but before Brett's death, he could fool most people. *Most* people. Lidia knew it was an issue, always trying to force him to get help before things got out of hand. It led to many arguments and fights, and that was *before* the cancer diagnosis. After they received that news, it was a complete downward spiral.

"Brett always wanted to hike and camp in this part of the White Mountains," Andy continued. "It was something he begged to do after he was diagnosed. But I... I was too fucked up to care. This is for him as much as it is for me, you know?"

What he didn't tell Sean was that his doctor was concerned about early signs of alcoholic cardiomyopathy. He'd told Andy to take it easy early on in recovery until they were able to do more tests. But that wasn't going to stop this trip; Andy had to do it. For him. For his son.

"I gotcha, man. You know I'm always gonna support you no matter what. Same with Amanda, right, hon?"

Behind them, the car trunk slammed shut. Sean's wife walked up to them carrying her hiking pack.

"Always. Hey, you guys sure we can park here overnight? Last thing I want is to come back down tomorrow and find our car gone."

"There was nothing on the website for the trails saying we couldn't," Sean stated and shrugged.

"Well, let's get a move on, shall we? Almost four thousand feet of beauty awaits us." Amanda smiled.

"Agreed," Sean said. "If we want to make it to the top and set up camp before dark, we need to get moving. Most of the tourists should be descending the mountain at this point, so we'll have peace and quiet."

"Okay. You guys get started without me. I'll be right behind. Just want to double-check and make sure I didn't forget anything," Andy said.

The couple gave one another an uncomfortable look but knew not to question him. They were here to support him and carry out the plan of camping at the peak of Mount Chocorua to honor his son. When they approached the trail, Andy walked around the side of the car. He kneeled and unzipped his backpack. Placed carefully inside was a bag of items that reminded him of his son. He removed a family picture taken when they had been happy and cherished every moment together.

The pristine White Mountains created the perfect backdrop to his son's amazing smile, so excited to go hiking during the fall foliage season. Lidia stood off to the side in the photo, leaning in with a smile that still warmed Andy's heart. Even after all they'd been through leading to the divorce, he still loved her. He put the picture in his pocket and grabbed the next item: Brett's necklace, which the boy wore every day after their first hike, all the way up until the last few painful months of his life in the hospital.

They'd found a small bone at the base of the mountain, and Brett begged them to keep it. Lidia had been disgusted, not wanting her son to touch it and catch some disease.

*All that worry for nothing, babe.*

Andy convinced her it would be fine, that they'd clean it up when they got home and make something cool for Brett. Now holding it in his hand, he fought back tears at the memory of placing the necklace over Brett's head for the first time, seeing how happy it made the boy. After moving to New Hampshire from Massachusetts in late summer, that hike was their first family adventure. They had only gone on one of the smaller trails, worried his little legs couldn't make it too far. Brett pleaded to keep going, wanting to reach the top.

Andy put the necklace in his pocket with the picture.

Lastly, he made sure his Baclofen pills were in the bag. Even though he no longer craved a drink, at least not on a regular basis, his doctor wanted him to take the pills to keep the obsession at bay. It wasn't perfect, but he realized early on that the medication helped. Lord knew how being at the top of the mountain without his son would make him feel, what he'd crave. Andy ensured that the baggie was sealed and put it in his backpack. After taking a deep breath, he headed for the trail, ready to overcome the pain that had been consuming him for months.

\*\*\*

They'd been hiking narrow granite paths and climbing steep embankments for over an hour. The scenery was stunning, and Andy couldn't help but feel a tinge of guilt that his son wasn't there to see it with him. Trees as far as he could see, so small in the distance that they resembled tips of spiky hair on top of an enormous head. Breathtaking waterfalls brought a relaxing ambience as they marched on. The sun had started its descent behind the mountain's peak, filling the forest with a radiant orange and pink backdrop.

"Let's stop for a sec. I need a few pics of this," Amanda said between heavy breaths.

She took out her cell phone and walked to the ledge, careful not to get so close she could slip to a sure death. Sean walked up and slapped Andy on the shoulder.

"How you feeling, pal?"

"I knew this wouldn't be easy, but it's fucking hard. *Real* hard. When we hiked the area before he got sick, Brett begged us to go to the top. Lidia and I got into a fight over me drinking the night before and she didn't want to go any farther. She demanded we turn around, gave Brett some made-up excuse for why we had to go, and said we'd come back another time."

"Well, you can't beat yourself up too much, man. People make mistakes. What matters now is that you're trying to make up for that," Sean said. And by the look in his eyes, Andy knew his friend wasn't sure if his effort was helping or not, so Andy decided to let it be.

"Yeah…"

"Do you know the history of this place? Where it got its name?" Sean asked.

Andy raised his brow, unaware of any local lore, and shook his head.

"Seriously? I forgot you didn't grow up around here. Well, you might not have let your boy come up here once you knew the truth."

"What the hell are you talking about, man?"

"Get this. Apparently, back in the 1700s, a Native American chief named Chocorua lived in the area surrounding these mountains. Most of his tribe had moved on when the settlers came, but he'd decided to stay. There are many versions of the story, but the one I heard most growing up said he became friends with a family of settlers with the last name Campbell. They got so close, in fact, that when the chief had to leave to attend business elsewhere, he felt comfortable enough to leave his young son with the family.

"Well, while he was gone, the camp supposedly had a fox that wouldn't leave them alone. Night after night, it came and killed their livestock. Don't ask me how people know all these details, but they do. Anyway, Mr. Campbell decided enough was enough. He set poison traps for the fox, ready to get rid of it once and for all. Only he forgot to take care of the bottle that contained the poison, and when they went to bed that night, the chief's son thought it was a drink and accidentally killed himself. They say he turned purple and had veins branching out all over his skin, and they found him the next morning dead with his hands frozen around his throat like he was trying to dig something out—"

"Are you fucking serious, Sean?" Amanda scolded as she came back from the ledge. "Andy's here trying to get over his own kid's death and you tell him a story about another kid dying! What the hell's wrong with you?"

"I—"

"Don't be an idiot."

"No, it's okay, really. What happened after that?" Andy asked, intrigued by the story as they resumed their climb up the mountain.

"So, Chocorua returns from his trip while Mr. Campbell—Cornelius was his name—was away. When the chief found out what had happened to his son, he lost his damn mind, supposedly killing Campbell's entire family. Once Cornelius discovered what the chief had done, he and a group of settlers chased him up these mountains for hours. Eventually, Chocorua had nowhere to go. They cornered him at the summit, where the famous ridge towers over the mountain. There are conflicting stories on whether he jumped off the ledge himself or if he was pushed by Campbell. But one thing all the versions say is that Chief Chocorua cursed the land before he died. That he wished 'The Evil One' upon them to bring death to their cattle and said the wolves would fatten on their bones..." Sean paused when he saw the smirk on Andy's face.

"Please tell me how they would know this much detail about what someone said almost three hundred years ago," Andy said. "Seems a bit like a drawn-out game of telephone if you ask me."

"Believe what you want, man. All I know is that there have been countless reports of strange occurrences over the years. Cattle died, plagued by an unknown disease. Bad things happened to people who lived around the mountain. And even to this day, it's said that you can hear voices whispering between the trees. That you can hear the screams of the dead who are stuck here—"

"Okay, that's enough. I let you go on long enough with this crap, Sean. Andy's just being polite listening to this stuff. Let's lighten the mood," Amanda insisted.

"You're quite the expert on the history of this place, huh?" Andy remarked.

"Hey man, try growing up out here in the middle of nowhere. Nothing better to do than pass the time telling ghost stories."

Andy shook his head and laughed at the tale. He assumed the legend had to be at least somewhat true, considering the mountain was named after the chief.

They trekked up the next section of the rocky trail. Individual stones placed three feet apart formed a makeshift path up the steep embankment. It was exhausting, but Andy found it cathartic. He took in the scenery once more, realizing the sun was now completely behind the trees but forcing its rays through the branches to create random lines of UV spotlights.

*Brett would love this.*

His focus shifted from the landscape to the story Sean had told him moments ago. In a way, he felt he had something in common with Chocorua: both lost their sons to something out of their control, and both wanted to seek revenge on those responsible.

*Except while Chocorua had the Campbell family to blame, who can you really hold responsible for Brett getting cancer? God? Family genetics? Maybe the additives in all the food kids eat these days?*

It didn't matter. While the chief killed those responsible for his son's death, all Andy *killed* was his marriage and any ounce of self-respect he had left. The guilt was something he needed to get over, or at least try to. Otherwise, the bottle would always be waiting right around the corner, calling his name.

After a few miles of strenuous rock climbing where the massive stones sloped at close to a forty-five-degree angle, the terrain transitioned back to a dirt path now entering the heart of the forest. Even though the trail wasn't quite four thousand feet, the paths elevated so quickly that it proved just as difficult as a much higher mountain would.

Andy was thankful his friends offered to tag along and camp in an area that wasn't exactly allowed. While there were a few adjacent campgrounds, such as Camp Penacook, he wanted to camp near the summit.

Technically, fires weren't permitted in the area, but after everything he'd been through the past year, he was willing to take the chance.

Amanda stopped and looked off to the side of the trail toward the woods. "The summit isn't too far ahead. I'm thinking maybe we should set up camp off the path here a bit, just in case any hikers are still out and about heading down the mountain. Plus, it's a bald summit, so there won't be any places to make camp up top. What do you guys say?"

Sean nodded. "Yeah, this seems like a good spot where we can find enough cover to remain hidden but be close enough to make it to the summit and back quickly. Andy?"

Andy looked to the woods off the path, then back toward the direction of the mountaintop. It would have to do. "Yeah, sure. Thank you, guys, again for doing this with me. I know it might seem like a strange request, to go camping in a place we aren't supposed to and all. It's just—"

"No need to explain, man. We get it. Brett wanted to camp out here. I'm proud of you for facing your demons. You're a hell of a lot stronger than I'd be in that spot."

"You're damn right," Amanda agreed.

"Hey! You see what she thinks of me? Unbelievable," Sean frowned in exaggeration.

They left the trail and entered the thicker portion of the forest. Andy wasn't sure where they'd even be able to set up a tent. Fingers crossed there would be an opening somewhere up ahead. Thankfully, they hadn't come across any other hikers before they left the trail. The trio continued through the dense woods for a while longer, marking trees as they went, and finally came to an opening where the ground looked flat enough to make camp. Andy turned and looked back in the direction they'd come, making sure they weren't followed by any stragglers who wandered off the trail.

A flash of movement passed between two trees in the distance.

"Shit. I think someone followed us," he said quietly.

Sean set his large backpack on the ground and turned to look.

"Nobody there, man. You're just nervous. Stop acting like you just robbed a bank, for Chrissake. We're just camping." Sean gave Andy a playful shove.

"Yeah. You're right."

He dropped his bag to the forest floor, allowing his eyes to linger between the trees a few seconds longer. When nothing moved, he shook his head and unzipped his bag.

"Maybe he spooked you with his stupid story," Amanda said.

"Nah. Just seeing things, I guess."

They found a level section on the ground and started setting up the tent. The sun was now completely blocked from the center of the forest, casting the area in dark shadows that made nightfall appear much closer. After the tent was up, Andy and Sean went to seek out firewood while Amanda got the fireplace situated.

"I'm proud of you, buddy. It's been a long road to get here, but you seem to be turning the corner. I think this weekend will help the closure."

"Thanks. It really does mean a lot that you guys still support me. I know you're close with Lidia, too. I'm grateful you didn't turn your back on me after how things ended between us."

"Please. You introduced me and Amanda to one another. Besides, it's not like Lidia stopped caring about you, you know? She'd never want you to lose some of your closest friends over what happened. And after all you went through. People deal with shit their own way. What matters is that you got the help you needed. It's been, what…almost a hundred days since your last drink?"

"One hundred and five, but who's counting?"

"Are you worried being up here will tempt you at all? Like the thought of Brett might put you over the edge?" Sean asked, picking up a few pieces of wood from fallen trees.

"Honestly? Yeah, I am. But that's why I'm doing this, you know? When I showed him pictures of the sunrise at the top of this mountain, you would've thought I got him a free pass to Santa's workshop. Wanting to come up here to see the sunrise was all he could talk about for days. And that's exactly what I plan to do: camp out, wake before the sun comes up, and hike to the summit to give him what he always wanted."

"You were a great dad to him." He patted Andy's back. "Let's get this wood back and start a fire, what do you say?"

"Sounds good. And thanks again for all of this, Sean. Means a lot."

They walked back to the tent, ready to settle in for the night.

\*\*\*

After sitting around the fire for a while, Sean and Amanda retreated to the tent and left Andy to himself, which, in truth, he didn't mind at all. He wanted time to reflect—to think back to all he could have done differently to save his marriage. He wondered if Lidia ever thought about him or getting back together. Now that he had cleaned up his act, Andy had this pipe dream of Lidia finding out and coming back into his life. But that wasn't fair to her. After all they'd been through, she had finally allowed herself to be at peace and move on. He knew he had to let go; that was another important step in his recovery. But fuck, was it hard.

The fire crackled and popped, burning through the remaining pieces of wood they had piled up near the tent.

Once the fire had burned down low enough, he planned to join his friends for some shut-eye and set his alarm to make sure he wouldn't miss the sunrise.

Andy zoned out, allowing the dancing flames to catch his attention while the nightly crickets chirped throughout the forest. His eyes forced themselves shut, the warmth of the fire relaxing him to the point that he didn't fight it. He was half asleep, thoughts swirling through his mind in rapid-fire succession. It was the first time all day he'd been in his own headspace for more than a few minutes, and he now found himself craving a drink. When he opened his eyes, the fire was much smaller.

*How long was I out?*

He stood and walked over to his bag outside the tent, opening the front pouch to retrieve his pills. At the same moment he pulled on the zipper, a distant cry moved through the trees.

*What the hell was that?*

He froze, listening for any other noises. A piece of wood popped in the fire behind him, and his heart almost exploded through his chest. Besides the crickets, no other sounds returned. He took out his pills and dry swallowed two, shaking his head. Sean's story must have gotten to him more than he let on. Thousands of hikers traveled these trails every single day, yet according to Amanda, only a handful said they experienced something. The sound he heard was likely some form of wildlife attacking another.

*The circle of life.*

The fire began to soften as the last few logs burned to completion. Andy watched the smoldering embers with their glowing orange outlines. Listening to the crickets' lullaby, he closed his eyes and pictured Brett running along the trail on his first hike. The boy smiled brighter than the campfire.

*...We can bring you your boy...*

Andy's eyes shot open.

"What the fuck?"

A soft whisper tickled his ear, and he thought he was hearing things.

"Who's there?"

*...Come be with us, Andy. Brett will be waiting for you at the top...*

Fear seized him in place. This couldn't be real. "Who's there?" he asked again.

Rustling from inside the tent let Andy know he'd woken his friends. The whispers were in his head, as if someone was sitting fireside.

*CRACK!*

This time, it wasn't a log popping but a branch off in the distance, out of the dimming illumination provided by the fire. Andy locked his eyes in the area of the sound when he heard it again. Then there were multiple branches snapping from each side, as if he was being surrounded by a group of invisible intruders.

"You're tired. It's not *really* there," he whispered to himself.

For a second, as the noises ceased, he believed his statement. But then he saw the outline of several figures spread out between the trees about twenty feet out. He couldn't make out any features, only the vague shapes of different-sized bodies. Andy swallowed down the fear, too afraid to move. The figures remained in the darkness, but Andy could feel their eyes on him. At that moment, he wished Sean and Amanda would wake up and come from the tent. He was about to yell for them when one of the figures stepped forward. Still too far back to see any detail, but it was the size of a small child. A boy.

*...Daddy. Come be with us...*

"Brett? How—how are you here?"

He knew it was impossible. That whatever was in front of him could not be his son. But the voice in his head absolutely sounded like Brett. Andy was so focused on the boy that he didn't realize all the other figures were now gone. He stood from the fire and prepared to enter the darkness, but now the boy was also gone.

*No. No, no, no!*

Andy ran to his bag and unzipped it again, pulling out his flashlight. If he was going to follow the boy, he needed to see where he was going. His friends were the last thing on his mind as he quickly left the campsite for the woods. Just up ahead, the boy passed between two trees, keeping his distance from Andy.

"Hey! Brett!"

He aimed the light at the kid, but as soon as the cone of brightness landed on the boy's location, there was nobody there. The path through the trees was anything but smooth; Andy picked up speed regardless. While he could no longer see the kid *(Brett, it has to be Brett)*, leaves crunched in the distance.

*...Yes. Keep going, you're almost there...*

The whispers were not the kid but the man he heard the first time.

"Who are you? How are you in my head?"

The man didn't respond, but Andy didn't care. He had to see if Brett was out here. In the back of his mind, he knew it couldn't be. His son had withered away to skin and bones, resembling a corpse even before he died. Andy and Lidia had watched as everyone they knew walked up to the open casket to say their final goodbyes. Then they'd buried him as family and friends cried uncontrollably over the small wooden box being lowered into the ground, never to see another day.

None of that mattered right now. He would do anything for one last look at his boy. Maybe it was the fact that they were on sacred land where spirits roamed the forest that allowed Brett to reveal himself? Maybe it was the pills causing an odd hallucination? Whatever it was, he had to know if it was Brett.

He grabbed a large walking stick, exited the wooded area, and made it back to the rocky trail heading toward the summit. It was dangerous enough to climb during the day, where any wrong move could lead to rolling an ankle or, worse, falling off the steep ledge to the rocky surface below. Now pitch black, every step was a death trap, waiting for a chance to grab hold of his foot and not let go.

The boy continued to appear at the edge of Andy's vision, and every time he aimed the flashlight toward the figure, all he saw was empty space. The moon was covered by evening clouds, making it even harder to see the path in front of him. Andy found himself alternating the light toward the ground to make sure he saw the terrain, then off in the distance to make sure he was still following the kid. Was he even on the trail from earlier? There were moments where the path looked familiar, and then he'd see something that looked completely foreign. His foot connected with something hard. He aimed the light toward the ground, expecting to see a tree limb or rock. What he saw instead prickled his skin in gooseflesh.

A large bone, lathered in blood, sat at his feet.

It looked far too large to belong to any sort of animal, and the blood appeared fresh, glistening in the beam of light. He leaned to get a closer look when the whispers returned.

*...Daddy... Commme to me...*

Andy took off in a sprint, forgetting about the bone, ignoring the rough terrain. He couldn't lose track of the voice again. After climbing a steep incline, he stopped to catch his breath, lights flashing across his vision as his heart tried to pump enough blood. He scanned the area, sweeping the light horizontally across the expanse like a laser cutting the world in half, and that's when he saw it: the infamous ledge that Chief Chocorua fell from to his unfortunate death, the place where he cursed this land and the people who resided here.

It was magnificent to look at, almost as if someone had placed a massive rectangular platform of granite at the mountaintop to overlook the land below. Andy stared in awe at the landscape, momentarily forgetting about the kid. He slowly walked out on its surface, approaching the ledge.

*...Yes. I'm right over here, Dad...*

The voice brought on too many good feelings to contemplate why Brett said "Dad" instead of "Daddy." He now found himself in the middle of the summit, his breath covering the cold space in front of him as he tried to get his heart rate down after the tough climb.

"Brett? Where are you?"

Instead of his son responding, it was multiple whispers, buzzing through the night sky like a horde of angry wasps. The sound intensified until Andy had no choice but to cover his ears to block it out. When the buzzing finally stopped, his ears continued to ring for a moment. Slowly, the sensation dulled, returning the world to silence.

Suddenly, rushing footsteps pounded off the crushed rocks behind him, the sound of someone sprinting. Running right at him.

He turned just in time to make out a larger figure, no longer a child, charging toward him. Andy took a step back quickly, losing his footing, and fell backward. His flashlight slipped from his grip and smashed off a rock on the way down, sending the mountaintop into darkness. The last image he saw before cracking his head on the stone ground was an older, giant of a man in what looked like a tattered colonial trench coat, with eyes darker than night itself.

\*\*\*

Screams from the forest woke Andy, and he was immediately welcomed by a throbbing pain shooting through the back of his skull. Panic grabbed hold of him when he opened his eyes and saw only blackness. The screams were everywhere around him. Something was wrong. It was as if the trees themselves were crying out for help. And then he realized that he was on his back staring up, and the darkness was just the night sky. Flashes of the man stalking toward him sent a chill down his spine. His eyes were as dark as obsidian.

The image jolted Andy up, sending a new shot of pain through his head. He blinked, attempting to get some semblance of his vision back. The flashlight's absence made him realize just how dark it was. He scanned the mountaintop, looking for any sign of the madman. Or for the boy.

*Brett, dammit, it was Brett!*

He heard footsteps approaching from the edge of the forest and trained his eyes on the trailhead, prepared to defend himself from the attacker. But it wasn't the stranger in the jacket he saw, it was Sean and Amanda. Their flashlight beams moved frantically as they climbed over the rocky path, exiting the forest.

"Andy!" Sean yelled, his voice echoing in the night.

"Are you okay?" Amanda asked.

As they got closer, their light path grew, and Andy realized the stranger wasn't gone after all. The large man was standing off to the side, hiding in the shadows of the tree line.

The man moved in their direction. Andy had to warn them.

"Guys! Look out!"

Either they couldn't hear what he said, or they ignored him because they climbed the final hurdle and Sean aimed his light at Andy, still sitting on the ground with the cliff right behind him.

"What the hell are you doing up here, man? We woke up and you were gone. You scared the shit out of us."

"We... We're not alone! Watch out!"

Sean whirled around, scanning the trees. When he saw an empty forest, he turned back to Andy.

"What's going on, Andy? Please tell me you didn't slip up. After all—"

"I didn't fucking drink! When I was sitting at the fire, there were people around our campsite. They told me to follow them. I—I saw a boy. He looked like Brett..." Andy trailed off, suddenly realizing how ridiculous it all sounded.

Sean stared at him blankly. Andy knew he had to elaborate.

"There was a guy. He wore a long jacket that looked old, and his eyes were pitch-black. I know it sounds stupid, but I'm telling you—" Before he could finish, Andy's eyes went wide as he saw a towering figure approaching over Sean's shoulder.

Sean turned and gasped. The man had a permanent snarl locked on his face as he marched forward, his long black hair stringy with sweat or grease. Sean backed up but was getting closer to the cliff. Amanda screamed, and at first, Andy assumed it was because she saw her husband getting near the edge. That's when he saw the other figures surrounding her a few feet away.

Just then, the clouds broke apart, allowing the moon full access to illuminate the surface below. For the first time, Andy got a good look at the group previously represented by blotchy silhouettes. A woman in an old-fashioned dress and her hair up in a bun grabbed Amanda by the throat. Two boys, not much younger than Brett would've been, flanked her on each side. Their skin glowed with the moonlight now reflecting off them.

Andy suddenly realized who these people must be. They were the settlers of almost three hundred years ago, Cornelius Campbell and his family.

*Why are they doing this?*

"Who the fuck are you?" Sean asked, peering over his shoulder, realizing he had moved past Andy and reached the edge with nowhere to go.

"You people think this is all some game. That these stories are fun to tell around a campfire. WE ARE STUCK HERE! For eternity!" Cornelius shouted.

He continued toward Sean, now only ten feet away. Sean attempted one more step back, but his foot reached the edge, slipping on the decline. He fell to his knee, grabbing for purchase as small rocks fell below. All Andy could do was watch. There was no time to react. Amanda continued to gasp for breath as Campbell's wife squeezed her windpipe. Everything was happening so fast.

"Please… We don't mean any harm. Let us go!" Sean begged.

Campbell ignored the plea, grabbing Sean by the hair and lifting him to his feet, now face-to-face.

"You can join Chocorua at the bottom of the cliff where his body has rotted for centuries," Campbell said in disgust.

Before Sean could respond, Campbell palmed his face. A sickening pop escaped beneath the man's massive hand as blood pooled between his fingers. Sean emitted a muffled scream. His body began to twitch as Campbell squeezed like he was juicing a lemon. With a quick snap, Campbell crushed Sean's jaw, revealing a sagging mouth that only remained intact thanks to the skin holding it in place.

Sean moaned incoherently, eyes fluttering. Andy tried to get to his feet and help, but a sharp pain shot through his chest, sending him back to one knee. He looked up, now only inches from his best friend. He reached out, grasping Campbell's ankle just as the bastard lifted Sean and chucked him over the edge into the black void below.

Andy couldn't move. A numb sensation tingled through his arm up into his shoulder. Sean's fading scream lasted just a second before a loud crack silenced it.

"No!" Amanda cried out.

She wrought free from her spectral attacker's grasp and scurried toward the cliff's edge. Mrs. Campbell and her kids turned and watched her go, their eyes matching the tar-black color of Cornelius's, sinister smiles spreading across their faces in unison. Amanda was so transfixed on getting to Sean that she completely ignored Andy and the towering brute, Cornelius.

"No, no! Sean! Please, no…" she trailed off.

Her focus remained below; eyes glued to the horrifying image Andy couldn't see from his crawling position. Not that he *wanted* to see it. The sound. That terrible sound. It replayed through Andy's head. The thought forced bile into his throat, and he leaned over and threw up.

Sean, who had stood by his side through his darkest moments when he contemplated suicide after losing his son and wife. Sean, who'd answered every single call that Andy made to him while on his many week-long benders feeling sorry for himself. Sean had been the one to convince Andy to go to rehab. He saved Andy's life.

Andy couldn't bring himself to move, instead he just continued to stare at the spot his friend had just been standing seconds before, hoping he'd come climbing up the mountainside to save him one last time.

Cornelius stood only a few feet from Amanda, watching her suffer. Andy had to do something. He remembered the walking stick he'd dropped when he was ambushed. He spotted it a few feet away and attempted to crawl toward it. Something grabbed his ankle, and he turned to see Campbell's wife clutching his pantleg, squeezing with an iron-tight grip. He attempted to kick free, but she refused to let go. She pulled him back and grabbed ahold of his neck, her nails piercing into his exposed skin. As she ripped back, he felt the warmth of blood pumping from the wound down his back.

"You pathetic fools don't even know what loss is. *I* lost everything. My family, my livelihood, my home. And you parade around here like it's some sort of amusement to pretend this land is haunted. Are you having fun now, little lady?"

Amanda pried her attention from below and glared at Cornelius. He grabbed her by the wrist, and she clawed at him with her free hand.

"Let go of me!"

"As you wish," he said, spitting the words.

He snapped her wrist, forcing one long bone to poke through her skin. She shrieked a bloodcurdling cry. Cornelius struck her in the face, crunching her nose upon impact. Amanda stumbled backward until she disappeared over the edge. A second of silence followed before the *thud* of her body below.

Andy's legs turned to jelly. He found himself frozen in place, wondering how it got to this. When Brett was diagnosed, it was Amanda who stopped by their house every single day to check in on them. She'd bring Brett stuffed animals and do everything in her power to make him smile while he suffered. She was his godmother. He called her "auntie," because she was more than just a friend to him.

"Why? We came to honor my dead son. Can't you see that? Isn't that what you were doing when you killed Chocorua?"

Cornelius bellowed an unsettling laugh and shook his head.

"He had what was coming to him, just like his nosy shit of a son. You call it honor. I call it vengeance."

With that, Cornelius closed in, his eyes somehow getting even darker than before. Andy forced himself to his feet, but something was terribly wrong. His chest tightened, and he had all he could do to stay upright. He tried to shake it off, but that only made him more light-headed. Campbell grabbed Andy by the throat and squeezed, then pushed him back with such force that Andy fell to the rocky surface once more, smashing his knee on a jagged piece of rock on the way down. Pain coursed through his kneecap, and the wind was knocked from his chest.

Andy looked up and saw all four of the Campbell family members surrounding him, inching closer. If this was how it would end, then so be it. How fitting for this to be the place Andy drew his final breath: the one spot his son wanted to visit before he died. He absentmindedly felt the outside of his pocket, knowing his son's photo and necklace were resting there and forced a smile.

"What are you smiling about, fool? You're about to suffer greatly," Cornelius menaced.

Andy ignored him, then pulled the photo from his pocket, and stared at it. Tears slid down his cheeks at the sight of his boy looking back at him and Lidia poking her head into the frame in one of the last happy moments of their marriage. He squeezed the photo close to his chest, knowing that his heart was giving out. After everything he'd been through, the alcohol was going to get the best of him. He felt a strong pulse pump through his body, unsure what was happening to him. While he knew he was dying, his heart was still full of not only loss, but the love he held for his son.

He looked up at the Campbell family. But instead of seeing their hateful stares, they were all looking toward the woods. It was fear that plastered their faces, not anger. Andy followed their gaze.

Emerging from the woods came a small figure, either crouched low or no bigger than a child. As the silhouette got closer, its features became apparent. Andy realized it was the boy he first saw at the camp before the others arrived. Although he never got a good look at the kid, he knew it in his heart. Whereas the Campbells made him feel nothing but coldness with their presence, this boy radiated a warmth that somehow eased Andy's concerns.

*Brett?*

"Get him, NOW!" Cornelius roared.

His sons ran toward the figure and Mrs. Campbell followed at a steady pace.

The boy got closer, and Andy realized it was not Brett. The boy's skin was a light shade of purple. Veins traveled along his shirtless torso up to his throat, which was a darker purple. This had to be the son of Chocorua. One look at him should have paralyzed Andy in fear, but it had the opposite effect. The boy was here to help. Andy clutched his chest, fighting for breath as he watched the boy come forward.

The boy stopped and waited for the Campbells to come closer. As they did, he opened his mouth wide and screamed. It was such a high octave that Andy had no choice but to cover his ears. The sound was deafening, swaying the forest around them with its power.

Mrs. Campbell stopped walking and violently shook her head. Her sons dropped to their knees, covering their ears. The veins visible beneath his purple skin began to glow a blueish-green as he continued screaming in their direction. Cornelius momentarily forgot about Andy and went to help his family. Each step he took looked forced, as if a tropical storm was blowing against him, trying to push him back.

Andy sat up, overcome with nausea, and watched as Mrs. Campbell and her kids dropped to the ground, their bodies flailing like they were having a violent seizure triggered by the boy's screams. They clawed at their ears, which began to leak liquid far too dark to be blood.

Cornelius made it about halfway to his family before he, too, was forced to his knees. Something beneath the skin of his face rippled, a current of bodily fluids swimming below the surface. The closer Chocorua's son got to the family, the more their bodies spasmed, like two magnets trying to force the same-sided poles to touch. The boy remained unfazed and continued toward the Campbells. He now stood over Cornelius's wife, who shook so violently that Andy heard her bones cracking as her spine went from fetal position to arched completely back, the top of her head now touching her heels. Her children did the same, writhing and gasping for air while the boy stared down at them, void of emotion.

The kids ripped and clawed at their faces, tearing away at the skin. Just like their dad, their skin was infested with movement beneath the surface. The cries were deafening, but eventually they faded. And then their bodies stopped moving, evaporating into thin air as if they were a figment of Andy's imagination. Cornelius, however, remained. He forced his head up to look at Chocorua's son.

"You…"

He couldn't say any more as the boy increased the volume of his scream, blasting another wave of force into Cornelius's face. An unsettling gurgle escaped Campbell's throat just before his head exploded like a potato in the microwave. He collapsed and then vanished with the rest of his family.

Finally, the screams stopped, but Andy's ears were still ringing. He looked to the boy, who stood far enough away that he couldn't make out every feature, but he was close enough that Andy saw a single purple tear travel down his face. He then lifted his hand and pointed toward the summit's edge behind Andy.

Andy turned to look, and what he saw coming up over the horizon was the most beautiful thing he'd ever seen. The sky began to fill with a bright pink hue, which pushed the darkness away to reveal a majestic sky. He held the picture of his son close, looked down at it, and then back to the sky.

"Here it is, buddy. It's beautiful."

He considered turning around but knew Chocorua's son would be gone.

And so, Andy laid down. He took his final breaths, but he wasn't worried. His vision was fading, and that was okay, too. He could see enough of the sun rising, but beyond that, he saw Brett.

As Andy reached for his son, he let go of the photo. He closed his eyes just as a warm breeze carried the photo over the summit like a child's kite taking flight for the first time.

# Luka and the Luchador

Francesca Maria

Black bits of charcoal hit the Arizona pavement as Luka's Harley skidded back to earth. The fire portal closed behind him, but not before he inhaled another rank whiff of brimstone. A small flame erupted on the back of his biker jacket.

"Fucking demons." He extinguished it with a quick pat. "That's real fucking leather!"

Both hands gripped the bars of the hog. A tattoo on the top of his left hand, aged by years of sun and sin, grinned back at him—a demon's head with a protruding tongue dangling between a mouth full of razor teeth, on his right, a smiling angel with a cherub face complete with wings behind each cheek. An angel on his right, demon on his left. The white of the ink had long faded, but the red, the red was as vibrant as the day he got it, a lifetime ago.

Luka's mane of black, once fashionable in the rocker days of the eighties, hung limp with patches of thinning at the very top. Gray hairs danced around his ears despite the constant Clairol he applied at home. He flipped the long strands behind his shoulders and continued down the dark lifeless road, straddling the yellow line all the way.

\*\*\*

Enrique exhaled as he laced his botas. His paunch made it a difficult task. A spike of pain snaked up each vertebrae like a hot poker. Scars on his arms, face, and chest littered his body like a schizophrenic spider web. The white of the scars was the only thing pale about him. Darkness loomed over every inch of the luchador, a shadow that soaked into his pores making him appear darker than his abuelita's Oaxacan skin.

*One more*, he kept telling himself. *One more then I'm done*. No more fighting, no more pain. Lying had always come easy to the five-time champion. As easy as throwing another pinche pendejo across the ring. Another lie. The once mighty luchador could no longer lift an opponent half his size for his trademark piledriver. Those days are collecting cobwebs—spinal fusion surgery saw to that. One more piledriver could cripple him for the rest of his life, however short that may be.

Marissa needed college tuition and Thomas, well, Thomas needed to stay out of trouble. Another big payday should do it, then he could retire on the little plot of land his abuelo left him and leave this godforsaken place. Leave behind the shame and find a new mask to hide behind.

\*\*\*

The flat rancho adobe rose up to meet Luka. The bone-white façade glared against crimson sand. A lone cactus as tall as Luka, stood in front of his home with its two limbs pointing in opposite directions, one toward Heaven, one toward Hell. Its inch-long needles grayed by the relentless sun.

"Hey, Skinny," Luka called out to his friend. It shimmered slightly in the heat's rays. Even with the sun long set behind the mountains, the Arizona heat was unbearable. Sweat plastered a ring of hair around Luka's face. He was used to the heat, and way hotter than this.

No one greeted him as he crossed the threshold, no spouse, kids, or furry companion. He liked it that way, but if he was honest with himself, some nights he could tolerate something other than his own company.

The first Corona went down fast, the second he carried with him along with a brick of cheese and a stale loaf of bread to the den. His leather jacket stared back at him from a hook behind his front door. His boots lay where he'd thrown them off like used condoms. Steam rose from the rounded ends where his toes were sardined not three minutes before.

With remote in hand, Luka switched on a wrestling match, sipped his beer, and fell into a deep sleep. Demon dealing was tiring business.

\*\*\*

Enrique's opponent was a newcomer to the scene, a kid half his age who went by the moniker, El Salvacíon. He had some buzz—they all did at first. The excitement of another luchador revved up the fickle audiences that grew tired of the old.

There was a time in the not-too-distant past when everyone chanted his name, El Rompe Huesos, aka The Bone Crusher. He could hear it in the locker room before every fight. It charged him up and gave him immeasurable strength. Little children would run to touch him, women would throw themselves at him, and opponents feared him.

After years of winning, followed by a decade of losing, the crowd no longer chanted his name. A few of the old timers did, and maybe a child here and there, but his fans had dried up, moved onto the next flashy entertainer. Now he was the villain of the week. No longer the champion, he became a nameless thug whose job it was to make the younger wrestlers look good.

The locker room door opened. "Cinco minutes, Huesos."

"Si, si, una momento." Enrique could hear chanting from the crowd, "Salvacíon, Salvacíon, Salvacíon." The cheers faded as the door closed, leaving him in silence once more.

El Rompe Huesos bowed his head and asked his abuelita and his god for protection and to survive his final match.

El Salvacíon's manager, Julio Vasquéz, a slimy snake oil salesman no taller than his twelve-year-old niece, had approached Enrique a month ago with a proposition. If Salvacíon can claim to defeat the once mighty El Rompe Huesos, then his rising star will shine all the brighter. Especially if he can overcome the famous piledriver!" The smell of sweat and cheap cologne had radiated off his bejeweled skin.

"No, no Señor. I can no longer do that maneuver. It may paralyze me." Enrique searched the man's eyes but he never met the champion's gaze. Enrique did not trust a man who would not look him in the eyes.

"I am prepared to offer you ten times your rate if you do this. I will not take no for an answer."

"I said no. It's not worth the money. It is too dangerous. I'm not even sure I can do it anymore." Enrique was struck by the honesty of his admission. He'd never before said, 'I can't do it anymore.' The words bit his heart.

"I was told you were stubborn." Julio Vasquéz took a small notebook from his pocket and scribbled something on a blank page with a broken pencil. "Here." He ripped out the paper and handed it to Enrique. "This is my final offer. Think about it. And here's my card." The small black card read simply 'Julio Vasquéz, Manager' with a phone number. There was nothing else on the card, save for an etching of some kind; it was shiny against the matte finish. When Enrique held it to the light, he saw a set of horns, a long face and a protruding tongue. When he opened the piece of paper, he nearly fell to his knees. It was more money and more zeroes than he had ever seen in his twenty-two-year career. When he looked up to see if it was a mistake, or worse, a joke, the stranger was gone.

*** 

A tickle, followed by a choking cough forced Luka awake. Something crawled into his snoring mouth and was fighting its way back out again. A few more spats and Luka freed the flying intruder which buzzed off in loud protest. The last few swigs of his second Corona eased the fire in his throat. It had never been the same since that first trip to Hell. Inhaling the toxic hellfire burned away part of his esophagus and vocal cords. It took months to heal and it still seized up on him causing occasional choking fits. When he spoke, his voice sounded like gravel grinding into powder. His singing voice was completely shot.

It had been a rookie move; going to Hell in his corporeal state, without protection, still flesh and blood—madness. Like sending a moth into an incinerator and expecting its wings to come out intact. Luka's lucky to be alive. The incantation had protected him just enough as he opened the portal to Hell, but he didn't think through what he'd do once he got there. It wasn't like he could ask someone for instructions. Most people spent their lifetimes trying to stay out of Hell, not trying to find a way in. But Luka was a stubborn S.O.B. and wanted to complain about his contract, formally.

Luka's band, The Death Stains, had played the L.A. clubs and started to get some airplay, albeit on college radio. Front-man Luka had dreams and aspirations beyond the local scene. He wanted to be the next Mick Jagger, Robert Plant, and Rodger Daltrey combined. The band's songs were passable, a few members knew how to play their instruments: Gregg on bass, Kyle on guitar, Jay on keyboards, and Frank on drums. They were all *his band*. Luka took credit for forming The Death Stains and considered the rest supporting musicians, there only to aid him on his path to rock stardom. If any of them stepped a toe out of line, Luka threatened to replace them.

It was October 31, 1984, Halloween, and The Death Stains had just finished their set at the Whiskey. Luka was drenched in sweat having *left it all* on stage. He ventured toward a buxom blonde who caught his eye but was interrupted when a diminutive bloke wearing a bowler too small for his bulbous head stepped in front of him.

"You are the leader of The Death Stains, are you not? Luka De LaCruz?"

"Depends on who's asking." Luka searched the crowd again for the blonde.

"Well, I represent a backer that can help take The Death Stains to the next level. Is there somewhere more private we can talk?"

Luka's eyes locked onto the man for the first time. He dropped his gaze a foot to the figure wearing dark sunglasses and heavy gold chains around his neck to match the bling on his swollen fingers. A chill ran through Luka despite the immovable heat vapor trapped in the club.

"Sure, yeah, there's a spot backstage." The two meandered through the thinning crowd to a dark hovel filled with amps, spilled beer, and spent cigarettes.

"So, who are you exactly?" Luka pulled out a Marlboro and lit it with his Zippo. The bedazzled stranger tried to find a place to sit and ended up leaning against a Marshall stack.

"It doesn't matter who I am, what matters is *who I represent*. Have you ever heard of Diablo Records?"

"Sure, wasn't that Robert Johnson's label? They signed some big names, Joplin, Hendrix, The Who, Led Zeppelin, the Stones."

"Too true. All wildly successful bands. They reached the stratosphere while others, dare I say *better* musicians, fell into obscurity. See, we at Diablo Records have something special that we offer our clients, something unique that will guarantee success."

"Go on, I'm listening." Luka stomped out his cigarette on the cement floor with his boot and lit another.

"It's all here, in the contract." In a blink, a black scroll appeared between them. Gold-ringed fingers unrolled what looked like ancient parchment. Red writing littered the page. The man produced a pen that glowed a fiery crimson. "All you gotta do is sign and The Death Stains will become legendary."

The little fucker lied. Sure, The Death Stains took off, played a few stadium shows, but then fizzled out as fast as the head on a beer. Not even close to the *legendary* status for which he signed away his soul. And no one, not even a demon-wielding record label, would get away with short-changing Luka. No one.

\*\*\*

Enrique finished lacing up his silver botas, specks of the coating fell as he tightened the laces. He considered getting a replacement pair, but remembered, if he survived tonight, he'd never need to step inside another ring again. The crowd had reached a fevered pitch, then his familiar theme music played, *El Diablo Viene Llamando*, his que.

The arena was packed, even the cheap seats at the top were taken. It was standing room only amidst a haze of smoke and body heat. The dull yellow spotlight followed

El Rompe Huesos through the crowd where a few chanted his name amongst a chorus of boos. When El Rompe Huesos entered the ring, he spotted Mexico City's elite in the front row. Even the mayor and his wife were in attendance.

Over the loudspeakers the announcer's booming voice shouted, "Now, what you've all been waiting for, the one, the only, El Salvacíooooooooon!" The spotlight shined brightly on the backstage door as it burst open revealing a mass of iridescent pastels and rhinestones. A flowing powder blue cape, tied around a brick-thick neck, did little to conceal cinderblock shoulders. A set of white wings protruded from the mask giving the luchador an other-worldly appearance. The crowd went nuts, screaming and throwing objects of adoration along the luchador's path.

El Salvacíon was taller than El Rompe Huesos but Huesos outweighed him easily by fifty pounds. Still, El Salvacíon's width and height would make the piledriver all the more challenging.

El Rompe Huesos continued to size up El Salvacíon as he paraded to the ring. The competitor was half Huesos' age. The seasoned luchador clenched and tightened his muscles, readying for what was to come. He ignored his aching back as he searched for El Salvacíon's eyes. They were locked onto the crowd, his arms waving back at his adoring fans. The young luchador's bright and perfect smile glittered as the light reflected off tiny diamonds embedded in two front teeth. With the crowd behind him, El Salvacíon looked toward the ring and met El Rompe Huesos' gaze for the first time. El Rompe Huesos saw fear. A quick indiscernible nod between the two luchadors signaled their unspoken agreement as El Salvacíon entered the ring.

The introduction, the handshake, the bell. The match was on. Pain sparked behind El Rompe Huesos' eyes as he took a right hook to the face. He ducked before the second swing and followed it with a body slam against the ropes. El Salvacíon appeared stunned but El Rompe Huesos knew better. They danced together, trading punches, kicks, one having the upper hand over the other, then they would switch. They appeared evenly matched, despite the height and age difference. The crowd was in a frenzy. The first bell rang and they retreated to their corners.

El Rompe Huesos spotted the tiny manager sitting in the bleachers behind El Salvacíon. He lowered his sunglasses revealing a set of flames. El Rompe Huesos shook his head to clear out his vision. *I must be hallucinating.* Julio Vasquéz smiled back with a grin too wide, revealing a row of sharpened teeth crammed into his child-size head. El Rompe Huesos felt his insides go cold as the bell rang again.

It was time. Time for the signature move. Time to get this over with. El Rompe Huesos searched the crowd to ensure his family was not in attendance. He made his wife Sylvia swear to keep herself and the kids away from tonight's match. It would make tonight even harder if he knew they were in the audience watching what could be a paralyzing, if not fatal, final maneuver.

The little manager's words from the fated phone call replayed in El Rompe Huesos' head. "If he can walk away from one of your famous piledrivers, El Salvacíon will become legendary and you will become rich beyond your dreams!"

Without another thought, the aged luchador raced up and grabbed his young competitor into a bear hug and squeezed with all his strength until his opponent went limp. When he released him, El Rompe Huesos took El Salvacíon's head and forced it in between his legs while grabbing at his mid-section. The two were locked together. El Salvacíon was upside down with his feet facing the arena lights and his head facing the mat, being held in place by the veteran's knees. El Rompe Huesos had been on the receiving end of a piledriver more times than he could count. He knew that if he tucked El Salvacíon's head above his legs his spine would take the impact, sparing his opponent's neck. He squeezed, lifted them both with a running jump and dropped hard onto the mat, tailbone first. Searing white pain gave way to merciful darkness. A bell rang in the distance…then all faded to black.

***

When Luka opened the portal to Hell on that first fateful trip, he fell through the pentagram he'd made on the dark wooden floor of his rockstar pad. The candles barely flickered as he plummeted down into darkness on an invisible elevator that had lost its brakes.

He smelled the brimstone first, the burning in his lungs second. His skin felt an instant scorch as if he lay in the sun on the hottest day of the year. A blinding red-orange glow like that of a late summer sunset seared his retinas and dropped him to his knees. He clenched his eyes and covered his ears as screams flooded his senses from every direction, vibrating his cells in a chorus of pain. His own screams joined those around him as patches of Luka's flesh began to burn off like ash from a campfire. His luxurious mane caught fire at the tips and proceeded to burn to the roots.

"I'm here about my contract!" Luka's voice, irreparably charred, echoed out into the vast nothingness.

A blue light appeared, engulfing him into a protective egg providing blessed relief from the burning fire and pain. Luka timidly opened his eyes to see himself being transported through Hell. Obsidian mountains, jagged with spire-like peaks encircled him. Impaled bodies, spiked by the mountaintops, writhed as they tried desperately to free themselves. Some of the bodies were headless, just torsos and limbs, moving up the spikes to freedom, only to slide back down by their own slippery blood. Luka threw up, having already lost his bowels upon entry.

Below him churned a lava lake which bubbled with torsos, heads, hands, and various body parts. When heads bobbed to the top, their opened mouths screamed before being drowned by the choking lava. Seeing and hearing the souls of the damned affected Luka on a level he had not expected.

As his transport progressed, Luka spotted a mammoth floating barge crammed with countless rows of desks—a thousand wide by a thousand deep—on the lava surface. Creatures dressed in ebony, three-piece suits with matching red ties, filled the desks. Their human-like faces gave way to horns protruding out of temples, flared nostrils the size of charging bulls, amphibious eyes that glistened in the heat, and grins that stretched into cuts at the edges meeting pointed ears on either side. Luka could not make out their color as every surface reflected the crimson lake, giving all within his vision a red-tinted glow.

Each being clamored away, typing furiously on ancient metal typewriters. Red lettering peppered black parchment after the keys were struck. When a page was complete, its author ripped the parchment out of the typewriter, where it disappeared in a crack of light. A new parchment was added and the process began again. The mass of clicks and dings broke up the screaming from the heads that bobbed below. A giant half-dog, half-sheep patrolled the edges of the floating monstrosity, shoving creeping human hands back down into the lake with a twenty-foot-long trident.

Luka's transport stopped in front of a pair of obsidian doors each the size of the Empire State Building. Luka made out carvings of human torture as the monoliths opened. The blue egg fell away leaving Luka exposed as he walked through the gates of Hell.

\*\*\*

El Rompe Huesos' limp body lay motionless on the mat. His competitor, El Salvacíon, cried out in pain, hands clutching his back. Medics rushed into the ring. The crowd, unsure if this was a stunt or a terrible accident, were on their feet. The longer El Rompe Huesos stayed motionless, the quieter the cheers became, leaving the sounds of the medics as they tried to resuscitate the unconscious luchador.

Enrique's eyes opened to a painfully bright red-orange glow and a heat he had never felt before. Every movement, every breath, was agony. The contract-wielding demon stood over him as the luchador lay on a lava stone. The manager, Julio Vasquéz, stripped off his human suit revealing reptilian scales. The color of raven feathers reflected the firelight. Wet bulging eyes, with a snout and full lips, made the demon appear frog-like. Spikes jutted out from a curved spine that bent over the prone wrestler.

"Welcome to Hell, El Rompe Huesos. I'm sure you will find your stay here unbearable." Enrique took in his surroundings and a nauseating wave of fear shook his entire being. "You did quite a number on El Salvacíon. I'm impressed. I didn't know you still had it in you." A snake-forked tongue slipped out from charcoal lips and licked its left eye.

"No, no, this can't be happening!" Every word, every movement was torture. Fire burned through Enrique's insides.

"We had a deal. And I must say, you fulfilled yours nicely. El Salvacíon will be joining us soon. The pills he'll overdose with from the pain will bring him here ahead of schedule. Nice work."

"No, you said that if I did this, my family and I would be taken care of, that I could retire. I never agreed to this." Enrique opened his arms indicating his surroundings. The pain was tortuous.

The demon leaned an elbow on Enrique's knee. "You know, you humans can be pretty thick sometimes. Read the fine print, luchador."

A contract appeared before them. "And I quote, 'Enrique Madrona Esponada aka El Rompe Huesos, will perform the piledriver on El Salvacíon and will receive $1.5 million in return for his soul which will be eternally condemned to Hell.' Demons lie, it's kind of our thing. That's why we put everything in the contract. It's not my fault if you failed to read it."

The faint sound of a motorcycle interrupted the demon. Its lizard eyes rolled up in its head. "Not this fucking guy." A man covered in leather wearing dark shades rode a Harley toward them. The presence of this being irritated the demon, causing Enrique to sit up and take notice.

"Well, well, what do we have here, Azazel? Another mouse caught in your trap?"

"Fuck you, Luka. What are you doing here? This doesn't concern you."

"Oh, I think it very much does." Luka's black hair blew in the fire breeze. Enrique could make out crow's feet from the side of the sunglasses. Luka lowered his shades and looked Enrique in the eye and gave him a wink. "I was given authority, by your boss, need I remind you, to oversee contract disputes due to your faux pas with me, remember?"

"There's nothing wrong with this contract. This human agreed to it as is."

"No, no, I never signed any contract and I never received any money for me and my family." Enrique stood near Luka.

"Oh for all the blood in Hades, that money would go to your widow in the event of your death, minus a 10% service fee. We must maintain our lava wells!" The demon smiled but not before he licked his right eyeball.

"Let's see here," Luka held up the familiar black parchment and swapped his shades for reading glasses. "I don't see any signatures."

"What?" Azazel snatched the contract from Luka and glowered over the red ink. The demon's skin turned a deep burgundy as he realized his mistake.

"Did the boys in the back office forget to check that tiny detail?"

Luka turned toward the still-masked luchador. "Did you sign this contract, Enrique?"

"No, no, Señor. I never signed anything."

"Did you at least shake on it?"

"No, we made the agreement over the phone after I met him in the locker room. He gave me his card and I called him after we talked that first time. The only other time I saw him was when I was fighting in the ring."

"That's just a technicality." Azazel pouted as he kicked at loose lava rocks on the ground.

"Ah, but an important one, making this whole situation null and void. Truly, I'm surprised the bossman lets you do *any* contracts, Azazel. You're so bad at this."

"Master said if I screwed up one more time I'd be stuck on torture duty." The deflated demon looked down and kicked more rocks.

"I think we should get this man back to his family."

"No, you can't. He's already marked for Hell, he's mine! I... I need him to fill my quota."

"Tsk, tsk. Even Hell has to abide by certain rules. Now run along Azazel and go explain your latest fuck-up to your master and why you'll be one short of making your precious quota."

"Fuck you."

"You're not my type."

Azazel disappeared in a huff and puff of grey smoke.

"Now let's see about getting you back, huh?"

"But aren't I dead, Señor?"

335

"Oh, no, not quite. You're still in the in-between. You can however, choose to stay here, if you'd like, or return to your family."

"Mi familia por favor. Muchas gracias. I am forever indebted to you. But, Señor, I must know, who are you and why are you doing this for me? Are you an angel?"

"Ha, no, that's a whole 'nother bunch of fuck-nuts. I'm just an average Joe like you. See, years ago, Hell tried to screw me over in a contract, too. I came down of my own accord and argued my case. So well in fact that the head chief of this godforsaken place said I could act as a human liaison, or advocate if you will, to prevent any further mishaps. One thing Hell doesn't abide by is disorder. Bureaucracy was invented in Hell. I know that may come as a shock, but it all runs like clockwork because of the unbreakable laws. When those rules get broken, well, all Hell breaks loose—pardon the pun. In return for my service, they granted me another shot at a new life, a chance to do better by others and not live solely for myself."

"Señor, I am forever grateful to you and for your service. A thousand, million times, thank you."

"Don't thank me, just doing my job. Oh, and I'll see to it that you get your money, you earned it! Now close your eyes and count backward from ten. When you get to zero, open your eyes."

Enrique obediently closed his eyes tightly and chanted, "Diez, nueve, ocho, siete, seis, cinco, cuatro, tres, dos, uno, cero." The bright lights of the arena welcomed El Rompe Huesos back to life. The crowd cheered his name and gave him a standing ovation. "El Rompe Huesos, El Rompe Huesos, El Rompe Huesos." It was a sound he never thought he'd hear again. His heart warmed as a lone tear slipped beneath his mask.

# Our New Church

James H. Longmore

The hollow, insistent knock on the front door pissed Mike Savage off.

For one, it was Sunday morning, for two it had riled his pit bull up to the point at which the dumbass dog was frothing at the mouth, and last—but not least—Mike was nursing the rear end of the hangover from hell; last night's beer session with the missus had been a doozy and a half—if the relentless pounding on the inside of his skull and his desert-dry mouth were anything to go by.

Mike rolled over, his broad shoulders taking most of the comforter along with them as the thing wrapped around his tight, lean, tattooed body like it didn't want him to leave. Mike cast one aching eye the length and breadth of his wife's freshly exposed, naked body and tried his damndest to will her to wake up. No luck there, Laura was dead to the world. She lay on her back, pert, pointy breasts pointing aggressively up at the slowly twirling ceiling fan. Her head was lolled back and she was snoring fit to burst.

The knock on the door again.

The dog barked with renewed fury and Mike heard Todd stirring in the bedroom across the landing. For a six-year-old, it certainly took a hell of a lot to wake up that boy.

"Goddammit," Mike growled to himself, his voice croaky and parched. He crawled out of bed, fighting to extricate himself from the bed sheets. Groaning, he pulled on the pair of gray sweatpants that lived permanently next to the bed and really would benefit from a run through the laundry sometime soon. Hopping comically on one foot, Mike struggled to avoid sticking both of his legs down one leg hole. "I'm coming, for fuck's sake," he grumbled as finally he exited the bedroom with one last glance at his beautiful wife.

*"Fifi!"* Mike called the barking dog away from the front door. "Here, girl."

Fifi ceased her noise and trotted over to Mike, tail wagging and fat, pink tongue lolling. Mike ushered his dog out into the backyard and approached the door with a nervous eye flicking to the tall, metal vase that stood sentry beside it—a souvenir from the African market Laura loved to frequent—in which was concealed his 12-gauge; one could never be too careful in Mike's line of work.

"Good morning, to you, sir." The cheerful, resonant voice that greeted Mike as he opened the door grated on his aching brain like nails down a chalkboard. "I hope you and your family are fit and well and happy with the Lord on this fine, fine day!"

Mike gave an inward groan; this was pretty much the last thing he needed right now, a God-botherer on a Sunday morning. He eyed the jolly-faced guy on his doorstep with great disdain and wondered just what on earth possessed these people to wear a three-piece woolen suit when it was already in the mid-eighties at nine in the goddamned morning.

"Allow me to introduce myself." The suited man stretched out a large, meaty hand for the shaking through the gap Mike had created in the doorway. Mike looked down at the hand as if it were some wholly unpleasant, alien thing invading his territory. He also noted that it was darkly perma-tanned like the guy's face and couldn't help but speculate if the rest of him was the same shade. "I'm Antonio D. Love, your spanking brand new, shiny as shit, God-appointed pastor!" Love announced like he was some cheesy, over-the-top game show host as he grasped Mike's hand and gave it a firm, moist shake. "And this here is my able assistant in the Lord's good work, Kayla Wyatt."

Mike squinted downward as the pastor ushered a short, chubby black girl from behind his legs. Mike hadn't noticed the miserable looking youngster standing dutifully behind Love in her demure, knee-length floral dress. The poor girl looked sweaty and uncomfortable but, nonetheless, she forced a weak smile. Mike smiled back and felt a little sorry for her.

The pastor plucked a crisp, white pamphlet from the stack the girl held tight in her small, sweaty hands and thrust it towards Mike's face.

"I come carrying our Lord's word," Love declared somewhat grandly, "and I simply *have* to share it with you, or I'll just go right ahead and burst, Mr....?"

"Savage," Mike grumbled. "Mike Savage." He stepped back into the cool of his hallway, seeking sanctuary from his throbbing head there. "You're wasting your time here, buddy."

"Ah, but am I?" the pastor grinned. He leaned in a tad, towering his tall, lanky frame over Mike who stood five-nine in his bare feet. "Can you put your hand on your heart, Mr. Savage—Mike, can I call you Mike? Of course I can, we're all friends under God's loving gaze—and tell me that you are truly not interested in hearing the glorious words of the Lord, our God?"

Mike fixed the pastor with his best steely glare, the one he held in reserve for the potheads and crack addicts who didn't pay him on time, and for the first time he noticed the clergyman's eyes. Dark, brooding, liquid, they were set deep into the smooth, golden skin of Love's impossibly handsome face, which was in turn framed by neatly trimmed hair that was by far the blackest shade of black Mike thought he'd ever laid eyes on. The pastor's eyes twinkled and smiled as they returned Mike's gaze. They were of the deepest, darkest brown. So much so as to be almost black.

"If I was interested, don't ya think I'd be in church now?" Mike gave his stock answer—religious types had become something of a nuisance in the subdivision recently, despite the gates and myriad signs that bluntly declared *no soliciting*; somehow they figured that selling their religion on Sunday mornings simply didn't count as solicitation. It annoyed Mike to no end how Love and his ilk seemed to prefer the more genteel estates to ply their ecumenical wares; he'd never had this problem growing up in the projects.

"Would you, Mr. Savage? Would you indeed?" Love persisted. "If that were the case, I wouldn't be interrupting your Sunday morning now, would I?" Again, with that shit-eating grin. "This is by far *the* perfect time for spreading the word of the Lord, as all of you heathens are home and ripe for the picking!" Love raised his hands to the heavens to emphasise his point.

Mike remained unimpressed.

"I'm just joshing with ya, Mr. Savage." Love tempered his smile somewhat and lowered his voice. "All I wanted to do was find a little time to make the acquaintance of my new flock."

"Then shouldn't you be in church?" Mike grumbled as with great reluctance he plucked the pamphlet from Love's long, spindly fingers.

"Not until eleven-thirty today, Mr. Savage." Love beamed. "Then again, you'd already know that if you were a Christian man." The pastor tipped Mike a smiling wink, which was met with an icy stare. "Perhaps we shall see you there?"

"I highly doubt that." Mike inched himself away from the door, easing it closed as he did so.

"You have yourself a great morning enjoying the Lord's miracles that dwell all around you." Love took a step backwards, turned on his heels, and ambled down Mike's driveway, skirting by Laura's *Panamera* with great care. The miserable little girl slouched along behind him, her brow decorated with shiny beads of perspiration.

"Who was that?" Laura's voice behind him startled Mike. He dropped the pastor's pamphlet and turned to face his wife.

"Just some Jesus freak," he told her. "Waking us up this time on a Sunday, who the fuck do they think they are?" Mike ran a shaky hand over his shiny bald pate and snorted.

"The guy with the little girl?"

"Yeah." Mike watched Love and his reluctant minion make their way down along the sidewalk in front of the house. He turned his attention to Laura and the all too familiar stirring in his pants. She looked mighty fine dressed in the oversized white T-shirt she'd bought him a couple of Christmases ago. It had a picture of Gizmo the pre-gremlin on the front because that had been Mike's favorite movie as a kid. Laura wore the shirt well, especially with her newly rounded belly, *sans* panties and fresh from their bed. Mike slipped an arm around his wife's waist and hoped that Todd had gone back to sleep.

"You didn't offer them a drink?" Laura shrugged his hand away.

"Why would I have?"

"Just look at that poor little girl." Laura pulled the door wide open and before Mike could protest she'd called out, "Would you like some water?"

Mike groaned as he watched the pastor's face light up. Laura was forever doing shit like this; always the champion of lost causes, mother hen to those she saw as weak and helpless. Mike reckoned it was his wife's way of remembering just where she and her husband had come from—perhaps even atonement for how they made their living. Or possibly it was nothing more than Laura Savage was just a sucker for a hard luck story. Either way, this was precisely why Mike steered her away from anything remotely charitable, and why he'd expressly banned her from the pet store on Pet Adoption Days.

"You are truly a gift from God, Ma'am." Love smiled once more with that capacious smile of his. "Didn't I tell you that the good Lord would provide?" he boomed into Kayla's upturned face that fair dripped with perspiration. Love trudged across Mike's meticulously manicured lawn, back toward the front door and Laura Savage and her warm, welcoming and most delightfully altruistic smile.

And before Mike could protest, Pastor Antonio D. Love and his young ward were firmly ensconced on his expensive, cream leather sofa sipping iced water from Laura's best cut-crystal tumblers. The young girl gulped hers down noisily, her throat bobbing up and down as the chill water quenched it, whilst the pastor took more genteel sips and watched pensively as the fat ice cubes danced around in his glass and chinked melodically against the sides.

It was cool in the house; the AC had been set to a positively Arctic 69 degrees for overnight—any warmer and Mike was guaranteed no Saturday night action because Laura would be *too hot*; and boy had they enjoyed some drunken action last night!

Mike watched as the pastor and the young girl cooled down some. Kayla, in particular, looked more comfortable by the minute, her face no longer looking sweaty and exhausted.

"I can't begin to thank you kind folks enough." Love sounded quite sincere. "It really is thirsty work delivering the Lord's word to folks such as yourselves in weather such as this." Mike found the smile that followed that particular statement to be patronizing at the very least. Just what did the pious fool mean by *folks such as yourselves*? "Or, as I like to call it, spreading the *Love*." The pastor guffawed at his own pun, although Mike figured this wasn't the first time he'd used it. He also thought it sounded wholly inappropriate coming from a man of the cloth, especially one whose name made him sound like a washed-up nineteen-seventies porn star.

"It's our pleasure," Laura said. "Isn't it, darling?" Aimed at Mike, her sweet smile caught him totally off guard.

"Yeah, sure.".

"Say, big guy," Love said to Todd as he sauntered into the lounge, his latest Lego creation clutched proudly in his hand. "Is that a space rocket I see there?"

Todd's face cracked into a broad grin and he held out the mismatched bundle of colored bricks for closer inspection, his usual reticence around strangers conspicuous by its absence.

Mike watched warily as the pastor took the toy from Todd's tiny hands and turned it over in his long fingers as if it were the most delicate thing in the world. As for himself, Mike really couldn't tell if his son's construction was a rocket, a car, a boat, or a damned robot. He also watched as his son's face lit up with pride and something akin to admiration for the strange man whom his mother had welcomed into their home.

"Ya know," Love said to Todd as he placed the Lego model with great care back into the boy's hands. "I'll bet Kayla here would just *love* to spend a little time on those swings of yours." He nodded out through the window toward the cedar wood swingset that dominated the backyard. "Why don't you two go play awhile whilst I chat to your mom and dad; save you gettin' bored with all the grown-up talk?"

Kayla was up and on her feet before Pastor Love could finish his sentence, the happy look on her face most out of place. Todd took the girl's hand and led her to the kitchen and then toward the back door to freedom.

All too late, Mike remembered the dog.

"No!" he yelled as he heard the door to the back-yard click open.

Too late.

Fifi bounded in, ears flapping, her panting mouth split wide open in a slobbering, rictus grin. Mike lunged for the dog as she raced by him, grabbing at the spiked collar around her neck, but missing by a clear mile. His heart sank as the pit bull made a beeline for the pastor.

"Hey there, sweet girl," Love greeted the charging dog with not so much as a flinch. Fifi in turn slowed up and approached him passively—tail wagging, eyes down, ears flattened to her broad skull. "Well, aren't you a beauty?" Love cooed as he scratched between the dog's ears.

Mike relaxed a little. Everyone, it would seem, loved Pastor Antonio D Love—even the stupid dog.

"What happened to Pastor Gregory?" Laura asked of Love. "He was nice."

"Alas, he passed on to join the Lord in his well-earned eternity." Love rolled his eyes heavenwards, their whites a startling contrast against his tanned skin.

"Oh dear," Laura said. "I am sorry."

"No need to be, young lady," Love soothed. "He had lived a long and fruitful life; it was merely his time to meet God, is all."

Mike remembered Gregory with a vague fondness. Their paths had crossed on occasion amongst the crowd of homeless lost souls who gathered beneath the towering columns of the downtown freeway—Mike to ply his trade and the pastor to save said lost souls from Mike's nefarious goods, amongst their other limited temptations.

Although Mike made his big money on the rich folk around town, he still sold to the desperate people once a week. He always took along his cheapest stuff, rocks of crack or meth' mostly, drugs that were easily affordable for those who'd made the effort to beg for spare change on the intersections for the quick escape from the abject misery life afforded them. Mike saw it as kind of his community service, giving back to where he clawed himself up from. It was his own perverse version of working the soup kitchens. Perhaps Mike Savage did have some soul left after all.

"I *thought* I hadn't seen him for some time," Mike added. In fact, he could not put a date to the last time he'd bumped into the ancient clergyman.

"He was old and not up to getting out and about in his final year or two," Love explained. "I guess that's how come many of his flock abandoned his church in preference for that mega-church over in Snake Bridge." Love shook his head and clasped his hands together. "Lord save those poor souls from that money-grasping, godless place," he said with reverence. "And it saddened me to hear that when the Chronicle printed his obituary, many of your fellow townsfolk were actually *surprised*. They'd thought the poor man had died years ago."

Mike admitted to himself that he was amongst that crowd. Learning now that Gregory had only just recently met his maker had come as a bit of a shock, the same way in which it does when an A-lister from Hollywood's golden era passes and one's first thought is *they were still alive?*

"So, can I expect to see you good folks at church later this morning?" Love spoke as if the three of them had actually had that conversation. "I'm sure that eleven-thirty will give you both plenty of time to make yourselves suitably presentable for an audience with the Lord." He tipped a wink at Laura. "You'd need hardly any time at all, why you're just as pretty as a picture as you are, Ma'am."

Laura giggled and Mike could have sworn she'd blushed; she looked like a silly little schoolgirl as she shuffled her ass nervously on the sofa opposite the pastor, and Mike hoped she'd remember to keep her legs closed.

"I really don't think-" Mike was cut off as his cell phone vibrated in his pocket, buzzing urgently against his thigh like an angry wasp. He fished out the phone and squinted at its bright screen. "I have to take this." He shot Laura a glance, not entirely comfortable at leaving her alone with the oddly charismatic new pastor but not able to take the call in the man's earshot. This was the deal he'd been waiting on for two days now; Molly, Crack, Colombian Coke, a thousand tabs of Ecstasy, and Christ only knew how much skunk they'd be wanting to go with all of that. Those rich folks up on the hill sure knew how to party hard.

"That's okay, honey," Laura dismissed her husband with a wave of the hand. "You go take care of your business."

With some reluctance, Mike took the call and retreated from his lounge, leaving his atheist wife chatting to the new pastor like they were old-school buddies.

\*\*\*

And so, that was how Mike Savage found himself sitting on a hard wooden pew at the rear of the ramshackle, wood-built Church of the Christian Fellowship in his Sunday-best suit and with trickles of sweat dripping down his back.

The place was packed to standing room only; it had been a mixed blessing that Mike, Laura, and Todd had arrived early (on Laura's insistence). While it had meant spending longer in the stuffy, airless church, at least they got to sit down, no matter how uncomfortable the seating. It had been quite possibly decades since the tiny church had been so full, and Mike feared that the sudden, sheer weight of all the townsfolk the new pastor had shamed into attending would likely cause the ancient floor to collapse and bring the whole place crashing down about their sinful, heathen ears.

"Good people of Waxahachie," Pastor Love's voice boomed out across the sea of sweat-shined, attentive faces, his tone full and resonant without the aid of a microphone. The congregation was hanging on his every word, enraptured by the man in the rickety old pulpit. Even Todd Savage, usually the most fidgety and easily distracted of children, sat stock still in awe of Love, a serene smile upon his thin lips. "It delights my very soul to see so many of you here today for my inaugural sermon, and I just *know* that our Lord is pleased, too. Praise Him!"

"Praise Him!" the congregation countered with gusto.

"And as I look around at all of these beautiful faces of God's children, do you know what I see?"

Silence met the pastor's wide-eyed stare.

"*I said*, do you know what I see?" Love raised his voice and startled the gathered people. Somewhere at the back of the church, a baby began to cry, its voice shrill.

"No, sir!" the people replied.

"I see a flock whose shepherd abandoned them." Love's voice was almost a growl at this revelation. "Yes indeed! He abandoned you all to the wastelands of sinfulness and neglect of prayer!"

This was greeted with nods and murmurs of acknowledgment, even an *amen* or two, and Mike pondered if *neglection* was actually a real word or not.

"And what I *see*," Love's tone rose once more and tears of raw emotion glinted in his deep, dark eyes, "are good, God-fearin' townsfolk who deserve so much better than this ruination, this *abomination*, of a church!"

"Amen!" a goodly number of the congregation chanted.

Love lowered his voice to a hissing stage-whisper. "Why, I can hardly bear to hear myself speak the word *church* in this place," he said. "For this is no church, and do you know why this is no church, good people of Waxahachie?"

"No, sir!" the people spoke, almost to a man, woman, and child.

"Because a church is supposed to be a place made for the people, *by* the people!" Love declared, his hands held aloft. "This place should be a place where the ten thousand lost souls of this great town can congregate to praise their Lord God and saviour, somewhere that brings the decent townsfolk of Waxahachie together with one purpose and one voice!"

"*Praise Him!*" The combined voice of three hundred or so souls reached the roof and once more Mike worried that it may just be enough to bring the whole thing crashing down about his ears. He glanced nervously upwards and whilst he was relieved to see the rafters were still very much intact, it niggled to see Laura's blank, entranced expression as she stared vacantly at the pastor. It was, Mike noted, an expression shared by the entire congregation. At this, a shiver darted up Mike's spine and nestled at the base of his skull like a small, frightened animal.

"So, ya know what we're gonna do, good people of Waxahachie?" Love persisted, his voice trembling with passion.

"What *are* we gonna do?" the people asked.

"What we're gonna do is tear down this repugnant facsimile of God's house and then we're gonna build Him, and you good people, the church that you *truly* deserve!"

As one, the congregation clambered to its feet and spontaneously clapped as Pastor Antonio D. Love soaked up their adoration from behind the flaky paint of the old wooden pulpit. Even Mike struggled to his feet, groaning loudly at the kink in his back.

"And we're gonna rebirth *your* church as the Waxahachie United Church of the People!"

At this, the applause was rapturous. Tears of joy streamed down the faces of some of the crowd and yet others stomped their feet as if the cacophony of six hundred hands slapping together wasn't enough.

"I can see some of you thinking *what is this gonna cost us, Pastor Love?!*" Love shouted above the row, which dampened considerably upon his mention of *cost*. He hushed the congregation with a downward motion of his hands, bid the gathered townsfolk to all sit down.

Mike allowed himself a wry smile. Here it comes; the rub, the hustle. For all of his crowd-pleasing rhetoric, the new pastor wasn't all that different than the thousand-dollar suit assholes that fleeced the little old ladies over at the mega-church.

"In times gone by, the people of a town would give up their time and skills as decreed by law to build their church," Love explained to the silenced audience—and even the baby quit its keening. "So yes, I do want your money for *our* new church, but more importantly than that, good people of Waxahachie, I need *you!*" And somehow Love's dark, almost black eyes managed to look at each and every one of those gathered before him, all at once. "Every single soul can contribute to God's new house. And to those who have no skills to offer, but are willing to give freely of their time—I say, we can teach you, we can guide your hands with the love of the Lord, and we will bring this beautiful town together."

"Praise Him!" the people cried in pious unison. *"Praise Him!"*

Praise Him, indeed, Mike thought to himself, too much the cynic to be swept up in Love's happy-clappy bullshit. He knew there'd be a catch, a scam somewhere along the line; it just remained to be revealed.

Nonetheless, the new pastor, Antonio D Love had promised to build the ten thousand or so Waxahachie townspeople a brand-new church, and that was precisely what he did.

\*\*\*

The old church had been torn down with such haste that it had seemed almost irreverent. The crumbling wooden structure had been reduced to its bare-bones foundations in a matter of days. And even for someone as decidedly irreligious as Mike Savage, the utter finality of seeing the town's familiar landmark stripped down so quickly seemed simply *wrong*.

Mike skirted around the tall, wooden perimeter fence that they'd erected around the construction site that was to be the new church. He'd opted to walk that way to his weekly rounds amongst Waxahachie's down and outs for the express purpose of sneaking a peek at the building work, his curiosity aroused by Laura's almost continual chatter about Pastor Love and his wondrous new celebration of the Good Lord.

Sadly, Mike's attempts at surveying the work in progress were thwarted. The fence around the site of the new church was easily nine feet tall and had not so much as the thinnest of gaps or a knothole through which a curious soul may peep. Even the gate that had been constructed to match the fence was good and solid, the work beyond shielded from the townsfolk's prying eyes.

And as he turned the corner, the mighty concrete freeway stretched out less than a half mile away, it occurred to Mike that for a construction site, the work on the new church was disconcertingly quiet.

"Early lunch, alright for some," Mike growled as he strode by, his head bowed against the oppressive heat that beat down against his shaven skull.

It was somewhat cooler beneath the stark concrete underbelly of the freeway, where the sun's baking rays simply couldn't reach. Above, the traffic thundered in a continuous roar, oblivious to the lost and lonely souls who huddled beneath to wait out the remainder of their wasted lives.

Today there were noticeably fewer of the bedraggled homeless folk than Mike had visited last week.

"They workin' at yon new church," Scruffy Joe explained to Mike, pronouncing the word as *noo*. "I hear tell that new pastor's givin' out free food an' work boots," he continued with undeniable envy in his voice.

"They took all of their stuff with them?" Mike quizzed. He squinted around at the lack of battered shopping carts, ragged cardboard boxes, and shitty old tents.

"They say Love's set up a campsite of sorts, with fancy tents an' lavatorials an' running water an' all." Scruffy Joe looked around at the towering walls of gray that rose around him and his remaining associates. "Sounds like one o' they refugee camps in Africa or someplace poor, but it's still gotta be better than this hell-hole." The vagrant sighed a melancholic sigh and stabbed his grubby fingers at his long, white-streaked beard as if he were searching for something.

Scruffy Joe was one of Mike's oldest and most loyal customers. He loved Mike's dirt-cheap Meth'—his prematurely aged, haggard features and lack of most of his teeth stood testimony to that. He'd been a Waxahachie bum for as long as anyone could remember, his shambling, reeking figure so common a sight around the town that he'd become something of a popular mascot. That Scruffy Joe's life had come to this; dwelling beneath the freeway, scavenging and begging for sustenance, living fix to fix and dreaming of a better life in a construction site tent, went way beyond sad.

In an uncharacteristic fit of empathy, Mike was tempted to slip the old man a freebie—just enough to allow him to take the edge off. However, Mike stopped himself. Business was business at the end of the day, and do that one time and they'd all expect it; his prices to these dregs of society were ridiculously low as it was.

"I'm sure I'll be gettin' my call up soon enough," Scruffy Joe told Mike with a grin that exposed the blackened, rotted carcasses of his three remaining teeth. "I reckon I still have a skill or two to offer."

Mike smiled back at the man, although he couldn't for the life of him think what those skills could possibly be.

\*\*\*

The next week, along with yet more of the freeway dwellers, Scruffy Joe was gone. Mike kinda missed the sad old bastard, and wished he'd given him that free hit of crystal now. It had been the same at the rehab clinics, both of which were markedly empty of residents, all lost to the Pastor's impressively ambitious project. It was beginning to grind Mike's gears; the homeless his business could survive without, but the clinics were filled with rich folk who'd happily pay well over the odds for his merchandise. They were the people who paid for his affluent lifestyle and who he was banking on to get Todd through college.

It was almost as if Love had become some bizarre one-man anti-drug crusader who's set out to ruin Mike's livelihood.

There was an air of excitement about town that morning as the new church—already considerably bigger than the old one, even though nowhere near finished—had emerged above the concealment of the imposing fence.

Even Mike had stopped to gawk up in wonder at the slender beams that rose out of the church's foundations like bleached, skeletal fingers that pointed accusingly up at the heavens. And around those, the emergence of the building's walls seemed most miraculous as the shape of the church was now clearly outlined in thick, white stone that shimmered like a desert mirage in the town's late morning heat.

Mike stood back at the other side of the road along with the small crowd of gathered fellow Waxahachians to marvel at Pastor Love's amazing feat of architecture. Just how they had gotten so far without scaffolding or some sort of crane was beyond Mike, but then again, he was no civil engineer. And the sheer speed at which the new church had grown was a far cry from the old days when such magnificent structures would take generations to complete. Not bad for a crew that seemed to have been made up almost exclusively of the town's degenerates and destitute.

And once again, Mike noted that the construction site was deathly quiet, and he wondered if perhaps they all worked through the night to avoid the brutal Texas summer sunshine.

\*\*\*

The following weekend, Laura dragged Mike along to Pastor Love's Sunday service. It was held in the Middle School's gymnasium, courtesy of the Principal who was both a fanatical Love supporter and chronic MDMA user.

*What ever happened to the separation of Church and state?* Mike had grumbled, decidedly unhappy at having to wear a shirt and tie, let alone being made to leave his bed on what had become his and Laura's sex morning.

"Welcome, welcome, one and all!" Love's dulcet tones radiated throughout the gymnasium, bouncing off of the cheerfully decorated walls. "It is truly God's miracle that I get to spend this precious time with you good people of Waxahachie," he boomed. "And it is also gratifying to see one or two new faces here today." Mike was positive that comment had been aimed squarely at him, and rather oddly he realized that he felt embarrassed.

"I am humbled here today before our Lord and saviour to see so many of you here in our church." Love waved his arms around to denote the gym, adorned as it was with past glories of the school's basketball team, the Waxahachie Ravens.

There were puzzled faces aplenty throughout the packed crowd at Love's use of the word *church*. The pastor smiled and it was as if he was smiling at each and every one of the gathered townsfolk.

"For what is a church, if not a gathering of good people in the common cause of praising the Lord?"

*"Praise Him!"* the crowd exalted, and Mike rolled his eyes.

"Mike!" Laura admonished her errant husband with a swift elbow to the ribs.

"Ouch!" Mike complained, and Todd grinned up at him like this was the most entertaining thing ever.

"A church—*our* church—is so much *more* than any building; it is the joyous coming together of like-minded souls." Love paused to soak up the adoration of his rapt audience. "And have we not all seen what such a coming together in God's name can achieve?"

"Yeah!" An over-enthusiastic voice rose high above the crowd. Mike glanced over his shoulder and saw that the owner of said voice was Charmaine Pemberthy, a rather stout young woman who had an expensive penchant for the finest Colombian marching powder that Mike could lay his hands on. In secret, the woman also happened to be the town's biggest slut and her poor husband had no idea that he was working himself into an early grave to provide for the children of three other men.

"How many amongst you have witnessed the miracle of our new church?" Love shouted, his arms out at his sides as if to gather in the warmth from his flock.

"I have!" The majority of the congregation yelled back at their pastor with such verve that it set the hairs on the back of Mike's neck on end as surely as a goose walking across his grave.

"An achievement attained only with the guidance of God's great hand!"

"*Hallelujah!*" the gathering erupted.

Love's countenance then fell serious. He leaned forward, hands braced against either side of the portable pulpit as if he were holding the rickety thing up. "And yet there are those amongst us who see you as nothing more than sheep," he said, his voice low.

And once again, Mike felt incredibly self-conscious.

"These people see themselves as holy sheepdogs, assigned by God to protect the sheep from harm." Love's face twisted in a grimace, like someone had just smeared fresh shit across his top lip. "They see fit to bring guns into our church, people," Love sounded suitably appalled and Mike felt relieved that the pastor's diatribe was not aimed at him. "And I have to ask them why. Why in the name of God, Jesus, and all that is holy do you think it necessary to arm yourself in God's house?!"

Love appeared to be directing his venom-filled words at Andy Saenz and his motley posse of open-carry rednecks. "Well let me tell *you*, good people of Waxahachie," Love growled. "If you are God's sheepdogs, then I am God's tapeworm!" A chuckle spread out across the congregation. "I will crawl up your ass and suck you dry of your self-aggrandizing vanity and false pride until the blinkers fall away and you can see the true beauty of the Lord our God! For you are no more special than anyone else here today—not the young, the old, the destitute, the addicted, the fornicators and the non-believers who stare constantly into the eternal void in which their only comfort is that when you're dead you don't know you're dead."

"*Amen!*" the people—with the notable exception of Saenz and his suitably humiliated cronies—cried out.

"All you do is posture and preen like ridiculous peacocks with your firearms on show." Love looked straight into Saenz's eyes and the man blushed a bright crimson. "Whilst others have brought their skills from every corner of this great town, from the city and from across the border; were it not for them, and we were to rely upon the likes of you, the labor of love that is the Lord's house would be little more than a hole in the ground!"

Mike stared at Saenz and took great delight in watching the gun-toting asshole wilt beneath the unrelenting gaze and harsh words of the pastor.

"Your time will come soon to serve Him and to make amends in his new house, for the Lord loves you as he does all of his children. You will have time to repent and see the error of your ways, and pray to your God that he forgives you for offending his justness," Love's voice mellowed as he played the crowd. "I am proud to call myself God's tapeworm, as lowly and vile as that creature may be, because it proves to us all that even God's self-proclaimed sheepdogs have a weakness."

Mike found the whole thing incredibly hard to swallow, particularly since the pastor's talk of intestinal parasites was making his breakfast pancakes churn around in his stomach as if they were trying to get out. But, seeing the joyful, rapt look on Laura's face, and the broad grin on Todd's, Mike could be at least happy that they were happy.

After the sermon, in which Love went on even further with the whole tapeworm analogy, and tuneless renditions of *The Lord's My Shepherd, Amazing Grace*, and another hymn that Mike couldn't recall from his childhood days in the old wooden church (not that the latter mattered too much, Mike moved his lips silently along to that one as he had the others), they stopped to chat to Pastor Love on the way out of the makeshift house of worship.

"Thank you for turning out, folks." Love beamed as he shook Laura's hand. "It is always an absolute delight to see you." Love then took hold of Todd's hand and shook it with enthusiasm. "You too, young man. I hope you are taking good care of your mom and your little brother—or is it *sister*?" Love glanced at the slight swell of Laura's belly and then at Laura.

"We don't know yet, it's too early to tell," she told the pastor.

"Mr. Savage!" Love turned his attention to Mike. "How simply perfect for you to have accompanied your beautiful family to our service! Welcome to the congregation."

Reluctantly, Mike shook hands with the pastor, and was surprised to find the tall man's hand warm, dry, and baby's butt smooth.

"He didn't want to, Mommy made him come," Todd blurted out at the top of his voice, much to everyone's amusement.

"Ah, but *did she*, young Master Savage?" Love grinned down at the boy. "Or was it God who persuaded your heathen father to join us on this most joyful of days?"

"Nah, it was Mom," Todd replied in earnest. "She said that if he didn't come along with us, there'd be no early night tonight."

"Todd!" Laura's face colored up a remarkable shade of red, and Mike smirked and held in the belly laugh that threatened to explode out through his nose.

Unphased by this innocent revelation, Pastor Love tousled Todd's neatly combed hair and replied, "No matter what the motivation, young man, *everyone* is welcome in God's house." His smile was quite serene as he turned his attention to Laura. "And on that particular note, I am hoping that I will be seeing you at our construction site this coming week. There is much work to be done and we could sure use a capable young woman such as yourself." Love's segue was a clumsy one but, nonetheless, Laura's face lit up with something other than sheer embarrassment.

"It's Spring Break," Mike chipped in with a distinct growl in his voice. Just what exactly Love had in mind for Laura, he couldn't imagine; she was a part-time waitress at Denny's for Christ's sake. "Laura has Todd home all day."

"Why, that is no problem whatsoever," Love's voice resounded about the gym, above the heads of the exiting congregation. "Bring the little fella along with you," Love told Laura. "There's a place for everyone in God's new house. Even you, Mr. Savage." His head snapped around to look directly at Mike.

Mike opened his mouth to protest, but Laura shot him a sideways glance that made him think better of it; pick your battles and all that. Still, it goaded Mike to think of his son being dragged along to Love's construction site on his week off from school, let alone having the opportunity to be brainwashed into the whole God thing by Love and his pious acolytes. With a derisory snort, Mike fixed Love with a steely stare and ushered his family towards the gymnasium's double doors.

\*\*\*

The frigid silence between Mike and Laura lasted all of two minutes into their short drive home.

"Well, that was a waste of my freakin' time," Mike grumbled as he gripped the Impala's steering wheel with such ferocity that his knuckles turned a stark white and the angular ridges of bone stood prominent against his skin. "I could have been out taking care of business."

"Selling drugs, you mean?" Laura snapped back. "Why don't you just call it as it is, Mike?" There was a sneer to his wife's voice that Mike didn't much care for.

Mike glanced in his rearview, concerned that Todd may have heard his mother's indiscretion; Mike's trade was something that was *never* discussed in front of the boy. Up until now, that is. Thankfully no, Todd sat silently in the back seat, earbuds jammed in his ears, watching *Sanjay and Craig* reruns on his iPad.

"Call it what you want, Laura, but it's how we pay for a nice house, your Corvette, the vacations –"

"Same old, Mike," Laura spat. "Change the goddamned record, why don't you?"

Mike was taken aback at this. His profession had never been a bone of contention between them before, even though he made no excuses for the fact that he was providing the good life for his family whilst destroying others'. Quite possibly, Mike figured, it had something to do with his wife's newfound admiration for one Pastor Antonio D Love.

"And I'm not happy you taking Todd to the new church," Mike threw in, might as well get all the dirty laundry aired while they were pulling it out. "Construction sites are dangerous places for kids."

"And you think I'll not take care of our son, Mike?"

"I think he'll be bored out of his brains and you'll be distracted by whatever it is Love has planned for you." Mike's tone dripped sarcasm.

"And just what do you mean by *that*?" Laura's hackles were up now—literally. Mike could see the hairs on the back of her neck looking all stiff and angry.

"You know damned well what I mean, Laura," Mike's accusing tone pretty much said it all.

As the 'f' in *fuck you Mike* formed on Laura's lips, they were both startled by the sharp, sudden *whoop* and flashing blue lights of the cop car that had pulled in behind them.

"Goddammit," Mike groaned. This was all he needed to top off a thoroughly shitty Sunday morning.

The cop, a particularly unpleasant individual who went by the name of Randy Salazar and who was universally disliked by everyone in Waxahachie, kept Mike waiting a good five minutes before hauling his stumpy, corpulent ass out of his blue and white. He sidled up to Mike's open window and leaned in, his breath stinking up the car with sour onions and last night's bourbon.

"Licence and insurance card," the cop growled at Mike—and then an almost polite, "Ma'am," to Laura who forced a wan smile back as Officer Salazar's eyes crawled across her chest like she was sitting there naked.

Mike handed over the required documents; he'd had them at the ready from the moment he'd pulled into the side of the road.

Unremarkably, he was all too familiar with this old routine. It was all part of the territory in his line of work.

"Could you step out of the vehicle please, sir?" The officer's hand absently crept to the butt of his gun that sat high on his flabby hip. "Slowly now."

Mike did as he was told, casting a glance at the troubled look on his wife's face and Todd's tearful expression. He knew from bitter experience what came next and he gave them both a wry smile that was meant to convey that they had nothing to worry themselves about and that all was going to be okay.

"Turn around, hands behind your back."

Of course, all was decidedly *not* okay, and although Mike viewed arrest as an occupational hazard—much the same in his book as shoulder pain in pro football players—it killed him a little inside to see his wife and kid look at him as if he were destroying their world one sorry sale of category A at a time.

There was a definite glint in the diminutive cop's squinting eyes as he 'cuffed Mike in front of his kid and pregnant wife. It had been a slow week, almost as if Waxahachie's criminal element had decided to take an impromptu vacation. Perhaps bringing in the town's one and only drug lord would cut through the boredom and give Salazar the appearance of having done something to justify his salary, even if it was an easy bust.

"Michael Savage, you are under arrest for the suspicion of supplying restricted substances," Salazar began the customary routine.

Mike snorted and ground his teeth together, struggling to keep his mouth shut as the cop manhandled him towards the awaiting squad car. He knew the drill well enough to know that any form of resistance now—even verbal—could result in longer jail time, a sound beating, or him being shot. Not one of those options sounded particularly appealing to Mike, particularly with Todd peering out the back window of the Impala.

"Call Cecil!" Mike called over his shoulder to Laura as she scooted over to the driver's seat of their family car.

Laura dismissed his instruction with a wave of the hand and a patronizing grimace. She was the Waxahachie drug kingpin's wife; of course she knew what to do.

\*\*\*

Cecil Tennenbaum had Mike out of county jail in two weeks, which by the attorney's standards was a little on the tardy side. He'd been on vacation over in Vermont for some of that period, and so Mike had spent a little more time than was usual behind bars. Still, Cecil was a good man, one hell of an attorney, and a great customer of Mike's; the two had a kind of reciprocity going on—Cecil would minimize Mike's jail time and Mike would keep Cecil supplied with whatever substances took his fancy at cost price.

Mike strode away from the jail with purpose in every step, determined to put distance between himself and the hellish place as quickly as possible. The stink of stale prison sweat, shit, and desperation clung to him like a second skin, his loose change, cell phone, and wallet dangled from his hand in a clear plastic baggie as he walked, swinging the thing in an almost jaunty fashion.

He'd heard nothing from Laura during his entire fourteen days inside, and Mike assumed this was because she was still mad at him. She'd done this before; it was Laura's silent protest, her way of assuaging her conscience at living on her husband's immoral earnings. This way she could fool herself that she didn't approve of his nefarious business dealings. Mike was confident though, that had his incarceration continued for longer than two weeks, his wife would have at least called him. She may even have applied to visit him, even though she knew how much he hated her coming to see him in jail. Mike didn't care much for his wife being ogled by the other sex-starved inmates, or for Todd to be exposed to the filthy, depressing jail atmosphere and oppressive stench.

The streets of Waxahachie were quiet, unusually so. Mike checked his phone to be sure of the day, but even for a Sunday, the place seemed unnaturally quiet. Surely *everyone* wasn't in church?

Mike took a detour and headed for the middle school, he figured he'd catch up with Laura there, as much as he despised Pastor Love's ranting *Praise be to God* sermons. The county jail didn't normally release on a weekend, but

Cecil Tennenbaum was on good golfing terms with Police Chief Cabera and had managed to pull a string or two. So, Mike had thought it would be nice to surprise his wife and son with an impromptu appearance at Love's makeshift church. It would lighten his prison-laden heart to see the sheer delight on their faces. And that alone would be worth having to sit through the back end of Love's dire proselytizing.

The route took Mike by the site of the new church and he was surprised to see the majestic white walls of the silent building reaching high above the once-concealing fence, its towering spires and pinnacles stretching as if trying to grab at the sky. All that remained to be done, as far as Mike could tell, was for the roof to be added. At this, he tut-tutted—it was rather remiss of Love's builders to have not spread a tarp over the exposed rafters, which shimmered and glinted in the harsh morning sun.

Laura and Todd weren't at the middle school.

In fact, no one was. The place was shut up tighter than a duck's ass and looked as if it hadn't been used in quite some time, although Spring Break had been over and done with a week ago. Mike skirted around the outside of the school, pulling on the doors just in case one had been left unlocked. All to no avail, the place was most definitely deserted; the locked doors as much a testimony to that fact as the empty parking lot.

Grinding his teeth together and fighting hard to suppress the temper that threatened to bubble up in his gut, Mike trudged home, his giddy delight at his plan to surprise his family dissipating with each and every step.

The Savage house was locked up and appeared to be devoid of life, and of course Mike had not had his keys about his person when he'd been arrested—they'd stayed behind with Laura and Todd in the car. And for as much as Mike rattled the doorknob and thumped on the front door, the only sign of life was Fifi barking in the backyard.

"Hey, girl," Mike cooed as he peeped over the fence at his dog.

Fifi wagged her tail in a lackluster greeting and waddled up to Mike as far as her chain would allow, her tongue lolling out the side of her mouth like some pink, slippery fish; it wasn't often they chained the dog up; she'd quit jumping the fence over a year ago now.

"You look thirsty," Mike said and Fifi cocked her head as if she'd understood him. Behind the dog, the large, stainless steel water bowl stood empty, likewise the food bowl that had pictures of Labradors frolicking around its perimeter—Todd had picked that one out.

Mike contemplated clambering over the fence to take care of his dog, but then thought better of it; the last thing he needed fresh from County was to have the nosey neighbors calling the cops on him again. Even if the houses across the street did appear to be equally as lifeless as his.

"I suppose they'll all be at the new church then," Mike said to the dog. He took some comfort in the sound of his own voice. It echoed around the stillness of the day and pierced the quiet with its exasperated tone.

Mike took a deep breath. He clenched his fists at his sides and chastised himself for having walked by the church earlier. It had seemed so quiet though, but upon second thought it was probable that Love was leading his congregation *en masse* in deep prayer, their collective heads bowed in reverence.

"I'll be back soon, girl," Mike reassured Fifi and she wagged her tail at the sound of her master's voice. At that, Mike ground his teeth together some more and set off towards the new church.

\*\*\*

There were but a handful of cars about on the main roads through Waxahachie, none that Mike recognized, but it was good to see them anyway as their presence helped relax the eerie feeling that had haunted him since finding the school empty. The gas station was open for business, as were the convenience store and the plant nursery. The suburban hum of lawn machinery kicked off somewhere far off in the distance, its thrumming noise sweet music to Mike's ears.

It seemed to Mike to have taken far less time to get back to the new church than it had walking home, something he put down to his eagerness to see and hold his wife and son again. The imposing building towered high above him, its stone facade shining bright white as if God Himself were illuminating its flagrant pomposity. The thick, solid bricks of the church's construction twinkled with a stark iridescence that made them appear liquid and it hurt the eyes to behold for too long.

Mike paced around the tall, foreboding fence that encircled the church, realizing that he had not actually seen so much as a doorway or a gate in the thing—where there had been a gate before was just a continuation of the fence. Naturally, he assumed, there had to be a new gate somewhere along the perimeter.

And naturally, there was.

Secreted at the very rear of the construction site, cowering like a timid, lost child, the gate was so well matched with the fence that surrounded it that Mike very nearly walked straight by it. Mike pressed against the gate, fully expecting it to be secured. But no, the tall wood swung open with ease, silent on its well-oiled hinges.

"Oh, wow," Mike muttered to himself as he stepped into the church grounds.

What greeted Mike's eyes was a veritable sea of tents—the small, two-man variety common at Boy Scout campouts the world over—each and every one that generic primary green color. And as Mike stepped over and around the myriad guide ropes that anchored the tents to the soft, virgin grass that surrounded Waxahachie's new church, Mike quickly discovered that every single tent was empty—in fact, they looked to have never been used at all.

It was then that Mike became aware of the soft murmur of voices, sweetly singing, the collective tone of praise, the dry tune of a hymn that Mike actually thought he recognized.

Mike's heart skipped a beat and he quickened his step towards the huge arched, double doors of the church. The wave of relief that swept over and through him was almost palpable; Laura and Todd had been in church all along, praising the God that Mike simply couldn't find in himself to believe in. That didn't matter now. All that concerned Mike right then and there was scooping the pair of them up and holding them tight—two weeks was a hell of a long time inside when you were used to seeing your wife and kid every single day. Of all the torments devised by man to inflict upon his fellows, such incarceration was in Mike's mind by far the worst.

Mike pressed his hand against the thick, wooden doors of the church, eager to be reunited with his family. He recoiled a little at the cold, clammy feel of the wood, its sweaty touch catching him off guard—as if the wood had been recently painted and the paint was still a tad tacky. Only, the wood was bare, rough and knotted, adorned with a thin film of moisture on the coarse grains. Undeterred, Mike shuddered and peered into the cavernous gloom of the church as the doors swung open.

The interior of the church was empty.

Mike could still hear the soft murmur of sung praises, the faint shuffling of weary feet on a stone floor, the occasional cough of the elderly, and cries of a small child. But nothing met his eyes as they adjusted to the dim light inside.

"Where are they?" Mike mumbled under his breath as he dared himself to step inside the cool, dank insides of the church, as if he were venturing into the belly of some vast and unspeakable beast.

"Why, they're here," a familiar voice spoke up from out of the murk. "They're *all* here."

Mike spun a ninety-degree turn and saw the unmistakable, lanky silhouette of Pastor Antonio D. Love as it stepped out from amongst the inky shadows that skulked by the font.

"Welcome to the new church, Mr. Savage." The pastor welcomed Mike with outstretched arms. "Welcome to *your* new church." The man beamed his broadest grin, his teeth sparkling white against the smooth darkness of his skin.

"Is this some kind of joke?" Mike could feel his hackles rising, his dislike of the ever-jolly pastor coming to the fore. He scanned the rows of empty pews with light-starved eyes as the sounds of praise caressed his ears.

"I can assure you that this is not *any* kind of joke, Mr. Savage," Pastor Love said. He paused just a handful of strides away from Mike, his rictus grin slipping ever so slightly. "Did I not promise you a church for the people, built *by* the people?" The pastor swept his long, spindle arms in wide arcs to emphasise the full glory of the brand-new Waxahachie United Church of the People.

Mike followed the man's arc, taking in the vast arches that supported the tall, concave roof beams and the intricate masonry around the detailed stained-glass windows that depicted countless Bible scenes—none of which Mike could distinguish.

And at that moment, the church's shimmering facade slipped away like the sloughed skin of some giant, malignant creature.

"Or perhaps I should say, a church built *with* the people," Pastor Love's voice resounded through the vast, hellish chasm of the new church. He laughed loudly, his tone high and maniacal, his eyes glinting wildly as he looked around at his handiwork.

Surrounding Mike and the pastor were people.

Hundreds, *thousands*, they made up the walls with their naked bodies, their arms and legs snapped and twisted and interwoven in a monstrous, infernal tapestry, each one pressed tightly against their neighbor like building blocks hewn from human flesh.

And worse, they were all—to a man, woman, and child—still very much alive.

The sounds that Mike's mind had interpreted as the sweet singing of praise for the God of all creation were nothing more than the pained moans and cries of those countless people, each and every one suffering in their own unthinkable agonies. And the soft shuffling sounds— simply the slick, bloodied, broken bodies as they writhed against one another, their snapped and dislocated bones serving only to add to their abject misery.

Every place Mike cared to look—and there were few of those—he saw people, many of whom he recognized as the townsfolk of Waxahachie. They made up the walls, the supports, the ceiling joists, and even the pews were a living, squirming mass of individuals, their tortured bare skin glistening and pulsing in the feeble light of Pastor Antonio D Love's grotesque place of worship.

"What have you done?" Mike stared into the insane face of the Pastor, searching in vain for some signs of humanity, desperate to run from this terrible place and just keep on running. "Where is my family?" He hardly dared ask the question.

"They are here, of course." Pastor Love's features once more resembled those of the affable, God-loving man Mike had first encountered on that Sunday morning a lifetime ago. "They have pride of place in this fine place of worship; you should be very proud, Mr. Savage."

Mike allowed himself to be guided towards the front of the church, where the pulpit stood high and dignified, towering over the altar like some grotesque, living totem.

And in front of the altar that was itself comprised of a multitude of shattered, crying young women, there sat the font.

"Oh no," Mike stammered, his legs threatening to abandon their duty and dump him unceremoniously onto the hard stone floor—the only part of that hellish place that was not comprised of living, tormented people. "Sweet Jesus, no." Mike felt the warm wetness of tears brim up in his eyes and cascade down along his cheeks.

Laura and Todd stared out at him from within the tangle of bodies that was the construct of the imposing font. Their eyes met his, imploring, so filled with pain and terror that Mike felt it deep down within his soul. Their bodies were broken and intertwined, along with those of the weeping people around them, arms and legs all but indiscernible from one another as if they were all part of the same living thing.

Mike rounded on the Pastor, his eyes sparking with pure hate, his fists clenched. "You fuc–"

Pastor Love caught Mike's fist with a powerful hand that crushed his fingers as if they were dry kindling. Mike yowled out his pain, his cry mingling with the sound of his snapping bones and soaking into the moans and wails of those around him. Mike dropped to his knees as the pastor twisted his arm up behind his back and, without further ado, dislocated his shoulder from its socket with a loud popping sound.

"There is a very special place alongside your adorable family, my non-believing friend," Pastor Love said with a broad grin. "I saved it especially for you." And with that, he snapped the twin bones in Mike's forearm with a deft flick of his wrist.

\*\*\*

Mike squirmed and fidgeted and the white heat of pain that shot through his body made him groan. Beside him, Laura's hot, sweat-clicked skin pressed hard into his, her twisted, shattered arms bent around his in some ghoulish semblance of a lover's embrace, her swollen belly pressed into his taut torso, the stirring life within nudging at his body. Between them lay their son, Todd, his small body so delicate, so frail, his thin legs shattered and doubled back on themselves and coiled around his mother's thigh.

At least they were all together, Mike told himself, although that really was cold comfort.

Around Mike, Laura, and Todd, the writhing walls of people cried out, each voice blending seamlessly into the next, their cries reaching high up into the arched ceiling as they all begged for the merciful relief of death that so cruelly evaded them; praying to a God that simply wasn't going to come. Mike tried to call out to Pastor Love, to beg for release in one form or another—for his wife and children, if not for himself—to perhaps strike a deal.

But no words would form in Mike's mouth as his chest was squeezed so tightly against Laura's, her breasts digging into his ribs and stealing his breath. Mike could only let out a low, wheezing grunt, and hope that would be enough.

Alas no.

Ignoring the plight of the newest recruit to his new church, Pastor Antonio D. Love—architect of this most wondrous accolade to the glory of the Lord—knelt down before the sweating, reeking flesh of the altar with his hands clasped firmly together and his eyes closed tight…and he prayed to his god.

# Fur-Baby

Rowan Hill

A soothing hand wiped sweat from Michael's brow, throbbing and raw after being hit with the car. He winced when the swelling egg above his left eye shot sparks of lightning and his eyelids fluttered like dying moths.

"*Shhhh,* hey, now. There you are. *Shhhhh.* You alright, young fella?"

Her voice, warm and maternal, caring and concerned, made Michael's muscles involuntarily relax, stirrings of flight or flight instincts melting away. The smooth lacquer of a coffee cup pressed his lips and tepid tea flowed onto his tongue. A gush threatened to go down wrong and Michael coughed. Chamomile, lemon, and something medicinal-tangy for his headache. It was the citrus that woke him, a sourness making him flinch and shivers cascading down his spine. He squinted and an unfamiliar, dim room materialized.

Heavy dust motes speckled the air like clogged pores, and a streak of light cut the floor, finishing on a small and dirty dog bed. A noonday sun beat on old red curtains, a musty rose tinting the small and claustrophobic room. Michael smacked his lips, the warm tea reviving him and he looked up from the ratty dog bed to the maternal voice and face sitting opposite him.

Apple cheeks with thready veins scoring their peaks, kind eyes droopy with crow's feet, a grey bun at her nape. His neighbor down the lane, Matilda. A geriatric, bush widow he hadn't spent more than five minutes with. Her skin had tanned boot-leather-brown after decades of Australian sun, wrinkles forming odd dykes and crevices everywhere.

"Maaatilda?" he mumbled and the throbbing in his head intensified.

"Oh, thank goodness! He speaks!" she exclaimed, her hands clapping just once. The elderly, big-boned woman pushed on her own knees like it was a chore to stand. "I thought for sure I did you in. I only meant to give you a nudge, but the truck just jumped out beneath my foot, you know?"

Michael blinked, grime and grit were mashed into the corners of his eyes. Matilda patted his knee before his brain caught her words. "Now you just wait here, yeah?" she gently commanded and, through his blurry sight, he saw her leave the bedroom via a door behind her. His body was heavy, lethargic, and sweaty from exercise and the accident.

"Wait…," he muttered, clarity coming too late as she closed the door. He raised his hand to stifle the pain burning his head when his wrist snapped back, bitten by a heavy metal tinkling against itself. With clearer vision, Michael looked down to his wrist and its new handcuff bracelet. He tugged at it, his pulse hurrying as metal clinked, his other limbs all handcuffed to the chair.

"Matilda?" he called. Panic clogged his throat, tightening it. He yanked, testing the cuffs, only to be rewarded with the stinging bite of metal cutting his tender flesh. "*Matilda!*"

Instead of her gruff voice, a dog answered. Dogs. Dogs barked and snarled. Feral and vicious mutts, certainly hungry, maybe even starving. The lump coalescing in Michael's throat hardened to rock and he jerked at his restraints. Metal bleeding him. How many fucking mongrels did she own? The mongrels were close. Was she one of these disgusting 'inside dog' people? Of course she was.

Michael closed his eyes, trying to guess the layout of her farmhouse. He only ever saw it in passing on his morning jog down the country lane. It sat far from the road, maybe twenty meters. Too far for details, but enough to know it wasn't much of a house. The house of a widowed retiree surviving on a pension. Enough for her and the feral rescues. Two bedrooms, maybe an eat-in kitchen, old and stained weatherboards wrapping the structure like a death shroud. And a new-ish chicken wire dog fence around the back, well hidden but peeking around wattle bushes.

The mongrels abruptly stopped their savagery, their silence even scarier in his imagination; when dogs stop barking, it means they're engaged in something else. Either eating…or finding new ways to get inside. Dogs always wanted to come inside. An image of a snarling mutt, drool running down yellow canines flashed in his mind. He knew Matilda had dogs, vicious ones.

The tread of heavy steps returned beyond the door with the unusual scrape of something heavy. Michael aggressively tugged at the chains, straining until warm blood snailed into his palm. He looked to the chair legs and noticed strange wheels sat on the back two and his cuffs were looped through metal holes. No escape.

"Matilda!" he called, his voice pitchy and high. The door flung open and Matilda's wide backside waddled in. She pulled something large, rolling it into the small, unadorned bedroom. A TV. A behemoth from a bygone era of classroom videos, when they needed their own carts and held VHS players beneath on a tray.

It wasn't the TV, nor the strange and unrecognizable leather strap hanging from the cart, that made his plea stick in his throat. Matilda now wore an apron, a white, industrial-grade apron covering her collarbone and down to her knees. The lower half was slick see-through plastic, the top half a rough calico with old bloodstains of brown and faded maroons. Their eyes met, his then pointedly staring at the memory of carnage on her wide bosom. She was made more sinister when she then laughed.

"This? Naw, this was me Larry's. Use' to be a butcher before he retired, though you wouldn't know cause you never asked. I could just never get the lamb's blood out for some reason. Every other animal came out with good ole' bleach and elbow grease. But lambs...just really stuck in there, ya know? Got in the threads nice 'n tight."

"Matilda, I don't know..."

"How's the house going?" she casually asked, wheeling the TV to the corner.

"Wha...what?"

She glanced at him as she bent to plug the cord into the electrical outlet.

"The house? The Miller's place was nearly in ruins last I saw it. You must have done it up since you moved in. A year is plenty of time to get some work done, yeah?"

Michael licked his lips, already dry again. The air in the room was too stale and had a filthy musty taste. He couldn't get a full lungful. He couldn't breathe. "Uhhh, yeah, yes. Had the roof redone. Bathroom's next."

Matilda nodded sagely and leaned on the cart. "And the yard? I drove by a week ago and saw you had put in a veggie patch."

Michael's gaze flicked to the window; the faded curtain camouflaged the shade of daylight. How long had he been unconscious? Couldn't have been more than a few hours. He was out for his 7 AM daily jog when he was struck from behind, the large rock by the roadside the last thing he recalled.

"Yes, planted some roots and some spinach."

She smiled, but not a genuine smile. The sarcastic smile of someone amused and humoring a townie playing farmer.

"Must be nice for a city fella to have all that space."

Michael worked to calm his shaky voice. He felt infirm, weak, vulnerable. His stomach rumbled. "Matilda, what is this about? Why am I cuffed? If it's about you accidentally hitting me with your car, I'm not hur-."

She turned her broad back on him and picked up a VHS tape, interrupting him. "Wasn't an accident."

She spoke with such indifference, such eerie tranquility, and there was silence as he registered what she'd said. All at once Michael convulsed, yanking the shackles frantically, metallic *clinks* filling the silent, unbearably hot, stuffy room. Matilda ignored him and injected the tape, a clunky *whurrl* of cogs accepting it, and the screen flared to life. She immediately pressed pause. Pulsing, horizontal lines of static turned the picture unrecognizable. Sweat trickled down Michael's forehead and into his eyes.

"People at work will notice I'm gone, Matilda. Please… I have money, some money."

She grinned with sharp, yellow teeth and crossed her arms over her chest, accentuating the lamb's blood. She had such broad forearms. How old was she? Michael couldn't recall it coming up in their one conversation at the Belcher's New Year's party months ago. Seventy?

Seventy-five? If this were the city, he would have thought she was on her way out. Holed up in her little apartment or house, rarely leaving except for the daily trip to the shops. But apparently, bush-widows kept the strength of younger women because the land needed them to.

"I'm sure you do," she replied offhand.

Matilda's dogs, several large beasts, began barking again. The kind of sounds indicating a fight within the pack, tearing themselves to pieces. Michael flinched with the abrupt noise, watching the doorway should they tear through the door. His gut now constantly churned, stewing with thoughts of the mutts Matilda likely trained to attack on command. One howled, reminiscent of the dingos he heard every now and then and wondered if she ever fed the wild beasts.

"You afraid of dogs, Michael?" she asked, noticing his unwavering stare on the door.

Michael pressed his cracked lips into a tight line. Saliva pooled in his cheeks and he swallowed it for his gurgling stomach, then shrugged. "A little, I… I was attacked by a big one when I was a…" Matilda frowned. "…a…kid."

Her frown deepened, big pouches of jowls lining either side of her pursed mouth, bloody capillaries coursing across the round of her cheeks. She didn't like that answer. He quickly offered another, honesty pouring out of him like never before for his captor, his mind only holding room for panic.

"But some dogs are okay."

"Some dogs?"

"Little dogs, maybe. When they're on a leash."

"Mmmm. Didn't get many dogs in the city, I guess?"

His eyes oscillated between Matilda, nonchalantly leaning against the cart, and the doorway with the barking. This was good, he realized, keep her talking. More time talking equaled more time people would realize he was missing. Someone would come looking.

"No, lots of people keep dogs. Even in their apartments. Good for security, I guess."

"Ahhhh, yes, of course, smart that. More crime in the city, I always forget, of course. Only been into the city a few times. No real need, and honestly, didn't like it. Not enough space for me. There's no horizon in a city, ya know?" She gave her attention to the staticky screen. "I always thought our little town was safe, too, ya know? Not my Larry, tho. Always suspicious, that one. Installed one of those CCTV security thingies one weekend years ago. Didn't even ask me about it. Just did it. The cheek, huh? Men are like that though, I guess."

Michael swallowed, the softening lump curdled once more. His gut hurt and a wave of fever raced across his body. His scalp shivered.

Matilda squared up on the VCR player, speaking while squinting at the small buttons. "Anyway, this dang thing just records the last ninety days, always *burring* in the corner of the kitchen pantry. All by itself. Never thought too much about it until last week. Would you like to see?"

\*\*\*

Matilda exhaled shakily, never able to grab a full breath since she dragged Michael inside. She pressed the tiny play button with trembling fingers as it stuck. She pressed harder. The video played from the very beginning, too far ahead, but she didn't want to fiddle with the fast forward in case it mucked up. Instead, she leaned on the far wall and watched Michael, cuffed, but now riveted to the screen.

Matilda herself didn't need to watch, obsessively viewing the footage more than what was healthy, breaking her heart into little fractals every time. Pieces chipped away only to be replaced with something ugly and vile, a need to howl her old worn voice into the bushland behind her house—in chorus with the roaming dingos that snatched a chicken every so often.

No, instead of sadism, she studied Michael. Manicured features with fancy waxed eyebrows. His gelled hair was matted with roadside grass strewed within, but his trimmed goatee was clean and his moisturized skin paired with possible eyeliner, though Matilda had never worn such stuff. He sweat profusely, but the only flaw on his face was the swelling bruise where his head had hit packed dirt.

Intent on the video, Michael squinted, concentrating on the fuzz until the screen cleared of static. Ghostly remnants of an old VHS recording over and over again, forever recording the view from her front door, angled down as the camera was attached to the corner of her roof. The front driveway filled eighty percent of the screen while the top narrow strip showed the main road. The timestamp at the bottom displayed 7:15 AM.

Michael's face flinched with recognition, his body tensing only slightly before schooling his immaculately prim features.

There.

Bastard.

The teacup on the small table beside him wafted slender ribbons of steam, caught in sunlight before evaporating into nothingness. Matilda circled her younger neighbor as he watched the video. He tried to ignore her, feigning ignorance, and she looked down at her baby's bed on the floor. Dust layered it like a carpet of memories.

"Matilda," Michael said, "I don't want to see you get into trouble and this is ridiculous, nothing is-"

She looked to the screen, catching it just turning over to 7:16 AM, and planted a firm hand on his shoulder, her strong fingers clenched and burrowed into his muscle and he wisely stopped talking.

Five.

Four.

Three.

Two.

One.

The screen door flung wide in the very bottom corner and a moment later her Milly ran onto screen, let out for her morning toilet. The old Shih Tzu sniffed around the edges of the front garden bordering the driveway and Matilda's eyes watered watching her cute little waddle. The banksias were always Milly's favorite watering bush, and after using them, her attention was stolen by a small butterfly fluttering between rose bushes. She promptly chased it, playfully jumping and snapping fruitlessly as if she could also fly and, although the video was mute, Matilda could perfectly remember her little high-pitched yap.

More unbidden memories of her little old girl flooded. The soft hair beneath her hand as they watched late-night TV together on the couch. Musty perfume as they settled to sleep for the night. The texture of her tongue on her palm. The way Milly's wet nose rubbed her face, nuzzling and comforting after Larry's funeral. They had each other in life. Two old girls who only had each other.

The butterfly, just a little white speck on-screen, rose too high and Milly watched it fly away, her tail wiggling. She stared at it for a moment longer before something off-screen grabbed her attention and Milly shot off running. Not very fast, given she was tiny and old. Just an old girl. She ran to the top of the drive just as a slender figure jogged past. The man, undeniably Michael in his trendy clothes and flash sneakers, skittered away from the small, barking dog that never went farther than the end of the driveway.

His hand flung out, something small and black flicking from his pocket and palm to the ground as he continued jogging down the road. Milly's attention immediately drew to the offering on the roadside, her snout scouring the dirt for whatever he'd flung at her. Her jaw opened and she ate it.

Matilda's hand had a mind of its own and reached into the apron's pocket for the remote control, promptly pressing RWD. She replayed the literal second of his hand flicking away, the black fleck flying to the ground. Milly snatching it. Again. Again, and again. Raptured by the moment over and over. Her mesmerized gaze finally filled with tears, spilling over her cheeks, cascading one after the other. She licked them off her upper lip. The tape continued playing, Milly returning from the top of the driveway and coming inside, nosing the door open by herself.

The worst was over and Matilda wiped her cheeks with the back of her wrist. This was the other side of grief, before the screaming. Crying. An old woman crying, she was nothing beyond a silly old woman crying alone in her house. Michael remained silent, still watching the tape or pretending to. She stepped around him, blocking his view and trying her best to quiet the trembling in her hand, in her body.

"What did you give my dog?"

His well-groomed head shook, the incredulity in his voice. "Nothing, Matilda-"

"What did you give my dog?"

"Nothin! I swear"

"*What did you give my Milly!*"

"Nothing! *NOTHING!*"

"*WHAT DID YOU GIVE MY BABY!*"

"CHRIST! A treat! A *treat!*"

Air left Matilda's body, her shoulders slumped from the fight, his answer long sought for. She might have leaned on the TV cart if she didn't want the bastard to have the satisfaction of seeing her discomposed.

"A treat?" she exhaled. He called it a treat.

He nodded, pursing his lips. His face had blanched a sickly yellow, the sweat on his forehead slimy and freely running down his temples like hell lit a fire beneath him. "Yeah, a little treat, doggie treats." He explained as if Matilda was stupid.

All she could do was stare at him, dumbfounded, and he continued lying, frustration edging his voice. "I keep them in my pocket when I run. With all the dingos and wild dogs around, I keep them so if I am approached by one I can keep myself safe and distract them, okay!? Okay?"

The tape continued playing and she sniffled, forcing herself to appear calm. It was a good answer. Plausible. There *were* dingos around. She knew that first-hand, of course. The scene on the TV hadn't changed. The breeze shuddered the bushes, the butterfly returned, the clock slowly ticked over. They watched in silence. Michael occasionally testing his handcuffs, and Matilda's gaze traveled down his body when he blinked heavy and woozy-like.

"You know, the Calders' dog was sick last week. A big mastiff breed. Too big for me, but seemed like a fun, energetic dog. Always happy. Anyway, last week it comes in and was throwing up for a good hour, shits everywhere, his legs went limp for a while. He was literally four sizes bigger than my little baby, Milly."

The screen all at once was a flurry of activity and she watched herself burst out the door, a baby bundled in her arms. Running to her truck with the swaddle, it quickly backed out of the driveway, racing out of the camera's view. The screen turned black and more tears cascaded down her face, and Matilda remembered the sting of her fist banging on the closed glass doors, frantic, panicked.

"Did you know the local vet don't open til eight-thirty?"

"Matilda…" he stopped talking, his throat visibly reflexing, gagging and his head turning ever so slightly to the table beside him. The teacup now cold.

"Matilda…what was in that…."

Matilda sniffled, her face indifferent, after all of it, she had no room for anything but indifference. She was empty, he had run her dry. From her apron pocket she pulled out the doggy biscuit she found on his unconscious body, lying in wait in his pocket. It was broken open, the little blue pill stashed inside missing. Her cheeks were cold with old tears as he looked up to her, recognizing the biscuit.

"A treat."

Michael gagged an awful wet sound, and Matilda sighed.

She reached for the altered muzzle.

Thick, creaky leather, strong and dry. He continued gagging, each gag spurring the next in disgusting domino effect. Dizzy and disorientated, Matilda looped it over his head without him noticing, the bottom strap beneath his chin. She tugged it, his eyes bulging mid-gag, and she cinched it behind his forehead hairline. His jaw closed for the last time.

"Sorry, youngin. I've got the apron but don't want that kinda mess inside." Michael struggled, his body convulsing back and forth like he could leave his shackled limbs behind. Panic. *Real* panic settled over him, jerky movements closer to a seizure, every muscle tense and fighting. Leveraging her weight, she tipped him backward and onto the chair's wheels, pushing him forward to reverse around and back out of the door. She pushed it open and his breathing grew louder. Frantic air through his closed lips, blowing them open in bursts and his gagging multiplied, followed by the recognizable, viscid sound of vomiting as they traversed the hallway.

"You know, then I remembered that the Wilson's golden retriever died about six months ago. Thought he got into some Daphne bushes. Though no one could ever remember seeing any. And one of the strays, a harmless little thing, was on the roadside, dead, about eight months ago. Strange isn't it?"

Michael vomited into his locked mouth as they wheeled past her little kitchen. The small dog bowl sat unused in the corner next to the fridge, her heart not ready to throw it away. If it remained, perhaps she could pretend. 'Milly' was painted on the side in fancy cursive.

"You know, cruelty to pets gets you a fine in this town. A *fine*. I think I heard it was something like five hundred bucks."

He choked on his own vomit, his throat undulating like he tried swallowing it back in a disgusting cycle of consuming and regurgitating. Matilda heard it in his nostrils, gunking up his orifices. Choking him on his own poison. Irony.

"But bush justice is a little more my style, you know? Bet you never got that in the city, huh?"

She pulled open the back door and the dingos began barking. Wrathful, ferocious yaps. They were skinny, serried rib bones stuck out at awkward angles of their bodies. Hungrily snapping as they began to turn on one another after a week of being starved. She yanked Michael's chair down the stairs, the struggling figure jolted as each step dropped him, still straining against his handcuffs. "It's so strange you mentioned those dingos. Caught a few myself the other day. Easy to trap dingos. Especially when they're hungry."

She turned Michael's chair to face them. He held a mouthful of poisonous vomit and his head tipped forward, oscillating between trying to breathe through his clogged nostrils and teeth and screaming a child-like primal fear. He squawked through his mumbled lips, maybe begging. Matilda wasn't interested in what he might say.

A few meters beyond her back stoop, was the cage.

An old chicken shed with a four by four meter enclosure, it was now devoid of chickens, all stolen by the dingos themselves. Matilda had reinforced its sides with more chicken mesh and sealed the entries. After taking a week to figure out and then constructing another entry chamber, the high fences were sturdy enough she could throw herself against them and the posts held them tight. Sturdy enough that dogs pressed their lithe, powerful bodies into it, searching for an escape, and it held fast. It would be enough for an effete dandy.

His chair juddered as they wheeled over weeds and dirt, Michael in front of her struggling, trying to tip his chair to the side. The three dingos currently roamed inside the shed, hidden, likely still driven mad by smelling fowl everywhere but having nothing to eat. Their yips reverberated and echoed loudly inside the tin box, making them out as behemoth monsters.

Michael screamed through his muzzle.

Matilda opened the first cage, the entry chamber, hinges squeaky with old rust and wheeled him inside. Michael understood this was the last of it and continued thrashing and pushing, flight or fight rocking side to side to stop his entry. Matilda was tempted to hit him over the head. The same way Larry did to lambs to make them sleep before slaughter. A mercy.

Matilda left him awake.

Beyond his strapped feet, she kicked open the second gate to the empty enclosure and wheeled him in just past the point of the open door. And then shut it.

Securing the two entry doors, the click of the gate latch sent shivers of a cathartic finality down Matilda's spine. She walked around the cage until she was directly beside him. Dribbles of viscous saliva, green with slivers of blood within, ran down his chin, his throat involuntarily convulsing. But his eyes. Matilda softly smiled. His eyes were gloriously terrified and staring not at her, but ahead to the chicken shed, and the little door, where the yips had quietened.

A dingo stuck his head out. Then two, then all three, flowing out of the coop like water. Beautiful golden animals, their gums had retracted from dehydration, a gummy rot settling in the corners of their mouths, frothing the edges. They sniffed the ground, smelling him from the distance, and then focused on Michael, pacing back and forth with an eerie, foreboding quality.

"Maybe when that dog bit you as a kid it was a warning. You know?"

Michael, still struggling, tipped his chair enough that it crashed into the fence between them, and he tilted at an odd angle. Neither lying on the ground nor sitting upright. Stuck. His gaze found hers and she smiled. Finally, tears ran down his muzzled face. Real emotion. A wet stain bloomed on his groin. He hollered a pitiful sound that might have been her name.

"Maybe they were telling you to be nice. Be polite. I don't know." She finished.

Pursing her lips, she made a small whistle, the same she had been using each time she fed the dingos their scraps over the last week, a signal for food, and the three skinny, half-starved dingos finally cautiously strolled closer, unafraid, sniffing the ground for meat, making their way towards dinner. Michael bayed through his jaw, sputtering vomit through his nose. His feet waved uselessly in the air as the curious, ferine dogs strutted to him. They sniffed at his bound ankles, discovering his sweaty flesh beneath his athletic socks.

Michael frenzied, something delicious about his movements and panic that rolled off him in putrid waves. That fear. That was justice.

Matilda left them, rattled growls sounding above muffled howls and tearing cloth. She shut the door to sounds of a weight crashing to the hard-packed dirt. She closed the front door on the muffled screams, having enough of it, and sat in her chair at the kitchen table. Larry's butchering knives, professional, thirty-year-guarantee type of knives, sat on the counter opposite.

Give them an hour, then she would shoo them away. They wouldn't reach his stomach and the poison in an hour. Wouldn't want to get any of that shit inside them. Wouldn't want another dog to be murdered by that metro-sexual or whatever he was. *She* wasn't the monster.

# MEET THE AUTHORS

*Lee Murray* *is a writer, editor, and poet from Aotearoa New Zealand, a Shirley Jackson Award and five-time Bram Stoker Award® winner. With more than forty titles to her credit, including novels, collections, anthologies, nonfiction, and several books for children, she holds a New Zealand Prime Minister's Award for Literary Achievement in Fiction, and is an Honorary Literary Fellow of the New Zealand Society of Authors. Read more at* <u>leemurray.info</u>

*James Aquilone* *is the owner of Monstrous Books, writer of the Dead Jack: Zombie Detective series, and editor of the anthologies* Classic Monsters Unleashed, Shakespeare Unleashed, *and the* 50th anniversary Kolchak: The Night Stalker *graphic novel. He's won the Bram Stoker Award for Best Graphic Novel, two Rondo Hatton Classic Horror Awards, and a Scribe Award from the International Association of Media Tie-In Writers.*

*Award winning author,* *Jasper Bark* *is infectious—and there's no known cure. If you're reading this you're already contaminated. The symptoms will manifest any time soon. There's nothing you can do about it. There's no itching or unfortunate rashes, but you'll become obsessed with his mind-bending books.*

*Then you'll want to tell everyone else about his visionary horror fiction. About its originality, its wild imagination and how it takes you to the edge of your sanity. We're afraid there's no way to avoid this. These words contain a power you're hopeless to resist. You're already in their thrall, you know you are. You're itching to read all of Jasper's bloodstained books. Don't fight this urge, embrace it. You've been bitten by the Bark bug and you love it!*

*Jay Bechtol* *likes to write, so he does. If you liked Jay's story, links to plenty more can be found at* www.JayBechtol.com. *If you prefer dad jokes, he can be found on Twitter @BechtolJay. And if you want to share a Dr Pepper, he can be found in person in Homer, Alaska. If you didn't like Jay' story, you are in luck. This book is filled with many more talented writers than him.*

*Felix Blackwell* *emerged from the bowels of Reddit during a botched summoning ritual. He writes in the horror and thriller genres, and is best known for* Stolen Tongues *(2017).*

*JP Behrens* *spends his days writing, reading, practicing Kung Fu, and spending time with his family. Besides graduating from the Yale Writers' Workshop, he has published numerous short stories, most in his new collection,* We Don't Talk Anymore and Other Dark Fictions. *His debut novel was* Portrait of a Nuclear Family.

*Devin Cabrera*, *a former filmmaker turned author, brings a cinematic edge to his gripping novels. With* Welcome to Nightmare Island *and* Jones 1963, *he ventures into the realms of suspense and horror, captivating readers with his vivid storytelling. Drawing from his experience in the film industry, Cabrera infuses his narratives with immersive scenes and dynamic characters. Through his transition to literature, he continues to showcase his talent for crafting compelling stories that linger in the imagination.*

*Kenneth W. Cain* *is an author of horror and dark fiction, and a Splatterpunk Award-nominated freelance editor. He is also the publisher and editor-in-chief at Crystal Lake: Torrid Waters. Cain is an Active member of the HWA and a Full member of the SFWA. To date, he has had over one hundred short stories and thirteen novels/novellas, as well as a handful each of nonfiction pieces, books for children, and poems released by many great publishers such as Crystal Lake Publishing, JournalStone, and Cemetery Gates Media. He has also edited ten anthologies, with a new one coming in 2024. Cain suffers from chronic pain, and as such, likes to keep busy. He lives in Chester County PA with his family and two furbabies, Butterbean and Bodhi. His full publishing history is available on his website at* kennethwcain.com.

**John Durgin** *is a proud active HWA member and lifelong horror fan. Growing up in New Hampshire, he discovered Stephen King much younger than most probably should have, reading IT before he reached high school—and knew from that moment on he wanted to write horror. He had his first story accepted in the summer of 2021 in the* Beach Bodies *anthology through DarkLit Press. His debut novel,* The Cursed Among Us *released June 3, 2022, and went on to become an Amazon bestseller. Next up, his sophomore novel titled* Inside The Devil's Nest, *released in January of 2023, followed by his debut collection,* Sleeping In The Fire *in June of 2023. In 2024 he is set to have two more novels and a novella released through DarkLit Press and Crystal Lake Publishing.*

*Twitter- @jdurgin1084*
*Website- www.johndurginauthor.com*
*Instagram- @durginpencildrawings*
*TikTok- @johndurgin_author*

*Two-time Bram Stoker Award Finalist* **Taylor Grant** *has written professionally in nearly every entertainment medium--from film, to TV, to comics, to radio, and everything in between. His critically-acclaimed horror fiction has been published by Random House, Cemetery*

*Dance, Weird Tales, Crystal Lake Publishing, Webtoon, Weirdbook Magazine and more. He is grateful to have shared pages with many of his literary heroes, including Stephen King, Neil Gaiman, and Clive Barker. Find him at* www.taylorgrant.com

**Gage Greenwood** *is the best-selling author of the Winter's Myths Saga, and* Bunker Dogs. *He's a proud member of the Horror Writers Association and Science Fiction and Fantasy Writers Association.*

He's been an actor, comedian, podcaster, and even the Vice President of an escape room company. Since childhood, he's been a big fan of comic books, horror movies, and depressing music that fills him with existential dread.

He lives in New England with his girlfriend and son, and he spends his time writing, hiking, and decorating for various holidays.

Find out more, or contact him: www.gagegreenwood.com

**Rowan Hill** *is an author of Sci-fi and Horror. She loves writing flawed women who occasionally murder and a plot twist within a plot twist. She has many stories of such things and her debut collection,* No Fair Maidens from Earth to Mars, *will be released July, 2024 with Trepidatio Press.*

**Naching T. Kassa** *is a wife, mother, and writer. She's created short stories, novellas, poems, and co-created three children. She resides in Eastern Washington State with her husband, Dan Kassa.*

*Naching is a member of the Horror Writers Association, Mystery Writers of America and The Science Fiction and Fantasy Writers Association. She's the Talent Relations*

*Manager for Crystal Lake Publishing and was a recipient of the 2022 HWA Diversity Grant.*

*Originally from Yorkshire, England,* **James H. Longmore** *became a US citizen in 2022. He has an honors degree in Zoology and a background in sales, marketing, and business. An accomplished, published author (and publisher in his role as co-founder/partner in HellBound Books Publishing LLC), and ghostwriter of popular fiction, Longmore writes across an incredibly wide range of genres and subjects in novel, short story, and screenplay formats. To date, he has four novels, five novellas, and a whole slew of short tales in print by various publishers (many can be found in his first collection,* Blood and Kisses*). He also runs and co-hosts the popular podcast/radio show (The New Panic Room), which is used to promote HellBound Books and indie authors, artists, audiobook narrators, and publishers of all genres. Longmore is an Affiliate Member of the Horror Writers Association.* www.jameslongmore.com / www.hellboundbooks.com

*Full-time family man, artist, musician, podcaster, and ferret owner with twenty books under his belt,* **Chad Lutzke** *dips his toe into all things dark: Crime, thrillers, noir, slice-of-life and horror, every one smothered in heartache with the occasional sliver of hope. Some of his books include:* Of Foster Homes & Flies, Stirring the Sheets, The Pale White, Skullface Boy, The Same Deep Water as You, Three-Smile Mile, *and The Neon Owl series. Lutzke's work has been praised by authors Jack Ketchum, Richard Chizmar, Joe R. Lansdale, Stephen Graham Jones, Tim Waggoner, and his own mother. He can be found lurking the internet at* www.chadlutzke.com

***Francesca Maria*** *writes dark fiction surrounded by cats near the Pacific Ocean. She is the award-winning, bestselling author of* They Hide: Short Stories to Tell in the Dark *from Brigids Gate Press which debuted as an Amazon #1 Best Seller. She is the creator of the Black Cat Chronicles, a true horror comic book series narrated by a mystical black cat. Her short stories and essays can be found in various publications including Crystal Lake Publishing's Shallow Waters, Death's Garden Revisited and Under the Stairs anthologies. Francesca is also the co-chair of the San Francisco Bay Area's Horror Writers Association Chapter. You can find her at* [francescamaria.com](francescamaria.com) *and on social media @writerofweird.*

***Joe Mynhardt*** *stands as a paragon in the horror literary world, a Bram Stoker Award-winning South African publisher, editor, and mentor with over a decade of experience. As the founder and CEO of Crystal Lake Entertainment, Joe has transformed a humble 2012 startup into a multifaceted Intellectual Property powerhouse. Under his visionary leadership, Crystal Lake Publishing has become just one of the many thriving divisions of his company.*

*Joe Mynhardt isn't just a figure in the horror industry—he's a driving force behind it, leading a successful online business that goes beyond the traditional boundaries of publishing. Joe is also the author of the Shadows & Ink series for authors. Discover more about Joe's journey and Crystal Lake's offerings at www.crystallakepub.com or connect with him on Facebook or Patreon (includes author tiers and a 7-day free trial), where he continues to inspire and lead the next generation of horror storytellers.*

***Bridgett Nelson*** *is a registered nurse turned horror author. Her first collection,* A Bouquet of Viscera, *is a* two-time *Splatterpunk Award* winner, *recognized both for the collection itself and its standout story, "Jinx." She is also the author of* What the Fuck Was That? *and* Sweet, Sour, & Spicy.

*Her work has appeared in the iconic Deathrealm Spirits, Splatterpunk's Basement of Horror, Dark Disasters, October Screams, The Never Dead, Razor Blade in the Fun Sized Candy, Y'all Ain't Right, Counting Bodies Like Sheep, Dead & Bloated, American Cannibal, and A Woman Unbecoming.*

*Bridgett is working on her first original novel and has been contracted by Encyclopocalypse Publications to write a novelization of the cult classic film* Deadgirl.

*Visit her website at* www.bridgettnelson.com.

**Colin J. Northwood** *is made of twigs and barbed wire. He writes fiction in exchange for scraps of human flesh. The bars of his cage are littered with the frantic scrawls from which his stories are assembled. Colin has surmised that he must appear docile, but only when someone is looking. This is the best way to minimize the punishments. Something inside him used to scream and scream, until he sold his soul to make it stop. Now, there is nothing left within him but the tranquil hush of a winter's day.*

**Diana Olney** *is a Seattle-based author, but she is most at home in the shadows, wandering the paths between nightmares and dreams. She writes in many shades of fiction, including horror, fantasy, science fiction, and LGBTQ dark romance. Her stories and poems have appeared in Dark Horses Magazine and anthologies by Crystal Lake Publishing, Worldstone Publishing, Last Waltz Publishing, and Critical Blast. She is also the creator of Siren's Song, an original comic series due to be released this year. Visit her website* dianaolney.com *or find her on Facebook for updates on her latest terrors.*

*Nick Roberts is a native West Virginian and a doctoral graduate of Marshall University. He is an active member of the Horror Writers Association and the Horror Authors Guild. His works include* Anathema, The Exorcist's House, It Haunts the Mind & Other Stories, *and* Mean Spirited. *He currently resides in South Carolina with his family.*

*Gregg Stewart is an author, songwriter, musician, screenwriter, journalist, and film composer whose dark fiction tales have appeared in* The Sirens Call, Crystal Lake Publishing's *Patreon contest series, and the anthologies* Shallow Waters, Vol. 9, *and* Dead Letters: Tales of Epistolary Horror. *He has recorded and published one hundred songs, toured the US and Europe countless times, scored multiple indie films (including the award-winning short "Beautiful Dead Things"), and provided songs for a dozen film/TV soundtracks from the cult-classic* 3,000 Miles to Graceland *to the hit show* Hart of Dixie. *Song highlights include "The Midnight Shift," a Folk category winner in the John Lennon Songwriting Competition, and "O Carry Me," featured in London's West End revival of* Little Women. *The 2024 film* Heart Strings *contains four co-written songs by Stewart, and his first co-written screenplay,* Western Gothic, *was runner-up in the 2023 Big Break Contest. Find him at* linktr.ee/greggstewart

*Jeff Strand is the Bram Stoker Award-winning author of sixty books, including* Pressure, Dweller, *and* Autumn Bleeds into Winter. *You can visit his Gleefully Macabre website at* www.JeffStrand.com.

*Kyle Toucher is the author of the novel* Live Wire, *from Crystal Lake Publishing, and the novella* Life Returns. *His most recent release is the Black Hare Press Short*

*Read,* Southpaw, *as well as an appearance in the anthology* Dead Letters: Episodes of Epistolary Horror.

*After writing a slew of Godzilla stories in grade school, he read* The Exorcist *at fourteen, then bought a guitar when* Black Sabbath: Volume 4 *changed his life. Through his twenties, he fronted the influential Nardcore crossover band Dr. Know, made records, and hit the road. Later, he moved into the Visual Effects field, earning eight Emmy nominations and two awards for* Firefly *and* Battlestar: Galactica. *Recent film credits include* Top Gun: Maverick *and* Devotion.

*He lives with a lovely woman, five cats, two dogs, and several guitars in a secure, undisclosed location.*

*Twitter: @kyletoucher*

# OTHER HELLBOUND BOOKS
### *www.hellboundbooks.com*

## The Horror Zine's Book of Monster Stories

With an introduction by Shirley Jackson Award-winner Gemma Files, this oustanding anthology of all things monstrous includes spine-chilling stories from Bentley Little, Simon Clark, Elizabeth Massie, Tim Waggoner, Sumiko Saulson, plus some of the best emerging horror writers working today.

"This anthology gives us a chilling glimpse at the dark and dangerous things prowling in the minds of some of today's best horror writers." – JG Faherty, author of *Ragman* and *Songs in the Key of Death*

"Throughout the pages are creepy tales by up-and-comers who you may have read, plus writers brand new to a horror reader's discerning eye. Embark on a journey to the realm where monsters—familiar or unique—dwell. Highly recommended to horror aficionados obsessed with eldritch fiction—this one's for you!" – Nancy Kilpatrick, author of *Thrones of Blood Series* and *the Darker Passions series*.

## Goodbye Stranger

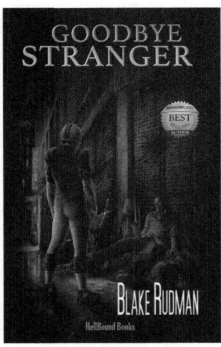

Another gripping noir thriller from the bestselling author of *The Gentleman's Choice* and *Dark Beauty* Danielle Harrington has the life many women envy: She's beautiful, rich, has two wonderful children, and is married to the Preston Harrington - the handsome, charismatic, retired quarterback who won two Super Bowls. Unfortunately, something is very wrong with Preston. Having suffered more than his fair share of injuries and concussions, he becomes quiet, withdrawn, and distant.

As Preston spends more time away from his family, Danielle begins suspect an affair without realizing her husband is involved in something much, much worse...

Following a series of tragic incidents and the return of an old nemesis from the past, things begin to spiral out of control for Danielle as Preston's dark side puts her and their children in terrible danger.

## Colleen

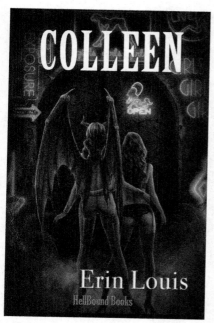

"Sexy, intriguing, terrifying - Colleen has it all! " - James H. Longmore, author of *Tenebrion*.

Lacey, a goth introvert with sketchy people skills, befriends Colleen, a dazzlingly beautiful ghost, during a solo Ouija board session. At last, her loneliness comes to an end.

An eclectic pairing indeed, but they form an odd-but-satisfying and far-from-platonic friendship.

When Lacey begins work as a stripper, she and Colleen find themselves with a conspiratorial mystery to solve in the strip club.

Unfortunately, Lacey's newfound supernatural lover has a secret... or two and isn't what she seems to be at all. Colleen is not a ghost at all, but a succubus with an unfortunate habit of killing people.

Accidentally.

It's not long before the mounting number of deaths occurring around Lacey draws the attention of a tenacious homicide detective...

Can Colleen uncover the shady happenings at the club and keep her beloved Lacey out of jail?

# Playground of the Dead

*Playground of the Dead* is a macabre tale set in a seaside California community of Clear View.

There have been a number of unexplained deaths of the town's citizens - all related to tragic incidents involving its children.

The police chief, Braden Powell, a man dealing with his own troubled, tragic history, has been investigating the mysterious occurrences with frustratingly minimal success,

Gradually, he comes to realize there may be a sinister, supernatural connection too horrifying to comprehend.

## Pede

*"A brutally affectionate homage to the creature feature!*

The once luxurious Mountainview Spa Hotel in the heart of California's Coachella valley lies decaying, abandoned and heavily boarded up - the site of a radioactive, "dirty" bomb explosion five years' previously. Zoology Professor, Jane Lucas, harbors a lifelong phobia of *Scolopendra gigantea,* the Giant Centipede, despite being the world's leading authority on the creature.

Following the savage deaths of two teenagers who broke into the hotel to cavort in the natural underground spa and the discovery of centipede remains almost three times natural size, the professor teams up with four of her students to investigate.

Their expedition soon becomes a fight for survival when they're trapped inside the hotel with a gang of violent thugs and a voracious swarm of oversized centipedes that infest the place - and then discover another creature even more terrifying is hunting in the Mountainview's deserted hallways: a centipede of impossibly monstrous proportions… ravenous and desperate to feed.

# The Horror Writer

*"The most definitive guide into the trials and tribulations of being a horror writer since Stephen King's 'On Writing.'"*

We have assembled some of the very best in the business from whom you can learn so much about the craft of horror writing: Bram Stoker Award© winners, bestselling authors, a President of the Horror Writers' Association, and myriad contemporary horror authors of distinction.

The Horror Writer covers how to connect with your market and carve out a sustainable niche in the independent horror genre, how to tackle the writer's ever-lurking nemesis of productivity, writing good horror stories with powerful, effective scenes, realistic, flowing dialogue and relatable characters without resorting to clichéd jump scares and well-worn gimmicks. Also covered is the delicate subject of handling rejection with good grace, and how to use those inevitable "not quite the right fit for us at this time" letters as an opportunity to hone your craft.

Plus... perceptive interviews to provide an intimate peek into the psyche of the horror author and the challenges they work through to bring their nefarious ideas to the page.

And, as if that – and so much more – was not enough, we have for your delectation Ramsey Campbell's beautifully insightful analysis of the tales of HP Lovecraft.

Featuring:

Ramsey Campbell, John Palisano, Chad Lutzke, Lisa Morton, Kenneth W. Cain, Kevin J. Kennedy, Monique Snyman, Scott Nicholson, Lucy A. Snyder, Richard Thomas, Gene O'Neill, Jess Landry, Luke Walker, Stephanie M. Wytovich, Marie O'Regan, Armand Rosamilia, Kevin Lucia, Ben Eads, Kelli Owen, Jasper Bark, and Bret McCormick.

And interviews with:

Steve Rasnic Tem, Stephen Graham Jones, David Owain Hughes, Tim Waggoner, and Mort Castle.

**A HellBound Books Publishing LLC Publication**

www.hellboundbookspublishing.com

**Printed in the United States of America**

Printed in Great Britain
by Amazon